ONE MORE KISS

A CONTEMPORARY ROMANCE ANTHOLOGY

DAWN BROWER

This is a work of fiction. Names, characters, places, and incidents are products of the author's imagination or are used fictitiously and are not to be construed as real. Any resemblance to actual locales, organizations, or persons, living or dead, is entirely coincidental.

One More Kiss Copyright © 2020 Dawn Brower

Edits by Victoria Miller Cover art by Mandy Koehler

CONTENTS

COWGIRL FEVER

EXCERPT: UNVEILED HEARTS

PASSION AND LIES

EXCERPT: DESIRE AND JEALOUSY

EXCERPT: NEVER DISREGARD A WALLFLOWER

USA TODAY BESTSELLING AUTHOR

DAWN BROWER

COWGIRL
FEVER

NOVAK
SPRINGS
1

This is a work of fiction. Names, characters, places, and incidents are products of the author's imagination or are used fictitiously and are not to be construed as real. Any resemblance to actual locales, organizations, or persons, living or dead, is entirely coincidental.

Cowgirl Fever Copyright © 2014 Dawn Brower

ACKNOWLEDGMENTS

This was the second book I ever wrote, and the first contemporary. There were a few people that helped me polish it and make it better. Christina S, Capri B, and Jennifer Z, I thank each one of you for your help. Without you this book wouldn't be what it is.

In life we are faced with many choices. One of the best choices I made was starting to write. Above that the only thing that tops it is my two boys. Luke and Nathan I love you so much and you are truly the biggest blessing and best thing to come into my life.

COWGIRL FEVER

Dallas Novak swore off women after his fiancée broke their engagement. His plans change when he becomes responsible for his family and their ranch, Novak Springs. Resigned to his new life, he throws himself into making the ranch successful.

Ginnifer Zeiss is a well-established journalist from New York. When approached to write an article on Cowgirl Yoga, she drops everything to experience what a real ranch is like. She secretly loves ranches and is attracted to sexy cowboys.

When Dallas meets Ginnifer he is instantly attracted to her. He tries his best to keep her at a distance, but fails. As he spends time in her company, he starts to wonder if it's possible to live without her. Can he move past the betrayal his ex-fiancée dealt him long enough to grab happiness?

The hot summer sun was beating down on the windowpane and making the room hotter than it should be with the central air blowing out on full blast. It was mid-July, and Dallas was looking over his sister Emma's business plan for Cowgirl Yoga. It was an addition to the already operational horse ranch they lived on. It was equally owned by Dallas, Wesley, and Emma, but Dallas had final say in everything that affected the ranch's bottom line. The three siblings had inherited Novak Springs when their parents passed away several years ago.

"I'm not buying it as a viable option, Emma," Dallas explained to his sister.

"Of course it is. We are not making any money in the fall months, and it's a great idea, admit it," Emma said, her heart-shaped lips lifting into an impish smile.

"Cowgirl Yoga?" He raised his eyebrows at her in disbelief, one of his blue eyes widening with the gesture. "A bunch of frilly, wanna-be cowgirls coming here for what? Exercise? It'll be one hell of an expensive venture when you throw in the cost of food, accommodations, and advertising. The turnaround isn't worth it. I have serious doubts we can make a profit off of this. I'm sorry, it isn't going to work."

A small tear formed in the corner of Emma's blue eyes. She clenched her fists and shook her head at him in defiance. Her cinnamon ponytail smacked her neck as it bounced sideways. He wanted to give her idea a chance. The problem was he hated taking unnecessary risks. Her business model was sound and did hold some promise of working though. He knew she had switched her plans and created some new goals. Her original plans hadn't been anywhere near working at the family ranch. This might be a good thing. He'd have to take a different approach with it for it to work. Dallas was capable of being reasonable, at times. When it suited his purposes, anyway.

"How about we agree to disagree on whether or not Cowgirl Yoga has a chance of working and look at this from a different angle?" she said with a gamine smile.

He nodded at her and said, "Okay I'm listening, what do you have in mind?"

"Give it a trial run. Let me do it in September, and if it fails, I'll let it go, but if it is a success, then you will let me continue to do it every fall. We can talk about expanding after a few years, provided it's profitable." After she got her spiel out, Emma sat quietly in her chair.

Leaning back in his own chair, Dallas started to tap the armrest as he silently stared at her. He gave no emotions away as he looked at Emma and contemplated what his next step should be. After a few moments, he said, "In your business plan you have your clients staying for two weeks. They would share the cabins on the ranch, with up to four per cabin. The price for this two-week vacation is $1,500 per week. Do you have any marketing ideas? I don't see it anywhere in your mockup who is going to run the yoga portion of this program, either. How are you going to afford to pay someone to run that?"

"Yes, I have one idea in place already. A magazine writer is coming for the first session. She is planning an article on Cowgirl Yoga for publication in the October issue. That is, of course, for future clientele. In the long term I want to utilize all of the social media that is available. As far as the yoga—the instructor I took classes with at school agreed to do the initial phase of the program. She is going to stay on at the ranch. Her only pay is going to be free room and board while she runs the yoga sessions and helps me finish up my certification to take over for any other sessions we have."

Dallas's lips formed a grim line of disapproval, and a hint of anger laced through each of his words as he asked, "Are you telling me that you already have someone coming and it wasn't even agreed that you could go ahead with this plan of yours?"

"Well, let's be honest. I deserve a chance to prove this is going to work. So what if I went ahead and scheduled her coming? You are going to give me this chance." Emma had a determined look on her face, and Dallas knew fighting her would prove to be futile.

Folding his arms across his chest, Dallas leaned back in his chair again and a half smile formed on his face. He knew how to deal with his baby sister. Too bad he was a sucker and usually gave in to her whims. "That's awfully presumptuous of you."

"But you love me anyway." She blew a kiss at Dallas, and crossing her legs, she sat back in her chair to wait for his response.

Dallas laughed at her antics; he loved his sister, and only she had the capability of getting him to lighten up. She was the adored younger sister, and there really wasn't much he wouldn't do to make her happy. He needed her to be the fun-loving girl he knew her to be.

Dallas picked up the mockup of her business model and asked, "Okay what can you do with social media and this magazine writer? Are you comping her stay? How can you make a profit if you start giving things away for free right from the start?"

"Well, for starters social media is free. We can create a business page and start the hype going early on. Give them contact information and some ideas of what the ranch currently does and how it is going to benefit them to participate in this new program we're going to run. I also plan on expanding our current web page to include links to the various social media pages and give them an idea of what Cowgirl Yoga has to offer."

That didn't sound too bad. The plan held a lot of appeal. Perhaps those business classes she had taken at college helped after all. Admittedly he didn't know a whole lot about marketing, that was Wes's area, but he didn't believe having a magazine writer come out for free was a good way to start out. Emma hadn't come out and said it, but usually that was how they enticed those types to attend a function. They wanted a free ride in order to give the much needed publicity.

"What about the media person, is she staying free?"

"Yes, she is. It is important to get her here so that I can get that advertising her article will give the new program. She writes for a prominent magazine and is an invaluable tool in promoting this venture. It's a good thing that she is coming, I promise. Let me worry about the profit margin. It is up to me to make a go of this if you agree to the trial."

Dallas sighed and looked at her with a grim face. "Okay. It's clear you have thought this out completely. The business plan is well written. I still have doubts, but I'm willing to give it a trial run. Just remember you agreed that if you don't turn a profit, we will not continue with the program."

"Thank you, Dallas, you won't regret this. I promise." Emma let out a squeal of delight and jumped up to hug her brother.

He hoped her Cowgirl Yoga plan worked as she planned it would. At the very least he had been able to extricate a smile from her. That alone made the added expense worth it. Emma had a hard time in her last semester of school. Her heart had gotten broken by her longtime boyfriend, Colt Lewis. The football player abandoned her for someone else when he signed a contract with a professional football team. It left Emma devastated, and she came home to lick her wounds.

"Okay easy now, there is a lot to be done to get your idea up and running. Do you know what you need to do first?" Dallas smiled.

Emma nodded her head in agreement as she said, "Yes,

I have so many lists of things that need to be done. Do you think Wes would help me? He's so good at this stuff, and he can charm anyone."

"Absolutely. He has believed in your idea from the start, so he should be willing to assist you with getting everything set."

"Awesomeness. I am the luckiest girl in the world to have you two as brothers. I hope you know that. I appreciate everything that you do for me." Emma's smile grew into a huge grin.

"It's only 'cause we have you for a sister. You're the devilish imp that keeps things interesting."

Emma let out a little chuckle. "All right, should I call Wes?"

"I will let him know that it's a go, and I'll make sure he calls you soon. He's a customer service genius and might be able to help with your marketing ideas too."

Wes was a great asset, and Dallas hoped she took advantage of his skills. The ranch wouldn't have been financially successful without his key insight. He had been instrumental in branching off and marketing the ranch in a different, more lucrative venture. Perhaps he could also make Emma's Cowgirl Yoga plan just as successful.

"I'm sure he will have a lot of helpful ideas. Have him call me when he is free to go over everything with me. In the meantime, I'm going to begin setting up the social media sites and give Ginnifer Zeiss a call. I need to confirm she'll be able to attend for the two weeks in September."

"You mean there's a chance she might not be able to come for your opening weekend?" he asked.

"Well I couldn't tell her to come when I hadn't gotten your permission to run the program yet. I had some details to iron out first. I will call her and see if she's still available. She seemed pretty excited about coming, though, so I don't foresee any problems."

Dallas gathered all of her paperwork together, placed it into a manila folder, and handed it to Emma. "All right, looks like everything is settled here. I have other matters to attend to unless you have something else you wanna talk 'bout?"

Emma grabbed the folder and stood up. "No, that's all I needed. I've lots to do, so I'll leave you alone now. Bubbye, big brother."

Emma turned on her heel and strolled out of the office. At least the meeting had gone relatively well. He believed he had been able to give her something to look forward to. She needed something to throw all of her energy into so she could forget her useless ex-boyfriend.

Dallas continued to stare at his office door after his sister left. Did he make a mistake in letting her try this latest idea of hers? He sure hoped not, but regardless of his reservations, he was still going to let her try it. Emma had wanted to try something new for a while now. The ranch was in a good place financially, and if Emma was going to experiment, this was the best time to let her try.

He let out a sigh and ran his hands through his chestnut hair in frustration. It was hard to be the oldest sibling. Sometimes he wished he didn't have so much responsibility. He had been the head of the family since their parents died in the car crash five years ago. Dallas barely reached the ripe old age of twenty-four when he found himself saddled with the responsibility of the family ranch, Novak Springs. The life he planned changed with the death of his parents. He barely graduated college before he had to take over Novak Springs in central Washington.

He grieved far more than the loss of his parents. Dallas also lost the life he had been planning with his then fiancée, Melody. She was everything that he thought he wanted in a lifelong partner. She was beautiful, smart, and tenacious. No other female had ever come close to meaning anything to him. They had made so many plans together, but they all came tumbling down when his parents died. Melody had not wanted to come with him to run the ranch. That wasn't in her plans. She wanted more out of life than to be holed up in a kitchen and taking care of their family. When Melody told him that she couldn't marry him, his heart shattered into a million pieces. Most of his family had never gotten a chance to meet her. The plan had been to bring her home the very week they died. In the span of a short time, he lost more than any normal person could handle. The only two people that mattered to him were his brother and sister. Melody was no longer important; she couldn't be. His heart hardened at any thought of her. It still baffled him that he could allow someone in his life who would abandon him when he needed her most. He vowed he would never give another woman that kind of control over him again.

Wesley, a year younger than he was, deferred his last year of college in order to help Dallas run Novak Springs. Emmaline was their baby sister, scarcely twenty-two years old now. They had to take over guardianship of her when their parents died in her senior year of high school. The vivacious teenager became sullen and withdrawn. Dallas was aware that she believed she was a burden to them, but it wasn't further from the truth. She was the glue that had held them together while they struggled to make a profit from the failing ranch. They still had some regular ranch hands for running the day-to-day operations of the ranch. Mrs. Henly, the housemaid, came in four days a week to clean the house and occasionally cook meals. She stocked a lot of casseroles in the freezer for them so they didn't starve.

Emma had been adamant she was not going to go away to college after high school graduation. It was Wes who convinced her that she needed to go away and earn her degree. He was able to make her see she could help them with sustaining the ranch if she got the right education. She wanted to help them run the ranch. Once she was there, she blossomed and had started to flourish into that cheerful girl again. The happiness bubbled out of her whenever she visited. She began dating a football player and couldn't have been happier with her life. Emma brought the guy home often on breaks until they broke up a couple weeks before her college graduation. Some of the happy energy left her, but it wasn't the same as when their parents died.

This was her first heartbreak, and it was in this new project of hers that she found a way to channel any restless energy. It was one of the reasons Wes had given Dallas to make sure he let her try it out. Wes was more tuned into her emotions. Pain flowed from her eyes more

17

clearly. They were both desperate to see a smile on her face and were willing to try anything to make it happen. Dallas understood heartbreak, and he hated that his little sister was experiencing it.

Wes was the charming and charismatic one and could talk anyone into anything. He was the golden boy in more ways than one, inheriting buttery-blond hair and blue-green eyes from their mother. It was his skills at talking to people that got the dude ranch going and the money flowing. Even with his happy-go-lucky attitude, it was obvious he held himself back from the world. He put up walls and only allowed people to see a small part of who he was. Appearances could be deceiving, something Dallas knew too well.

Dallas picked up the phone and pressed his brother's name in his contact list. The call was answered immediately as he heard a hello on the other end. He took a deep breath before saying, "I gave her the okay to do it. She's expecting your call to help her set it up. I'm trusting you to guide her in every step."

"What made you change your mind?" Wes asked.

"The look on her face, she was so eager to prove herself. I still have doubts it'll be successful, but you're right—she needs to try."

A shout of laughter came through the connection. "Haven't you learned by now I'm always right?"

"No, because you rarely are. Your ego is too big for the state of Washington. You should branch off east a bit and let the residents of Idaho and Montana enjoy the experience of all that is Wes Novak."

Wes chuckled at his brother's response. "You're just jealous that everyone loves me."

"Not at all," Dallas said smoothly, "I'm more selective than you are."

"Of course you are. More like you can't find a woman to put up with your crap."

"Not likely. I'm not looking for a woman to put up with a darn thing." Dallas visibly shuddered at the idea of allowing another woman the opportunity to shatter him again. No, he would never make that mistake again.

"You can't let what one woman did to you rule the rest of your life," Wes said. "Someday you'll find a woman that adores you, hell, they may even like you too."

"So generous of you. As I said, I don't want or need one."

"Famous last words. I can't wait for the right woman to come along and knock you for a loop," Wes snickered.

Even though Wes couldn't see it, Dallas rolled his eyes. "Whatever."

"She's out there and she is going to turn you inside out. I'm gonna make sure I've got front row seats for the show."

Yeah, he already met a woman that turned him inside out. No thanks, he would pass on a repeat experience. "Now I know you're delusional. I'm not letting a woman run my life. Ever."

All he could hear was laughing and decided the conversation was over. Dallas ended the call; Wes knew what he needed to do, anyway.

*G*innifer sat at her desk going through her workload for the week. She had a lot to get accomplished and not enough time in the day. Her schedule didn't allow her a lot of free time. That didn't bother her too much because she didn't have anyone to go home to. So work gave her something to focus on. The only person around to give her any kind of companionship was her best friend, Vitoria. If not for Tori, she probably wouldn't leave the office or home that much. Vitoria made sure she got out and even took an occasional vacation. That didn't include her working vacations. She took at least four of those a year to review places for the magazine she worked at. It had been Tori's idea to schedule a yearly vacation for the two of them. Usually someplace warm with sandy beaches.

Ginnifer looked down startled when her phone began to ring. Usually her personal line didn't ring. She had an assistant to answer phones. It must be someone important for them to have her direct line. Well only one way to find out.

She picked up her phone and answered it. "Ginnifer Zeiss, how can I help you?"

"Hi this is Emmaline Novak; I spoke to you a few weeks ago about our Cowgirl Yoga program. I wanted to confirm you would still be able to attend the first two weeks in September."

"Hmm, let me check my calendar, the first two weeks of September you said? I do remember talking to you about attending. I thought we hadn't nailed down a specific time."

"That's correct. I was getting things scheduled, and I realized we hadn't touched base again. I hope you're still willing to come out and review our program."

Ginnifer checked her calendar and looked over her schedule. Darn it, that's the two weeks of her annual vacation with Vitoria. They had planned on going to the Virgin Islands for this trip. She hadn't ever been there and she loved beaches. Not nearly as much as Vitoria, but it held a lot of appeal. Not as much appeal as spending a couple weeks on a ranch with cowboys. Something about a man in a cowboy hat always made her sit up and take notice. She had hoped to find a sexy cowboy to ogle at her heart's content when she visited the ranch. Perhaps there could be a way to still make it work. Vitoria could be persuaded with the right incentive. She needed to let Emma know that it might not work, though.

"Well I have those two weeks scheduled for a vacation, but I'm supposed to be going away with my best friend. We do it every year. I was afraid they would clash when you mentioned September. Is there any way I can come another time?" Ginnifer explained.

"Oh that's too bad. I was so hoping you would be able to come then. I don't know when I can squeeze you in again," Emma said with a small sigh. "There's absolutely no way you can come during those two weeks?"

Ginnifer tapped her desk with her fingers as she contemplated what she should do. She really did want to go to the ranch. She had always been slightly fascinated by cowboys and ranches. Perhaps she should lay it all on the table for her to consider. Ultimately she would prefer to still have her vacation time with Vitoria. She might be able to persuade her to go. Tori knew how much she loved to look at cowboys. Of course she would point out she could do more than stare at them. Tori liked to touch and didn't understand why Ginnifer didn't jump at the chance herself.

"I was really looking forward to visiting your ranch. It'd be awful to miss out on the opportunity. Are you completely booked? Maybe I can talk Tori into coming along for it. She isn't the roughing it type, but I'm sure she would at least enjoy the yoga and all of the other activities you've planned."

"Well I could put her in a cabin with you. I was going to put you in your own accommodations anyway instead of making you share as the program dictates. If she is willing to come, I could give her a discounted rate. Of course your stay is completely comped like we discussed, but I can't afford to let your friend stay for free. I hope you understand."

"I'll run everything by her and get back to you by the

end of the day tomorrow. She can be hard to pin down because she's out of the office a lot, but I'll leave a message, and she'll get back to me. I should know something for sure when I call you back."

"Excellent. I'll look forward to hearing from you then."

Ginnifer said good-bye and hit End on her phone. She set the phone down on her desk and picked up her to-do list. No need worrying about something she couldn't change, there was plenty of stuff she needed to finish. She would discuss all of the possibilities with Vitoria later today. In the meantime she had some deadlines to meet before she could call it a day at the office. Ginnifer picked up her coffee and took a big drink. She could feel the warmth slide down her throat and settle in her stomach. Coffee was her favorite drink. Nothing compared to its lovely energy, and she couldn't get through a day without it.

"Excuse me, Ms. Zeiss, you have a phone call."

"Thanks, Alison," Ginnifer said. "What is it regarding?"

"It's Mr. Tolliver from that beach resort on the Hawaiian islands you visited three months ago."

Ginnifer reached over and picked up the phone.

"Hello, Mr. Tolliver. How can I help you?"

"I wanted to call and thank you for the lovely review you gave us in your article. I finished reading it a moment ago. I'm glad you were able to enjoy your stay."

"Hawaii was lovely. Thank you for inviting me out. I

don't usually get to visit beach resorts unless it's on my own dime."

"It must get to be expensive traveling all over the place to write articles."

"It can be. I try to visit places that don't have a vested interest in my visit. It makes my articles more valid. I'm always honest, though. If there is some area that can be improved, I don't hold back, as you could tell from my article."

"Yes. We are taking all of your suggestions to heart. We want to give all of our guests a stay worth remembering."

"I'm glad I could help. Overall it was one of the best places I've ever stayed. You did a good job of meeting my needs and making me want to come again. I hope to visit again sometime in the future," she said.

"We look forward to seeing you again. Have a wonderful day," Mr. Tolliver said.

"You too. Good-bye, Mr. Tolliver. It was lovely hearing from you."

Ginnifer hung up her phone and considered her options while braiding a lock of her wavy butterscotch-blonde hair out of habit. Her mind had wandered to the issue with the Cowgirl Yoga program. She really needed to talk to Tori and make a decision. Did the story mean as much to her as her relationship with her best friend? Ginnifer knew it really was more than that, though. She always wanted to visit a ranch, and this was a prime opportunity to get to scratch the experience off of her bucket list. She had to consider all angles and figure out how to make it work.

Tori was looking forward to sunny beaches and sexy

men. What mattered most to her were the sexy men, especially if they were long-haired blonds. The question was how to spin it so she wanted to go on this vacation more than lounge on a beach and ogle the hot guys that could stroll by. Ginnifer wanted to get away, and if she could get her vacation free, even better. Add some possible cowboys to boot? Mmmm nothing sexier than that. Hell did it really matter? She'd approach Tori with the idea, but when push came to shove, she knew she was going to that ranch in September. It would be more fun if she could bring her best friend along for the ride, though. So she hoped Tori wouldn't put up too much resistance to the idea.

As if she knew that Ginnifer had been thinking about her, Tori breezed into her office like one of New York's fashion models, her high heels clicking on the tile floor. Her long caramel-blonde hair pulled up in a messy bun with strands spilling over her face, blue eyes sparkling with mischief, she threw her purse on Ginnifer's desk and sat in one of the chairs nearest to her. Tori scooted the chair up closer to the desk and brought her elbows up to the desk, folding her hands under her chin.

"You will not believe the day I have had," she proclaimed.

Ginnifer smiled at Tori before saying, "I'm sure I won't. Your days are inherently more interesting than mine, but do tell. I'm all ears." Ginnifer leaned her chair back in a more relaxed position, awaiting Tori to tell her the latest tidbit in the entertainment world. The stories she weaved were always interesting and full of the juiciest gossip.

"Well you remember that new client of mine? The sexy football player, that signed a two-year multimillion dollar deal with the Seattle Starlings? Well it appears he needs a little hand holding. I am going to have to fly out to Washington and deal with some issues he created in the tabloids." She rolled her eyes. "Apparently he's going to be a proud poppa in oh about eight months give or take a few weeks, except he swears he has never laid a hand on the baby mama."

"What are the chances he's telling the truth?" Ginnifer asked.

"With this one I'd say the odds are in his favor. The bastard doesn't know how to flirt and totally ignored my suggestions for a little side fun. I swear he acts like a monk. This woman's getting a little money hungry and is trying to saddle him with her bill."

Ginnifer sat up and looked at Tori with shock on her face as she asked, "You actually hit on him?"

"Don't look at me like that, have you seen him? All rock-hard muscle and a face that would put a Greek god to shame. I wanted to run my hands through that unruly mahogany mane of his." Tori shivered as she sighed. "You know I have a weakness for long hair, but no, it didn't happen. Thankfully he doesn't bend easily. Trust me, I gave it my all, and most men can't resist all things Vitoria Miene."

Ginnifer rolled her eyes at her best friend. "You did this knowing you were going to work with him? Isn't it taboo to hit on your potential clients?" Tori was gorgeous, and she's right, most men fawned all over her. She's very choosy who she picks as a lover, though. It could be a little disconcerting to go out with her at times. Sometimes Ginnifer thought she should bring a stick or cane along to beat them off of her best friend, but she knew how much Tori enjoyed the attention. Having them close in on you was a little suffocating, and she had no idea how Tori managed them all.

"Well I actually tried before we signed a contract. You should know I don't like to mix business with pleasure, besides he wasn't biting." After a long drawn out breath and sigh, Tori said, "I didn't honestly think he'd take me up on the offer. It was a test to see how far he was willing to go."

Tori continued to make herself comfortable in Ginnifer's office, pushing the chair back into its original position and leaning against its comfortable cushions. She took one of her crimson stilettos off and began to rub the bottom of her left foot. It wasn't easy walking around in four-inch heels all day, but Tori had a height issue. She was barely two inches above five feet. She made up the difference by wearing very high heels on a daily basis. She often told Ginnifer how lucky she was to be at least five feet five. Tori would love to be taller so that it would be easier to access the tall men she adored so much.

Ginnifer nodded her head at Tori in understanding and asked, "So when do you leave?"

Tori reached down and replaced one shoe and took off the other one to give each foot equal attention as she said, "Well that's partly why I came by here. Not that I don't love you, but this isn't entirely a social call."

Ginnifer groaned and she was almost afraid to ask, "What do you need?"

"Well could you do a nice little interview with him? Publish it in next month's edition? He needs to give his side of the story, and I know you'll give him a fair interview."

The reason Tori and Ginnifer had met was because of their career choices. Tori was a successful publicist. Ginnifer worked for a prominent magazine and also did some freelance work if the magazine didn't want to pick up one of the articles she wrote. She made a decent living writing and traveling when the story made it necessary. They met at a media conference and hit it off immediately. Because of their mutual interests and similar tastes, they had been best friends since that fateful encounter. A little tit for tat was commonplace for them, and if it was possible to help each other out, they didn't think twice about it. That didn't mean they didn't make each other work for the favors they bestowed. Nothing should ever come easy, even between best friends.

Which gave Ginnifer a brilliant idea on how to get Tori to agree to change their vacation from a tropical island getaway to a ranch. "Well I'll consider it on one condition."

Tori looked at her with skepticism in her eyes. "That was almost too easy. Am I going to like this?"

With a shrug, Ginnifer said, "That depends. How do you feel about changing our yearly vacation plans? Instead of sunny beaches, we're going to a ranch for horse riding and yoga."

Tori raised her eyes at her with shock and disdain radiating from them. "You're joking, right? That doesn't sound very relaxing to me. That sounds like some sort of torture, not a vacation."

Ginnifer frowned before saying, "I forgot I agreed to do a story on the ranch. I need to go out there the first two weeks of September."

"I don't think this is actually a fair trade. If we change our plans, you'll owe me."

Ginnifer shook her head as she said, "No, it's either you go with me or I go alone. I made a promise, and it's one I plan on keeping. This could be a good thing. Please say you'll go, and I'll definitely make your football player look better than a Greek god."

"I don't think that's even possible." Her voice was tinged with disbelief. "What could be better than a god?"

A knowing smile formed on Ginnifer's face. "A sexy cowboy."

With that, Tori grinned at Ginnifer as if it occurred to her there would be men on a ranch and the things she was capable of doing with them. Tori loved to flirt; it was by far her favorite hobby. "That's a good point, don't know if they're better, though. I'll have to play with a few to find out."

"So are you gonna go?"

"Yeah count me in. I'll cancel our other vacation plans. Where's this ranch, anyway?" Tori asked as she grabbed her purse and started to rifle through it. She located her phone, opened her calendar, and updated the vacation plans to show a ranch in September. "I need to input it in my calendar."

"Washington state, not too far from Seattle. I've seen

some pictures on their website. It's breathtaking. I can't wait to see it in person."

Tori rolled her eyes. "Only you'd be excited to visit a ranch."

"You know how I feel about cowboys." Ginnifer shrugged. "Maybe you'll get lucky and find a long-haired blond cowboy."

"Unlikely. Don't they like their hair more manageable? As in too short for my tastes?" Tori winked at her. "You don't mind that as long as they're wearing a hat and some cowboy boots, but would you know what to do with one if you found him?"

Ginnifer laughed so hard tears started to come out of her green eyes. Trust Tori to get right to the heart of the matter. With her, the point was always how do I get this one to fall in love with me the fastest.

"Oh I hope I'd know what to do with the right one," she told her best friend.

"Well no worries. I'll be there to help you out if you need to sexify yourself." Tori wiggled her eyebrows suggestively at Ginnifer.

"Thanks, Tori. You truly are the bestest."

"Don't I know it. Washington state? Maybe I can mix with a little business and pleasure on this trip too. I am sure Colt Lewis, quarterback extraordinaire, will continue to need my help after training camp and preseason are over with. I believe the first game is at home the beginning of September too, I'll have to double check the schedule. He has to be a little shell-shocked at all of this. His first NFL season, and he gets a scandal at the top of it. This is going to be an eventful summer."

Reaching for her desk calendar, Ginnifer asked, "When do you want to set the interview up?"

"Let me get back to you on that. I'll need to clarify his schedule with him. I'll call you sometime tomorrow so we can compare schedules. It'll be easier to find something that works when I know more. And with that, I'm off."

Tori blew a kiss at Ginnifer as she walked out of her office in much the same fashion as she entered it, with flair only she could pull off. Her purse was swinging on her shoulder and both stilettos once again on her feet, clicking as she sashayed down the hall.

Well at least that was settled. Tori and she were definitely visiting a ranch for some yoga. The only thing left to do was to make a phone call to Emmaline Novak and tell her to expect both of them in September. Maybe they would be lucky and each find a sexy cowboy on the ranch. It had been a long time since she had met a man she wanted to spend time with, let alone get naked with. She was on one hell of a dry spell lately. Maybe a vacation at a ranch was something she needed to get back in the saddle again, so to speak.

CHAPTER 3

*M*rs. Henly left moments ago, leaving directions sitting on the counter next to the lasagna she fixed. The instructions were included so it would be baked correctly. Mrs. Henly learned the hard way that none of the Novak siblings knew a damned thing about cooking when they burned the first casserole she left. So every time she made them something to heat later, directions were neatly written and placed on the counter. She also left some fresh bread cooling on top of the oven. The scents were tantalizing and a minor distraction to Dallas's productivity. He was sitting at the kitchen table working on the financial reports and going over what they needed for the livestock in the fall months. The sun was streaming through the kitchen window with rays so bright they bounced off of Dallas's iced tea and created a rainbow of colors across the alabaster walls. They were appealing, but frustrating to his concentration. Perhaps he needed to take a break. The warm sunshine made him want to go to the barn and take one of the horses out for a ride. He hated paperwork, but it was a necessary evil.

Dallas had been working on the damned reports all weekend, making sure every aspect was completed. He believed he had managed to think of every possible detail that could arise. He had even considered Emma's Cowgirl Yoga plan. He knew she had a lot cooking in that brain of hers. He wanted her to succeed, but he also knew a lot of business ventures failed. He would have to do what he could to help her plan be a success. It weighed on his mind that she could end up being upset if her idea failed. She already hurt too damn much in her short life.

Emma had told him she managed to nail down every last detail she could think of in planning for her program, including contacting Ginnifer Zeiss to attend her opening. He understood it would be beneficial to have her come but didn't understand why they had to give her a free stay. Plus Emma had discounted her friend's reservation to entice them both to come. He hoped they proved to be worth it.

Dallas also noted the social media sites had all been set up and were a huge hit. They already had several followers and a large interest in what Cowgirl Yoga had to offer. His little sister had even managed to catch the interest of a few bloggers. With the hype she was able to garner in a short time, she managed to completely book the entire two weeks at the beginning of September. There were several people that were only going to be there for one of the weeks, but that didn't matter as long as both weeks were booked solid. He was in the process of looking over the final details when his brother Wesley walked into the kitchen.

"What's up?"

"What? Nothing," he said in a distracted voice.

Dallas continued to work on his lists, ignoring his brother's presence. It wasn't anything he did, but more that he was that wrapped into what he was trying to do. "Hello, Earth to Dallas. I asked you a question."

Dallas looked up at Wes as if seeing him for the first time. He had gotten himself his own glass of iced tea and took a seat at the kitchen table next to him. His aquamarine eyes were glued on him, watching and waiting for him to reply to his question. Wes's face was red and dripping with sweat. The white T-shirt he was wearing was glued to him and drenched down the front, outlining his lean muscular frame. His long buttery-blond hair was pulled into a short stubby ponytail at the nape of his neck. It was clear to Dallas that he had just come in from working hard around Novak Springs.

With a shrug Dallas said, "I'm sorry. I'm trying to iron out some last minute paperwork. Emma's retreat is happening sooner than I realized. Everyone will be here in a week. I can't believe how fast time has flown by."

Wes took a drink of his tea before saying, "That happens. What can I do to help? I have a free afternoon if you need me. I'm finished working for the day. I was going to drive up to Seattle, but I can change my plans if you need me."

"I don't think there's anything that you can do to help. Emma should be here shortly, though. She said she has something to discuss with me. You should stick around to find out what it is she wanted. Maybe it's something you can help with as well."

Wes looked at him with a small amount of fear in his eyes. "Why does that scare me?"

"Probably because our baby sister has a way of making us do things we don't particularly like to do."

"You're not building a solid case here. Tell me something that might make me want to stick around," Wes said.

"Don't be an ass. You know you want to help."

"You're right," he said with a sigh. "I will wait for her to turn up, then."

Just as he said the words, Emma breezed into the kitchen carrying a couple of folders. "Oh good, you are both here. I can use both of your help. Now I know you're going to try to find a way out of it, but I'm not going to take no for an answer."

"What is it?" Wes asked.

Emma walked over to the table and set everything down. Walking over to one of the kitchen cupboards, she opened it and pulled out a tall clear glass. Next, she strolled over to the refrigerator and placed it under the ice cube dispenser and filled it. Picking up the pitcher of tea already located on the counter, she filled the glass to the brim and set it down on the table next to her various folders. She stood next to the table and gave Wes and Dallas her full attention.

"I have this idea for one of the weekends, and you two are essential to making it happen. It's important that I keep them occupied as much as possible. I want them to have a full ranch experience and not have an opportunity to get bored."

"Quit stalling and tell me what it is," Dallas demanded.

"A scavenger hunt."

"Okay I'm confused. Why would you need our help with a scavenger hunt?" Wes asked.

"I can't let them all go around the ranch alone. I need someone that knows every inch of it with them to supervise, and well, we're the only ones that truly do."

Wes put both hands on his forehead, his fingers running up into his golden locks, pulling some of them loose from his ponytail, and looked down at the table. He shook his head from side to side without saying a word for several minutes.

"So let me see if I understand this. You want me and Dallas to escort a bunch of women around this ranch looking for certain items on a scavenger hunt?"

"Um, yes?" she said. "But I'll have a group too."

Wes shook his head. "Not a good idea, Em."

"Why not?"

"Because it's a lot of women. Most of them don't know a lick about anything to do with a ranch. They also tend to do whatever the hell they please. They only care about themselves, not how their actions will impact those around them," Dallas said. He hated women. Okay, maybe hate was too strong of a word. He liked them fine enough for certain activities. He didn't tolerate them all that much for anything other than extracurricular activities. The only woman he liked was his sister. He learned the hard way they were not to be trusted. He didn't want any hands-on duty while they were traipsing around the ranch. He thought he had made that perfectly clear to Emma in an earlier discussion.

Crinkles developed around Emma's eyes as her lips formed her favorite pout. "I need this. You have to help. I know that you have your reasons for not wanting to help, Dallas. But it's dumb. It's not my fault some stupid woman broke your heart. You won't even tell me her name so I can hate her properly. The point is, though, you need to let it go and help me make this work. Not all women are your ex-fiancée."

Wes raised his hands up in frustration. "All right, I can help. I don't like it, but I'm more likely to get along with the women than Dallas, anyway."

"Bullshit. I'm capable of charming a woman if I feel like it. I don't want to. You know why I'd be so adamantly against doing this."

"I thought you were on board to help with whatever's necessary to get this project of hers going. What am I missing?" Wes asked.

"It requires more hands-on activities than I planned on helping with," Dallas shot back.

"Bullshit. What is the real reason you don't wanna help?" Wes turned toward Emma and said, "I'm sorry he's being a jerk, but you can count me in."

"It is nothing really, Dallas, just a game. Surely you can take time out of your day to help with it," Emma pleaded.

Wes looked at Dallas with an evil gleam in his eye. "It's a wittle, wittle game, Dallas, can you come out and play with us?"

Dallas shook his head as he said, "No, I didn't agree to any of this. I don't want any hands-on duties with your Cowgirl Yoga program. Count me out."

"There's that. The big question really is, why are you

afraid of a little game? Is losing money worth a little bit of your time to help your baby sister out?"

"That's enough," Emma told her two brothers. "If you're not willing to help me out, I'll plan something else. I don't need you two if you're going to whine about participating in a freaking game."

The two brothers looked at their sister with guilt shining from their eyes. Dallas began to shuffle his feet from side to side, opening and closing his mouth like a fish out of water. He hadn't meant to disappoint her, but she didn't understand why he felt the way he did. That was his fault. He could explain what had happened with Melody. It had been a really hard time for him, and he didn't like to discuss it.

Wes sat quietly at the table, his hands folded in front of him, waiting for his older brother to find the words he was searching for. No doubt, Dallas thought, if they were not her only family, she would never speak to them again. Emma stood up and began to gather her papers to leave the room. Her frustration showed as her mouth pursed up in displeasure, and she shut each folder harder than necessary. She gathered her paperwork into her arms and started to storm out of the kitchen.

"Emma wait," Dallas pleaded.

Emma turned around and looked at her brother. Her anger was palpable, face flushed red and her breaths coming out in heavy pants. "You wanna know what pisses me off the most? That you didn't even bother to ask why it was so important to me. Oh no, the great Dallas help? Pfft, as if. What the hell is wrong with you? Can't get off that high horse long enough to join the rest of us minions? Don't worry, I will find someone else to help me. I don't need you."

Dallas wasn't able to get another word out as she breezed out of the room faster than he could blink. Apparently Emma believed the conversation was over. Nothing else needed to be discussed. He knew he was acting like an asshole, but sometimes he couldn't help himself. It was his go-to attitude.

"Fuck," Dallas said under his breath.

Wesley slowly clapped his hands as he watched his brother stalk toward the kitchen door after their sister. Dallas turned around and gave him a look that would have withered a lesser man, but Wes was used to dealing with his brother's ornery side and laughed at his attempts of putting him in his place. "Nice try, but I think you've bigger things to worry about now."

Dallas was stunned. "What's that supposed to mean?" he asked.

"You pissed Emma off. Now what are you going to to do to fix it?"

"What the fuck do you mean, what am I going to do to fix it? Seems to me you were clearly a part of that discussion. You've an equal part in fixing it."

"Oh no, that's totally about you. You forget I told her I'd help." He looked Dallas directly in the eyes. "I didn't think you would give in and help, though. You proved me right. If she means anything to you, then yes, you will make this right. If I find what you do to make it better agreeable, I might still go along with what you decide."

Dallas ran his hands through his short chestnut hair and rumpled the strands out of their normally well-groomed existence. He sighed in frustration and rambled aimlessly around the kitchen lost in thought. When an idea came to him, he stopped and turned toward his brother and then slowly walked over and pulled out a chair to sit down at the kitchen table. The iced tea that Emma had abandoned was still sitting on the table directly in front of him. He watched as tiny droplets of water trailed down the side of the glass from the condensation. With each drop of water, he felt his insides turn to mush at the idea that he had hurt his baby sister in any way. She was the only woman that mattered to him, and he did something that made her feel like he didn't care about her.

Resigned to helping her out, Dallas said, "Okay, I will help. I need more information. Do you have any idea what this scavenger hunt involves? I know I didn't give her much of a chance to explain it, but maybe you saw it when you were helping her out."

"Well I don't have the complete details. She didn't get past the fact that she needed both of us to help with it."

"Okay what does she need help with?" Dallas asked.

"She needs us each to lead a team. From what I gather, there'll be three groups total, and she doesn't want her guests to wander aimlessly around the ranch. She said we knew the ranch best, so she wanted each of us to head a set of players."

"I still can't believe she wants me to take time away from the ranch to lead a fucking bunch of women around for a damn scavenger hunt. Has she lost her mind?" Dallas didn't want Emma to be upset, but the more he thought about it, the more he hated this idea of hers. She knew how busy he was around the ranch. Did she really think taking time away from his many duties was such a good idea?

"That is the problem right there. You're just seeing how much this is going to be a nuisance for you. Why don't you look at this from Emma's point of view? She needs us to help with this venture so that she is successful, or have you forgotten why we thought this idea of hers was good for her?"

Dallas let out a breath and once again started to push his fingers through his hair. At this rate he was going to pull out some of the strands and eventually go bald. Maybe the women wouldn't try to fawn all over him if he didn't have any hair on his head. He shook that thought out of his head. Only one problem at a time, and the current dilemma was how to make his baby sister happy again. Damn harpies would still think he was a good catch regardless of the state of his hair, bald or not. If they didn't have the idea of getting him to settle down and marry them, it wouldn't bother him so much. He wasn't a long-term kind of guy. He could deal with some women trying to get close to him for a short time if it helped Emma out.

"No, I haven't forgotten. I know that she needs to get her head wrapped around something other than the guy who broke her heart. I'll make it up to her," Dallas said.

Wes nodded his head in agreement. "Good, we can both talk to her and tell her we are willing to help with the scavenger hunt."

"Yes, damn it. I'll help lead one of the teams on her scavenger hunt," Dallas grudgingly agreed.

"Fine. Then we should go look for her to make her realize we're willing to help her in any way possible to make sure this goes off without a hitch."

Dallas sighed and got up to stroll out of the kitchen. He turned and looked at Wes. "Are you coming?"

"Right behind you," Wes said as he got up to follow him.

As they left the kitchen, Dallas thought it was going to take a lot of groveling to get Emma to forgive them. She could hold a grudge longer than anyone he knew. He would have to promise damn near anything to get back in her good graces. Dallas had forgotten why they had really decided it was a good idea for her to start her Cowgirl Yoga program. She wasn't that happy girl they all knew anymore. The goal had been to try to get her to a place where her smiles were not forced but the bright sunshine they were used to seeing on her face. They went through a small kind of hell after their parents died, and they worked hard to get her to a good place. Dallas didn't want to lose her to that kind of depression ever again. He grimaced at the idea of what was going to have to happen to make that smile shine on her face again. The only hope he had was that it would be worth it if at least one of them found some kind of happiness.

Ginnifer was packed and getting ready to go to the airport when her phone started to blare the words of "I Like It, I Love It" by Tim McGraw. She looked down and saw a picture of Tori coming across her screen. She pressed the button to accept the call and raised it up to her ear, saying hello.

"Good. I caught you before you left for the airport," Tori said breathlessly on the other end.

"What do you mean before I left for the airport? I thought you were meeting me here and we were going over together," Ginnifer replied. Her anger could be heard in every word she said. Her mouth crunched up in displeasure, and she held her phone tight in her hand.

"Damn, I forgot we were going to do that. Please don't be mad at me," Tori begged.

Ginnifer sighed in frustration. What the hell did Tori do now? She was always changing plans last minute. It was one of the few things that irritated her about her best friend. She always had some last minute emergency and forgot to let the people around her know her plans had changed.

"Well, I hit a snag with my latest client. I finally was able to get him to agree to do that interview with you, but I had to fly to Seattle last night. So, um, yeah I am already in Washington. I was wondering if you could delay going to the ranch and do the interview with him first."

"No," Ginnifer told her. "I'm going to the ranch. If he is willing to do the interview, tell him to come out to the ranch and I can make time for him there. He's been hem-hawing around about doing it. Tell him to man up and take a stand. I'm not going to cater to him when this is a favor I'm doing for him." The damn idiot had been putting the interview off for weeks. She was not going to go out of her way to cater to him when it was her vacation he was getting ready to interrupt. What kind of entitled asshole did he think he was?

"Fine. I think I can make that work. I could have him drive me out to the ranch tomorrow. I'm going to be a day late. Please let our host know that I will be there tomor-row," Tori said. "I wish you'd take care of it in Seattle, though."

"Sorry, no can do. If he wanted me to come to him, he should have agreed a lot sooner. You know how I feel about people that do that. I don't do last minute crap without a damn good reason. My time is too valuable for that."

Tori sighed on the other end of the call. "Okay. I'll text you when we leave Seattle. Don't grab all the hot cowboys for yourself before I get there."

Ginnifer chuckled to herself. Tori always did have

certain priorities. "I'll try to save you at least one. I'm generous, after all."

"Pfft, you better save more than one. I have needs."

"I don't know. You might have to make do with only one. I hear that they have a lot of stamina. I'm sure you could make do."

"Stamina? We will have to see how much they actually have. I bet I could wear them out." A hint of devilishness filled Tori's voice.

"If anyone could do it, Tori, no doubt it would be you," Ginnifer agreed.

"Okay I have to go. I need to go tell Colt that he has to drive me to the ranch tomorrow to meet with you. Wish me luck. He's one stubborn quarterback."

"You don't need luck. I'll see you tomorrow," Ginnifer said and hit End on her phone.

The first order of business was to call a cab. She hadn't already called one because she thought Tori was meeting her. The plan was to share a cab to the airport. She picked up her phone and called the cab company. She accepted there would now be a twenty-minute wait until she could go to the airport. While she was waiting, she thought about everything she needed to do before she got to the ranch. She made a mental note to make sure she packed her tablet. She would need it to complete her notes and article while she was on vacation. Ginnifer walked around and made sure she had everything she needed one last time so she would be ready to leave her apartment when the cab arrived. She sat by the large window in her apartment staring out the window until her ride to the airport appeared.

She thought again about her upcoming vacation and her impending interview with Colt Lewis. She hoped she didn't regret agreeing to do it for Tori. So far it had turned out to be more hassle than it was worth. This vacation better be everything she hoped it would be. Ginnifer would be pissed if this interview hindered it in some way. The break was supposed to be fun. Yes, it was a working vacation, but it was also something she had always wanted to do.

Looking out the window from her apartment, Ginnifer saw the cab had pulled up and parked next to the curb. She grabbed her luggage and got into the elevator outside her apartment to make her way down to the first floor. She lived on the fifth floor, and she was grateful she didn't have to carry her luggage down five flights of stairs. She exited the building and walked over the cab. Once she was there, the cab driver got out and helped her put her luggage in the trunk. She walked to the back of the car, opened the door, and climbed inside to get comfortable for the ride to the airport. She had two layovers from New York to Washington. It was going to be a very long trip, and she was looking forward to relaxing once she arrived at her final destination. The ranch sounded so peaceful, and she prayed it lived up to all of her expectations. Visiting a ranch and experiencing everything it had to offer had always appealed to her. She hoped it lived up to every one of her desires, including the hot cowboys of her imagination.

~

DALLAS WALKED into the den and found his sister sitting at the table going through a bunch of lists. She was so completely engrossed in her plans she hadn't realized he walked into the room. That appeared to be a family trait. They tended to get lost in their own worlds from time to time.

"Hey, sis, what are you working on?"

"Oh last minute details. I am checking off items on my lists. I had all the cabins scrubbed clean. Fresh linens put on the beds. Mrs. Henly agreed to cook all of the meals for our guests. You know, those kinds of things you stopped caring if I told you about."

"You know it's not like that. I've been trying to talk to you to apologize. You know that I do care. Please don't stay mad at me," Dallas pleaded.

"Are you willing to help with the scavenger hunt?"

"Yes. I don't like it. But I'll help."

"It's going to take more than that for me to forgive you. I don't think you helping with the scavenger hunt is enough."

She had a wicked glint shining from her eyes. His sister was up to something. He didn't think he would like it much, either. There was a price to pay, though, and he was more than willing to pay it. Hurting Emma had never sat right with him. She had always depended on him to fix things, not make them worse.

"What do you want from me? I will do whatever you ask. I do have responsibilities on the ranch, though, so please take that into consideration as you exact your revenge on me for making a mess of things."

"I want you to be part of the prize for winning the scavenger hunt."

"Okay…" he started to agree. "Wait, what?"

"You heard me."

"I don't understand. You are going to pimp me out to a bunch of women? That's taking things a bit far, don't you think?" Dallas said, appalled at her suggestion. He didn't think Emma had an evil bone in her body. He had to rethink his opinion of his little sister if she was going to torture him that way.

"Well it isn't quite like that. I am also going to need Wes to be part of the prize as well."

"I'm so glad you clarified that. It's not just me you are going to throw to the wolves. You're going to throw both of your brothers, I feel so much better now. Thanks for making it easier to understand." Dallas shook his head.

"No, silly. I want you both to take them on an overnight campout. It'll be fun."

"I think your idea of fun differs greatly than mine. Are you sure Wes is open to doing this?"

"Not in the slightest. I'm going to count on you to make that a reality. You said you would do anything to help." Emma batted her eyelashes at him.

"Fine. I will talk to Wes and make sure he will participate. He said he would help. Don't think this was exactly what he had in mind, though."

"You'll both be fine. Like I said, it will be fun. I'm getting excited, guests should be coming soon."

"You said Mrs. Henly agreed to cook the meals. Is she going to stay at the ranch for the two weeks?"

"No. She said she'd rather go home. She has the

kitchen fully stocked for everything she needs. She'll come out each morning and make breakfast and lunch. She said she'd prepare something we could heat up for dinner. So I'll have to be done with everything in time to make sure dinner is ready for our guests each night. I'm grateful for her help. This is a lot more work than I thought it would be when I started it out."

It sounded like Emma had everything organized and planned out to the last intricate detail. For a brief moment he let his pride for her roll over him. She accomplished a lot in a short amount of time, and he started to believe this business idea of hers might be successful.

"It will be great. I'm sure you will make everything run smoothly. I believe in you. I know I was reluctant in the beginning, but I understand how much this means to you. That will make all the difference," Dallas said.

"Thanks. I appreciate you saying that. I will make this work. I'm determined."

"Excuse me, Emma," Mrs. Henly said as she walked into the den. "You have some guests arriving already. Do you want me to show them to their cabins, or do you want to greet them first?"

"Go ahead and show them to their cabins and get them settled. Tell them that I'll meet with everyone this evening before we have dinner to explain what we're going to be doing over the next several days," Emma told her. "And Mrs. Henly, thank you so much for agreeing to help out over the next couple of weeks. I couldn't have done all of this without your help."

Mrs. Henly beamed at her with a huge smile on her weathered face; her soft blue eyes glowed with the praise.

"It's nice to be helpful. I enjoy helping your family out. I'd do anything for you three. I'll go make sure the guests get settled in. Do you have a list of all of the guests so I can check them off and make sure they get into their assigned cabins?"

Dallas watched as Emma looked over some papers in front of her until she found a list of names and handed it to Mrs. Henly. "Here it is. I have every guest name listed under the cabin they are going to be in. There are three to a cabin except in the blue and green cabins. We have twelve total guests each week. The blue cabin has four guests. The green cabin has Ginnifer Zeiss and Vitoria Miene. They're our special guests, so make sure they're settled in and let me know once they're here. I want to speak to them before this evening."

Mrs. Henly took the list and left Emma and Dallas alone in the den. Yes, it looked like Emma really had thought of everything. She had a decent plan, and it all had been organized down to the last detail. Dallas was proud of her. He hadn't been lying when he told her he believed she could make it work. If anyone could do it, his little sister could. He knew he had a large amount of cynicism that he carried around inside of him. It spilled out into most of the areas of his life. He didn't want it to become such a huge part of him that he couldn't support his family. They needed to depend on him, and he couldn't let his own demons into that equation. Melody had hurt him, his family hadn't. That made all the difference in the world.

"I have some paperwork to go over. Do you need me to do anything before I leave?"

"No I have this. Go talk to Wes for me. Tell him we will have three groups for the scavenger hunt, each led by one of us. The prize is an overnight campout reminiscent of the old days. Open skies, campfires, and cookouts… You get the idea."

"Yes I see where you are going with it. I still think it's an awful idea, but I will do it."

"Thanks, I appreciate it. You know I'd never really stay mad at you, right?"

"I do. We're family, we forgive each other. That doesn't mean we don't pay the price for hurting each other. You can always depend on me."

"I know that, Dallas. You and Wes are the only men I can count on."

Oh hell his sister had sunk down to his level. He needed to work on his attitude toward women. Maybe somewhere along the way he could find a good one. He'd need to step up and show her that not all men were bad. Maybe all women weren't, either. He didn't like the idea of opening himself up to that kind of hurt again.

"You shouldn't close yourself off, Em."

"You don't have a lot of room to talk."

"I know, but I'm not someone you should aspire to be."

"I don't see it that way. You're a good man, Dallas. I think you should take your own advice. Find a good woman. Take a risk. Try to feel again."

"I'll take it under advisement. You could be right."

"I'm always right."

"No, you're not." He laughed. "But in this case you might be. I have to go. Let me know if you need anything else."

"I will. Now go take care of the ranch. I'd hate for it to go down in ashes before I have a chance of trying out the Cowgirl Yoga program."

Dallas laughed as he left the room. At least he had been able to get her to smile. Mission accomplished. He had a few things he needed to take care of. Number one on his list was locating Wes and getting him to help with Emma's scavenger hunt. He couldn't wait to see the look on his face when he realized what her prize was. That alone was worth tracking him down and giving him the good news.

*D*allas still couldn't believe he let Emma talk him not only into leading one of the groups on that blasted scavenger hunt but also to take the winners out on an overnight camping trip. Why did he let her talk her into doing these things to entertain her guests? Oh yeah, he wanted to make her happy. He remembered now. It still irked him a bit. The only good thing was Wes's reaction to it had been priceless. It should be entertaining at least to spend the evening with his brother on that campout.

He had a lot of things to do and most of them involved running the ranch. He sometimes wished he didn't love his family quite as much as he did. They were the only ones he allowed inside his heart. After what he went through with Melody, he didn't trust anyone he hadn't known his whole life, and if he was being honest, sometimes he didn't trust them. He learned that women were fickle and that he really only needed one thing from them. As long as they understood he wasn't the staying kind, he would form a relationship of sorts with them. The relationship consisted of one night of no-holds-barred sex and he left them. Once the night was over, he didn't give any of them a second thought. Why bother? All he needed was to occasionally have his needs met, and he had no problem finding a willing female to give him what he desired most. Of course in light of his discussion with Emma, he believed it was time to make a change. He had no clue how he'd go about making that happen. It was hard to let go of already ingrained attitudes.

As he sauntered out of the barn to walk to the main house, he saw a navy blue Honda Civic pull up in the long driveway. The driver pulled it up to the front of the house and parked it by the white wraparound porch attached to the sunny-yellow house. She got out of the car, closing the door with a small thud. She began to pull her long butterscotch locks up into a messy ponytail that left random strands to fall all over her head and face. The woman adjusted her oversized sunglasses that covered her high cheekbones while her heart-shaped mouth lifted into a smile as she looked at the house. Dallas was awestruck at how beautiful she was; her breasts were full and high, and her waist narrowed into a plump ass. He had never seen hair quite that shade, and he wanted to touch it to feel if it was as soft as it looked. As she leaned forward to smooth away the wrinkles on her shirt, he got a better look at her ass. His mouth watered at the sight, and he ached to reach over and give it a hard squeeze while he took the time to sink his mouth into her lush bosom. It gave him ideas of what he could do with her once he got her naked and in that exact position.

She turned toward him, and as she looked at him, her tongue slowly ran over her lips. In that moment he knew that she was going to be the one woman he couldn't resist. She was going to be his, if only for a little while. Miss Butterscotch Locks would be the exception to his one night rule. Oh yes, she will be in my bed for as many nights as I can charm her into it, he thought as he hoped she was one of the program's two-week guests. That might be enough time to get her out of his system. Heavy emphasis on the might. He suspected it wouldn't nearly be enough time to satisfy his lust for her. He brushed his sweaty hands on the side of his dusty jeans and walked toward her. As he neared her, she looked him over as if trying to figure him out. He must be quite a sight. The chores in the barn had gotten quite dirty, and he was covered in dust from head to toe. A shower was calling his name, and he had been aiming to get inside of one when he stepped outside of the barn.

"Can I help you, ma'am?" he asked.

"Ma'am? Seriously, do I look like a ma'am?" the woman said sarcastically and shook her head. "I'm sorry, it's been one hell of a long trip to get here. I'm looking for Emmaline Novak."

"I might be able to help you with that." The corner of his lip curved up into a half smile. "I happen to know her very well. Are you one of her guests?"

"Ginnifer Zeiss," she said as she held her hand out to him. "I need to tell her that Tori won't be here until tomorrow and to, well, get settled in. I need to rest, I've been traveling since eight o'clock this morning. The trip from New York was hell, and I could seriously use some down time. God, I am rambling, I'm sorry. I didn't expect jet lag to hit me quite this hard."

I sure would like to hit you hard. He shook the idea out of his head. One thing at a time; she needs to get settled in. Ginnifer. It was too long. He needed to think of a fitting nickname for the gorgeous woman standing in front of him. He had never been swayed by someone's appearance, but he believed by the time she left, he was going to know this female quite well. It would be a vacation she wouldn't soon forget, and the bonus was that she was leaving in two weeks and he wouldn't have to see her again. Sounded like a win-win situation in his mind. The key was to try to charm her from the start and maybe they could get a lot closer and soon. Who was he kidding? He wasn't capable of real charm. She would be his, though, make no mistake about it.

Dallas reached out and shook her hand. "Nice to meet you, Gin. If you follow me inside, I'll see if I can find Emma."

Ginnifer raised her eyebrows, mocking him. "Gin? I'm not some kind of alcohol you can swill at your convenience. Please call me Ginnifer if you're going to be less formal."

Dallas's lips lifted into a smile that could only be described as cocky. The corners of his mouth lifted partially up and his eyes narrowed. His gaze traveled her body upward from her feet, slowing over her torso and chest, and then up to stare boldly in her sea-green eyes. "Trust me, I'd take the time to savor every inch of you. Swill isn't in my vocabulary. Come along, Gin, and I'll get my sister for you."

Dallas started to walk to the front door as Ginnifer followed. They walked in, and he led her into a bright sunny kitchen. The whole room was squeaky clean. There were several fresh rolls cooling on the counters and a huge pot of vegetable beef soup simmering on the stove. The aroma was mouthwatering. It had been ages since he had eaten anything and couldn't wait to taste what Mrs. Henly had created.

Ginnifer rubbed her hands over the legs of her pants, once again wiping the moisture that was gathering on them. "Emma's your sister? She didn't mention she had a brother."

Dallas raised one of his eyes at her question. "I didn't realize you two had gotten real cozy and shared personal info. There are the three of us—Emma, Wes, and, well, me."

"Mr. Novak, I really don't like being called Gin."

His mouth twitched into another cocky smile. "Dallas."

A puzzled look was on her face. "What?"

"Call me Dallas, not Mr. Novak."

"Right, if you had bothered to tell me your name sooner, I may have addressed you as such. Has anyone ever told you how rude you are?" she asked.

"On occasion."

Gin raised her eyebrow up and asked, "And you never bothered to question if they were right or not?"

Dallas's laughter rumbled out of him, and it reverberated through the room. "Oh no, I know I'm rude. It's an art form, really. Why be nice? It's a waste of time."

She rolled her eyes. "Right, I wouldn't want to waste your time."

Dallas was quick to reassure her. "Oh this isn't a waste of my time. I was coming in here anyway."

"Oh soooo glad I'm not keeping you from something much more important. Please don't let me keep you any longer. Do go run off and well, do whatever it is you do here. I'm sure that Emma will be around here at some point. I don't need you to stay here and babysit me. Actually I would prefer that you didn't."

"I think that it would be best if I stayed here and kept you company." He ran his tongue over his teeth. "I am finding your company—very stimulating."

Ginnifer's lips pursed in displeasure. "In case you were wondering, I don't like you. In fact, I'm starting to think that most people don't."

Oh his Gin had some spunk. Oh yes, he was going to enjoy her very much. The battle of wits was almost as orgasmic as it was going to be once he found a way to be inside her. He needed to fuck her, and well, it was only a matter of time before he got what he wanted. Dallas was used to getting what he wanted, and Gin was the newest acquisition he would add to his portfolio. The foreplay before they got to the real stuff was only going to make it that much sweeter. Once he had her naked, he could taste every last inch of her. When he finally got her ass in his hands and as he licked her nipples to pull them inside of his mouth, it would be one of his greatest moments. That idea would have to be tabled for now. Gin wasn't nearly ready to go down that road with him, but it didn't mean he couldn't start preparing her for the idea. "I don't care if other people like me. As long as I get what I want." He ran his fingers gently down the side of her face as he leaned in closer and whispered in her ear, "And rest assured, I always get what I want."

Ginnifer jerked away from him and moved across the room to gain some distance between them. "What the hell is that supposed to mean?"

"Exactly what you think it means."

With an appalled look on her face, Ginnifer said, "Well I don't plan on getting any closer to you than I have to. Find your sister so I can go rest in my cabin in relative peace."

A slow, lazy smile formed on his face. "Oh, I don't think so darlin'. We'll have plenty of time to get to know all the intimate details about each other."

Ginnifer's faced turned a bright red at his suggestive comments. He couldn't wait to see if her whole body blushed as brightly when they got around to getting naked together. This was one time that Dallas wanted to whoop with joy at his sister's lame-brained idea of Cowgirl Yoga. At this point in time, it was the best idea she had ever had. In fact, maybe he should start encouraging her to make this project a little more long-term.

Ginnifer stared at him, shocked at his innuendos. "Uh-huh, that's a bit presumptuous of you. I think I'll pass."

"Not at all." Dallas sauntered over to her, leaned in close, and spoke softly in her ear. "I look forward to seeing if you blush all over."

With that comment, Dallas strolled out of the door. That would give her something to think about. Anticipation was part of the game. The more time she had to think about it, the more eager she would be. He knew over time she would want him as much as he wanted her. He would be only too happy to accommodate her when she walked willingly over to the dark side.

GINNIFER COULD NOT BELIEVE he said those things to her. When she first saw him, he was the sexy cowboy of her dreams. Well he was filthy, but she still wanted to rub her hands all over his body. She had a deep desire to feel if he was as rock-hard all over as he looked. The cowboy was truly a beautiful man. He had some light stubble on his face, adding to his appeal. His blue eyes were steel traps that sucked you in and begged you to touch him. Ginnifer wanted to give in, at least until he opened his mouth and started speaking. That was when he ruined the fantasy. What an ass. She was torn between wanting to slap him and kiss him. Her emotions were so conflicting, she couldn't make heads or tails out of the jumbled mess going across her body.

Could I possibly give in to that desire? He had such kissable lips. It had been a very long time since she came across a man that made her want to get naked. It was more than that. The desire she felt in his presence was something she had never truly felt before. It was both overwhelming and exciting at the same time. It didn't matter that he was a rude asshole. His attitude told her he would be able to carry out everything his demeanor said he was capable of. That man would be able to make her scream, and Ginnifer had never come across a man so sure of himself. It was so damn attractive, and she had to wonder if she was willing to put up with his rudeness in order to find out how good he actually was. *Mmm, Dallas might indeed be the man I've been waiting for my whole life.* Ginnifer was still lost in thought and staring out of the kitchen window when a woman with reddish-brown hair walked in.

"Hi you must be Ginnifer. I'm Emma. Dallas told me you were waiting in here for me. I apologize if he was rude. He doesn't like strangers," she explained.

Ginnifer brushed the comment away with her hands. "It's no big deal. I've dealt with worse. It's nice to finally meet you, but I'm desperate to lie down and rest. It's been a long day."

Emma nodded her head. "I'm sorry I kept you waiting. If you'll follow me, I can show you to your cabin."

They walked out of the kitchen and made their way out the front door and onto the white wraparound porch. When they were down the steps and near Ginnifer's rental car, Emma stopped and looked at her saying, "Do you need help with your bags?"

Ginnifer had completely forgotten about her bags. When Dallas had walked up, all reasonable thoughts had left her sleep-deprived brain and focused solely on him. It's a good thing Emma had reminded her, or she very well may have left them in the trunk of her rental car. She turned to Emma and said, "Oh yeah, I should stop and get those out of the trunk. I wasn't sure where you wanted me to park. Don't worry, I can handle them myself. I only have the two bags, and one of them is on wheels." Ginnifer stopped and popped the trunk and removed her two bags. She lifted the handle on the one and got ready to roll it over to her cabin. Swinging the remaining bag on her shoulder, she turned toward Emma and blew a stray piece of hair out of her face. Ginnifer nodded to Emma indicating she was prepared for the trek to her home away from home. They began to make their way over toward the cabin and talked on the way.

Emma waved toward the Civic and said, "Leave your car where it is. If it needs to be moved, we can have it relocated later. Where's your friend?"

"Oh Tori will be here tomorrow. She's having someone drive her up here. I actually have to do an interview with him when he gets here. It shouldn't take too much time. Then he'll leave afterward. I hope that isn't a problem."

Emma shook her head to reassure her. "Not at all. Do you have any idea what time they'll be here?"

She had gotten a text from Tori as she drove to the ranch, complaining about having to bring Colt all the way to Novak Springs. All Ginnifer could think was too damn bad, but Emma didn't need to know all of that, so all she told her was, "Not until after lunch. She texted me earlier and said it would be close to two o'clock before they arrived."

Emma rustled through the folder she was carrying and pulled out some papers. She turned her face toward Ginnifer and smiled. "Good, then you'll be able to get up with us at sunrise to do our first round of yoga. We are going to do horseback riding this evening if you're interested."

"No, I want to rest tonight. I'm not even sure if I can manage to come up for dinner."

Emma had two sheets of paper and a set of keys in her hands. She handed them over to Ginnifer. "Well, here is a list of our two-week itinerary and the keys to your cabin. If you have any questions, feel free to ask at any time. Here is your cabin now, we have you staying in the green cabin. In case you get confused, it has a green door. We painted all the doors different colors to help guests remember which one they are in because they all look alike sitting like ducks in a row. Dinner is in two hours if you decide to join us. The itinerary has details about everything, including when and where we'll have each meal."

"Thanks, I appreciate it."

With that, Emma walked away as Ginnifer unlocked the door and entered the cabin. Everything was clean and smelled heavenly. It was really too bad she was too tired to enjoy it all. She scanned the room and walked to the nearest full-size bed. It had the prettiest green and blue patchwork quilt on it with two matching fluffy pillows. That was what she really needed, someplace to lay down and leave the rest of the world for a little while. She would get a good look at everything else in the cabin once she had some more sleep. Ginnifer dropped her bags, kicked off her shoes, and fell face first onto the bed. It didn't take long for her to fall asleep and enter the world of dreams. She didn't know that a certain sexy cowboy was going to star in them, or she might have held off trying to get the sleep she desperately needed. All she got out of the deal was a frustration she wasn't prepared to handle.

CHAPTER 6

a loud noise erupted through the stillness and echoed louder with each bounce of acoustics across the cabin's walls. When the sound reached Ginnifer's ears, she shot out of bed and pounced on the offending object to make it stop. Damn phone, who the hell tries to call at five a.m.? The reverberation of the phone was the equivalent of getting a bucket of cold water thrown on her face, successfully jerking her awake. She picked up her phone to see who dared to disturb her sleep. She had been tossing and turning all night from the erotic dreams her subconscious decided to bestow upon on her. Stupid sexy cowboy had to make a starring role in those erotic dreams too. A happy camper she was not; patience was not a virtue when you were jolted awake before the sun rose in the sky. If they were expecting her to have a charitable mood, they were in for a not so pleasant surprise. She slid the unlock button on her phone and scrolled to her missed calls. Damn it, Tori. She should know better than to try to call her this early in the morning. If there was anyone on the planet that should realize how she hated mornings, it was her best friend.

Crap! What if something happened? She needed to call her back to find out why she had called her before even a rooster was awake to cock-a-doodle-doo with the sun's morning rays. Tori hated mornings even more than Ginnifer did. If she called, there should be a damn good reason for it. There must be something seriously wrong. Ginnifer raised her hands to her face and rubbed her eyes rapidly to scrub the sleep from them. To make sure she was as alert as possible, she lightly tapped her cheeks with the palm of her hand to get the circulation flowing and help remove the cobwebs from her sluggish brain. Some serious stimulation was in order—well that and a strong cup of coffee. Ginnifer pulled her phone up and hit Send on Tori's name. It rang several times and went to her voice mail. What the hell is going on? She just called and then didn't bother to answer her own phone. When Tori got there later today, she was going to get a mouthful on the many ways she was going to die for doing something so diabolical.

Ginnifer listened to the recording and waited for the beep, debating what she should say on Tori's voice mail. After the beep sounded in her ear, she began to speak, "You're dead to me. When you get here, I'm gonna make you regret that you're still breathing. There better be a damn good reason for calling me at this unspeakable time and an even better reason for not answering your damn phone when I called back. Be prepared for hell once you get here."

She clicked End on the phone and placed it on a

nearby table. Ginnifer chewed her lower lip and debated what her options were. She looked over at the itinerary that Emma had given her yesterday and decided to see what was on the schedule for the day. She rolled her eyes over the agenda and landed on the first activity. Yoga outside in the south pasture at seven o'clock in the morning with breakfast to follow at eight thirty. She had a little less than two hours before anything was happening on the schedule. Where the hell was the dining area and south pasture, anyway? She looked at the papers again and noticed a detailed map on the back. Well, she would say one thing about Emma Novak, the young woman was certainly prepared for everything.

Ginnifer let out a breath and contemplated what she should do for the next two hours. She could check her e-mails and see if there was anything that needed attending before she started her day and make some notes of what little she experienced so far on the ranch for her article. What she needed, though, was a hot shower and some coffee to get her moving. Going back to sleep was out of the question at this point. Once she was awake and moving, it was futile to attempt to gain any more shut eye. Her brain was not wired to doze back off once she was jolted awake.

Maybe if she got the shower out of the way, she could see if she could locate the coffee somewhere on the ranch. Surely there was someone awake taking care of things, or at least they should be by the time she was done with her shower, anyway. She might as well go bathe and get ready for the day. Coffee would be helpful if she was going to make it through the morning. It was a little slice of heaven she was not used to denying herself. It would be worth almost any price to her to get her hands on a cup of hot java with a side of cream and sugar. She would even consider putting up with Dallas's sexual innuendos to get her mouth around the rim of a cup filled with the blissfulness the caffeinated drink would bring. The man was so unnerving to all of her senses. The promises in his eyes made her want to give in and see if he could keep each one of them. She would have to steel herself for the onslaught of emotions that he evoked in her. If she had one hope, it was that she wouldn't run into him in her hunt for her morning brew. That male had the power to make her forget what she wanted most.

She went to her bags and picked up her largest one, dragged it over, and plopped it on top of her bed, unzipping the sides to release the top. The top of the luggage was thrown open as she began to dig through its contents. She pulled out a pair of soft black yoga pants trimmed with black and white polka dots, the matching top, a pair of panties, and a sports bra. She zipped the suitcase closed and placed it on the floor. Bundling everything up in her arms, she made her way to the bathroom to take a hot shower. It was going to be a lot longer than she had originally planned, and she had Tori to thank for the impromptu wake-up call. Something she would make sure she paid for once she arrived at the ranch later on in the afternoon. In the meantime, she would make the best of the situation and start her day without snarling at anyone, well, hopefully not too much anyway.

After she was finished with her shower, she dried herself off and threw the wet towel into a nearby hamper.

Picking up the clothes she had pulled out of her suitcase, she dressed as quickly as possible to stop the chill of the morning from seeping through to her bones any more than it already had. Her brush was lying on the bed where she had dumped it when she pulled her toiletries out, so she grabbed it and ran it through her hair, untangling the knots that had developed overnight. With a flick of her wrist, she twisted her long hair between her fingers. A thick braid formed and fell down the middle of her back. She grabbed a hair tie and wrapped it around the end of the braid. Ginnifer strolled over to her small bag and began to sort through it. She pulled out a small, clear lip gloss and ran it over her dry lips; the sweet strawberry flavor of the lip gloss rolled over her tongue. She picked up the jacket, pulled her arms through it, and zipped it up. Her cell phone was still lying on the table where she had placed it earlier after her unsuccessful attempt at calling Tori back. She grabbed it and placed it into her other pocket in case Tori tried to call or text her again.

Ginnifer looked around the cabin one last time to make sure she wasn't forgetting anything and then made her way over to the door. She pulled her phone out of her pocket and looked at the time. A whoosh of air left her mouth as she sighed when she saw it was past six in the morning. The key to the cabin still rested upon the table she had tossed it on when she walked in, so she grabbed it as she exited the cabin so she could lock up as she left. It was time to go see if there was anyone else awake. She began the short trek to the main house, hoping that someone could help her find some coffee. In a small part of her subconscious, she was actually hoping the angel of mercy making her favorite beverage was a sexy cowboy by the name of Dallas. If caffeine didn't work to boost her liveliness, a dose of him would work wonders in bringing her energy level to a brand new point of existence. She pushed thoughts of the sinful man out of her brain and continued her journey to the house. It wasn't conducive to her mood to be reminded about how she was struggling with the combination of instant lust and loathing for the man.

THE SUN WAS BEGINNING to rise, and its rays were bouncing off of the walls in the kitchen, displaying various hues across the white walls. Dallas had just poured himself a cup of coffee, black and strong the way he liked it. He didn't understand how anyone could drink it with sugar or cream. In his mind that ruined a perfectly good cup of his favorite morning brew. With the drink in hand, he began to carry it over to the table so he could sip at it and slowly let its caffeine infuse into the cells of his body. Out of the corner of his eye he noticed a movement outside. The cup was placed on the table and forgotten as he spied his target through the window directly over the kitchen sink. The object of his latest fantasies was wandering outside, and it looked like she was headed directly to the house. He couldn't have asked for a better start to his morning. Forgetting about his coffee, he decided to seek her out and further his agenda. All he had to do was cross paths with her and get her into the position he wanted. Well the position he was capable of achieving this morning, anyway. The other positions he wanted her in would have to wait for an even more opportune time. This was only the beginning of his plans for the blonde beauty he was planning on intersecting paths with. He was pleasantly surprised when he realized she was the reporter doing the article for his sister's program. With that knowledge, he knew she was going to be around for the next two weeks. It would give him plenty of time to play with her, and he could take his time a tad bit. Not too much, just enough to get exactly what he wanted. What Dallas wanted was to savor her, and sex was only part of that equation.

Dallas walked outside and headed her off along the path. When she looked up and saw him standing there, she stopped dead in her tracks. She looked like she couldn't decide if she wanted to turn around and walk back where she came or to continue on her current path. She pulled her lip between her teeth and bit down with indecision spreading through her green eyes. After she made a decision, it became evident as she continued toward him with a purposeful stride. Once she reached him, she stopped and looked directly into his eyes. "Please tell me you have coffee. I would sell my soul for a cup."

Dallas couldn't help but laugh at her begging him for a simple cup of coffee. The question was how to use it to his best advantage. She said she would sell her soul for one cup. Surely she would give him something a little less valuable in the grand scheme of things. A smile grew on his face when he realized what he was going to get from her. "I might. I'd even be willing to give you a cup, for a price of course."

Frustration lacing through her voice, Ginnifer said, "I already offered up my soul. Being one of hell's demons, I figured that'd be payment enough to give your boss for a piece of heaven."

The smirk on his face should have been a warning for her to run; luckily for Dallas she didn't take the hint. "Well a piece of heaven might be worth your soul, but I wouldn't be giving that up for anyone. I want you all to myself. So it's a good thing I don't work for anyone but me. Give the devil his due, darlin', I'm needing a little heaven of my own, and your soul alone won't get the job done."

Ginnifer took a step back away from him and glared up into his eyes. "I don't have the time or patience to play right now. Please have a heart and gimme some damn coffee. It would be my preference to not snarl at every living creature today."

Dallas took a step toward her and leaned in close with his eyes mere inches away from hers. "I'm not a giving person. If you want something from me, I expect a payment of equal value. I'm willing to make a deal and give you one of the best damn cups of coffee this ranch has to offer. Say the word and it can be all yours."

"What do you want for a freaking cup of coffee?"

His eyes raked over her body, his desire shining through. Her tongue darted out of her mouth, and she licked her bottom lip. The corner of his mouth turned upward into a cocky smile. Oh yes, he was going to get exactly what he wanted from his Gin today. "Well do you want a piece of heaven?" he asked her.

She nodded her head in agreement, sarcasm filling her

voice. "I want some caffeine pumping through my veins. That's my own personal heaven at this time of day."

With his voice growing a bit husky, Dallas said, "I bet I could get your blood pumping in other ways, and because I'm so altruistic, I'm willing to give you both."

"What the hell are you getting at? Didn't I mention already I'm not a morning person?"

He leaned in and whispered in her ear, "Don't worry, darlin', we'll fix that soon enough. Are you prepared to give me what I want?"

She glared at him and stomped her foot. "Quit playing games with me and give me what I want, damn it."

He grabbed her and pulled her into his arms. "Well all you had to do was ask nicely." He leaned into her as she looked up at him in shock. Her mouth gaped open in surprise, and he took the opportunity to swoop in and claim it as his own. Glossy lips with the taste of strawberries and cream filled his mouth, and he couldn't get enough. He pulled her closer, intertwining her tongue with his. No protest came from her. She lifted her arms up, wrapping them around his neck, and rested her hands at the base of his neck. Her fingers wandered up and raked through his hair on the back of his head. He took the opportunity to explore her face with his lips, trailing kisses across her cheeks and sucking her neck below her ear. She sighed in his ear as she relaxed in his embrace. He drew back and looked in her lust-filled gaze. It wouldn't take long at all to have her in every way he wanted.

He pulled away from her, and his arms felt empty without her lush figure filling them. "Now how about that cup of coffee?"

Ginnifer reached up and slapped him across the face. "Damn you, why couldn't you have given me the coffee without groping me first?"

His laugh rumbled loudly over the quietness of the morning. "What fun would that be? Come inside and have a cup. I think you need some time to adjust."

"Clearly you are losing your mind. You're in need of a reality check. Give me some damn coffee before I get the urge to slap you again."

"Darlin', if you go slapping me again, you best be prepared for something else afterward. I only give you one free shot. As you already used it, well, you do it again and you'll find yourself over my knee."

Ginnifer's cheeks started to flush a little at his comment. Hot damn, his little spitfire wanted to be spanked. He would have to keep that in mind for a later date. "Don't worry. If you want, we can always do that for fun too."

"Damn it, I don't need coffee this bad." She turned around and marched in the opposite direction. All Dallas could do was laugh as he watched her cute little derriere walk away from him. This morning sure was the best one he had in a very long time. He couldn't wait to find out what the afternoon would bring.

*G*innifer was stressed out after her encounter with Dallas. She was afraid if she had actually gotten some coffee in her system, she would be a jittery mess. Normally she needed at least two cups in her system before she could function. Apparently one conversation and a hot kiss with Dallas were enough to not only get her through the day, but the rest of her life. She couldn't have stopped moving if she wanted to. The things that man had made her feel were beyond her comprehension. What would happen to her if she had to deal with him on a daily basis? Would she even need any caffeine to start her day? She stopped in mid stride as the thought rolled through her mind, and she let out a sigh at the thought of waking up with him every morning. Frustrations aside, it would be pretty awesome to wake up beside a sexy man that got her motor running faster than any strange brew ever would.

She made her way back to her cabin and pulled out her tablet to make some notes for her interview with Colt

Lewis. She walked over to the small table and chairs in the cabin and sat down to work. There were some key questions she wanted to make sure she asked him when he arrived later that day. If she was organized enough, she could write the article and send it to her editor to make next month's publication. She would save the article on Novak Spring's yoga retreat for the Thanksgiving issue. It would be a good idea for potential Christmas gifts. If it was featured before Christmas, it would help both the magazine and the ranch's new program. Sitting up straight and raising her arms above her head, Ginnifer started to stretch her tight, aching muscles. The tension of the morning was starting to take its toll on her body. She picked up her phone and looked at the time. It was almost seven a.m., and she needed to get walking if she was going to make it to the south pasture for the morning yoga session. It turned out the south pasture was near the main house to make it easier for the guests to find it. Near the south pasture there was a building they had renovated into a small dining area and kitchen for hosting a large group of people. She had spotted the building when she was walking to the house earlier in her quest to find coffee. That building had raised some questions in her mind. More specifically, she wanted to know everything they used the building for and if it had ever been used for something besides hosting cowboy wannabes. She understood it was the dining hall, but she was curious if they utilized it for other events. If so, it could be something she included in her article to draw other individuals to the ranch and help their business grow. It might be the perfect spot to hold wedding receptions or anniversary parties. The ideas going through her head were endless, and she needed more information before she would decide exactly what would be included in her article.

Crossing through the yard, she made her way over to the south pasture where she saw a group of women gathering. There were groups of women in various spots gathered around each other making conversation and laughing. The clusters were all preparing for the yoga session across the grassy field near one of the fences, stretching and warming up in the cool morning sun. As she drew closer, Ginnifer spotted Emma pulling out the things they would need for the yoga class and standing next to another woman with a clipboard in her hands. It appeared that some of the women had either known each other before they arrived or had made time to bond once they checked in at the ranch.

At that moment she was annoyed with Tori again for not already being there to help ease their way into the group. She shouldn't care, but it always bothered her to be thrown into a social situation where she didn't know any of the people that were part of the gathering. It also didn't help she decided to skip having a cup of coffee earlier when Dallas offered it to her. Her energy levels were starting to droop a little bit, and she was regretting not taking him up on his offer. She had been so frustrated with him that she couldn't stand to be around him any longer. Her feelings concerning the man were a little overwhelming, and she hadn't been able to handle being around him a moment longer. It had not been worth it, even if it would have gotten a jolt of caffeine in her system. If she was going to be around him, she needed to understand what was going on inside of her first. Her face started to flush at the memory of how it felt to have his arms wrapped around her and his mouth pressed against hers. No doubt that kiss scorched her inside and out, but one kiss wasn't enough to get through the day like she had originally thought.

Ginnifer looked over all of the participants and tried to decide where she should go. A petite, busty brunette was talking with the host of the program. Emma looked up and spotted Ginnifer and called out to her. "Ginnifer please come join us, we are getting ready to start. This is Melody. She is going to be the yoga instructor for all of our sessions throughout the next several weeks. She is a yoga genius. It was with her help I designed the program. She has graciously also agreed to participate in some of our other events if I need even numbers."

Walking over to join the two women, Ginnifer raised her hand to shake Melody's hand as she approached. "It's nice to meet you. I haven't had time to meet anyone yet. I got in pretty late yesterday. Jet lag hit me hard, and all I could think about was crashing for several hours as soon as I got to my cabin."

Melody's face lit up with a smile only a true morning person could demonstrate to the world past seven a.m. "I'm so glad you could make it to our first yoga session. Today we're going to mix things up a little bit and do some things besides yoga. We are putting a new twist on things and throwing in some techniques you can only learn in the Cowgirl Yoga program. The beginning is going to be a bit faster paced—to get our motors running.

Then we will slow it down and do some more traditional yoga."

Ginnifer hated cheery people. Did she ever shut up? Someone should stab Melody's brown eyes with a sharp stick, or at the very least pull her black hair and smack her head into one of the fence posts. Good God, when did I get such violent thoughts? Maybe she should have taken that damn coffee from Dallas. Clearly she wasn't fit for decent company. Cruelty was something she didn't condone, and this innocent woman was only trying to be nice. It became very clear in that moment she needed to keep her distance away from everyone so she could get her nasty thoughts under control. Once the yoga session and breakfast were over, she would head back to her cabin for some extra face time with her pillow. Doing her best to fake a smile of excitement, Ginnifer nodded her head vigorously and lifted the corners of her mouth up with all the effort she could muster. "That is marvelous. I can't wait to see what you have planned for us." She turned her back away from Melody the cheerleader and let the corners of her mouth relax into the grimace she was more comfortable donning. Even though she knew she was a bit on the grumpy side, she couldn't help thinking all that hyperness was not normal before noon. Little Miss Bubbly was the kind of person she had always avoided like the plague. She really was the cheerleader type—all curves and high, perky breasts. All the boys would have followed after her with their tongues hanging out with the hope she would notice they existed. How was she going to stomach an hour listening to her all chirpy-like? Kill me now.

Melody walked over to a set of speakers and plugged in an iPod. "Okay everyone, if you would grab one of the yoga mats and line up in front of the fence into three rows, we will get started."

Ginnifer trekked over and grabbed the first mat she could get her hands on and went to find a spot among the other women. There were three rows forming with four in each row. She wandered over and took a spot next to Emma in the first row. At least she knew her on some level and not everyone was a complete stranger to her.

Melody's voice rang out to bring her back to reality for a minute. "Okay everybody, we are going to loosen up a bit first. We are going to walk like toy soldiers for ten steps. One hand up and bring it down and take a step and repeat until you do the whole ten steps, and then turn around and do it all again until you are back in your original spot." Melody walked a few steps, demonstrating the movements that she wanted the women to make and returned to her original spot. "Okay, let's start moving."

Toy soldiers? Um, whatever. This would at least be a good stress reliever, and Ginnifer was willing to try it. The opening lines to "Country Girl (Shake it For Me)" began to pour out of the speakers. Luke Bryan's voice saying, "Hey girl and shake it for me" was almost enough to get Ginnifer's pulse racing. Oh yeah, she would shake anything to the sound of his voice crooning to her. At least Melody had good taste in music.

At the end of the song, Melody skipped over to put on some softer music and said, "Okay everyone, we are going to start with a mountain pose. Stand tall with feet together, shoulders relaxed, weight evenly distributed through your soles, arms at sides." Melody stood in front of everyone to demonstrate the position she wanted them in. She looked over at the group and nodded her head in approval at the women. She started to do the next step of the exercise as she spoke. "Take a deep breath and raise your hands overhead, palms facing each other with arms straight. Reach up toward the sky with your fingertips."

Once they were done with that position, Melody took them through the steps of each pose she wanted them to do that morning. The session went by without an incident. Maybe this wouldn't be so bad. She could go get some coffee and breakfast. It was starting to look like her day would maybe not be so bad after all. The corners of her mouth started to lift into a true smile, and she let out a breath of relief that she made it through yoga without harming anyone.

"All right, that's all the yoga we have for today," Melody said as she turned the music off.

"We have a little surprise, though; we are going to learn a few cowgirl tricks after each class. Today we are going to learn how to tie a knot." Emma winked at the group of women. "This is, of course, handy when you want to tie your favorite cowboy up when he's been naughty."

Every one of them started to laugh except for Ginnifer. Her mouth turned up into an evil smile, and pure wickedness shone through her eyes. Well now this was interesting. There was definitely one wayward cowboy she wouldn't mind tying in knots. It might come in handy to get even with him for this morning's groping session. If the opportunity arose to actually use her knot-tying skills on him, well it would mean that God was truly a female and understood women sometimes needed the upper hand when dealing with ornery men. Emma was going to find a very willing student in all these cowgirl tricks she was going to share with them. If Dallas was going to constantly ambush her and throw numerous innuendos her way, it was time she started to fight fire with fire, or she would never make it through the entire two weeks.

Ginnifer sat back and prepared to learn all the different ways to tie a knot and the best situations to use them. In all her life she had never been so excited to learn something. Emma really had something with this Cowgirl Yoga program. She was simply a genius. The article she wrote was going to outline everything so well, Emma would have to start turning people away because she wouldn't be able to accommodate them all. When Tori realized the things they would learn, she was going to be just as excited. Well that is if she ever made it to the ranch so she could tell her. With a soft sigh, she pulled her phone out of her pocket to once again check the time. It was a quarter to eight. The lesson should be over soon, and they would be heading over to get breakfast. If Tori didn't get a hold of her by the end of breakfast, she would call her again. Hopefully everything was okay and the five a.m. call wasn't anything she needed to worry about.

Once all of the women knew everything there was to know about tying a good knot, Emma announced they were going to head over to eat breakfast. The next meeting would be at noon for lunch, and then they would have horseback riding at two and eight for those who were interested. The evening yoga session was after dinner at six.

Ginnifer was starting to get extremely hungry. Her stomach rumbled and made a growling sound when she thought about food. She had worked up quite an appetite and couldn't wait to get something in her stomach. There were several things she wanted to accomplish, but the first thing she was going to do after she got sustenance was go back to the cabin and take a nap until lunch. Tori should arrive around two, and then she could get Colt's interview out of the way before dinner. She was not going to miss the evening's yoga lesson. Whatever cowgirl lesson was happening was surely going to be useful in her repertoire and essential for her struggle to get the upper hand against Dallas. Ginnifer had never looked forward to a mêlée with another person quite so much. She was going to be the victor in their battle of wills, and if she did one thing well, it was always coming out on top.

CHAPTER 8

*G*innifer slowly strolled toward the breakfast hall. She had never been so exhausted in her life. Yoga was part of her daily life in New York, but for some reason today's session drained all of her energy reserves. It could be the residual effects of jet lag making her feel so fatigued. She seriously doubted it was the extra lessons on how to tie a knot. They didn't require much stamina to complete. In fact, learning how to tie a knot was one of the most mind stimulating activities she had ever completed. The constrictor and bowline knots might be the most useful—for tying someone in place anyway. She wasn't sure what the actual uses for them were.

The sound of a car's engine drew her attention toward the front of the house. She looked over and noticed a burnt orange Jaguar convertible pull to a stop in front of the wide porch steps, directly behind her meager Honda Civic. Ginnifer wanted to go over and run her hands over the car and stroke its exterior. It was so pretty and she had always had a soft spot for expensive sports cars.

Struck dumb at the Jag's appearance, it had distracted her from its occupants. So when she saw her best friend Tori getting out of the driver's side of the vehicle, her mouth dropped open in shock. The lucky bitch was driving that drool-worthy machine? Ginnifer quickly made her way over to Tori, barely noticing the passenger of the automobile. She saw him lingering in the corner of her eye as she made a beeline for Tori.

Tori, wearing a pair of cobalt four-inch stilettos, slammed the car door and waltzed over to Ginnifer as she pushed her designer sunglasses on top of her head. Her caramel-blonde locks floated over her back in long, luscious waves. The sapphire halter dress she was wearing hugged her breasts, narrowed around her waist, and flowed over her hips, stopping above her knees. Ginnifer was starting to feel inferior standing in the vicinity of her best friend. Tori's skin glowed with warmth, and it looked like she had gotten some much needed beauty sleep. Something that Ginnifer had been denied by her early morning wake up call. It took all of her reserves not to growl at the sight of Tori's exuberance.

Tori's face lit up with a radiant smile. "Oh good, I don't have to send out a search party for you. As you can see, we arrived a bit earlier than planned. I had to take over driving at one point. It was easier than fighting with him. This car here is his baby, and once it was clear I was going to drive on without him, he jumped in the passenger seat faster than the Flash."

Ginnifer looked over at Colt Lewis and nodded her head at him. He walked over to stand next to her and Tori. She turned back to Tori and said, "I'm confused. Why did he need to be forced to come here? I'm not doing an interview with a reluctant participant."

Tori turned and sent Colt a scathing look of disdain. Ginnifer was familiar with this particular look. She was disgusted with her client and was about to throw him to the wolves. This was his last chance to make things right before she washed her hands of him. Tori turned her attention back to her best friend. "He was fine until he found out where we were going. He hadn't realized that Novak Springs was our final destination until we were an hour away. We had stopped to fill up the gas tank when it had occurred to him he had been on that particular stretch of road before and asked what the name of the ranch was. He was about to turn tail and run. I didn't know he had history with the place, or I would have worked harder at getting you to do the interview in Seattle. No matter, though, we are here and he's all yours."

Ginnifer raised an eyebrow and looked over at Colt with a questioning expression in her green eyes. What history? Well this was definitely going to be more interesting than it had started out to be. Ginnifer couldn't help wondering what this ranch had to do with Colt Lewis. She turned to Tori and gestured to the two of them to follow her. As she started to turn, she saw the front door of the ranch open and a man she had not met before walk out. He had long citrine-blond hair pulled into a short ponytail at the nape of his neck. A few strands had escaped and were falling over the side of his head, hugging his cheekbones and stopping short of his chin. A black T-shirt hugged his rock-hard muscles across his chest and left little to the imagination. His jeans were slung low over his hips and were covering some black cowboy boots. Not bad, not as good as Dallas, but he might do in a pinch…

His face turned a bright shade of red as he approached and asked, "What the hell are you doing here, Colt? You can get back in that overpriced contraption and drive on back to Seattle. I know you don't want us to bust you up just as the season is starting."

Tori leaned over and whispered in Ginnifer's ear, "Please tell me who that scorching hot cowboy is." Her eyes were glazed over and lust was pouring out of them. This was her ideal man. Longish blond hair, chiseled face with light stubble across the lower half of his face, muscles everywhere. Oh yeah, Tori was in sexy man heaven.

Ginnifer shrugged her shoulders at her and told her, "I have no idea."

Colt looked over at Tori, running his hands through his long mahogany hair in frustration. "I told you this was a bad idea. Do you listen? Noooo, 'cause you think you know best. Come on, let's leave."

He started to walk back to the car, but Tori put herself in front of him and held out her hands in protest. "I will deal with this Colt. Hold your horses and you will be able to leave in no time."

The sexy cowboy turned his steely eyes on Tori. "He can leave now, or I'll not be held responsible for what happens to him."

Tori turned on her charm and smiled up at him, flipping her shiny caramel locks back over her shoulder. If she were a kitten, she would already be purring in delight.

As it was, she was damn near close to rubbing herself all over him. If she got any closer, Ginnifer would need a crow bar to dislodge Tori from the cowboy's body. Of course then her claws would come out because nothing pissed her off more than being interrupted when she was on the prowl. Her lips curved into a sultry smile as she narrowed in on her target and trailed her fingers across his firm chest and skimmed down his abdomen, a move that had never failed to achieve her goals with a man in the past.

"Well, darlin', I am sure we can work something out. Ginny needs to do a quick lil' interview, and then Colt will be gone. Where is the harm in that? She got permission from the lady running this shindig. Didn't you?" she asked as she turned her head toward Ginnifer, leaning it slightly into the guy's chest, a soft moan escaping from her mouth.

Sometimes Tori really had no shame. Ginnifer was used to her shenanigans, and it would make things easier if the guy fell willingly under her spell. It helped that she was right and she had gotten permission from Emma the night before when she arrived. Nodding her head in agreement, Ginnifer said, "Yes, I asked yesterday when I arrived, and she said it wouldn't be a problem."

The man snorted in disbelief. "I don't believe Emma gave anyone permission to have Colt Lewis anywhere near this property. She wouldn't have agreed to that for any reason."

Ginnifer's face screwed up in puzzlement, and she tilted her head at him with questions streaming from her eyes. For once Tori's charms were not working to distract someone of the male persuasion. Maybe she was losing her touch a bit. She was shocked as he pushed Tori aside and stalked over toward Ginnifer and Colt, leaving Tori stunned in his wake. She stepped in front of him before he could reach Colt's side. Holding her hand out to him, she said, "I don't believe we have met. I'm Ginnifer Zeiss and over there, that is my friend, Vitoria Miene. The one that you damn near pushed onto the ground to storm over here," she said.

He stopped and grudgingly said, "Ah yeah, the reporter Emma asked to do an article on this venture of hers. I'm glad you're here, but Colt still needs to disappear and fast. I don't particularly like your friend, either, but I understand she is a guest, so she can stay."

As he said that, they heard a scream coming from the direction of the dining hall. A female with cinnamon hair pulled up into a high ponytail had stopped before the main house, shock covering her face. It didn't take long for her to regain her composure. Ginnifer watched as Emma rushed toward them, her face as white as a ghost. She walked over and stood next to the cowboy pointing at Colt as she said, "Wes, what the hell is he doing here?"

"I don't know, Em, he hasn't said much. If I were to hazard a guess, it's something to do with these two ladies here." Contempt covered every inch of his gaze as it landed on Tori and Ginnifer. Wow, Tori really had lost her charm because this man was disgusted looking at her.

Tori took exception to the look. "I have no idea what your problem is, mister, but you're making this a lot harder than it needs to be. Ginny could have already been done with Colt, but you had to hold us up and be an ass."

"I stand corrected, that one isn't a lady. She's a harpy." He squeezed the bridge of his nose between his thumb and index finger, bending his head down in frustration.

"Well, as if. Ugh. Ginny do something," Tori demanded.

Ginnifer sighed and looked over at Wes and Emma. "I swear it won't take long. I don't know what issues you have with Colt here, but I did ask you yesterday, Emma, if it was okay if I did a quick interview here today."

Emma turned toward Ginnifer with shock on her face. Her mouth opened and closed several times. "You never said it was with Colt Lewis, though."

Ginnifer rubbed her temples and breathed in a deep breath. "I never said it wasn't with him, either. You didn't ask who I had to interview, and honestly, it didn't cross my mind to tell you. Please let me get this done. This day hasn't started the best, and I want to rest. If I can knock this out, I might be able to salvage the day."

"What do you mean it hasn't been the best? I thought you had fun at yoga earlier," Emma said. A tinge of pain laced through each of her words.

"Yoga was fine. I enjoyed it. My day went to hell when my phone rang at five a.m. and woke me up before I was ready." Ginnifer turned to glare at Tori.

A sheepish look formed on Tori's face. "I'm sorry, Ginny, I was going to give you a heads up to expect us, but at the last minute I realized it was dumb to call you that early and hung up."

"You could have answered when I called back, but that's for another time." Ginnifer turned toward her hosts. "Is it okay if I get this done, Emma?"

"I'm not gonna lie, I don't like it. I'll give you an hour and he better be gone. I'm sorry. I know I invited you here, but he isn't welcome on this ranch. Ever." Emma stressed the last word vehemently.

"I'll make sure he's gone in an hour, Em." Wes continued to glare at Colt.

Emma nodded her head at him and walked up the stairs and into the house. Wes turned to the three of them and folded his arms in front of his chest. "The clock is ticking; you better get started."

Ginnifer looked over at Colt, and Tori and waved them toward her. "Follow me, we can go to the cabin and finish. It really shouldn't take long."

Tori looked over at Wes and said, "It really is too bad."

Wes looked puzzled at Tori's words. "What is?"

"That such a smoking hot body is wasted on such an asshat," she said as she turned to follow Ginnifer and Colt to the cabin. Her stilettos pushing into the dirt path making it difficult to storm away, still Tori did her best to sashay as she escaped from Wes's presence. She only stopped briefly when she heard him say, "I can overlook you being a bitch long enough for a good fuck if you change your mind."

Tori turned her head, looking over her shoulder as she coolly replied, "You wouldn't be able to keep your mouth closed long enough. The fantasy would be ruined in ten seconds flat. No thanks, I have better uses for my time."

Ginnifer had stopped to stare at her best friend's exchange with Wes. Colt was standing next to her with his arms folded across his chest. Tori never could leave well enough alone; she always had to get the last word in.

It was going to be an interesting two weeks if Tori was going to cross barbs with Wes whenever she saw him. Come to think of it, she had her own cowboy to fend off. At least Dallas was being rude in a different way. She didn't think Wes and Tori would ever get along. There were sparks between them that bounced all over the place. If anger and instant dislike hadn't ignited between them, they might have found a useful way to dislodge those flames. Now though, it was a lost cause because Tori had written him off as useless.

When Tori reached them, she said, "What are you waiting for? We have to get this shizzle done before the Terminator comes and throws us off the planet or something."

With those words, they silently turned and walked toward to their cabin. Ginnifer sighed with discontent. She was never going to get a cup of coffee at this rate.

CHAPTER 9

*I*t didn't take them long to get back to the cabin
and settle in for the interview. Ginnifer was
still reeling from the tension in front of the main house
between the Novaks and Colt Lewis. She couldn't wait to
get this interview over and send the quarterback on his
way back to Seattle. Tori was going to owe her for this
one, and she didn't care about their previous deal. Colt
Lewis was enemy Numero Uno in Casa de Novak.
Ginnifer didn't deal well with hostile environments. If she
had wanted to work in a dangerous terrain, she would
have become a political journalist or something of a
similar nature. She dealt mostly in entertainment and
fashion, which held its own pitfalls but generally was
harmless. This was crap she didn't need to take.

Ginnifer rummaged through her bag, pulled out a
small recorder, and grabbed her notes. Colt was already
sitting in one of the chairs by the little table in the cabin.
Tori took one look at the room and told them she needed
to get her luggage out of the Jaguar. Palming the keys, she

left the room, leaving Ginnifer alone with Colt. Ginnifer shrugged and went to sit down at the table with Colt. Tori had some steam to let off, and the walk back to get her belongings might help her relieve some of the pressure brewing inside of her. Ginnifer set the recorder and notebook on the table and pulled out the chair. Once she was seated, she turned toward Colt and gave him her full attention. "Are you ready to begin?"

He nodded his head at her indicating he was ready. "Yeah, I want out of here before Wes decides to eject me himself. I tried to tell Tori they didn't like me here."

Ginnifer turned her recorder on and took the opportunity to ask him, "Yeah about that, why do they hate you so much? Emma is such a nice person. I hadn't met Wes before, but he really wanted to pummel you."

"Yeah, well, um," he started to say and then changed direction with his words. He looked up at her with a lot of guilt shining through his eyes. "Emma and I used to date. Well, before all this crap came out. I love her and I wouldn't ever hurt her, willingly. I tried to tell her Missy was lying. At first she believed me, but well, something changed her mind."

The man's features were wracked with pain. His brown eyes bled misery into anyone that looked at him, causing them to feel every ounce of the hurt he was barely holding inside of him. He should be angry at the injustices that were dealt him, but all Ginnifer noticed was his inner turmoil and agony. She needed to remember why they were here and doing this interview. It might not be enough, but maybe it could help him find a way out of the mess that had found its way into his life. Ginnifer set her notes down, deciding to take a different approach to the interview. She looked up at Colt and asked, "Missy is the girl that says she is having your baby."

Colt looked directly in Ginnifer's eyes. "Yeah, and until the paternity test comes back, I have to deal with her lies. I honestly don't care what anyone thinks about me. I know it isn't my baby. It's Emma that mattered. I lost her because of this. When she broke up with me, I wanted to punch something. Thank God for football practice, it gives me a good outlet for most of my frustrations. I didn't want to come back here until I had proof the baby wasn't mine. It was part of the reason I freaked out when Tori told me where we were heading. You want to know the saddest part, though?"

"What's that?" Ginnifer asked.

He scrubbed his hands over his face, trying to erase the desolation away. "I don't think she will ever believe that I never had sex with Missy, even if that baby isn't mine. She could very well be lost to me forever. My life isn't right...without her in it. I don't know what to do without her. I don't know what to do. If only I could make her understand, make her see that I didn't betray her. It's useless, though, football is all I have left."

Ginnifer ached listening to his sad story. She had to do something to ease the sadness falling off of him in waves of despair. If someone had asked her if she believed someone could love another person as much as Colt appeared to love Emma, she would never have believed it was possible. In Ginnifer's mind love was a fantasy and rare in the harsh world she lived in. If she could find a way to help him repair his relationship, she was going to do everything in her power to make it happen. Sometimes a person needed to believe fairy tales did exist. She took Colt's hand in hers and looked him in the eyes as she said, "Maybe this article is the first step in getting her to realize that she was wrong. Tell me your story, Colt. How did this Missy get her claws into you?"

Ginnifer sat back and listened to the long, sordid tale. Colt had been signed to a two-year deal with the Seattle Starlings as a second-string quarterback. He had gone out celebrating with some of his teammates, excited at signing his first professional football contract. They got drunk, and Colt passed out and woke up in a hotel room next to Missy. He had been fully clothed and barely remembered the previous night. But he did remember everything he had done up to the point he had passed out in the hotel room. Missy had been drinking with the whole team and had been cozying up to the tight end of the Starlings most of the night. She didn't rate much of a blip on his radar. Colt didn't think anything of her until she claimed to be pregnant with his kid.

"I'm telling you, I didn't have sex with anyone that night. Did I get drunk? Yeah. I don't know who Missy's baby's daddy is. I know it isn't me. I remember everything from that night, and all I did was go to sleep. She passed out next to me or someone else put her there after I was asleep. I don't know what their end game is, but it's a media frenzy I hadn't planned on dealing with in the early stages of my career. If only I knew why they were doing this to me, or if Emma had stood by me, it would be more bearable. I'm floundering here, lost with no one to turn to for help. Vitoria is a pain in the ass, but if not for her, I don't know what I would have done."

Ginnifer turned her recorder off and placed it in her pocket. She had enough to write the article and would work on it later that evening. The sooner it was written, the quicker it would hit publication. She had enough time to get it in the next edition before it went to print. This was a story that would make the magazine fly off the shelves. Hot new football quarterback embroiled in a hefty sex scandal, priceless. She was going to do the man a solid, though, and write in how it ruined his relationship with the hopes that Emma read it. Maybe if she saw it in print, she would be more willing to forgive him. Besides, it humanized him and made his struggles real to the readers. They needed to connect to him in a way they could understand, and losing the love of his life would help them to relate to him.

She turned toward Colt and rested her hands on the table. "I think that's all we need. Don't worry too much about it. At least you know that some of the truth will come out. When will you have the results from the paternity test?"

"Next week. Honestly I'm not really worried about it. Not the baby, anyway. Like I said, I know it isn't mine. It's the hassle and losing Emma over this mess. Nothing else I can do but follow Tori's instructions." He raised his hands in frustration.

"Chin up, it might get better. You just have a rough patch to get through. Come on, I'll walk you to your car. We got done in record time. Look, we have a whole fifteen minutes to spare. The asshat, as Tori called him, won't have a reason to boot you out."

Colt let out a small laugh at her attempt at a joke. His smile brightened with pleasure. "Yeah, Wes and Vitoria sure didn't hit it off. Don't get me wrong, she is a sexy woman, but sometimes she comes on a bit too strong. She is kind of Wes's type, though. I'm surprised he reacted so negatively toward her."

Well, isn't that a bit of interesting news? Ginnifer couldn't help but wonder why the sexy cowboy had pushed Tori away. The reporter in her smelled a story she was dying to dig into. No doubt Tori would be just as willing to dig up dirt on Wes Novak as well. The man had sneered at her and degraded her in front of an audience. If Ginnifer didn't look deeper, Tori might dig a hole she wouldn't be able to get herself out of.

"Tori isn't all she seems to be. She only comes on strong to get a point across. Inside she is a marshmallow. All squishy sweetness, don't let her sharklike outer appearance fool you."

Colt nodded his head in agreement. "She knows how to get the job done and isn't afraid to jump in full throttle. I can't say I've seen that sweet side, but I respect her. She hasn't steered me wrong yet."

They got up and strolled toward the door as Tori pushed it open. She walked in carrying her luggage and grumbling about jerks and getting even. It was humorous to watch her struggle with the overly large suitcase as she pulled it over to a nearby bed in the cabin. She looked up at Ginnifer with surprise falling across her face. "What?"

Ginnifer hid a small smirk by flattening her lips and

shook her head. "Nothing, nothing at all. I'm going to walk Colt to his vehicle. Did you get everything out of it?"

Tori was a bit flabbergasted. Her hands began to flail with her continued frustration. "Yeah, believe it or not, I only have the one suitcase."

Ginnifer raised one of her eyebrows in amazement at Tori's pronouncement. "Um, you do realize that is a ginormous suitcase, Tori. I could fit both of my bags in it and still have room to squeeze myself next to them inside that monstrosity."

"Whatever," Tori said as she waved her hands at them. "Get Colt out of here before Rambo decides to go all first-blood on him."

Ginnifer laughed as they left Tori to unpack in the cabin. Ginnifer and Colt quickly walked to his car, and he got in and left immediately. Wes was nowhere to be seen, but that didn't mean he wasn't watching for Colt. He didn't want to take any chance of meeting up with the Novaks again and was in hurry to leave. Once Colt was in the Jaguar and safely on his way from Novak Springs, Ginnifer was able to let out a breath of relief. It was short-lived, though, when she heard someone behind her say, "Was that Colt Lewis? What the fuck was he doing here?"

Ginnifer turned to find Dallas standing behind her. Sweat was already dripping down the front of his navy T-shirt. It was sticking to him like glue, and Ginnifer had to stop herself from reaching over to peel it off of his chis-eled body. Damn the man had a nice chest, and she hadn't even had the chance to see it bare yet. She licked her lower lip and looked up at him. His eyes were battling equally between lust and anger as he looked from

Ginnifer to the departing car down the ranch's long driveway.

Looking directly into his cobalt-blue eyes, she asked, "Does it matter? He's gone."

"Hell yeah, it matters. He isn't welcome here. Ever."

"Yeah, I got the memo from Wes and Emma. No worries, he won't be back. Ever," she said, sarcasm dripping through every word.

A devilish smile formed on his lips. "Well, since he's already gone, how about you and I take a break together?"

How did the man jump from being pissed to flirting with her so fast? Ginnifer's hands curled up into fists. He frustrated her and made her want to hit something. It didn't help she never did get any caffeine in her system.

"I don't think that's a good idea."

"Of course it is. Did you ever get some coffee?" A gamine grin settled on his face.

Ginnifer groaned at his mention of coffee. It was already late morning, and it didn't look like she was going to get her daily indulgence. Damn him, why did he have to remind her she didn't get any this morning? She would have to make do with a nap and hope for the best in the afternoon. She glared up and let her irritation flow out of her. "I don't have time to trade barbs with you right now and have way more important things to do. I'm going back to my cabin to deal with Tori. Bye, Dallas. I'd say it was a pleasure, but well—that would be a lie and I try to keep things simple."

Dallas's lips curved up into an even more sinful smile. "I'll take that as a no on the coffee. I was willing to give you a cup. You should've taken me up on my offer. It would have been worth it."

A look of disbelief came across Ginnifer's face. The man took conceit to a whole new level. "Nothing would've been worth putting up with your company any longer. You make me want to scream."

He wiggled his eyebrows suggestively. "I know. I bet you can't wait until your mouth releases that scream of pleasure only I can give you."

Her mouth gaped open in surprise. She couldn't believe he actually went there. Well actually she did; the man knew no boundaries. Oh God, she didn't know how much longer she could deal with his sexual innuendos. It had been less than a day, and if she had allowed her hormones control, she'd have been crawling all over him the moment they met. She sighed in frustration. If only she had the energy to find out if he could put his money where his mouth was—yeah he would definitely hear her scream. Ginnifer didn't have time or the stamina to deal with him at the moment, though. She looked over at him and raised her eyebrows, unable to resist saying, "Oh, I can scream right now. You want me to demonstrate?"

His mouth formed a sexy half smile with laziness filling his drawl, "Definitely, give me a taste of what I have in store for me."

She should have known better than to bait him. Ginnifer rolled her eyes at him. "Never mind. Go play with yourself, Dallas. I'm not here for your entertainment. I'm sure you can find a way of getting satisfaction all by yourself. I don't have any desire to indulge you right now."

She turned and started to walk away when she heard him say, "That's 'cause you're running scared, Gin. If you want to experience true ecstasy, you know where to find me."

She stopped and looked back at him with a sneer on her face. "Don't hold your breath."

All she could hear as she walked away was his laugh thundering across the wind. Bastard knew how much she desired him. It was almost futile to resist him. She was determined to hold off as long as possible, though. Ginnifer had a lot on her plate. The first thing was a nap and then an article to write before dinner. Dallas Novak would have to wait until she wanted him so much she couldn't resist him any longer. What he didn't know was that Ginnifer didn't really believe in denying herself once she made up her mind about something. She had already decided she was going to give Dallas Novak the ride of his life. But she would choose the time and place and wouldn't be goaded into doing something until she was good and ready.

CHAPTER 10

*G*innifer stormed into the cabin and slammed the door shut. Pissed wasn't quite the word to describe the level of anger flowing over every inch of her body as she made her way across the room. In all her life she had never been as furious as she was in that moment. When she told Dallas she had to deal with Tori, she had meant it. There was about to be a reckoning, and she wouldn't be held responsible for the damage inflicted. Tori was lounging on her bed browsing through a fashion magazine and chewing on her bottom lip. Her legs were crossed at the ankles, and she was leaning against the headboard as she flipped the pages. She didn't even bother to look up when Ginnifer stalked toward her with a purposeful stride. As she neared the bed, Ginnifer noticed the wires of headphones peeking out from behind Tori's long caramel hair and her phone sitting next to her on the bed. Music blaring through the headphones completely blocked out all the noise of her surroundings. Tori must seriously need some de-stressing if she was listening to music. It was her way of drowning out the world around her and recalibrating her senses. Well, too damn bad. They had some things to discuss, and Ginnifer didn't give a rat's ass if Tori needed to relax. Stomping the remaining distance to the bed, Ginnifer yanked the headphones out of Tori's ears and angrily said, "You created a mess, damn it, and now it's time to help fix it. Get off your ass and help me figure this shit out."

Tori looked stunned at Ginnifer's angry gesture. It didn't take her long to gain her composure. She raised one eyebrow, looked up at her, and said, "What the hell crawled up your ass and died? Since when are you the psycho bitch in this relationship? Who the hell are you and what did you do with my best friend?"

Ginnifer started pacing back and forth across the cabin with her arms flying up and down. Each motion jerked out as her anger heightened. Her face was flushed red, and her breaths came out in heavy pants. She began to talk nonstop with each step of her foot across the wooden floor. "I've had the worst twenty-four hours of my life. First, I had jet lag from hell. I get here to be damn near groped by this hot cowboy who turns out to be Emma's older brother, Dallas. The things that man has said to me—I, wow, there are no words to explain it all. He is so sexy and he always leaves me feeling flustered. Never in my life has a man made me feel so twisted up inside. And damn it, you—you, it's your fault I haven't had any coffee today. If you hadn't woke me up this morning, I wouldn't be the raving bitch I am right now. Why the fuck didn't you answer your phone when I called back?" Ginnifer had stopped ranting to look at Tori with daggers shooting from her eyes and her lips pursed up in displeasure. Her hands rested on her hips, and she started to tap her foot, waiting for a response from Tori.

Tori's lips curled up into a half smirk as she watched her best friend rant and rave about the hell the past day had been for her. She looked her over, amusement glowing through her periwinkle-blue eyes. "Well, aren't you a hot mess? I must meet this Dallas if he has you all hot and bothered. Clearly he's of better stock than Wes is, that bastard. You won't believe the crap he said to me when I went back to get my bags."

If Ginnifer was capable of getting any angrier, steam would start pouring out of her ears to relieve the pressure building inside of her. Damn Tori and her selfish nature. It had never bothered her before. She began to feel her face crawling toward the color of a ripe tomato. She stopped, and with barely controlled fury compressed inside, demanded. "Why would I care what Wes said to you? Maybe you should've gotten the whole story out of Colt before dragging him here. Did it ever occur to you to check everything out before deciding it was a good idea? All of them went through some unnecessary anxiety because you took a shortcut to get what you want. Did you even hear a word I said?"

It looked like Tori had been ignoring everything that Ginnifer had said. She continued to flip through the magazine and stopped occasionally to admire something on the pages. She set the magazine aside and grabbed her purse off a nearby table. Tori pulled a file out of her purse and started to run it across her well-manicured nails in nonchalance. "Of course I did. You met a hot man that gets your motor running. The rest is incidental. Damn straight I did my homework. I knew that Emma was his ex. It didn't mean anything to me in the grand scheme of things. It's why I didn't tell him exactly where we were going until we were almost here. He never would have come otherwise. The article needed to be written, Ginny. I'm sorry it stressed you out, but I have to look out for the best interests of my client. You do understand that, right?"

Earlier she had said that she hadn't known what Novak Springs meant for Colt. It shouldn't surprise her that Tori lied, but in that moment it did. Ginnifer was ready to pull every strand of Tori's blonde hair out of her head. She was willing to bet everything she owned that Tori would look hideous bald. Let's see how well her flirting attracted a man when she looks like a plucked chicken. She paused a minute in her thoughts to admire the creation her imagination had pulled inside her mind. It didn't take long for her to find the humor of it all. The image was so amusing she started to laugh hysterically and had trouble breathing. Gasping for breath with each eruption of laughter made Tori sit up and take notice of the hilarity causing Ginnifer to grasp her chest and fall over on her bed.

"What the hell is so funny?" Tori asked.

All Ginnifer could manage to get out were the words, "hairless chicken."

"I have no idea what your problem is, Ginny, but this is ridiculous. Seriously, what is going through that brain of yours? What the hell does a hairless chicken have to do with what we were talking about? You do realize chickens don't have hair, right? They have feathers, damn it stop laughing."

Ginnifer had finally managed to get her breathing under control and sat up on the bed. The smile never left her face as she pictured what Tori would look like without any hair on her head. Comical didn't even come close to describing what that image looked like floating through her brain. She really didn't want to explain that Tori being bald was her amusement of choice, so she shrugged it off. "No need to worry about it. I am seriously slap happy right now and desperately in need of a nap. I want you to know one thing before I crash until dinner, though."

Tori raised her eyebrow questioningly at Ginnifer. "What's that?"

"If you ever pull any of that bullshit on me again, I will quit speaking to you. Listen to me when I say this. I'm not a tool in your repertoire to use to further your agenda. What I'm supposed to be is your best friend, and if you want my help, you owe me all of the details. I don't give a fuck what your reasons are, we'll be done forever if you pull another stunt like this. Do you understand me?"

Tori pursed her lips in displeasure. "Loud and clear, Ginny. I honestly didn't comprehend what the big deal was, though. If it means that much to you, I won't do it again."

"Good. Now I need to get some shuteye. Do. Not. Wake. Me," she said, stressing the last four words to make sure her point got across. She knew she was being a raging bitch, but she honestly couldn't stop herself. The best course of action was to get her much needed rest.

Reaching down, she untied her shoes and kicked them off onto the floor. Once that was completed, she pulled the covers down and slid under them. As her eyes closed, she only had one thought before she let herself fall into oblivion. Nothing had better disturb her in the next several hours.

AFTER GINNIFER LEFT to go to her cabin, Dallas went in search of his brother and sister. He found them in the kitchen drinking a glass of lemonade and snacking on some of Mrs. Henly's oatmeal raisin cookies. Emma's face was devoid of color except dark shadows forming under her eyes. Wes's was close to resuming its natural color, but his cheeks were still tinged with red. They both hadn't had enough time to adjust to their recent visitor's arrival and departure from Novak Springs to completely regain their composure. Dallas strolled into the kitchen, grabbed a glass out of the cupboard, and filled it with lemonade. Setting his glass down on the table, he pulled a chair out and sat down. A plate of oatmeal cookies was in the center of the table, and he grabbed one off of the plate and broke it in half. Before he shoved half into his mouth, he said to the room in general, "So who wants to explain to me why Colt Lewis was driving away from the ranch?"

If it was possible for her face to get any whiter at his words, Emma's would have. She looked up at him and explained, "I told Ginnifer it would be okay to do a brief interview today. It didn't occur to me to ask who she'd be interviewing or why. If I'd known, I'd have told her no. Seeing him here was a shock."

Wes slammed his fist on the table and practically screamed, "That bastard knew. He didn't have to come here and prance around in front of you."

Emma leaned over and rested her hand on Wes's arm and said, "I would hardly call what he was doing prancing. He actually looked very uncomfortable."

Wes snorted at Emma's description. "It had a lot to do with that harpy that he came with. Vitoria Miene."

Dallas raised his eyebrow and asked, "Who is she?"

Emma sighed and told him, "She is Ginnifer's best friend and apparently Colt's new agent. I hadn't met her before today. From the little I understand, she brought him here for Ginnifer to interview. Of course she would want his side of the story published somewhere. It helps when you have a best friend with the right connections."

"Ah well, that makes a bit of sense. He wasn't here too long was he? I saw him leaving, but I had no idea he was here until I saw him practically run to get into the driver's seat of his car and race down the driveway. The way he peeled out of here, you would think a bunch of hell-hounds were chasing him," Dallas said.

With those words, a bark of laugher escaped Wes's mouth. A smile formed on his face for the first time since Dallas had walked into the room. Emma's own lips turned up into a half smile as Wes said, "Well, that would be my doing. I saw him pull up almost immediately. I told him he only had an hour to get it all done, or I was going to break every bone in his body. It wouldn't do for the new star quarterback to be incapacitated just as the season begins. Emma grudgingly gave them permission to finish the interview, and I kept watch to make sure they kept their word. Ms. Zeiss didn't even use forty-five minutes before she walked him back to his car."

Dallas nodded his head at his two siblings. "I'm sorry I wasn't here to help you guys out. I got wrapped up in the back pasture. One of the horses threw a shoe, and I had to fix it before the mare hurt herself. While I was out there, I noticed some of the fencing needed to be fixed. Before I knew it, I'd been out there for hours. I have some paperwork to do in the office, so I made myself come back in. That's when I saw him drive off."

Emma smiled and tried to reassure him, "Dallas, there isn't anything you could have done. We handled it. No harm, no foul, right? Well, I've work to do before lunch in an hour. I'll leave you guys here to finish talking. I know you'll want to discuss how to prevent this from happening again." With that she got up and slowly walked out of the kitchen.

After she had left the room, Dallas turned to Wes and asked, "Is she really okay?"

"Yeah it was more of a surprise than anything. She really didn't expect to see him here," Wes said.

Dallas sighed in frustration. He ran his hands over his mouth, trying to find the right words to express what he was thinking. It really pissed him off that Colt had come to Novak Springs, and he needed to get to the bottom as to why the guy thought it was okay to show up on the ranch, even if it was a brief interview. The prick should've known that he wasn't welcome on the ranch. It had to be something with that other woman. He looked over at Wes and asked, "What do you make of this agent of his?"

"A real piece of work. You know the type—chews men up and spits them out when she's done with them. What do they call them? A man-eater. Real charming while she's trying to get what she wants out of you, see ya later when she's done," Wes summed up Vitoria for Dallas.

Dallas raised an eyebrow at his description of Vitoria Miene. From the little Dallas knew of her, Vitoria seemed to be the opposite of her best friend, Ginnifer. How had the two polar opposites become friends? It would be interesting to find out more about the woman. He needed to make sure she didn't feel free to invite Colt back to the ranch. What surprised him the most in Wes's description was how bitter he sounded when he described Vitoria. He sounded almost pissed off that she was on the ranch. It made Dallas wonder if perhaps he knew her from somewhere else. He shrugged the idea as nonsense and said to Wes, "Well, I will take care of it and make sure he never comes back here again. Don't worry about dealing with the matter, I'm aware it pissed you off. Go find something to relieve the stress."

"I'm fine, bro. I needed to cool off a bit. If you need help with anything, I'm willing to pitch in."

Dallas shook his head at him attempting to dissuade him. "No I'm serious. Go find something or someone else to do. You need to let this go before you see Emma again. You were stressing her out when she was already too pale to begin with. Go to town and take the night off. Come back here and be the carefree Wes we know and love. There can only be one asshole on this ranch at a time.

Otherwise we might scare away the help or, God forbid, Emma's guests."

"I don't really want to go out. I'm not really in the mood. I'd rather find something around the ranch to occupy my time."

"You need to go out and do something. The ranch is the last place you need to be right now," Dallas explained. "Something is seriously bothering you. I don't know how much of it has to do with this Tori person. If you don't want to talk about it, I understand. I've closed myself off before. But I can't have you ruining Emma's program with your bad mood."

"You know me too well. I do have some stuff on my mind. I can't talk about it right now."

"You know where to find me when you're ready. I may be an ass at times, but you're my family. I'll always be here if you need me."

"I know that. It's not something I like to admit to. If anyone would understand, it'd be you. When I'm ready, I'll find you. It may be a while."

"Good. Go and have fun, but be warned. Once you get back, I'll have a list of chores for you to do tomorrow. I have a few fences that are going to need mending. I'm sure it will help you keep your mind from rolling over your problems."

"Okay that sounds like a plan." Wes laughed and stood up. He slapped Dallas on the back and said, "Fine, I'll drive into town and see what kind of trouble I can find."

"It shouldn't take much. Everyone knows you're the real trouble as soon as you walk in the door."

"Ha ha. I'm outta here. Talk to you later, bro." Wes waved at Dallas and walked out of the kitchen.

Dallas was alone in the kitchen with his own thoughts. It was never going to be easy being the oldest sibling. At least he got them both calmed down. Now he needed to find something to relieve his own stress levels. He thought of Ginnifer and knew what he needed to make himself feel better. When he was around her, he felt lighter somehow, like he could be more of the person he used to be before all life had landed heavy responsibilities on his shoulders. He knew he was way too serious at times. It came with being prematurely the head of his family. It was time to start looking out for himself. His timetable was about to be pushed up where the sexy writer was concerned. What he needed to figure out was how to push her in the direction he was looking for her to go. He smiled when an idea occurred to him. In a few short days he was going to head a scavenger hunt, and he was going to make sure Ms. Zeiss was on the team he was leading. When he saw Emma again, he was going to insist that she be put on the same team as him so he could keep an eye on her. For good measure he decided that Vitoria needed to be on the same team as Wes. For some reason, she stirred something in him, and if anyone was going to keep a good eye on the publicist, it would be his brother.

CHAPTER 11

*T*ime wasn't on her side. That was what Ginnifer was thinking as she woke up from a four-hour nap. She had only meant to sleep for a couple hours and then get up to write her article on Colt Lewis. When she had lain down on the bed, it had been barely noon. Looking at the clock, she saw that it was already four o'clock in the afternoon. A quick perusal of the cabin showed that Tori was nowhere in sight. Her overly large suitcase was open on her bed, clothes spread everywhere, indicating Hurricane Tori had decimated the tidiness of the cabin. A smile formed on her lips recognizing that at least some things never changed. Ginnifer got up and walked to the window and looked outside. The sun was still shining brightly in the sky. It was possible to get something out of the day, but with a sigh, she resigned herself to knocking out her article on Colt first. There was no way she would be able to enjoy the day with that hanging over her head.

Strolling over to her bag, she pulled out her small

tablet and folded out its keyboard. Opening up her word processing application, she began to type her article. She detailed Colt's struggles and his denial at Missy Claybourn's claim that he was her baby's father. Ginnifer weaved a tale of tragedy-filled heartbreak and betrayal. Once she had it written, she double checked her grammar and spelling. Feeling satisfied it was one of her best pieces of work, she sent it off to her editor for approval. Stretching her arms above her head, Ginnifer caught a glance at the clock from the corner of her eye. Damn it, had it really taken her two hours to get that article done? Dinner was in fifteen minutes, and she would have to practically run to get there in time. With a rush, she grabbed her shoes and slid them on her feet. She ran out the door, practically knocking Tori down in her haste to get there in time.

"What the hell, Ginny, you tryin' to kill me here?" Tori asked.

"Of course not. I lost track of time and didn't realize it was dinner time. Are you going to eat?"

Tori wrinkled her nose up in distaste. "I'm hoping that Wes is nowhere to be found during dinner, but I need to eat, so yeah I'm going. I need to grab my phone. I forgot it in the cabin. I need to see if Colt called me and check up on him. If you wait a sec, I'll walk back with you."

Nodding her head at Tori, she agreed that she would wait outside for her to retrieve her phone and asked, "Do you have your key? I forgot mine inside the cabin."

"Yeah it's in my pocket. Do you want me to nab yours while I'm inside?"

She thought about it and told Tori, "It might be a good

idea in case we come back separately. It's on the table by my tablet."

Tori laughed as she headed inside the cabin to retrieve her phone and Ginnifer's key. Once she came out of the cabin, they started their journey to the dining hall. While they were walking, Ginnifer told her, "I did finish the article on Colt and sent it to my editor."

Tori stopped dead in her tracks. Turning toward Ginnifer, she stated, "I had hoped you'd let me read it before you sent it off to get published. Why didn't you run it by me first?"

"Because my job is to write articles as I see them. It shouldn't matter whether the publicist likes what is written or not. Besides I didn't write anything that would harm Colt. Why don't you trust me to do what is right?"

"Probably because sometimes we have a different idea of what is right and what's not."

Ginnifer had to agree with that. "True enough. That's probably because your version is skewed."

Tori's face started to turn scarlet as she attempted to control her temper. It was a wasted endeavor because she had anger issues. A burst of fury sprouted from deep within Tori as she shrieked at Ginnifer, "Well excuse me, Miss Perfect. Have you ever stopped to take a long look at yourself in the mirror?"

Ginnifer was baffled at that. What could she possibly mean? So she raised her eyebrow at her questioning, "I'm at a loss here, Tori. I don't have a freaking clue what you're talking about."

Sarcasm was weaved through her words as Tori articulated them. "Well we're being honest here, right?"

Ginnifer's heart skipped a beat. Hadn't they always been honest with each other? She looked into Tori's eyes, sadness reflected out from under the anger. They needed to stop fighting, but Ginnifer had no idea how to stop it. It had already gone past the point of no return. So she looked her best friend in the eye and said, "I thought we were always honest with each other."

Tori tilted her head and with a lot of bitterness uttered, "Only as much as you allow me, Ginny."

"When have I ever held you back, Tori?"

"Always. Tori don't do that, or I can't believe what you did. The list goes on. You're a straight-laced prude. If I flirt too much, I get an evil eye from you. God forbid if I take a guy home with me. When did you get like this? Do you hate yourself, or is it just me?"

A look of pure shock took over Ginnifer's face. She couldn't believe Tori thought she hated her. What did she do to make her ever think that? It was a horrible thing for her to believe. Surprise washed over her face. Ginnifer attempted to reassure her, "Of course I don't hate you. Why would you think that?"

Tori had tears forming in her eyes and turned away from Ginnifer. "I need to call Colt, so I can't deal with this right now. I'm going to have to take your word that the article is good for him." Tori stormed in the opposite direction of Ginnifer to gain some distance between them. She had an easier time of it than she had earlier trying to escape Wes. A pair of sneakers now graced her feet, having traded her stilettos in for something sensible for once. "Tori, wait. We should talk about this."

Tori stopped and turned around, looking at her with

sadness permeating her expression. "No, I think we talked it all out." With that she continued her trek toward the cabin, leaving Ginnifer stunned. How had this happened to their friendship? How evil am I to make my best friend feel this way? Maybe they needed a little space for now. She would try talking to Tori later after they both had time to calm down.

In the meantime she would go and eat dinner. Ginnifer continued to walk to the dining hall and met Emma on her way over.

"Oh good, Ginnifer, I'm glad I ran into you. I have some things I'd like to talk to you about."

"If it's about Colt, I'm sorry it disturbed you. He won't be coming back."

"No. I mean, yes it disturbed me, but you didn't know about our previous relationship. I can't hold that against you. It's a different matter I need to talk to you about."

"What do you need to discuss?"

"I had a small mishap come to my attention in one of the other cabins. The pipes in the bathroom broke and flooded the room. I am going to have to relocate the guests."

"Oh that's terrible."

"I hope you don't mind. I need to move two of them into the cabin with you and Vitoria. I know I promised you your own cabin…"

Maybe having two other people in the room would be a good thing. Normally the idea would have irritated Ginnifer, but having a buffer between her and Tori probably would be a blessing in disguise.

"No, that should be okay."

"Oh thank you. I hate that this has happened. Everything else has gone so well."

"These things happen. It's part of starting and owning a business. Don't let it worry you too much."

"I know. I have so much I want to prove to my brothers. I probably shouldn't be telling you all of this, but I think maybe you understand on some level. With everything that happened with Colt, I needed this program. It gave me something to focus on when everything else was falling apart."

Ginnifer understood. She didn't want to, but she did. Her interview with Colt had told her a lot about their relationship. Maybe she could help her with more than allowing two people to move into her cabin.

"Maybe you should try focusing on more than this business."

"I don't know what you mean."

"I know Colt hurt you, but maybe you should consider letting that go."

"I can't. It hurts too much."

"Are you sure you can't forgive him?"

"Yes. I tried. The betrayal was more than I could handle." Emma hugged herself as she said the words.

"I'm not going to pressure you into doing something you don't want to do. I think maybe you are wrong, and you might regret it if you don't find out. It's your life and your decision. We all have to do what we think is best for us. At the end of the day there isn't much else we can do," Ginnifer said.

"I know. Maybe one day I will talk to him. I doubt it, though. Like I said, it hurt too much."

"I respect how you feel. Maybe one day you can look at in a different light."

"Maybe. Maybe in time I can forgive him. I don't think I can ever be with him again. Right now the wounds are way too fresh and real."

"I suppose I can relate on a small level. Sometimes it's hard to look past the pain." Ginnifer couldn't help relating to her pain.

They continued to talk as they walked to the dining hall. Ginnifer wished she could take away her pain. It had to hurt an awful lot to have your heart ripped out of your chest. It was clear to her that both Emma and Colt still loved each other. She hoped they could find their way back to each other someday. They clearly cared what happened to each of them. They said time healed all wounds. Maybe it would be kind to the both of them and allow them to find each other again.

"Thank you for listening to me," Emma smiled. "The subject of Colt isn't a favorite topic of mine, but you made it easy for me to tell you how I feel. That's a gift. You listen really well."

"I don't mind. If I can help even a little, I can walk away happy. When can we expect our new cabin mates?"

"Soon. Probably tomorrow. I'm not exactly sure. I will let you know when I know more. I do know it will be two women. Probably Melody and Shelly if I remember correctly from my notes."

"I will let Tori know when I see her later."

"She isn't coming to dinner?"

"No. She had some calls to make. A situation to check on."

"Oh you mean Colt. I may no longer be in a relationship with him, but I don't hate him. I can't make myself quite feel that for him. A small part of me will always love him. Sometimes two people just are not right for each other. I wish him happiness, and I truly do hope that Vitoria can help him. Deep down I know he's a good man. He made some mistakes. Someone doesn't change that much in such a short time."

"You're a very mature young woman, Emma Novak. If I didn't respect you before, I do now in spades. For what it's worth, I believe you are right. Deep down he didn't change. In fact, I believe he was actually taken advantage of. It's an unfortunate aspect of being thrown into a world you know next to nothing about."

"I don't know if he was or not. It's not for me to say. I just know what happened between us. It's all I have to go on. It's up to him to figure out where to go from here. I can't be that person for him anymore. I need to figure out what I want out of my own life. So far it's starting the Cowgirl Yoga program. That has to be enough for now."

"You have time to figure it out."

"That I do."

"Well let's go inside and get something to eat. I'm suddenly starving."

They both walked into the dining hall and were greeted by the other women. In a short time she and Tori would have to welcome two of them into their cabin. She didn't generally like to get to know new people and didn't really plan on changing that outlook for them. All she saw them as was a way of gaining some much needed relief from the tension she had to deal with when she was around Tori. Nothing else really mattered because she had no intention of seeing any of them again. She did truly like Emma and was glad she had a chance to talk with her. It helped her to shake off the uneasiness she carried around after Tori had left her. The talk with Emma gave her something else to focus her energy on.

THE TENSION REMAINED thick between Ginnifer and Tori. Staying inside a cabin with her made it difficult to breathe. So instead of going to bed, Ginnifer decided to go for a walk to clear her head. The night sky was pitch black and sprinkled with a bazillion stars. They twinkled at Ginnifer during her walk. The stars didn't shine quite like this in New York, so she couldn't help staring at them as she strolled along one of the paths on the ranch. She found herself at one of the main stables and heard a horse whinny inside. A gentle voice followed the noise. It was a decibel barely above a whisper, making it difficult to hear, but she could still make out the sound of Dallas's voice saying, "That's right girl, I'm here to help you."

Ginnifer found it difficult to resist the lull of his voice and wandered inside to find out what he was doing. When she walked inside, she found him leaning down with a white mare having difficulty delivering her foal. The poor horse was breathing heavy as she attempted to expel the baby from her body. Ginnifer shuffled her feet to get a closer look at the horse, causing Dallas to stop and look up at her. Surprise filled his eyes followed with a tiny smile. "Well looky here, Olympia. We have an angel of mercy come to help us out."

Ginnifer was floored he thought she could help. No way, absolutely not, she knew nothing about horses. She would be useless to him in this situation. So she told him as much by saying, "Uh, I don't know anything about horses. I doubt I will be able to do anything to help her."

Dallas shook his head disagreeing. "You're wrong. I was trying to figure out how I can help her, and here you are just when I need you. I can't get inside of her and keep her calm. Come on, Gin, you can do it, stroke her face and talk in a nice soothing voice while I help her. I will be here with you every step of the way."

Ginnifer's face lost all color. Did he ask her to pet a horse as she gave birth? What if it got wild? Clearly he was delusional. With bewilderment she asked, "Uh... exactly what do you want me to do again?"

"Come a little closer. You will have to get down on your knees here and take off your jacket. It will be a bit messy to get this done," Dallas explained as he gestured her to come closer. Not knowing what else she should do, Ginnifer quickly peeled her jacket off and followed his instructions.

"That's it. Now I need you kneel closer to her head and with a soft voice reassure her. I'm gonna try to pull the baby with her contractions to help the baby come out easier. It's her first delivery, and she's not doing well with it," he told her.

Ginnifer slowly sat down next to the horse. Raising her hand up to her mane, she gently stroked her as she spoke about anything and everything. It wasn't long before she saw Dallas pull a small horse completely out of the mare. Dallas looked up at her with delight in his eyes. "Looky here, we have us a baby colt."

Ginnifer had no idea what had been preventing the horse from delivering the foal on her own, but she was glad she was able to help. She looked up at Dallas in wonder. Ginnifer still couldn't believe she helped even in a small way for a horse to give birth. A huge grin spread over her face. Turning to look Dallas in the eyes and with wonderment in her voice, "That's absolutely amazing."

Dallas took advantage of the pure bliss in her expression and pulled her into his arms, kissing her senseless. His mouth moved over her lips with light caresses. With a moan, Ginnifer turned around to face him and placed one of her hands lightly over his chest. For a brief minute Ginnifer let herself forget about the horse and the foal, allowed herself to feel. Dallas deepened the kiss and held her tightly against his chest. For a few short moments they both were lost in each other. The sound of the horse behind them broke the spell. With a sigh Dallas released her and took a step back. His stared into her eyes with an intensity Ginnifer didn't understand.

"Well, we have to get the little guy cleaned up. Are you going to stay and help me?" he asked.

"Oh yes, I want to make sure he's okay."

A soft smile formed on his face. It was an intimate moment, and for a brief second Ginnifer felt like she could really like this man. In this moment it felt wonderful to be with him, and she didn't want to go back to her cabin anyway. So she smiled back at him as Dallas expressed, "Good. For a fleeting moment there I thought you were going to flake out on me."

The light mood changed and the air was charged with something else. She needed to get more control of the situation, and really? She couldn't believe he had just said that to her.

So Ginnifer gave him a look of pure vexation as she proclaimed, "Well, it isn't like I've ever helped a horse have a baby before. Hell, for that matter I've never seen any baby born, let alone a freaking horse. Give me some credit for not bolting out the door immediately."

Dallas looked into her eyes and with complete sincerity agreed, "I know, and really I do appreciate your helping me out here. I was going to call the vet, but I was afraid he would be too late getting here. You helped me save both their lives tonight. Thank you, Gin. I owe you."

Wow. It was the only thing that Ginnifer could think when she looked at him. Where had this sensitive guy come from? Gone were the sexual innuendos she had gotten used to hearing, and instead she saw compassion and sincerity. If she wasn't careful, she was going to start seeing him in a different light. That wouldn't do her heart any good. She was already wildly attracted to him. Ginnifer cleared her throat, trying to get the lump forming inside to disappear. With an uneasy smile, she stared into his eyes. Shaking away the jittery feeling growing inside of her belly, she contemplated what she should say to him. She had never been so nervous in her life. This was a game changer, and she had no idea how to handle it. This cowboy could end up being her undoing.

Her voice taking on a husky tone, she muttered, "I'm glad I could help."

Dallas grabbed her into his arms. Hugging her tightly in his embrace, he whispered in her ear, "Come on, Gin, let's go get our new baby settled in for the night."

With that he released her and they began working together to get the newborn foal settled in with his mama. They worked together like they had been doing it for years. The entire time Dallas didn't express one sexual innuendo to Ginnifer. The man was continuously surprising her. If he kept it up, she wouldn't know which way was up. She leaned against the wall while watching him add some straw to the stall. He turned to look at her and smiled. She couldn't do anything but smile back at him. *Damn him for making me feel things I'm not ready for...*

CHAPTER 12

*L*ife is full of insanity at every turn. It is just a matter of how it's handled and the amount of chaos that erupts each day. The madness touching your mind also plays a huge part. Some people can't handle the stress of life and check out when it gets too difficult. Everyone has their own demons to keep in check, and it isn't always easy to be the strong one in every situation. In fact, it is damn irritating when it is expected of you every time something happens to disrupt the status quo. At some point a little bit will give, and the world will come crumbling down. Ginnifer was at the crevice of her existence and was about to find herself shattering into a bazillion pieces. She managed to get some sleep and make it through a few days without disaster striking, but she could feel the tension with Tori every time they were in the same room. It was getting harder and harder to breathe around her. Tori didn't usually hold things inside, and she had to be bursting with explosive energy. It had always been expected for

Ginnifer to be the glue that held things together, but a person really could only take on so much before they splintered. Their disagreement could very well erupt in ways that could destroy the very fabric of their friendship. Tori still wouldn't talk about their eye-opening argument. Her response to any inquiry Ginnifer made was that there wasn't anything left to discuss. So Ginnifer had no choice but to continue on and avoid conflict with her. She was tiptoeing around her, and the stress of it all was taking its toll on her.

Today Ginnifer had a mission. One that could prove to be impossible to complete depending on the person she was seeking out. Yeah, she was also avoiding Tori as much as possible. So much so that she was actively looking for Dallas. She had asked Emma some questions about the ranch that morning after their yoga session and had been told that Dallas was the one to bounce her questions off of. She had been told she could find him in the main barn because he was working with the newborn foal they had delivered a couple nights ago. With a grimace, she steeled herself for the task at hand and wandered into the barn. Dallas really was the lesser of two evils at this point. She was damned if she did and damned if she didn't. The two people turning her life upside down were also the two people she couldn't avoid forever, but if she could put off Tori for as long as possible, their friendship might weather this storm. It would be devastating to lose her at this juncture of their relationship.

The small problem that came to light in one of the cabins Emma hadn't foreseen resulted in extra individuals in her and Tori's cabin. One of the cabins had a pipe burst and flooded the entire cabin floor. She moved two of them into the cabin with Ginnifer and Tori because they had the most extra room. Their two new cabin mates were Melody and Shelly. So before she ran off to do her errand, she had made sure that she moved all of her belongings near the bed she was occupying. As far as Tori's belongings went, it would take a miracle to wrangle them all up, so she left it to her to complete on her own. Having two other people in the cabin might help ease some of the tension. It would give Tori some new targets for her angst.

Emma had also informed them during breakfast that after dinner they were going to assign teams for Friday night's activity. It had been explained that it was going to be a scavenger hunt led by Dallas, Wes, and Emma. Ginnifer prayed she didn't get put on Dallas's team because it could only lead to trouble. She was already growing attached to him in the worst possible way. Hell, this little excursion of hers was bound to lead her down a dangerous path. She told herself it was only for work, but if she was being honest with herself, she really did want to see him. He must have been extra busy the past couple of days because he had been scarce around the ranch. It galled her to admit she missed his sexual innuendos and devilish smile. It still baffled her he hadn't tried to do more with her when they delivered the foal. Ginnifer was actually craving his attention. Not that she would admit that, ever. Still, she figured at the very least this activity might prove to be the stress reliever she needed in order to make it until the end of this vacation. Who the hell was she kidding? There really was only one place this would eventually lead to, and it was a matter of time before she gave in and jumped the man.

There was a noise coming from one of the stalls, so Ginnifer wandered over to see if she could find Dallas inside. When she reached the stall, she looked inside and saw a beautiful white colt with a mane and tail mixed with a combination of black and silver. The baby she had helped Dallas deliver was truly beautiful. He was a stunning horse. When he was fully grown, he would be breathtaking. Ginnifer wanted to stroke his mane and hug him. While she watched him move inside the stall, she wondered where his mama was. She heard a whinny from behind her and watched as Dallas led the solid white mare inside. He stopped when he noticed Ginnifer standing in front of the stall and stared at her for several minutes before he continued on his path. Once he arrived at the stall, he gestured with his head for her to move aside and allow him to open the gate for the mare to get back inside with her baby. After she was inside, he closed the stall door and secured the lock on the outside. Dallas turned to face Ginnifer and stalked toward her, stopping in front of her. He leaned over and brushed his cheek against hers, the stubble from his facial hair lightly scraping against her sensitive skin to whisper in her ear, "Did you come to visit our baby, or are you ready to play with me yet?"

Ginnifer took a step back in a feeble attempt to gain some distance between them. She knew if she ventured in here on her own, he would take it as a sign of surrender. It was up to her to gain the upper hand and fast before things got way out of control. With a shaky voice, she looked at him and said, "No I, uh, Emma said I should ask you about some of the stuff concerning the ranch. So I was forced to seek you out to get the answers to those questions."

A look of disbelief crossed his face, and after a brief moment his lips turned up into a sinful smile. "Darlin', don't ya know you don't need an excuse to come looking for me? I've been waiting for you to give in to the inevitable."

Ginnifer gasped as he grabbed her and pulled her into his embrace. His breath mingled with hers as their faces were almost close enough to touch noses. She looked up into his cobalt-blue eyes and tried to explain, "No, seriously, I'm looking for some information for my article. If this isn't a good time, I can come back later."

"Now's as good a time as any. Ask away."

Ginnifer sputtered over her words but managed to get out, "Aren't you going to let me go?"

"Don't much see the point. We both know this is where you really wanna be. I don't expect those questions of yours taking very long—this position will give us a better advantage for the fun stuff." Dallas winked at her.

Ginnifer's mouth dropped open in surprise, and it took her several seconds to get words out of her mouth. "Well, I never. Really this is the only way you will talk with me?"

"Well, we can skip the talking part if you want. I kinda like having you in my arms, and if I'm being honest, there are other things I'd like to be doing. So's you know, talking isn't involved in any part of them." He leaned in closer and dropped a tiny kiss at the base of her neck.

Ginnifer was in trouble with a capital *T*. She came

looking for a distraction, and Dallas was definitely up to the task. The question being how far she was willing to let him go along this path they were heading down? She already knew his kisses were scorching, but he was currently doing some stuff with his hands across her ass that made her want to lean farther into him and beg for more. Damn if it felt this good with clothes on, what could he do once we both got naked? Ginnifer was fast getting breathless, and he hadn't even really kissed her yet. The fight in her slowly left as she leaned her head back with a final attempt at getting information out of him. "I really do need to talk." Lust filled her eyes as she licked her bottom lip in anticipation.

"We can talk later." He leaned down and pressed his lips to hers. The kiss escalated out of control, and before she knew what was happening, she was backed up against the wall of the barn with her arms wrapped around Dallas's neck. He had let her go, and his hands were pushing against the barn's side as he continued to devour her mouth with his kiss. She reached up and pushed her hands through his hair, knocking his black Stetson to the ground. Ginnifer brought herself as close as she could to him while rubbing her body all over his. Dallas took it as an invitation to reach down and pull her ass up under his hands. Ginnifer wrapped her legs around his waist, and he pushed her back securely against the wall. Her ass was firmly sitting inside the palms of his hands, and Dallas took the opportunity to squeeze it as he held her in place. Ginnifer moaned, leaned down, and deepened the kiss further, her hands grabbing his hair tighter with each sweep of her tongue with his. She could feel his dick harden between her thighs as she tightened her legs around his waist. Oh God, she needed to feel him inside her now. Dallas's hands wandered up and inside her white tank top. She felt the clasp of her bra come undone. He quickly pulled both off of her in one quick motion and bent her body back against the solid panel of the barn. Ginnifer grabbed a post in each hand above her to hang onto as his palms brushed across her nipples. He palmed one breast in his hand as he brought the other one's nipple inside his mouth. His tongue swirled around her nipple as his teeth grazed over it with a small bite. Dallas lifted his head up and blew on the sensitive nub. He turned his attention to the other breast to drive her wild with need. Ginnifer moaned when his tongue slowly ran over her other breast, and then he pinched it between his lips.

"That's right, Gin, let me hear how much you like this."

"Do it again now," Ginnifer demanded.

A small chuckle escaped his mouth, but he leaned down and did as she had asked. While he was giving her breasts his attention, he took it a step further and snapped open her jeans, pushing them open. He slid his hands inside and brought them down below her ass. His hands circled around each cheek as he whispered in her ear, "Untangle your legs, darlin'. I need these jeans off of you."

Ginnifer quickly did as he asked because for once he was speaking her language. Hell, he had been all along, but she chose to ignore it. She even took it a step further, and once her feet hit the ground, she kicked off her shoes to make things easier. Dallas made quick work of pulling her jeans and panties off. When the barrier was out of his way, he pulled her back into his arms and carried her inside one of the empty stalls and closed the gate. He set her down on a nearby stack of hay bales already covered with a saddle blanket and spread her legs wide across his shoulder. Dallas removed his black T-shirt and stepped out of his jeans before he turned his attention back to her. He spread her legs to give him better access as he leaned down and slanted his mouth over her clit to run his tongue over it. While his tongue caressed the sensitive nub, his finger eased inside of her. With each stroke of his tongue, he brought her closer to climax.

"More, Dallas, I need you to fuck me now," Ginnifer pleaded.

He raised his head up just enough to say, "Not yet, I'm not done playing yet." He resumed his attention between her legs as he brought her clit between his lips, rubbing his tongue and teeth over the hypersensitive bud. His finger kept stroking her inside and hit her sweet spot as he rubbed his tongue over her sensitive core. She screamed as the orgasm erupted through her whole body. As she was starting to feel the calm from the storm, Ginnifer felt his cock probing at her entrance. Dallas slowly inched his way inside of her until he was fully seated to the hilt.

"Are you ready, Gin? I'm going to fuck you so hard you're going to scream the rafters down."

"Yes, damn it. Quit talking and do it already," she yelled at him. With her words, Dallas began to fuck her in earnest. Each stroke was fast and deep. She could feel his balls slapping against her ass with each thrust. Dallas's breath got heavier the faster he pushed himself inside her narrow passage. It wasn't long before she was screaming like he promised. She peaked faster and harder the second time, squeezing him with each convulsion. Dallas leaned down and rested his head between her breasts as his own orgasm overtook him. He reached down and pulled her closer to him while his breathing started to even out. It was quiet inside the barn for several minutes as he held her close stroking her back. Ginnifer had to admit that not only was the sex mind blowing but the afterward felt damn nice too.

Dallas was quiet. Too quiet, it was almost unnerving, so it was a relief to finally hear him speak. "I forgot protection. I never do that."

"Is that why you're so quiet? I'm on the pill, so you don't have to worry about a baby. This isn't normal behavior for me...by that I mean I don't sleep around and I'm clean."

He nodded his head at her reassuring, "Good. I mean I am too. Damn, this isn't how I wanted this to end." He tilted his head and looked at her as if he was seeing her for the first time. He smiled and said, "I mean this wasn't how I planned on spending the afternoon, but damn if I'd change that for anything."

Ginnifer smiled back at him. Disaster was averted, and the devil was back out to play. That was a relief in itself. His grin was infectious, and she had to admit this had been what she needed. "You still need to answer my questions. This was by no means a way of sidestepping that."

Dallas began to stroke her breasts again, wickedness glazing over and through his eyes. "Well darlin', I did promise we'd talk later. I'm a man of my word. Come by the house after dinner and we'll talk—among other things if you're willing."

Her laughter floated through the barn. "You keep doing that, neither one of us is going anywhere. We need to get dressed before we start all over again."

He lifted his eyebrow up questioning, "And what is wrong with that idea? I definitely have not had enough of you yet."

"We both have things to do. Let me go so I can get dressed." She pushed him away from her.

"Fine, if you have to go and ruin a perfectly good moment by putting some clothes on, I suppose I'm gonna have to let you."

Ginnifer laughed as she walked out of the stall to gather her clothes. She put them all on and turned to look at him finish getting dressed. Damn, he was sexy. Ginnifer didn't think she would ever get enough of looking at him. It may have been a mistake to have sex with him, but she wasn't going to let that bother her. For the time being, she was going to enjoy the time she had with him. It was the best damn sex she had ever had in her life.

He turned and found her staring at him. "What are you looking at?"

"Enjoying the view." She slowly ran her tongue across her lips.

"Now don't be doing that, or those clothes you insisted on putting back on over that gorgeous body are going to be torn to shreds."

She wiggled her eyebrows at him and teased, "Promises, promises."

Dallas sauntered over, reaching for her as he muttered, "Come here."

Ginnifer scooted out of his reach. "Later, cowboy. I have things to do. You can make me scream again tonight."

"I'm going to hold you to that."

"Oh me too." She gave him a naughty smile.

"You sure you want to leave?"

"No. I need to, though. I can't stay in the barn with you all day."

"I don't know about that. It has its appeals."

"Quit trying to talk me into staying."

"No, because it's working. I want you to stay with me."

"I wish I could. I really do. This has been…fun."

"Then stay."

Ginnifer mulled over his words. She would like to stay, but she didn't think it would be a good idea. He made her feel way too much, and she needed to gain some distance between them. That didn't mean she couldn't maintain the playful attitude. It had been amazing.

"No, babe. I'm gonna go. I promise, though, that the wait will be worth it. I'll see you later."

She sashayed out of the barn and headed back to her cabin with a huge smile across her face. Yeah, it was definitely the distraction she had been looking for. It had been worth it to seek him out. Ginnifer had doubts she would be seeing much of Tori if she spent her nights in Dallas's bed. It was a win-win situation. She got hot sex each night and was able to get out of dealing with one of Tori's hissy fits. Ginnifer couldn't have asked for a better way to handle her rising stress levels. Dallas had skills she planned on taking every advantage of. The only real problem she could see was that it wasn't just Tori in the cabin with them anymore. Their new cabin mates were going to be joining them in a short time. They might already have moved into the cabin. Sneaking out to spend time with Dallas would be harder to manage with three sets of eyes watching her every move. She didn't know why it mattered to her to keep her extracurricular activities secret, but it did. Ginnifer didn't see any reason to let the world know she was having a sexual relationship with anyone. What happened with her and Dallas was a private matter. She had never been known for her ability to share. Some things were meant to be kept to yourself. How Dallas made her really feel and what she did with him was one of those things. Maybe someday she'd consider telling Tori some of it, but never would she spill all of the details.

*G*innifer wandered into the cabin she shared with her best friend and two new occupants, hoping she would have the room to herself. Luck had never been a friend of hers, and it wouldn't make any exceptions at this juncture of her life. Once the door opened fully, she saw Tori standing with bare feet in the middle of the room tapping her foot impatiently, waiting for her to come inside. Her hair was in a loose ponytail with strands falling out all over the place in a complete mess. Tori's face normally had perfectly applied makeup but now had streaks of dirt all over her forehead, nose, and left cheek. Ginnifer stopped abruptly as she got closer to her when a putrid smell reached her nose and she asked, "Good God, what is that horrible scent?"

Tori stopped tapping her foot and crossed her arms across her chest. Her bottom lip popped out as a small sob escaped her mouth. Tears started to fall in earnest when she looked up at Ginnifer. Her whole body started to shake as her misery found a way to release her pent up frustrations. Tori did her best to get words out of her mouth, but with each attempt, gasped for breath. "I hate—himmmm," she screamed.

Ginnifer stopped short and really looked at Tori. Her clothes were filthy. Her jeans were smeared with...yes, manure. Well that explains the smell... The strap on her white tank top was broken on one side and fell down across her chest. Something or someone had put her through some kind of hell. It made Ginnifer feel kind of guilty for avoiding Tori over the past couple of days.

"Do I want to know what happened to you?" Ginnifer asked wearily.

"That Indiana Jones wannabe lassoed me and pulled me literally into a pile of shit."

Ginnifer asked with an appalled tone, "Excuse me? Who would do that?"

"After we got invaded by Melody and Shelly, I wanted to escape the cabin ya know, and well, I missed my best friend. So, well I went out looking for you and ran into that jerk, Wes. The more I see him, the less I like him," Tori explained

"I'm not following you. Why would he make sure you fell into a pile of manure?"

Tori let out a breath and started to explain what happened to her. "Well it wasn't exactly a pile. There were a bunch of horses, and they had got done taking a dump—Anyway, we were arguing, and he took the rope he was holding, formed this circle thingy, and started twirling it in the air. Next thing I knew, I landed in the recently excreted horse crap. In my haste, I rolled away, getting it smeared all over, and well, you see how I look."

Ginnifer just shook her head, trying to wrap her head around Tori's tale. Something didn't make sense. Why would Wes do that to Tori? There had to be something she wasn't telling her. Narrowing her eyes into small slits, she pinned her gaze on Tori and asked, "Exactly what did you do to provoke him?"

"Why do you always assume I did something? I'm innocent, I swear." She shuffled her feet as she protested Ginnifer's question. She had a look of guilt all over her dirt-smeared face. Chewing on her bottom lip, Tori mumbled a few words that sounded like, "I may have…"

"Speak louder, Tori, I'm not good at deciphering mumbled words."

"It wasn't my fault, Ginny. I don't get why he's so sensitive."

Ginnifer rubbed her temples at the start of a headache forming. Closing her eyes as she tried to rub the pain away, she demanded, "Tell me everything and quit avoiding it."

Tori sighed and started to peel off her soiled clothes. When her tank top hit the floor she turned her attention toward Ginnifer. "Well I tried to have an honest conversation with him. Okay, I flirted—and he got all grumpy and said something about how I would never change. It confused me. I've never met him before and said as much. It escalated from there…"

"I'm still having a hard time following this. Get to the point. What did you do?" Ginnifer asked.

"Well, I insulted him. He pissed me off. In my defense, he said some really mean things to me first. I'm not generally a rude person, you know that." Tori continued to pace around the cabin as she talked.

"I know. What did he say to get you so rattled?"

Tori stopped and looked at Ginnifer as she began to chew on her bottom lip again. It was a sign of how nervous she was to admit what had happened. It wasn't usually a problem for them to tell anything to each other. When she finally started to speak, her voice trembled with emotion. "He called me a whore. I know that I'm not innocent, but I'm not a whore. I don't sleep around nearly as much as people think I do. I just flirt a lot. It would be more accurate to call me a tease, ya know? I play around, but I'm choosy with my lovers."

Yes, she knew that Tori liked men. Ginnifer was aware of every lover she ever had because there wasn't much they didn't share with each other. Even her hitting on Colt Lewis was a scam. Tori could usually tell if a man was interested and took advantage of it. Hitting on Colt promoted the image that she wanted to portray. She wanted people to think she was a man-eater. It helped her further her career if people were half afraid of her or what she might do. If she had read Colt wrong and he took her up on her offer, she would have found a way to extricate herself from the situation. Tori had explained later that she needed to know what his character was like if she was going to work with him. Rumors had already been spreading about him, and she needed to measure them to the man himself. Lucky for him, he passed with flying colors and earned her respect. Tori worked much harder to clear his name because she believed his story. She would still have signed a contract if he fell for her charms, but it would have given her an idea what to expect from him. Ginnifer had only been surprised because Tori generally didn't hit on her potential clients. It's usually one of Tori's unwritten forbidden rules.

"I need to shower. Good God, I reek," Tori stated as she tossed her jeans on the floor next to her tank top. She was standing in the room in only her bra and panties. Gesturing to the soiled clothes, she looked at Ginnifer and said, "Can you get rid of those? I'm never putting them on again."

"Absolutely, consider them gone," Ginnifer reassured her. "Where are our new roommates, anyway?"

"Melody was apparently annoying Shelly, so she stormed out of the cabin almost as soon as she moved in. The yoga instructor stuck around to annoy me. She didn't seem that rude during the yoga sessions, but let me tell you, she's a real trip from the one conversation I had with her before I took off. You might be interested to know she seemed awfully curious about you. I don't know why, but something about you is making her curious."

"Well I don't know why, I barely know her. In fact I don't even really speak to her at yoga. Something about her grates on my nerves."

"After talking to her, I can see why."

"Yeah well if she's going to be so damned curious about me, having her in the cabin is going to get on my nerves even faster. I wish she had been put in a different cabin."

"Maybe you can talk to Emma and get her to make a switch."

"No. I mean she probably would, but I don't want to add to her stress. I will deal with her."

"It's up to you." Tori shrugged her shoulders. "Personally I'd find a way to get rid of her."

"I know you would. But for now I think you should worry about cleaning yourself up. You kind of stink."

Tori stuck her tongue out at her. "I know. No need to point out the obvious."

"That's what friends are for." Ginnifer laughed.

Tori started to walk toward the bathroom and turned to her with amusement in her voice, "Oh, and Ginny, one thing before I lose myself inside of a hot steaming shower..."

"What's that?"

Peeking her head out of the bathroom door briefly, she said with a gamine smile on her face, "You and I are going to have a talk later. You can tell me exactly what you were doing this afternoon to get hay tangled through your hair."

A sheepish smile formed on her lips. Raising a hand to brush the hay out of her hair, she looked over at Tori and muttered, "Uh, well um..."

A smile formed on Tori's face for the first time since Ginnifer walked into the room. Tori let out a small chuckle as she ducked inside the bathroom. Her voice could be heard as she started to close the bathroom door. "Those words hold promise. Make sure you get back here ASAP so we can discuss their full meaning." With that she disappeared completely into the bathroom.

Ginnifer heard the shower running as she grabbed Tori's stinky clothes to dispose of them. Yeah, things would be fine between them. She had no idea why she had been so worried about the status of their friendship. A smile showcasing how happy she was that she and Tori were still best friends spread across her face as she exited the cabin. Ginnifer couldn't wait to tell her about her afternoon with Dallas. She also needed to get more details on her conversations with their new roommates. Melody had struck her as off from the first day, but she had chalked that up to caffeine withdrawal. It would be interesting to get her take on the situation. What could she have possibly done for the yoga instructor to take such an interest in her? Ginnifer got along with people, but as a rule she didn't particularly like them. For that reason she didn't go out of her way to strike up a conversation. Melody's bubbly personality was off-putting to her. She found her annoying and logic dictated she should do everything possible to avoid her. She sure hoped the woman didn't become too annoying staying with her in the small cabin.

She couldn't worry too much about it, though. Ginnifer had other things on her mind. Like what she had planned with Dallas later that night. Maybe Melody wouldn't be so bad to have around because she'd find a reason to be absent from the cabin as much as possible. Dallas gave her a lot of incentive to disappear.

IT IS AMAZING how a day could start out mundane and turn into one of the best days ever. That was the thought Dallas had, whistling while he worked. It was an unusual activity for him, so Wes expressed his surprise at not only finding him with a huge grin on his face but also having a happy tune emitting from his vocal chords.

"Yo bro, did hell freeze over or something?" Wes asked.

Dallas continued to grin at him. Nothing could diminish his happiness. Ginnifer's visit to the barn had brightened his day, and he wasn't about to let anyone bring him down. Her helping with the foal's birth had been the turning point in their liaison. Dallas had been engrossed in the chore of feeding the mares in the main horse barn and hadn't heard Wes walk in. He had finished tossing some hay into the last stalls when Wes spoke. So he stopped and pulled off his work gloves, tossing them on a bench as he spoke, "Not that I'm aware of."

Wes narrowed his eyes on his brother. Confusion filled his words as he asked, "What do you have to smile about? It's creeping me out."

A bark of laughter emerged from deep inside Dallas. It was loud enough to disturb the birds nesting in the rafters of the barn. A few of them flew out of the open door to escape the noise. When he was done laughing, he found Wes looking at him with bafflement. "I'm in a good mood. Leave it at that."

"Right. Do you honestly believe it's that easy?"

It was Dallas's turn to be baffled. What the hell was he talking about? So he came out and asked him, "What the hell are you talking about?"

"I know you. Something must have happened. You do not smile. Ever."

"I asked you to leave it alone, Wes. Don't ruin the first good day I've had in a long time."

Wes held both hands up and backed away. He nodded at Dallas with agreement. "Fine. I won't push. So ya know, I'm happy for you, and I can't wait to meet her."

"What the fuck are you talking about now?" Dallas demanded.

"Like I said. I know you. Nothing makes you smile on this ranch. It has to be a woman."

A frown formed on Dallas's face. *Do I really never smile? What does that say about me?* He brushed those thoughts away as trivial. "You don't know what you're talking about, as usual. I don't have a woman in my life."

A huge grin came over Wes's face. "Keep denying it. It's not going to make it any less true, bro. You're falling and hard this time."

Dallas wasn't going to argue with his brother. Wes had no clue what he was talking about. He was not falling for Ginnifer. They were only having fun with each other. They barely knew each other. A few conversations and one romp of sex did not mean he wanted more from her. She was leaving in a little over a week, and then they would be done. Instead he decided he needed to change the subject, so he looked over at Wes and said, "Why don't you tell me what happened to you. You're a mess. I thought you were going to check on the stallion over in the back pasture."

Wes's lips pressed together as anger filled his eyes. His forehead crinkled and his eyebrows pressed down with displeasure. He looked over at Dallas and said, "Well yeah, that was the plan, and I did manage to get out there."

"You make it sound like something went wrong. What could've happened while you were checking on a horse?"

"Anything with that damned nuisance currently on the ranch."

Dallas raised his eyebrow and stated, "Nuisance?"

"Vitoria Miene," Wes uttered, contempt filling each syllable of her name as he damn near spit it out of his mouth. From his expression, it was clear how much he disliked the woman. Wes had never reacted this strongly to a woman before. Wes got along with everyone, literally. He could walk up and have a conversation about the weather and leave the person with a smile on their face. Wes was capable of making the most depressed person on the planet laugh. There had to be something about Vitoria that disturbed him for him to have that strong of a reaction to her. Dallas had no idea exactly what those feelings were, but he would bet Novak Springs it didn't start out as hatred.

With a smile still firmly in place, Dallas looked at his brother and intoned, "Ah."

"That's all you have to say?" Wes asked.

"Yup."

A look of surprise crossed Wes's face as he asked, "You don't even want to know what happened?"

"Nope," Dallas said.

"Wow. I can't believe you're not going to lecture me. I know something is up now."

"Nah. Nothing's up. I'll say one thing, though." Dallas began to stroll toward the door to exit from the stables.

"What's that?" Wes asked.

Dallas stopped at the entrance of the barn. Before he left, he turned around with a parting shot at his brother, "I couldn't have picked a better woman for you if I'd tried."

Throwing back words very similar to the ones Wes had said to him earlier. Turnabout was fair play after all.

He could hear his brother's exclamations of anger as he strolled toward the house. Dallas wasn't going to let Wes's comments get to him. Yeah, he had started an affair of sorts with Gin, but that's all it was. They didn't have a relationship, at least not the long-term kind. It was understood it was only a fling while she was on the ranch. Wasn't it? He needed to talk to her and make sure they were on the same page as far as that went. The last thing he wanted was some misunderstandings to color the short time they had together. Yeah the first thing he needed to do when he saw her again was set down some ground rules. Dallas had messed up by skipping that and jumping in with her. He hadn't expected her to give in as easily as she had, not that he wasn't grateful. There wasn't a damn thing he would change about their afternoon in the barn, but he had to backpedal a bit. With that decision made, Dallas walked into the house. It was well past dinner time. Gin had said she would come to see him after dinner to discuss her questions about the ranch to include in her article. He would get those formalities out of the way when she came to see him. After that they could continue to enjoy each other...

*G*innifer and Tori were laughing as they strolled back to their cabin. They had taken advantage of the horseback riding that evening and enjoyed their time together. All was right in their world, at least as far as their friendship went. They had taken the time to discuss everything and hashed it all out. They let their tempers lead them instead of what they knew of each other. They set their differences aside for the sake of their friendship. Tori reviewed Ginnifer's article and talked to Colt. Everything looked good, and it was cleared to appear in the next issue of the magazine that Ginnifer worked for.

Tori reached up to the caramel ponytail swinging on top of her head and pulled the hair tie tighter as she said, "Colt seems to be handling things as well as to be expected. I might have to leave the ranch a few days early. It didn't occur to me that I might have to handle the shit storm surrounding the results of the paternity test."

"I hadn't considered that, either. When did he say they were coming in again?" Ginnifer asked.

"At the end of next week, Thursday I believe. We're supposed to be here until Sunday afternoon, correct?" Tori asked.

Ginnifer's mind began to race as she thought about all the things she still wanted to do on the ranch. She didn't really want to leave early. As things stood, she only had a short time with Dallas. Leaving earlier than planned would deprive her of what little time she was allowing herself to have with him. Only one option would allow her to remain and let Tori go to Seattle on Thursday. Looking over at Tori she said, "I don't really want to leave here on Thursday. Do you think you can take the rental car to Seattle, do everything you need to, and then come back and pick me up on Sunday?"

"I don't understand why not. It may not be necessary, though. I'll call Colt tomorrow and get a better grasp on how things are going and decide then."

"All right, let's play it by ear."

"So what do you think about our assigned teams for the scavenger hunt tomorrow?" Tori asked.

During dinner Emma had announced the teams, and they were both disappointed they were not on the same team. Tori was actually pissed because she had been put on the team led by Wes. With as much animosity that was floating between the two of them, that pair up was sure to be a disaster. Ginnifer, on the other hand, was happy to find out she was on Dallas's team. Two days ago that would have upset her. It was strange how quick a person's feelings could change. Imagine what could happen if they had more time together. It was a scary thought. After they had assigned teams, it turned out that Dallas's team had been short a person. That was when the yoga instructor piped up and volunteered to even the numbers, so both of her new cabin mates had been assigned to her team, Shelly and Melody. Ginnifer wasn't too happy she would have to deal with Ms. Happy Pants through the whole scavenger hunt. The few times she had actually made it to yoga, she had to restrain herself from snapping at the woman. It still surprised her it wasn't just lack of coffee that made her want to smack her silly. That woman was way too perky to be normal. It made her wonder if she was hiding something nefarious, and her chirpy nature was a mask of some sort. Clearly she had an overactive imagination. Melody probably was exactly what she appeared to be, a perky yoga instructor out to lead them to a new plane of peace and love.

While they were walking, they began to talk about what was weighing on their minds. For Tori it was the aggressive way that Wes was targeting her. He really appeared to have it out for her, and Ginnifer couldn't comprehend why he had such an intense hatred for Tori. It was baffling how much animosity he held for her. There were so many sparks flying around when they were together a match would set them to flame. It was both terrifying and awe inspiring all at once.

All Ginnifer could think to say was, "It should be an interesting event."

Tori sighed and with a grim look on her face she asked, "Ginny, do you think I'm overreacting where Wes is concerned?"

Ginnifer tilted her head to the side thinking about it. Wes had made it clear that he didn't like her. So she probably was only reacting to his actions. She couldn't actually be sure, though, so she said, "I don't know. He has very strong reactions to you. Are you sure you've never met him?"

Tori shook her head no. "I'm positive. I've never met that man in my life. He acts like he knows me, though. I've thought a lot about it, and there truly can only be one possible explanation."

"Really? What do you think it is?"

With a long sigh, Tori stopped and looked at her. She said the one name that said everything for her, "Vivian."

"Oh God, you're right. I forgot about her. What has your evil twin been up to?" Ginnifer asked.

She shrugged her shoulders with uncertainty. "I've no idea. I haven't spoken to her in a couple of years. What do you think she did to Wes? I mean I love her, she is my sister, but she is capable of anything. I wonder where Wes went to school? It's possible he went to the same place she did. We scattered to the opposite ends of the Earth after we graduated high school. We couldn't get far enough away from each other. She went west and I stayed east."

"Oh God, I had the most horrible thought go through my mind."

Tori looked at her and asked, "What?"

"The Wicked Witch of the West flew home."

Tori laughed with pure amusement to Ginnifer's comment. It was good to see her smile and laugh after the last few days. Their vacation had gotten off to a rotten start. Once Tori's laughter began to subside, she held her hand up, gesturing for them to stop walking. She looked at Ginnifer and told her, "I think my movie obsession is finally starting to rub off on you. I never thought I'd hear something referring to a movie come flying out of your mouth. It does a heart good to see my good work start to pay off."

"Pfft, seriously. I don't like movies. I prefer books, you know that. There's no way to prevent that stuff you make me watch from sticking in my brain." Ginnifer blabbered.

Tori had a warm smile on her face as she looked at Ginnifer. "I know, but you watch them for me. I do appreciate it."

"Well back to the subject at hand, where did Vivian go to school?" Ginnifer asked.

"University of California, Berkeley. Vivian thought it was the best school for what she wanted to study. It also had the added benefit of being located on the other side of the country."

"What did she study?" Ginnifer asked. She looked up at Tori and waited for her answer.

Tori was chewing on her bottom lip, so what she had to say wasn't completely an easy answer. "Political Science, Prelaw. Last I checked, she graduated law school and was working at a top corporate firm in San Francisco. Strange that we started on similar paths but ended up in different careers. I have a law degree but chose to work in public relations. I use my knowledge of law to negotiate the best contract possible for my clients. It's part of why I'm so good at my job. After I graduated, I kept thinking do I really want to do this? The answer was no. Of course, you know most of that already. I never talk much about Vivian with her being such a sore subject." Tori looked at Ginnifer as she finished speaking. Sadness was shining clear out of her blue eyes. It must really be hard for her to have a twin so completely distant from her. Their relationship bordered on hatred. They really could not stand to be around each other and ended up fighting constantly. Their issues stemmed from the rivalry cultivated by their parents. Tori had told her how her parents believed they could garner superior children by pitting them against each other. It was their belief that by having them compete against each other they would both want to succeed, resulting in award-winning academics and stellar careers. They were so successful, both girls had earned full scholarships to their schools of choice and ended up resenting each other in the process. Vivian was hell to be around. The few times Ginnifer had met her, she couldn't wait to get away from her. She was intensely jealous of Tori and tried to undermine everything she did. It was for the best they didn't contact each other that much.

"So what are you going to do if Vivian really is the reason that Wes has taken an instant dislike to you?" Ginnifer asked.

With a resigned smile Tori told her, "Nothing. I don't see the point. We'll be gone in a week. I don't plan on ever seeing him again. What's sad is that I'm willing to bet he's a really nice guy once you get to know him, but we're oil and water. There is zilch that's going to make us mix well together. Why fight it when there isn't any reason to?"

"I guess I understand. Still, the scavenger hunt is going

to be difficult. I hope he doesn't make things hard on you. Maybe you should at least ask him about Vivian."

"No. Even if it was Viv that he met before, he clearly doesn't remember her name. Either that or he never even knew it to begin with. He wouldn't believe me. Trust me, she has that effect on people," Tori told her.

Ginnifer sighed with discontent. "I'm going to have to take your word on it. I don't like it, though."

Ginnifer and Tori continued to walk to their cabin. Presumably they were going to crawl in bed for the night. What Ginnifer didn't tell her best friend was she had no plans to sleep that night. She still had to talk to Dallas. He had expected her to show up after dinner, but Ginnifer chose to spend some time with Tori instead. She didn't regret that decision. It was essential to their friendship, and they needed the bonding time. After the hellish last couple of days, they needed the time to regroup and remember why they were friends. Dallas wasn't in that equation. He wasn't even a real blip on her radar. When it was all said and done, all Dallas ever could be was her temporary lover. No matter what feelings she was starting to develop for him, she couldn't see how it could ever be more than what they had at this tiny moment in time. Tori was her friend for life and couldn't be put on hold.

So the plan was that once Tori was sound asleep, she was going to sneak out and go visit Dallas. Hopefully it didn't take too long for her to go to sleep because Ginnifer was overly anxious to see him. She was desperate to feel his arms around her again. Nothing had ever made her feel more alive than having all of his attention completely on her. It was the best thrill ride she had ever been on, and she wanted to get as much of it as she could in whatever time they had left together.

Ginnifer looked at Tori and asked, "Do you think our new roommates are in the cabin already?"

Tori sighed at the mention of dealing with their new cabin mates. "Probably. Curse that damn cabin for having a pipe burst in it. I'm sure Emma isn't too happy about it, either, but damn it's annoying to have to share the cabin with those two. Okay Shelly seems like good peeps, but the jury is still out on Melody."

"Why do you say that?"

"I don't know...she seems off. Fake, like a plastic Barbie doll. I'm still trying to figure her out. She seems sugary sweet, but I don't buy it."

Ginnifer laughed at her description. "Well when you decide, let me know. I'm not so sure about her myself."

They walked into the cabin and found their two roommates sitting on their beds. Melody was flipping through Tori's fashion magazine, and Shelly was reading on her Kindle. Tori strolled over to the bed and asked, "Can I have my magazine?"

Melody looked up as if surprised to see them in the cabin. Her eyes grew big, and she put on one of her supersweet smiles. "Oh this is yours? It looked interesting. I hope you didn't mind me borrowing it. Some of my reading material got ruined in the other cabin. I was closest to the bathroom." She folded the magazine and tossed it on Tori's bed instead of handing it to her. Swinging her feet over the side of the bed, she raised her arms above her head and stretched. A catty smile formed on her face as she looked at Ginnifer and asked, "What are your plans for tonight?"

She acted like she knew what she was going to do. It couldn't be possible, though. How would she know that she had planned on meeting Dallas? That had only been between the two of them. So she shrugged it off as nonsense. "Not much, probably going to take a shower and go to bed. What are your plans?"

"Oh I don't know. I'm considering meeting a sexy cowboy tonight."

Huh? Maybe she did know something, but Ginnifer refused to acknowledge anything, "Well good luck with that. I'm sure it will be fun with whomever you visit with. I'm going to go take that shower now."

Ginnifer turned away from her and walked over to her suitcase to gather her items for her shower. She hadn't really planned on taking a shower yet, but it was a good enough excuse to get away from their yoga instructor. If Melody really did know she wanted to meet up with Dallas, it would be even more difficult to sneak away. She couldn't worry about that, though. If she was meant to spend more time with him, it would happen. It wasn't like they had any long-term commitments to each other after all.

*I*t had taken forever for all the women to fall asleep. Ginnifer wanted to sneak out to go visit Dallas, but she was starting to think it might be a bad idea, especially since Melody had hinted at knowing about her plans. What if he was asleep? It was well past midnight, and she had no clue where his bedroom was located. Standing outside of the main house looking up, Ginnifer chewed her bottom lip trying to decide what to do. It was ridiculous to even come out here expecting that he would still be awake. She would have to resign herself to spending time with the foal she helped deliver. Visiting with Dallas was clearly out of the question. Ginnifer turned around and headed to the horse barn where the new foal was being stabled. As she walked in, she saw a small light was lit in the back of the barn. Strolling through the paddock, she stopped at the stall that held the baby horse and his mama. Olympia looked up at her, made a small noise, and trotted over to the gate. Ginnifer took it as a sign she was happy to see her. Reaching over into the tiny bucket hanging next to the stall, she pulled out a couple sugar cubes and fed them to the horse. Olympia greedily ate up the two cubes and nudged her head into Ginnifer's chest. *At least someone is happy to see me...*

"I should've known I could find you here." Ginnifer turned to find Dallas leaning against one of the posts in the barn. "I think you may have made a friend for life," he said.

"She's a beautiful horse," Ginnifer replied as she was petting Olympia's mane. "I thought it would be too late to come and visit you, so I decided to stay with these two wonderful creatures."

Dallas sauntered over to where Ginnifer was standing and pulled her into his arms. Once she was fully seated within his embrace, she looked up into his eyes. A smile only a man could possibly portray crossed his face. Leaning his face closer to hers, he told her, "It's never too late for you to come visit me, Gin."

Ginnifer crinkled her nose up and shook her head at him. "Yes, tonight would've been, but only because I had no idea where to find you in that house or if it was unlocked for me to find you."

Dallas pulled her closer as he leaned down and brushed his lips against her cheek. Bringing his mouth up to her ear, he whispered, "Well, we can remedy that now. I can show you exactly where you can find me each night."

Ginnifer laughed and pulled away from him. "In a bit of a hurry are you?"

With a devilish grin Dallas said, "Absolutely."

"I don't know that I'm done visiting with Olympia and her baby. Does he have a name yet?" she asked.

Dallas shook his head. "No, why don't you name him?"

Excitement filling her voice, she said, "Really? Oh, I have to think about this...he's so beautiful, he needs a name to match."

Dallas laughed as Ginnifer bubbled with excitement. "Do you have anything in mind to fit such lofty expectations?"

"What do you think about calling him Eros?" she asked.

Dallas pulled back and looked at her, shock evident on his face. "The God of Love?"

"Yes, because everyone that looks at him will fall instantly in love with him. I think it's very appropriate."

Smiling down at her, Dallas nodded his head in agreement. He leaned down and kissed her forehead before saying, "It is perfect. Are you ready to stay the night with me, or do you want to visit with Olympia and Eros longer?"

Ginnifer was more than ready to spend the night with him. The more time she spent with him, the harder it was to leave. She was already in too deep to pull herself out. It was starting to look like she might be nursing a broken heart when she went back to New York. There was no way she was going to deny herself whatever time she had with him. So with that decision made, she nodded her head in affirmation. "Yes, take me to your bed."

Dallas smiled as he pulled away from her. He grabbed her hand in his and pulled her along with him out of the barn. Ginnifer thought he would be in a hurry to get her inside of his bedroom, but he strolled along in a slow, lazy pace as they followed the path to the house. Dallas confused her at every turn. She thought all he wanted from her was sex, but the more she got to know him, it seemed like he genuinely liked to spend time with her. It was a conundrum she couldn't pick apart and solve. When they got to the steps leading to the front door, Dallas stopped and pulled her into his arms. He brought his lips to hers in a quick scorching kiss before letting her go. Ginnifer felt butterflies growing inside of her stomach. The man was constantly surprising her.

Brushing his hands alongside her cheek, he pushed back her hair. "I needed to do that once before I got you inside."

"You don't see me complaining."

A bark of laughter floated through the air. "That's what I love about you, Gin. You constantly surprise me. Come on, let's get inside," he said as he grabbed her hand again. They stepped quietly into the house as he led her to his bedroom.

If Ginnifer was confused before, she was even more so now. What did he mean when he said he loved that about me? Those words scared her, but she wasn't going to allow them to interfere with her night. She had been looking forward to spending this time with Dallas all day. She needed it. So when Dallas opened his bedroom door, Ginnifer left her reservations behind as she followed him inside.

DALLAS COULDN'T BELIEVE he had finally gotten Ginnifer inside of his bedroom. He needed to strip every ounce of her clothing off of her. Their time in the barn had been rushed. Now that he had her where he wanted her, Dallas planned on taking his time. He needed to savor every inch of her. Gin was becoming a distraction, and he thought about her all the time. Dallas figured if he could get her out of his system, he would quit thinking about her so much.

Once they were fully inside the room, Dallas closed the door and locked it. He twisted Ginnifer around and pulled her into his arms. He turned and pushed her up against the wall and captured her mouth with his. When she gasped in surprise, he took advantage of her open mouth and tangled his tongue with hers. They stayed in that position for several seconds, letting their tongues dance together. Dallas slowly trailed his hand under her shirt to cup her breast. He lightly squeezed it as his thumb caressed her nipple. He pulled his mouth off of hers so he could yank her shirt over her head and took a step back to admire her in the dim light of his room. His Gin had on one of the sexiest bras he had ever seen. It was sheer black with lace cupping her breasts. Her nipples poked through the black fabric, so he leaned down and pulled one of them inside his mouth. Dallas sucked on it through the barrier of her bra. He heard her whimper as he let it go and took the other breast in his hand. With fast fingers he unsnapped her bra and let it fall from her shoulders. Her beautiful breasts were begging him for more attention, so he pinched them between his fingers as he nuzzled her neck.

"You have too many clothes on," Ginnifer said as she tried to push his shirt off of him. Dallas stepped back and tore his shirt off. He watched as she pushed her pants down, revealing matching panties. The woman had some enticing lingerie. He kicked his own jeans off before pulling her back toward him.

He led her over to the bed, sitting her on it as he ran his hands over her already naked flesh. "Let's have some real fun tonight."

"I thought we were having fun."

He shot her a sinful smile. "You haven't seen fun yet." He left her lying on the bed as he pulled a drawer out. He pulled out some silk ropes, holding them out for her to see.

"You expect me to let you tie me up?" she asked with bewilderment.

"Have you ever let someone tie you up, Gin?"

"Um, no…"

"You'll love it, I promise, but if for any reason you don't, say the word and I will untie you. Do you trust me?"

Ginnifer started to chew on her bottom lip as she kept looking between the ropes and his face. Finally with a half-smile, she looked at him and told him, "Okay, I want to. Tie me up good, Dallas."

Dallas couldn't believe his luck. For a minute there he thought she was going to say no. He had a desperate need to see her tied up in his bed and spread out for his pleasure. With a cocky smile on his lips, he gestured her to scoot up on the bed as he said, "Spread your arms above your head, darlin'. I can't wait to hear you scream with pleasure." He tied her up quickly with the silk ropes and then reached into the drawer, pulling out a silk blindfold.

"You're feeling real kinky tonight, aren't you?" Ginnifer asked.

With a small chuckle, he put the blindfold on her. Now that he had her where he wanted her, he needed to decide how he wanted to start. He leaned over her and licked from her navel to her breast. Her nipples puckered up when his mouth hovered over them, not quite taking them in his mouth but letting his hot breath coat them. Ginnifer moaned in pleasure and began to squirm on the bed, pulling on the ropes. Dallas trailed his fingers down her stomach and rested them on the edge of her panties. He ran the palm of his hand over her mound and rubbed it over the outside of her black panties.

"Please, Dallas, you're torturing me," she pleaded with him.

Dallas ignored her pleading and slowly pulled the panties down her legs. Once she was fully naked he began in earnest to drive her wild. He licked the inside of her thighs and skirted over her most sensitive flesh. He lay down next to her and stroked her hips and left small kisses on her neck. When she started to thrash in earnest, he whispered in her ear, "Are you ready?"

With frustration Ginnifer muttered, "I've been ready forever. Do something before I scream."

"Oh, you're going to scream. Give me a little time, and you'll be screaming so much your throat will be raw."

Dallas pulled away from her and spread her legs wide, leaning down to lick her core. He pushed a finger inside and stroked his fingers over her clit. Ginnifer pushed up at him and began to beg him, "Please, Dallas, I need more." He brought his mouth down again and licked her overly sensitive clit, and she screamed as the orgasm rocked through her body. Dallas continued to roll his tongue over her sensitive flesh as she came, causing another volcanic eruption from her. Ginnifer screamed again as the second orgasm hit.

Dallas pulled away and crawled up on the bed over the top of her. He pushed her legs farther apart as he probed her entrance with his cock. He slowly pushed himself inside her. Her entrance, still contracting from orgasm, made him pause with each thrust. Once he was fully seated, he reached up and untied the silk restraints and pushed off the mask. He pulled her into his embrace and began to slowly push himself in and out of her tight channel. Ginnifer bent her knees and lifted her hips to meet his thrusts. She wrapped her arms around him and met each of his thrusts with her own. Nothing had ever felt as good as this.

How am I ever going to let her go in a week? Dallas could feel Ginnifer start to quiver in orgasm again. He reached down and rubbed his thumb over her clit, setting her off. With a loud moan, she squeezed his shaft, throwing him into the most explosive orgasm he had ever felt. For several seconds Dallas couldn't think as he released himself inside of her. When he was capable of thought again, he realized he was probably crushing her with his weight. He wrapped his arms around her and rolled them both onto their sides. With a satisfied smile, Dallas leaned down and looked at Ginnifer. Her eyes were closed and a sultry smile remained on her lips. He unwrapped one of his arms from around her waist and pulled the blanket up on top of them. He reached for her and pulled her securely back into his embrace. With a contented smile, he let himself breathe in her scent, memorizing it. It was definitely going to be hard to watch her walk away from him. No one had ever pulled him in as completely as Gin already had.

CHAPTER 16

*G*innifer had a smile she couldn't get rid of if she wanted to. Dallas had woken her up before the sun rose with a kiss and some wild morning sex. She hadn't slept so little in her life. If she was lucky, she had actually gotten three hours of sleep. Who was she kidding, that had nothing to do with luck. Luck hated her. That night was absolutely amazing, no matter how much sleep she did or did not get. It had been totally worth every second. She would sacrifice sleep for the rest of her life if she was treated to Dallas's brand of lovemaking. No one had ever satisfied her the way he had. He took his time savoring every inch of her body. He took pleasure in exploring what she liked. Dallas was an amazing lover, and Ginnifer promised herself she would never regret this time with him.

Ginnifer was currently at breakfast enjoying a meal before they were handed their scavenger hunt assignments. Dallas and Wes were still nowhere to be seen, probably choosing to breeze in at the last minute. Dallas had mentioned he needed to try to get as much done as he could before he was tied up with Emma's guests. As far as she knew, he didn't know who was on his team, and they would be sort of spending the day together. She kind of felt bad for her best friend. Tori was bound to have a bad day dealing with Wes's animosity.

She frowned as she looked over at Tori. When she had gone back to the cabin, Tori was still sound asleep, so she jumped in the shower. There wasn't any reason to go back to bed because she planned on attending the morning yoga session. Ginnifer knew that Tori planned on skipping it so she could call Colt before breakfast. For a half a second Ginnifer had thought about skipping it herself. She only reconsidered when she thought it might look odd if she bailed out on her plans. Tori expected her to go, and it might appear strange if she changed her mind. What it really boiled down to was Ginnifer didn't want to explain to Tori why she had changed her mind. She had told Tori about her budding romance with Dallas but had left out a lot of details. For instance, she didn't tell her they had actually had sex. It felt wrong to divulge those intimate details. For the first time, it felt bad to tell her best friend everything. Saying it aloud would somehow taint how special it felt.

Ginnifer looked up at the sound of Emma's voice announcing she was going to pass out the scavenger hunt list. Emma looked at the group and said, "Could everyone assemble into your teams? I have one list per team for you each to look over. The instructions are on the list. Please look it over and see if you have any questions."

They all got up and assembled into the teams they had been assigned to the previous night. Ginnifer's team was Cassidy, Shelly, and Melody. She liked Cassidy and Shelly, but she could have done without dealing with Melody. She still really bugged her. Her skin crawled whenever she was near. It was unreasonable, she knew that, but she couldn't help feeling like the woman was spying on her. She had disliked the woman since the first day she met her. It was time to admit her instincts were on par as far as the woman was concerned. Coffee hadn't been necessary to understand the woman was off. With a grimace, Ginnifer and Tori separated and went to their respective teams. Tori hated having to spend even a second in Wes's company, and Ginnifer wasn't happy because Melody was being super annoying that morning. During yoga she had come over to her, bubbling over with happy tidings. The last thing she remembered her saying was that she was glad they had been assigned to Dallas's team. She couldn't fathom why the perky yoga instructor wanted to be on Dallas's team, but she knew she was going to have to restrain herself from punching her the whole time. Ginnifer still couldn't pinpoint what it was about Melody that bothered her. The woman was the bane of her existence though, and she couldn't wait until the day she no longer had to deal with her. She had to agree with Melody on one point. It was awesome to be on Team Dallas. After her night with him, she didn't think it was possible to tire of being around him. He was more than capable of wearing her out, but it was more that her appetite for him was insatiable.

Melody bounced over and stood next to Ginnifer

while they awaited their scavenger hunt list. Her black curls were spilling all over her head as she kept hopping up and down in place. She really was incapable of standing still. Maybe that was what was so irritating about the woman; she constantly was moving some part of her body. Emma walked over and handed the coveted list to Ginnifer, the members of her group crowding around to read the list.

"This is going to be sooo much fun, roomie," Melody practically screamed in Ginnifer's ear. She reached up and rubbed it, trying to settle the vibrations within. Looking over at Melody and giving her a scathing look, Ginnifer started to read the list out loud, "Bull rope, lariat, riding crop, riding gloves, spurs, saddle, chaps, cowboy boots, leather vest, cowboy hat, mechanical bull, spur sleeves, goat, horse, water trough, barbwire fence, corral, and a grazing pasture."

With a shrug of disbelief, Melody asked, "Is that all we have to find? Those are boring."

Ginnifer rolled her eyes and refrained from stating her true feelings about her roommate's lack of excitement. "It's a ranch scavenger hunt. What did you expect? There are some items listed as bonus finds. They are worth extra points if we find them."

"Well, what are those items?" Melody asked with some enthusiasm returning to her voice.

Ginnifer couldn't wait for the scavenger hunt to be over with. She only hoped her team won so she could go on the overnight camping trip with Dallas and Wes. She didn't want to be apart from him for the night. She looked down at the list and started to read the items that were worth extra points. "Bitter root, gray wolf, and a gopher snake."

Melody smirked at the items on the bonus list. "Those aren't much better. I hope there's something more entertaining that happens while we are doing this scavenger hunt. I could've come up with a better list than this."

Ginnifer frowned at the normally vivacious woman and asked, "Why the hell are you doing this if you find it so distasteful?"

Melody shrugged her shoulders. "It seemed like a good idea when Emma said your team needed another player. Plus have you taken a good look at Dallas? I only agreed to participate if she put me on his team. It was the only way I could get a little closer to him. The man is like a ghost never to be seen around this place."

Ginnifer's mind wandered as Melody kept talking about how sexy Dallas was. She only had one thought cross through her mind as she attempted to block out Melody's incessant chatter. Good God, Melody was interested in Dallas. Maybe she *had* been spying on them. Clearly the woman had a death wish. Ginnifer sighed as that thought crossed her mind. She didn't know for sure if she had been spying on them, but it felt right. Melody saw a good-looking man and wanted to get to know him better, so it probably hadn't crossed her mind that she was being invasive. Still it was grating her nerves raw to listen to her go on and on about all of Dallas's physical attractions. Didn't she realize he was more than a human stud? She had better stop talking about him soon, or there was no stopping Ginnifer from smacking her silly.

Ginnifer looked up and noticed that Melody had been

talking the entire time she had been lost in her own mind. She didn't even need someone to pay attention to her. Clearly the woman enjoyed the sound of her own voice. Ginnifer did her best to tune back in, but Melody was not one of her favorite people, so it was an excruciating task to complete. Turning her head in Melody's direction, she heard her say, "Plus, we have a history, so I know once he sees me, it will make him extremely happy."

Ginnifer turned toward the energetic woman and with a stunned look on her face asked, "Wait a minute, what did you say?"

Melody beamed as she gloated, "Dallas and I go way back. He asked me to marry him. I had to break things off because I wasn't ready at the time. I am now, so it's partially why I took this job. I needed to get close to him again."

All Ginnifer could think about when Melody uttered those words were, why me? If Dallas had cared enough about this woman to actually ask her to marry him, she really must mean a lot to him. For the life of her she couldn't comprehend what he could possibly have seen in Melody. On the other hand, Melody was incredibly beautiful. It was her personality that made Ginnifer cringe. Perhaps Dallas saw a side of her no one else did, but Ginnifer seriously doubted that. It was much more likely he was blinded by lust.

After all it wasn't like Dallas owed her anything. They hadn't made any promises to each other. If he wanted to get back together with the gorgeous chatterbox, she had no say in the matter. It still irked her that she had to spend the day with Melody fawning all over him. It was time she started to distance herself from him. Nothing but hurt could come out of the situation. So with a forced smile, she looked up at Melody and said, "Well, I wish you luck with that. I hope things go the way you have planned. "

For a brief moment it looked like triumph flashed through her eyes as Melody tilted her head and said, "Of course they will. Dallie loves me. Why wouldn't everything go the way I have planned?"

Ginnifer shrugged her shoulders. "I don't know. Maybe he's changed. Aword of caution, sometimes things look better in your head while the reality of it sucks."

Melody waved her hands, brushing off Ginnifer's comment. "Not a possibility. I know that man better than anyone. There's no way he changed."

Ginnifer wanted to laugh at her. Was she really that naïve? Melody was going to do what she wanted no matter what anyone said to her. If anything, it should be interesting to witness Dallas's reaction to seeing his ex-fiancée on his scavenger hunt team. How would he possibly juggle her with his current lover? If her heart wasn't breaking into a million pieces, Ginnifer would laugh at the situation. As it was, she had to gear herself for a hell of an afternoon.

In the distance she heard Emma tell the teams to look on their scavenger hunt list to find out where they had to meet their team leader. So Ginnifer looked down at the list to find out that they were supposed to meet Dallas in the stables near the house. Well at least she was familiar with their starting location. She looked up at her team members and asked, "Are you guys ready for a scavenger hunt? Let's go meet our team leader." Melody bounced out in front of them, stopping only when she realized they hadn't all followed her out.

Cassidy and Shelly looked at her with disbelief on their faces. Clearly Ginnifer wasn't the only one who didn't like Ms. Happy Pants. Shelly shook her head in denial. "I can't believe that woman's audacity."

Cassidy agreed. "Don't let her get to you. She is horrid. I don't think she will last long on this scavenger hunt. Want to bet she hangs all over Dallas the whole time and doesn't help us?" She visibly shuddered. "I don't envy you two having to share a cabin with her."

Shelly grimaced at Cassidy. "Yeah lucky you. You got to escape her company." Looking over at Ginnifer she said, "She insisted on being in your cabin, did you know that? Emma agreed because she needs her here for the yoga program."

Well that was interesting. Why would Melody want to be in the same cabin as her and Tori? This wasn't adding up to anything good. Over time it would make more sense, but at that moment nothing did, so she laughed at their comments and nodded her head in agreement. "Well, we need to go catch up with her. Let's get this thing done, ladies."

Even through the shock of Melody's news, she saw them as two women she could get along with. Maybe they would help her to forget the ache in her chest. They all walked out following Ginnifer to where Dallas was located. All Ginnifer could think about as she led the way was that she wished she could find a way out of doing the damned scavenger hunt. Something she had looked forward to had turned into something that would potentially be the worst experience of her life. She didn't really look forward to Dallas's reaction to seeing his ex-whatever she supposedly used to be again. No, watching that reunion was Ginnifer's equivalent of hell.

*D*allas had finished feeding the horses in the barn and started stacking some bales of hay when he heard a group of female voices chattering outside. He had lost track of time trying to get as many chores done as he could before having to deal with the scavenger hunt Emma had planned. The only bright spot in the situation was that he had guaranteed that Ginnifer would be on his team. The night he had spent with her wrapped in his arms had to be the best night of his life. If he got his way, she would be there every night. He stopped as he thought about that. Yeah, he wanted her there every single night. Not just while she was on vacation at Novak Springs. It shocked him to realize how much she had begun to mean to him in a very short time. He still wasn't ready to make any commitments. The last time he tried that it had been a disaster. When he proposed to Melody, he had believed she was the love of his life. He was blinded by her beauty and energetic personality. He wasn't sure what he felt for Ginnifer. The only thing he was certain of was he was nowhere near ready for things to end between them. There had to be a way for them to continue seeing each other. He tabled that idea, a bale of hay still in his hands as he turned to find four women approaching from behind. He didn't get a clear look at the other three. Dallas had eyes for only one of them. Ginnifer was leading the pack with a grimace on her face. It took everything he had not to laugh at her expression. Apparently she wasn't too happy with the chattering females behind her. If he had any doubts about how perfect she was for him, that look erased all doubt. There was no one else he would rather spend time with than her. Dallas admired her for her beauty and charm. Ginnifer was brilliant and full of spunk. It also helped a great deal that she was willing to try just about anything. Gin was his equal in every way.

Ginnifer stopped directly in front of him and tilted her head, gesturing to the group behind her as she said in a mocking tone, "We're ready for you to lead us, oh Great One."

Dallas laughed at her sarcastic remark. He wanted to pull her into his arms and kiss her. Unfortunately he knew she wouldn't allow that in front of the other women. The only thing really stopping him was he didn't know how it would make her feel. Not at this stage of their relationship anyway. They were still on very shaky ground in this tumultuous liaison; they were embroiled with each other. He looked over at the three females and dropped the bale of hay he had been holding. A beautiful woman with dark-black curly hair was practically bounding around in front of him. Her curves were endless, and her breasts were as perky as he remembered. He had only one thought before she threw herself at him. What the fuck is Melody doing at Novak Springs?

Melody wrapped her arms around him and brought his head down for a kiss. Dallas was too stunned to stop her. He stood there immobilized for what seemed like an eternity before he was able to push her away. He was baffled because he had no clue how to deal with his ex-fiancée standing in front of him. If someone had asked him the last person he thought would ever show up on the ranch, Melody would have topped the list in bold letters and triple starred. When she ended their relationship, she had made it obvious she never wanted to see him again. She had made it clear in no uncertain terms that she wasn't made out to be a rancher's wife. All she wanted to do was open her own studio and teach yoga. Dallas groaned as he remembered exactly what the name of his sister's program was, fucking Cowgirl Yoga. There was no way he could have ever foreseen this possibility. Emma had no clue that Melody was his ex-fiancée and probably hadn't thought twice about hiring her. They had never been introduced, and Dallas refused to talk about her. Her name never left his lips once it had ended between them. Hell, he hadn't even asked her who she hired to help with her program. Wes was the only one that actually knew his ex-fiancée's name. Melody knew everything about his family, though. Dallas talked about them all constantly with her. He had wanted her prepared to meet them when he introduced her to his family. It was important to him that she understood his family and gained acceptance. Melody had been his everything back then. So she had probably used her knowledge of his family to get hired for the Cowgirl Yoga program. It wouldn't surprise him if she hadn't bothered to inform Emma of her previous relationship with him. There was no way Emma would have hired her if she had known exactly who Melody was.

He tried to block her out, but Melody's energy was infectious. It couldn't be ignored, even when that was all you wanted to do. She was bouncing around in front of him, her mouth going a mile a minute. Dallas hadn't heard a word she said while he was lost in his own horror. He stopped when he heard her say, "It's so good we are getting back together, Dallie. I'm so glad I found you again. I've been on this ranch for days, and you've been nowhere to be seen."

"Wait a minute, what?" He couldn't have heard her right. Did she say they were back together? Had the woman lost her fucking mind since they broke up?

Melody kept rubbing herself all over him and petting his chest. She was doing her best to gain his attention. Unfortunately it was working, just not in the way she was hoping it would. Her breasts jutted out as she leaned back to show them at their best advantage. "I've missed you sooo much. Aren't you glad to see me?"

He couldn't deal with her right now. Dallas needed to put as much distance as he could between the two of them before he did something he would regret. Melody hadn't changed at all. She was as selfish as she was beautiful. It was like watching a cobra and waiting for it to strike. Its beauty was as mesmerizing as it was deadly. Staying clear of its poison was almost impossible. Once you allowed yourself to be sucked in, the venom would destroy your soul. All Dallas could think about as he looked at her was he hoped the scavenger hunt got over in record speed. This shit storm was about to become one for the record books.

He pushed Melody to the side and asked the group in general, "Who's got the list?"

Ginnifer stepped over and handed him the scavenger hunt list. The look of betrayal in her eyes seared him to his soul. Dallas couldn't deal with her any more than he could deal with Melody. He needed space to breathe—to think. This damned scavenger hunt needed to end and fast. He gritted his teeth and took the list from Ginnifer. Looking over the list, he turned away from the group and barked out orders to them. With irritation filling his voice he said, "Okay, ladies, follow me. I don't have a lot of time for nonsense." He started to walk away, hoping they were following him because he wasn't stopping to make sure.

WHEN GINNIFER HAD FIRST WALKED into the barn, Dallas's face had lit up when he saw her. For a brief moment she felt her heart skip a beat as it hoped his feelings mirrored her own. So it was a disappointment to her core to witness his reaction to Melody. Her heart sank to a bottomless pit as she watched him interact with Miss Chatterbox. His face had lost all of its color when she had entered his sight. Melody didn't notice her effect on him or she didn't care. She threw herself into his arms and started kissing him. Ginnifer wanted to rip her hair out, but she knew she didn't really have a claim on Dallas. Her chest hurt, and she rubbed her hand over it trying to make the agony go away. Dallas didn't contradict anything Melody was saying or bother to stop her or correct her assumptions about getting back together. Ginnifer thought, maybe he had really loved the woman. She had not thought it was possible until she saw how he reacted to seeing her. Melody had meant something to him. What she was unsure of was if the little sneak still meant something to him.

When Dallas had ordered them to follow him, there wasn't anything she could do but follow his orders. She could have taken the easy road and detoured back to her cabin, but Ginnifer never did do things the simple way. She faced her problems head on and wasn't about to change now when her heart was being ripped from her chest. The only time she gave up was when it was obvious that fighting would be a wasted effort. It was starting to look like she was heading down a path to nowhere. Going on a scavenger hunt was one thing, continuing to smash your heart to pieces was the act of a masochist. Ginnifer had never been overly fond of extreme pain and wasn't about to find pleasure in it now. If only she had some answers about how he felt about Melody, this whole situation would be so much easier. The pain stinging her heart wasn't lessening any. If anything, it grew more excruciating the more time she spent in his company.

No, she would follow his lead on the scavenger hunt, but then she needed to step away and never look back. Ginnifer continued to follow Dallas to wherever he was leading them. He was their group leader, after all, and knew the ranch better than they ever could. Melody had skipped ahead and wrapped her arm around Dallas's. She was chirping away as they walked, talking about everything and anything. Ginnifer tried to block her out as she stayed back with Cassidy and Shelly. She tried to numb her feelings. Nothing was working to make the ache go away. A piece of her soul had been ripped out of her body. That kind of hurt didn't lessen with a few deep breaths and a will to make it stop. Ginnifer shrugged her shoulders and braced herself with all of the energy she could muster. It was going to take everything she had to not kill Dallas and his strumpet.

"What's the first thing we are going to find, Dallie?" Melody asked.

Lord help her. If she keeps calling him that, Ginnifer wouldn't be able to help herself. The woman would become a bloody mess lying at her feet. Dallas must have had a similar thought because he looked at Melody and practically growled his displeasure. "Stop calling me that. It's annoying."

"You never minded before." A full pout developed on Melody's face.

"It never bothered me before, Mel. Let go of me, I need to get a look at this list."

Well, that was a little better. At least he stopped her from hanging all over him. Is this day ever going to end? Ginnifer had serious doubts that it would. She was seriously in hell. One of the fates surely hated her for subjecting her to this torture.

"Most of this stuff is over in the barn we use for the rodeo roundup camp. Follow me. We can get more than half of this done in thirty minutes. The rest will require a hike out to the back pasture," Dallas told the group.

They all tromped behind him as he led them to the barn. He was right; a lot of the stuff listed was in the barn. They quickly took pictures of it all and checked it off of the list. Ginnifer sincerely hoped the rest of the list would go equally as fast. All they had left was a pasture, goat, horse, and barbed-wire fence. There were the bonus point items, but they didn't have to find those. Once they were done with the items inside of the barn, he told them to follow him. They had a bit of a hike to make it to the pasture with the horse and goat in it. Ginnifer geared herself for the hike with the hope she would only be subjected to their company for no more than an hour.

The trek to the back pasture didn't take more than twenty minutes. The items on the list took less than five minutes to catalog and take pictures of with Ginnifer's phone. The only things left on the list were the stupid snake, a wolf, and some plant she had never heard of. As she made sure the pictures she had taken were saved on her phone, she felt something slither across her foot. She looked down and screamed as a huge snake was winding its way around her leg. Ginnifer stood still as fear spread throughout her body. She couldn't move if she wanted to, afraid of what would happen if she did. The snake that was crawling all over her leg was at least six-feet long with dark reddish-brown spots on its yellow back. There was a dark stripe running from its eye around its jaw. Underneath it looked like it had a yellow belly with more dark spots.

When she screamed, Dallas turned to look at her.

When she hadn't moved, he must have thought it was serious because after a few minutes he started walking over to figure out what the problem was. When he looked down and saw the snake twining around her legs, amusement glowed from his expression. His laugher floated around her like a strong wind enveloping her whole body. "Looky here, Gin found you guys a gopher snake. Take a picture of that so you can add it to your bonus board."

Her group stood there with their mouths gaping open. All three of the women were in as much shock as Ginnifer was. They gained their composure quicker, though. They didn't have the experience of having the damned snake crawling all over them. Ginnifer was still stunned by the experience and didn't move an inch. When he instructed her to take a picture of it, she couldn't move to save her life. Snakes and her did not get along. She hated the damn things, and there was no way she was moving until it was no longer wrapping its body around hers. Dallas shook his head at her, took her phone out of her hands, and snapped a picture. After the picture was taken, he put the phone in his back pocket and reached down and untangled the snake from Ginnifer. He walked away and placed it on the other side of the pasture. When he turned around, he saw that Ginnifer still hadn't moved from the spot she was standing in.

Dallas strolled over to her to her side. "It's okay to move now. That snake isn't going to come back here to bother you."

With eyes still glazed over in shock, the only word she could get out was, "Promise?"

A soft smile crossed his face. "Absolutely."

With that Ginnifer allowed herself to relax for the first time in several minutes. She started to shake with relief, and Dallas pulled her into his arms. He hugged her close until she no longer felt the tremors overcoming her body. "Ssh, it's okay, Gin, the big bad snake is long gone."

A laugh escaped her mouth when he whispered those words in her ear. She looked up at him with a wobbly smile. "I'm okay, thank you. I'm petrified of snakes."

He nodded at her, a hint of sarcasm in his voice, "I never would have guessed."

Ginnifer rolled her eyes at him. "Why'd you have to go and ruin a perfectly good moment and turn into an ass."

Dallas had a cocky smile on his face. "You should know by now, Gin, that I'm not a good guy." He turned and walked away from her and gathered the rest of the group. "It's time for us to head back. We need to check in with Emma at the dining hall."

They all followed him, and as they made their way back, Ginnifer hoped that finding the snake didn't make them the winner of the scavenger hunt. She didn't want to go on a campout with Dallas anymore. All she wanted to do was go back to her cabin and lick her wounds. It was time to accept that the time they had together had come to an end. Unfortunately finding that snake changed everything. The thing she had previously wanted was the one thing she now dreaded. After all the tallies were in, it looked like she had to prepare for the overnight camping trip from hell. Ginnifer felt like she was in a living nightmare. Earlier in the day she had thought, if only wishing made it so... Now she had that thought for entirely different reasons. The day had started out with such promise, and now it was ending filled with misery. She had no way of escaping. If Tori could manage going on a scavenger hunt with a man who blatantly hated her, surely Ginnifer could manage to go on an overnight camping trip with her lover and his ex-fiancée. Her mind filled with cynicism as she thought, isn't life grand?

CHAPTER 18

The walls were closing in on her. The longer Ginnifer remained in that building, the more her lungs failed to work properly. Each breath she took burned her lungs, causing her to choke as she exhaled. The extent of her luck held—that being she still had none to speak of. Winning the scavenger hunt should have been a good thing. In Ginnifer's case it happened to be something she wanted to lose. That damned snake ensured they had gotten the most points. No other team had found any extra items. To top it all off, they had also made it back first. So even if they hadn't found the blasted snake, they would most likely have won anyway. The freaking snake deciding to make a home around Ginnifer's leg ensured they would be more difficult to beat. The more she looked at it, she realized she was in a lose-lose situation. Damned if she did and damned no matter what she freaking didn't do. *Could my day possibly get any worse?*

The directions that Emma had given the winning team

were to pack a light bag and return to the dining hall at seven that evening. It would give them time to go over the rules and get out to the campsite Wes and Dallas had set up. Ginnifer, Melody, Cassidy, and Shelly were the team that won. The men would go over what was expected of each of them before they left for camp. Oh joy…

Once she escaped the confinement of the dining hall, she was able to finally allow herself a deep breath. Space, she needed lots of space in order to make it through the next twenty-four hours. Fuck, like she was going to actually get any room to breathe. She couldn't fully escape Melody or Dallas. Of course Melody wanted to share a cabin with her. It all made sense. She must have seen Dallas with her and was jealous. She had been scouting out the competition and lying in wait to strike when the iron was hot. At least she appeared temporarily occupied with Dallas, so it would give her a few moments away from the two of them. Ginnifer practically ran back to her cabin to gain some much needed distance between her and Dallas. He had stood there the entire time, letting Melody fawn all over him. Ginnifer didn't know why they broke up in the first place, but why would he make it so easy for her to jump back into his life?

She was supposed to be packing a very small overnight bag. As in essentials only because everyone was responsible for their own belongings as they traveled to the campsite. It was reiterated several times they shouldn't expect anyone to carry their stuff for them. Ginnifer was willing to bet that Ms. Hot Pants would try to talk another person into lugging around her stuff. That woman was the most irritating person in all creation.

Okay maybe she was being harsh, but really in her defense, she hadn't liked Melody before she knew of her former relationship with Dallas. So it wasn't like she instantly hated her because Melody acted like a growth permanently attached to Dallas's arm. Ginnifer needed to cut her losses and move on. Right? How many times was she going to tell herself before she believed it? It didn't matter how many times she said it in her mind, she knew it wouldn't stick. She didn't really want to give up on him, but knew there was no reason to continue the fling with Dallas. So she tried to beat it into her head it was a useless endeavor to hope he still wanted to be with her. She was a conundrum of emotions. One minute she was cursing him and ready to cut her losses. The next she got all sappy and thought about how much she wanted him. Clearly she was falling apart and needed someone to tell her what to do. For once in her life Ginnifer was at a loss and incapable of making a decision.

No, she needed to stop bouncing around. A choice needed to be made. She deserved better than whatever it was Dallas was offering her. So what if the sex was good? That didn't mean she had to continue beating her heart to smithereens just to have a few more days of amazingly awesome lovemaking. It was very possible that she was overreacting to the situation, but she chose to believe it was self-preservation. She needed to guard her heart from further agony, and the only way to accomplish that was to put a guard up.

She had been inside of the cabin she shared with Tori for fifteen minutes before her best friend made her way back. She looked up as Tori walked into the cabin. Her hair was in a mess, but at least she didn't stink this time. In fact she almost looked well tousled instead of terrorized. Maybe she had a better time on the scavenger hunt than either of them anticipated. There hadn't been a lot of opportunity for them to talk while the teams reported back. They had to stay near their respective teams until everything was tallied up. Tori had no clue about all the discoveries that Ginnifer had made during the course of the scavenger hunt. She didn't even know where to begin to explain how horrible her day had been. So it was no surprise that Tori stopped and with a look of surprise on her face. "Why do you look so depressed? Your team won. Shouldn't that make you happy...more time with your potential lover and all that?" Her hands waved in the air, brushing the comment aside as she strolled farther inside the room.

Oh where to begin? My depression, the win, or my broken heart? They were all intertwined together as one painful experience, so with those things all at the forefront of her mind, there really was only one thing that Ginnifer could mutter, "Stupid eff'ing snake. Had to go and ruin everything."

Her words echoed through the room. It remained eerily silent for several seconds before Ginnifer looked up at Tori and saw that she had a puzzled look on her face. She kept staring at Ginnifer, trying to dissect her. After several minutes, she finally began to speak, "I'm almost afraid to ask, but why are you cursing a snake? Is it a literal snake or a metaphorical one? Better yet, are you talking about a man because I get that too, but I need more information. I'm confused 'cause didn't finding that snake give you a shoo-in to win this competition, explain yourself."

With a long sigh, Ginnifer geared herself for answering Tori's questions. What was the best way to answer them? Was Dallas a snake? She doubted it. The only promise he made was that she would find pleasure in his bed. He fulfilled that promise in spades. She now had a craving for his touch that rivaled any addiction known to man. No, Dallas was honest. It wasn't his fault she had fallen for him. Trying not to love Dallas had been a futile mission. She had been doomed to fail from the start. So there really was only one snake to truly blame. That wretched creature that almost made her faint with fear as it twirled its body around her leg. So with a grimace Ginnifer was forced to admit, "The snake that made it possible for us to win the scavenger hunt."

Surprise filled her voice as Tori expressed her bewilderment, "I'm confused. I thought you wanted to win the scavenger hunt."

Yeah, Tori was correct. Earlier that morning she had said as much as she was getting ready for yoga. She had been so happy having woken up in the best possible way. So when Tori had finally tumbled out of bed, Ginnifer couldn't stop talking. She'd been so excited at the prospect of spending some time with Dallas, even if it had been in a group. She loved being around him. There was no way she could have known how her outlook would change. She was still basking in the glow of Dallas's expert lovemaking skills. With a sigh, Ginnifer walked over and plopped down on her bed and frowned up at Tori. "Originally, yes I did."

Talking a mile a minute, Tori started bouncing her thoughts out loud as she roamed around the room, her hands flailing with each statement. "Well what changed? I need you to explain what possibly could have happened in a few short hours that would make you want to abandon the idea of spending some possible alone time with your latest man candy."

With a small laugh at Tori's rambling, Ginnifer resigned herself to telling her exactly what her problem was in the simplest terms possible. "Melody is his ex-fiancée."

"Oh, you mean Audrey 2?" Tori asked.

Ginnifer burst out laughing at Tori's interpretation of Melody, wiping a tear from her eye she looked at her and said, "Oh. My. God. I can't believe you compared her to a man-eating plant. I thought I was the only one that gave her snide nicknames in my head."

"Please. There is no better comparison than that. I finally figured her out. It took me a minute to see underneath that fake exterior. She is a man-eater. She's a predator of the worst kind. I feel sorry for Dallas if she wants her hooks back in him. He's doomed."

With a confused look Ginnifer asked, "Why do you say that? I know I hated her on contact and all, but that was before I knew she was his ex. Why'd you instantly dislike her?"

Tori strolled over to sit on the bed next to Ginnifer. "She sees us as competitors. She brings her claws out to warn us off. She starts out nice until she knows how to warn you off. You notice how she is sugary sweet with

Emma? It's 'cause Emma can help her attain her goal of latching back onto Dallas."

Ginnifer scrunched her mouth up in disapproval before saying, "So you think he'll get sucked back into her bullshit? I couldn't tell if he wanted to push her away or if he actually enjoyed the attention."

Tori wrapped her arms around her in a half hug, laying her head on Ginnifer's shoulder. "What can I say? He's a man. They aren't to be trusted."

"I know you have issues with men, Tori. They are not all bad."

Tori raised her head and looked Ginnifer in the eye. "I appreciate that you believe that, but you're wrong. They're all selfish bastards. Don't get me wrong, they do have their uses. It's best not to trust them with your heart."

Ginnifer frowned and sadly had to agree with Tori's assessment. "Yeah too little too late. I really tried, Tori. I didn't want to feel anything for him. Dallas surprised me, and before I knew it, he wormed his way inside. He's sneaky that way. How am I going to get through a night watching her fawn all over him?"

With an evil smile on her face, Tori stood up and told her, "By using every weapon you have in your arsenal. You have to fight fire with fire. Under no uncertain terms are you to allow him to realize how much you're hurting."

"But I am hurting, Tori. I can't fake happy."

Tori laughed. "No, but you can be the sexiest damn cowgirl on the range."

With horror Ginnifer asked, "Do I want to know what you have in mind?"

Clapping her hands in excitement, Tori began to dig through one of her bags. "Of course you do. Don't worry your pretty little brain. I'm going to take care of you, and in the process Dallas won't know what hit him."

With a resigned sigh, Ginnifer stood up and asked, "Okay, I don't really have the energy to fight you. What do you need me to do?"

Tori marched over and began shooing Ginnifer to do her bidding. "First go get your ass in the shower. I'm in charge until you leave. In fact, I'm even going to pack your overnight bag."

"Now I know I'm terrified. Do you have any idea what needs to go in that bag?"

With glee slicing through her words, Tori announced, "Yes. And no, it's none of the bullshit they listed off. This bag will be filled with all of the tools you'll need to not only drive Dallas crazy but make sure he leaves you alone as well."

"I still have my doubts, but I'll leave it in your capable hands, oh Wise One."

Tori laughed and gestured for her to get moving. So with some reluctance, she did as she was told and walked into the bathroom. There really was no arguing with her once she got something in her mind. Ginnifer might as well get up and do what she wanted. She needed to take a shower, anyway. The hot steam would be cathartic in helping relieve some of the tension from her muscles. If what Tori had planned truly helped her get through the night, the torture would be worth it. Otherwise she had no clue what she could do to make the night go by any faster. As it was, she already dreaded seeing Dallas again.

Ginnifer reached into the pocket of her jeans looking for her phone so she could listen to some music while she showered only to realize it wasn't there. Oh God, Dallas had put it in his pocket after taking a picture of the freaking snake. How could she have forgotten to get it back from him? The blasted man should have handed it back to her instead of putting it in his own pocket. There was nothing she could do about it now. It was something that would have to be dealt with later. But the only thing she could really think about was, damn it I will have to actually talk to him so she could get it back.

CHAPTER 19

*A*fter Ginnifer got out of the shower, she wrapped a towel around herself and walked out to find out what Tori had planned. She had gone into warp speed to get everything ready while Ginnifer was in the shower. She had dug through her own clothes as well as Ginnifer's to gather the items she deemed necessary to make her into a sexy cowgirl. Luckily they wore the same size clothing. Tori was a little shorter than Ginnifer, but that only became a problem with her tailored pants. Her skirts and anything meant to be on the short side still fit Ginnifer's lean body. In this instance, Tori had actually raided Ginnifer's clothing to pull out a pair of skin-tight black jeans hemmed into a boot cut. When she wore them, she didn't have any extra room because they hugged the curve of her ass and were tight all the way down her leg until it flared slightly at the ankle to allow for boots. From her own wardrobe she pulled out a black leather vest with three tiny silver buttons down the middle and a cutout in the shape of a *V* at the bottom of it. It curved up over her shoulders in the fashion of a halter top. The back of the vest was nearly non- existent, with only a couple of inches to leave her back almost entirely bare. She finished the look with a black leather belt that held a holster for a knife and a flashlight. She looked closer and thought it looked like a black lasso was thrown on the bed as well. A pair of black cowgirl boots with silver buckles was sitting on the floor next to the bed.

There was no shirt anywhere among the items on the bed. Terrified as to what her answer might be, Ginnifer looked at Tori and asked, "Where's the shirt? Please tell me that isn't a whip."

An evil laugh floated through the room as Tori sashayed over to stand next to Ginnifer. She picked up the vest and showed it to her. "This is all you are wearing. No bra, either. Just this to hug your breasts as you parade around camp. His tongue will be hanging out when he sees you wearing this outfit. I guarantee it."

Ginnifer was scandalized. She had never worn anything quite like the outfit Tori had laid out for her. So she addressed her biggest issue with it as she said, "Um, won't this be a little cold to sleep in? I mean, um, it is a camping trip."

Tori nodded her head in the affirmative as she began giving Ginnifer detailed instructions. "You'll absolutely freeze. It's why I'm packing a nice sweatshirt in your backpack for emergencies only. Do not take it out unless you can't bear the cold. You need to walk around as long as possible in this get-up so Dallas can't keep his eyes off of you. It's a sacrifice we women have to make in order to get our point across. Why do you think I wear those nose-bleed-inducing shoes every day? It's a statement. I don't like wearing them. Now remember you're not to encourage him. Do not look at him. Do not acknowledge him unless he asks you a direct question. Even then, be abrupt and walk away. It is imperative that you are blasé about the whole situation. It has to appear like what is going on between him and Melody doesn't mean a damn thing to you. Be your usual sarcastic self, but at a distance. Do you understand me?"

Ginnifer didn't know if she was going to remember all that. It was a lot of information to process when her brain was barely functioning as it was. She decided to pretend she had heard it all. "Okay fine. I understand all that. But please explain what the whip is for. I get the flashlight, but what the hell do I need this thing for?"

Tori waved her hands at the item in question. "Oh that's just for looks. I'm going to attach it to your belt loop so it hangs down. Trust me, he is going to eye it up. It's sure to give him ideas. Just do not give in to them. Oh, and it's a lasso, not a whip."

With exasperation Ginnifer asked, "What the hell's the difference?"

Tori laughed at Ginnifer's question. "Well normally a lasso is a rope that is used to form a circle and catch an animal, like a calf. I had to look that up after Wes used that damned rope on me. Well, this was part of a costume I bought and had no idea what it was. I packed it up as something I might use. It's not meant to be used for real. The material of the rope isn't very strong, and it's not quite long enough to do a real lasso justice. I'm sure you can find something useful for it, though, so I want you to take it."

"Fine, it's not worth arguing over. Besides, if it's attached at my belt, it's not like I have to carry it."

"True enough. Now get dressed. You have thirty minutes before you have to be at the dining hall to leave, and we still need to blow dry your hair."

Ginnifer grabbed the clothes and put them on quickly. The jeans fit as snuggly as she remembered, and the vest felt decadent against her breasts. It was a little weird not wearing a bra, but it also felt sexy as hell. It's too bad she couldn't let Dallas peel it off of her. No, bad Ginnifer. She wasn't supposed to be having those kinds of thoughts. There was no denying that the outfit did make her feel good. By putting it on, it felt like she had a chance of pulling off indifference. It was something she never would have picked out herself because it would have felt wrong. Ginnifer didn't generally do blatantly sexual. She preferred the subtle approach. Tori knew how to get a man's attention. She had a lot more practice at doing this than Ginnifer did, so she trusted her directions. The whole purpose of all of this was to make Dallas lust after her and regret pushing her aside for Ms. Grabby Hands. She laughed in her head again at Tori's description of her. She was so right in comparing her to the bloodthirsty foliage from *Little Shop of Horrors*.

Once the outfit was on, she sat down and slipped the boots on her feet. After adjusting the pant legs, she stood up so Tori could add her attachments around the belt loops. The rope wasn't even noticeable once it was attached. The flashlight was mildly annoying, but it was tiny and only lightly tapped her hip as she walked. Tori did a circle around her, inspecting everything to make sure it was in place. "Okay sit down. We are going to dry your hair so it falls down like butterscotch waves across your back."

Ginnifer seriously doubted it was a good idea to keep her hair down. She didn't generally like to wear it hanging loose over her shoulders and back. It became annoying pretty fast, so she was constantly pulling it up in a pony-tail or braid. She forced herself to say, "Um, won't it get annoying being down like that, Tori? I mean, it's camping. Can't I at some point pull it up in a ponytail or something?"

With a flick of her hand gesturing agreement, Tori said, "Sure, once you are ready to go to sleep, by all means do something else with it. But don't do anything until then. It needs to float around as much as possible. Even when you pull it up, make it a messy ponytail so strands fall down and entice."

There was no way to talk Tori into putting her hair up and out of the way, so with a sigh Ginnifer nodded her head in agreement. "Fine."

It didn't take long for Tori to have her hair arranged the way she had described it. Then she took some lip gloss and swiped it over Ginnifer's lips. "This should be all you need. You have a great complexion, Ginny. You should put the lip gloss in your pocket in case you need it later."

Ginnifer stood up and grabbed the small bag Tori had packed for her. She had no idea what was actually in it, but she trusted her. It was probably filled with items she never would have included, but she chose to look at it as an adventure she would never have again. She looked at Tori and said, "Okay, I guess it's time to get this show on the road. I have five minutes to get over to the dining hall. Wish me luck."

Tori folded her arms across her chest and surveyed her handiwork. "You don't need luck. You're fabulous and make things happen without it."

Ginnifer laughed at her friend's assessment of the situation. "You're right. Luck and I don't get along, anyway. Okay, I'm off. I will see you sometime tomorrow."

"Oh before you run off. I should warn you that Melody was already here. She packed extra light. Grabbed a small knapsack and ran off. I don't think she wanted to be in the cabin for very long. I have to wonder what that's all about."

Ginnifer raised an eyebrow in wonder. "Hmm, maybe she's avoiding me for some reason. Kind of dumb when we are going on a camping trip and will be required to spend time together. I'm not going to stress over it. I'll see you in the morning." She walked out the door and started the journey toward the meeting place. With determination of steel, she kept putting one foot in front of the other so she could make it there in time. At this point there wasn't a thing that would keep her away from the camping trip. It was a matter of pride. She needed to save face and show Dallas she didn't care if he got back together with Melody. Ginnifer was an intelligent and independent woman. She didn't need a man to cement her happiness. Tori was right, she made things happen. She didn't wait for them to happen to her.

When she got to the dining hall, everyone was already

there waiting on her. Dallas looked up and saw her with shock in his eyes. Ginnifer turned away quickly and walked over to Emma and asked, "Are you coming too?"

Emma smiled at her before saying, "No, I wanted to see you all off and make sure everything went well. I'm glad you are going tonight. It'll give you more things to write in your article. Did you get Dallas to answer all of your questions?"

Ginnifer shook her head back and forth expressing the negative outcome of the interview with Dallas. "Um, no we kind of got sidetracked with the birth of the foal."

Emma nodded her head in understanding. "Ah. I understand how you'd lose sight of what you had sought him out for in light of that happening. If you make up a list of your questions, I can sit down and make him answer them. I know how difficult he can be."

That was an excellent idea. If she could get Emma to have Dallas answer those remaining questions, it would be one less thing she had to deal with. If it was Emma that answered the questions, it wouldn't bother her, but she really had no desire to have any extra conversations with Dallas. So she nodded in agreement. "Do you think I could e-mail them to you? It might be easier that way, and you can work on them even after I leave. I have time to get it all written before I send it to the editor. It'll be at least two weeks before it's due for the publication once I return to New York."

Emma nodded her head affirming the suggestion. "Sure, that would work. Are you excited about the camping trip?"

That would be a negative, Emma. The camping trip

was going to be awful. She didn't want to tell the woman that, so instead Ginnifer said, "Yeah, I've never been on a real rodeo campout. Are we using tents?"

A voice from behind her said, "Of course not. Cowboys camp under the stars." Ginnifer turned to find Dallas standing behind her as he said, "We're leaving, Gin, are you ready?"

He kept clenching his hands open and closed into a fist. It looked like he wanted to grab a hold of something but thought better of it. His face was contorted with frustration. Ginnifer chose to only give him a courtesy nod in concurrence. "Yes, lead the way." After that she ignored him as she turned back toward Emma. "I'll e-mail that to you sometime tomorrow after we get back. I already have it written out, I need to attach it to the e-mail before I send it to you."

Emma nodded at her. "Okay, I'll remember to look for it. Have fun."

Avoiding Dallas, Ginnifer turned and walked toward the rest of the group. She stood next to Cassidy and Shelly, hoping Melody would leave her alone. There was no way she would be able to handle being around her for long. She looked over and realized there was no reason to worry that Melody would be a problem. Like a leech out for blood, she had latched on tightly once again to Dallas's arm. Dallas turned to stare at her with confusion pouring out of his eyes. The poor man looked lost. Well, Melody was his problem, not hers. He needed to find a way to extricate himself from her grasp all on his own. If that's what he wanted, anyway…

In the meantime she would have to find something

else to occupy her mind with. Ginnifer turned and walked over to Wes with a sultry smile on her face. "Are you our leader, cowboy?" It was time to get to know her best friend's current nemesis.

With a smile dripping with sin, he looped her arm around his. "Well darlin', I'd happily lead you anywhere. Just follow me. I promise I won't steer you wrong."

The group started walking toward the campsite. They had been informed that everything they needed was already there and set up. There was a chance they would need to gather extra firewood, but there was a small amount already in camp. All they had to bring was the small bags they had brought with them. So they all started the journey toward the pasture they would be camping under the stars in. Wes and Ginnifer led the pack. As they sauntered past Dallas, she saw his mouth form a grim line of displeasure. Well looky there, Dallie isn't happy. Melody better do something fast because her hook wasn't quite as tight as she thought it was...

CHAPTER 20

*D*allas had no idea what was going through Gin's mind, but if she was trying to piss him off, she was doing a splendid job of it. When she had walked up, he had to use every bit of his self-control not to drag her away and strip that outfit off of her. There wasn't a doubt in his mind she wore that outfit to drive him crazy. She had fuck me written all over her from her long blonde tresses floating down her back to her skin-tight black jeans. He eyed the vest and wondered if she was bare underneath it. Dallas hoped not, or there was no way he would be held responsible for what he did. There was a very high possibility he'd go all cave man on her. She needed to learn exactly what would happen if she wore an outfit like that in his presence. This really wasn't the time or place to give her that lesson. Soon though, very soon, she would know what she was doing to him.

As much as he wanted to get Ginnifer naked, he also wanted to strangle Melody. He was trying to be polite and not embarrass her, but her constant petting and groping was starting to get on his nerves. What the hell had I ever seen in her? The more time he spent with her, the more he wanted to distance himself. Melody was the most irritating female he knew. He couldn't understand how he had expected to spend the rest of his life with her. True, she was beautiful, but she was also annoying as hell. Had she always been this buoyant? The level of her enthusiasm was grating on his nerves. Melody was bubbling over with unrepressed energy. Damned if he couldn't remember anything about her except that she had been wild in bed. That had to be the reason he'd been so attached to her five years ago. The more he pushed her off of him, the harder she latched back on when she got the chance. Melody's sugary sweetness was making him miserable. If she didn't stop touching him, Dallas would get mean and fast. She wouldn't be happy with his reaction, but at least he'd be able to finally shake her free.

In the meantime he was making plans on how to murder his own brother and exactly where to bury the traitor's body. He couldn't believe how he had grabbed a hold of his Gin and led her to the campsite. Admittedly, Wes didn't know that Dallas considered Gin to be his, but that didn't mean he still didn't deserve to be bashed in the head for his actions. It pissed him off watching them walk in front of him, laughing each step of the way. Each stride their legs made along the weathered path caused Dallas's anger to grow. He was a hot kettle about to burst wide open, releasing some trapped steam. The only benefit to following them was that he got a good view of Ginnifer's ass. After they were settled in the camp, he was going to have a long talk with her. Besides he had her phone in his pocket. It gave him a good excuse to force her to talk to him.

She had to be pissed off about Melody fawning all over him. A part of him agreed with her. He didn't like it, either, but he felt he owed Melody a certain amount of respect, even if she had been the one to break things off and break his heart. Looking back, he realized she had done him a favor. They wouldn't have lasted very long before their relationship fizzled if they had stayed together. The clues had always been there, and Dallas had chosen to ignore them. Melody had been his everything back then. Not a damn thing would've made him sit up and say hey maybe we aren't meant to be together forever. He was blinded by his love for her. It's funny how clear things looked when you took the time to glance back. At the time, it had devastated him to the point he hadn't let anyone into his heart again. It led to Dallas's belief that love was for fools. His faith in that emotion had been crushed to oblivion with Melody's departure from his life. She had been his reason for losing all trust in a woman's ability to stick around. They were not reliable. Until he had met Ginnifer, he hadn't believed he would ever find a woman worth fighting for. Dallas still wasn't sure that she was, but he wanted to find out. She made him want to believe love was possible.

Melody was walking next to him. She had tried to grab hold of his arm, but he had shaken her off a while ago. She had settled in for incessant chatter as they made the trek to camp. Thank God they were almost there. Dallas had no idea what she was talking about because he had blocked her out. Listening to her was akin to shooting yourself in the head. If given the choice, Dallas would have asked for a gun to end his misery. Clearly, listening to Melody was a fate worse than death. Again he had to wonder what he ever saw in her; she drove him insane in a very short time. That was when he remembered how he used to shut her up. The quickest way to get her to stop talking was to keep her mouth busy doing something else. Dallas almost stopped in his tracks at the memory of what else her mouth was good for. Oh yeah, it was definitely a good reason to keep her around back then. It didn't mean he still felt that way. The last thing he wanted was to get intimate with his ex-fiancée. He looked up and sighed with relief when he saw the campsite a few feet in front of them. Ginnifer and Wes had already stopped and were idly chatting as they waited for Dallas and Melody to reach them. Cassidy and Shelly were trailing a short distance in front of him. Dallas had insisted that one of them lead and the other follow to ensure they didn't lose anyone on the way. So the other two ladies walked in between them on the way up.

As Dallas reached camp, he looked Ginnifer directly in the eyes, letting her know without words that he wasn't happy with her. The saucy wench smiled seductively at him and nodded her head. She bent down and adjusted her pant leg and gave him a good look down her vest. The damn woman wasn't wearing a bra. His fucking brother probably got a good look at her perfect breasts the whole way to the back pasture. Oh yeah he was going to kill him, making sure no one found the body. Wes was going to pay for laying his grubby hands on Ginnifer. As soon as he got a chance, he was going to show his little brother why it was wrong for him to touch her in any way. Right now he had other priorities. For instance the women needed to get settled into camp. The faster that happened, the quicker he could have a little chat with Ginnifer. Dallas strolled over to Wes. "Let's divide them up and show them how to set up their bedrolls. Do me a solid and keep Melody occupied before I slap her. I can't take any more of her right now."

Wes nodded at him. "Is she who I think she is?"

"Yes. Don't say another word about it. Keep her away from me." Dallas stalked over to Ginnifer's side.

He stopped in front of her as she picked up a bedroll, examining it. She looked up at him and raised her eyebrow questioning, "Yes?"

"Do you know how to set that up?" he asked.

With a shrug she said, "Not exactly, but I think I can figure it out."

He shot her a pissed-off look. "Or you can let me help you."

With sarcasm lacing through her voice, she expressed her displeasure at the idea, "No, I think I've got this." Then gesturing toward the other two females in the group, she attempted to send him in a different direction. "Shelly and Cassidy might need help. Why don't you go do the manly thing with them?"

She turned her back and ignored him. She was fucking putting up a wall between them, and he wasn't going to have it. He went to grab her and shake some sense into her when he heard a scream. He looked over and saw Melody jumping around and pointing at the ground. Wes, a short distance away, didn't get to her in time before they saw a snake slithering near her. "There's a snake!" she shouted at them.

"Damn it, Melody, stand still so we can figure out what kind of snake it is. I'd hate for you to feel what it's like to get bitten by a snake. If it's poisonous, we might not have enough time to get you to the hospital for antivenin," Wes told her.

Dallas shook his head and walked over to deal with it. When he got closer, he saw that it was another gopher snake. "It's all right, Wes. It's not poisonous. Let me get it out of the way so we can set up camp. We don't need any more screaming females." Damn Melody for distracting them. He grabbed the snake and walked it away from the camp. He turned around and saw that Ginnifer had her bedroll in place and was helping the other two women with theirs. Wes had his hands full comforting a crying Melody. Dallas started to walk away when he saw Melody look up and stare at him. Wes's arms were still wrapped around her, but she was doing her best to try and lure Dallas to her side. Well she would have to be disappointed. As far as Dallas was concerned there wasn't any good reason to take over for his brother. Wes had her under control, and he wasn't about to get between them. That was a headache he didn't want or need. Instead, he went to find out if he could help the other females set up their bedrolls.

"Do you ladies have this all figured out?" he asked.

"Oh yes, Ginnifer has been great about helping us," Cassidy told him.

"Please tell me that snake is long gone." Shelly shuddered.

He shot them an evil grin. "Yeah it was slithering off in the opposite direction when I left it. They are harmless, anyway. It's the rattlers you have to keep an eye out for. Let me know if you see one of those, but remain as calm as possible so they don't strike you."

The color drained from Ginnifer's face. "Oh God."

Cassidy and Shelly nodded their head at him in agreement. "We'll do that. What's a rattler look like?" she asked

"Very similar to a gopher snake," he told them.

"Well how can we tell the difference?" Cassidy asked.

"Well if it hisses at you and there's a rattle in its tail, there's a good chance it's not a snake you should mess with."

With a grimace on her face, Ginnifer shook her head. "In my opinion no snake is worth messing with. They can all keep their distance from me."

Dallas nodded at her. "Well, Gin, if you see another one, let me know. I will gladly untangle it from your legs."

"Right. 'Cause that would be my damned luck a snake would choose to twine itself around my leg again," Ginnifer muttered under her breath.

A smirk on his face, Dallas looked at her. "Well, they are mighty fine legs. Can't fault their taste."

Ginnifer rolled her eyes at him and with heavy sarcasm made her displeasure known, "Sure I can. Snakes are evil creatures. I don't want them slithering all over me leaving a taint on my skin. It's best to avoid that at all cost."

Dallas frowned and heard her double meaning laced through her words. She was warning him away from her. Damned if he was going to let her go that easy, so he said,

211

"No reason to take out your anger on the poor snakes, Gin. Make sure you aim at your true target with that pessimism."

With disdain in her eyes, she looked directly at him. "Oh, I thought I had. Snakes. Evil. Taint. Those are all things I'll avoid as much as possible in the future. Isn't that clear?"

Pissed that she thought of brushing him off like garbage, he returned her look with equal measure. "Crystal." Fuck if he was going to deal with her while she was in this mood. He would have to wait until she was alone and deal with her then. He saw a small rope around her belt loop and thought it might be a good idea to make use of it. If he tied her down, she wouldn't be able to escape him. It would definitely ensure she had to listen to him. He didn't give a damn if she was mad about Melody. She could have at least given him some time to explain the situation. Instead she had gotten all moody about it and decided they were done. Gin was wrong. They were far from done, and he was going to prove it. He had a plan, and once everyone was asleep, he would make it happen. While he waited, he would make sure everyone else was settled in and the campfire was lit. They were going to roast some food over the fire for dinner and tell stories around the fire. He had a good one about snakes sure to make his Gin a bit nervous.

His plan firmly in his mind, he walked over to Wes and told him he was going to gather some wood for the fire.

Wes looked at him in confusion. "But we already have some gathered."

Was his brother seriously that dense? "I know that. I

need to get away. Gathering more wood is an excuse. Just pretend it's a good one and let me leave."

"Ah. Okay. Take as long as you need."

"Please keep the women busy while I'm gone. I need a breather from all the estrogen," he said as he walked away. In reality he needed a bit of time to cool off and solidify his strategy for dealing with Ginnifer. If she thought they were over, she was dead wrong. He didn't give a damn about Melody. Their relationship had ended years ago. She was next to nothing to him. Dallas would have a long talk with both women so they knew where he stood. Melody was going to be sent back to whatever hole she had crawled out of. Ginnifer, well she was going to get a lesson in what would happen if she ever ignored him again. She needed to realize there were penalties for her actions. It was time she got that spanking she wanted so much...

CHAPTER 21

*G*innifer was far from amused. Dallas had walked off over an hour ago to only God knew where. Night had already fallen, and the temperature was starting to drop. The time to abandon the sexy cowgirl look for something on the warmer side was fast approaching. A shiver rolled over her making her glance at her bag and think about the warm sweatshirt encased inside. Tori was nuts if she thought she was sacrificing warmth just to make a point. However, she didn't want to grab the sweatshirt yet. If torturing Dallas was the goal, she couldn't accomplish it with him absent from the camp. So the bastard had better come back soon so she could commence with the torment she wanted to inflict upon him. She didn't know how long she could go without pulling the sweatshirt over her freezing limbs.

There wasn't a damn thing she could do about the situation until he returned. Instead of making him feel like an ass, all she had accomplished was some bonding time with the other two women in her group. Shelly and

Cassidy were great, but she wasn't looking to make any new friends. She wanted to make Dallas burn. Whether it was with anger or passion, she didn't really care. As long as the flames licked him to the point only ashes remained. In her mind the end totally justified the means.

If only she could get rid of Melody, her life would be so much sweeter right now. At least she was bugging Wes instead of her. Poor Wes looked like he wanted to shoot himself. He clearly wasn't impressed with Melody and her numerous charms. The last thing Ginnifer had heard her ask him was when Dallas would be back. Good question, when was he going to show his face again? If only Melody didn't want him back as much as she did. It was a funny thing that she simultaneously wanted him both at camp and wherever he was at the same time. She wished she didn't yearn for his attention as much as she did. It shouldn't matter so much if he wanted her, but sadly it was all she could think about.

With a sigh of resignation, she turned to look at Melody and Wes again. The woman had a one-track mind where Dallas was concerned. *Like you're any different?* Okay, so she had a one-track mind lately too. Didn't make Melody any less annoying or predatory. Tori was right about her personality. She didn't do anything to try to get to know any of the women. She did her best to pretend they didn't exist. With Dallas gone, the only one in the group that mattered to her was Wes. The women didn't help to further her agenda, so they were not important to her.

Ginnifer figured Melody didn't need any additional of her attention, so she decided to walk back to her bedroll and relax. She was so lost in thought she hadn't heard anyone approach until she heard a voice behind her. "I need you to come with me." With a gasp she turned around and saw Dallas standing right next to her. When the hell had he sneaked back into camp? Ginnifer thought she had surveyed the whole area a minute ago, and he hadn't been anywhere to be seen.

"When did you sneak back in?" she asked him.

Dallas's voice filled with indignation, "I didn't sneak anywhere. I walked right here in the wide open. It's not my fault you were lost in your own world."

Ginnifer sneered at him before saying, "Yeah, whatever. I don't have time to deal with you right now. Go away."

Dallas raised his eyebrow questioning, "What, you have a hot date or something?"

Her anger began rolling off of her in waves, and she could feel her cheeks start to heat and pursed her lips in displeasure. What right did he have to question her? Fuck that, she wasn't going to give in, so she said, "Definitely. So hot it'd burn you alive."

"Prove it."

Ginnifer shrugged her shoulders, dismissing him. "Don't have to. Go away, Dallas."

"No."

Ginnifer didn't know why she had let Tori talk her into this. She really wasn't fond of confrontations. So she did the only thing that felt right. She picked up her small bag to walk away. "Fine. I don't have to deal with you. Do whatever you want. I'm going back to my nice warm cabin."

"Like hell you are. I swear I'm going to put you over my knee and spank your ass. It's dark, and you don't know the ranch that well. It won't take you long to get lost, and I'll be damned if I'm searching for your stubborn ass in the dark."

Ginnifer pinched the bridge of her nose between her thumb and forefinger. The man was so frustrating. Why wouldn't he leave her alone? "Spank me? As if I'd let you. No man is ever going to slap my ass. I'll be fine, get out of my way." She shoved past him and started to stomp away. She stopped only briefly when she saw Melody look in their direction. It was at that point Melody noticed Dallas had returned. She practically skipped her way over to them shouting, "Oh Dallie, your back. I've missed you so much." She damn near jumped into his arms and started to kiss him. With a disgusted look at the spectacle, Ginnifer turned around and continued walking away from the group. No one noticed her absence. Dallas had been too occupied with Melody to stop her.

She had walked quite a distance when she got an odd feeling and stopped. A sound made her turn her head, and she saw a snake slithering toward her. Damn it, she really didn't have any luck where the creepy creatures were concerned. There wasn't anything she liked less than snakes. Here was the third freaking one in less than twelve hours. Surely this was some kind of record. A rattle caused her to stand still as she remembered Dallas's earlier warning. Wasn't that her freaking luck? She would have to come across a damn rattler. Ginnifer looked around and thought about her options. The snake was maybe two feet away with the damned thing heading straight for her. Her options were to stand as still as possible and hope it would slither on past her or to try to move as far away from it as she could. Ginnifer was petrified of snakes, and that fear had left her standing frozen. So option one it was...

Ginnifer must have stood there for an hour before Dallas found her. At least it had felt like a really long time as the rattler moved at a snail's pace across her boot. Maybe it was longer, maybe it was shorter. All she knew was her heart was beating a mile a minute. Ginnifer didn't know if she could stand still for much longer. When she heard his voice, she wanted to cry with relief.

"Gin, why are you standing there?"

Her voice shook with fear. "I want to tell you to go away. But I think I need your help. Don't come closer, Dallas, I mean it."

His voice was full of confusion as he asked, "How can I help you if I don't get close to you?"

"There's a snake. It's a rattler. It's like crawling over my boot." She did her best to remain still as she could feel it slither across the top of her foot.

She looked over and could barely see him shaking his head in the pitch black night. Ginnifer wouldn't have known that the snake was there if she hadn't heard it. She hadn't even had a chance to use her flashlight to guide her back to the ranch. "I'm going to have to get a little closer if I'm going to help you," he told her. "The problem is it's really dark, and I can't see that well."

"Then stay where you are. It's got to leave at some point, right?"

Dallas shrugged his shoulder, not giving her an affirmation either way. "Maybe. Snakes do what they want, though. You might be standing there an awful long time. You think you can handle that?"

Ginnifer seriously doubted her ability to stand still for very much longer. She didn't want him to get hurt, though, so she started to say, "I don't know. Ouch."

With a worry in his voice, Dallas asked, "Gin, what happened? Don't move. I'm coming over there."

She tried to stop him before he got closer by saying, "No. I'm fine. I promise. I got a cramp in my leg."

When Dallas got closer, the snake started to hiss. Ginnifer could barely see in front of her under the dark night sky, but with horror she saw it rear back ready to strike. She closed her eyes, bracing for the impact of the bite, but was surprised when none came. The next thing she knew she was wrapped inside of Dallas's arms. He hugged her tight, practically squeezing the breath out of her. Ginnifer looked up into his eyes and started to cry in relief.

Dallas tried to comfort her by saying, "Ssh, it's okay. It's dead. Look."

Ginnifer just shook her head, weeping. She could see a knife in the snake's head. Dallas must have thrown it at the snake as he rushed to her side. Ginnifer couldn't handle it anymore. It was all too much. So in between sobs she said, "Take me back to the cabin. I don't want to do this anymore."

With a resigned sigh, Dallas looked at her and agreed, "Okay. I'll take you back."

They walked back in silence. It took them less than thirty minutes to get back to her cabin without much light from the dark night sky. She didn't say anything until they were at her door. Turning toward him, she expressed her gratitude, "Thanks. I'm going to go in and sleep."

"We still need to talk."

She shook her head at him. "Not now, Dallas. I've had enough. Whatever you have to say can wait."

The look on his face said he wanted to push her into dealing with it. Something stopped him from doing it, though, so he shrugged his shoulders. "Fine. I have to get back and help Wes with the other women. Try to get some rest. We'll talk tomorrow."

Ginnifer nodded her head at him. She would have done anything to get him to leave. "Okay."

He stared at her with a piercing gaze. "I mean it, Gin. This isn't over. Be prepared to deal with this when I get back tomorrow afternoon."

"I get it. Go. You're needed elsewhere," Ginnifer agreed before she turned and walked into the cabin. What he didn't know was that Gin had no intention of dealing with anything. They were done. She accepted that as she walked back to the cabin with him in silence. This was her last hurrah before she went back to New York. In fact, as far as she was concerned, she there wasn't any good reason to stay the whole second week. She had enough information to write the article she promised Emma. The e-mail with her remaining questions would detail anything else she might need. So once she was in the cabin, she woke Tori up and told her, "Start packing. We're leaving when the sun rises."

CHAPTER 22

Ginnifer worked fast in packing all of their belongings. The little Honda Civic's trunk was loaded up and ready to leave before the sun rose in the sky. Ginnifer didn't think they had ever packed quite that fast. Tori was motivated, though. She had wanted to leave as badly as Ginnifer had. Wes hadn't terrorized her as much on the scavenger hunt, but she was ready to put some distance between them. The Cowgirl Yoga vacation didn't quite go as she wanted it to. In some ways it was the one vacation she would never forget. On the other hand, it was also the one she hoped she could. Her heart was filled with agonizing pain. Dallas only wanted to let her down easy. It was the only thing she could think that he possibly wanted to talk to her about. He wanted to break things off easily or tell her he was going to try again with Melody. Every time she saw them together, Melody was hanging all over him or kissing him. He didn't do a thing to stop it. It must mean he wanted to be with her. There was no reason to prolong the torture and listen to his spiel on why they should end things. It's not like it would have gone anywhere, anyway. No promises had been broken, and he had the love of his life back. It didn't matter that Ginnifer didn't understand what he saw in Melody. As long as Dallas was happy, she would try to be happy for him.

With the keys in her hand, she walked over to the driver's side of the car and turned toward Tori saying, "Are you ready?"

Tori nodded in her direction. "I am. Are you sure you want to leave like this?"

Ginnifer had never been so sure of anything in her life. "Yes. I don't do drama. I want some distance between us and this ranch."

The front door of the ranch closed on a bang. Ginnifer looked back noticed Emma walking down the front steps. Her cinnamon hair was pulled back into a French braid, and she was dressed in yoga gear. She stopped in front of them. "I thought I saw you out here. Why are you here? I thought you were on the campout, Ginnifer."

Damn. She had hoped to leave without talking to anyone. Ginnifer pasted a bright smile on her face before saying, "Yeah, something came up. We need to leave early. I thought you might be sleeping and planned on contacting you later. I already sent you an e-mail with those remaining questions."

Emma frowned before saying, "Oh. I'm sorry you had to leave early. I hope you enjoyed your stay."

Ginnifer did her best to reassure her the vacation was great. It wasn't her fault she had fallen in love with her older brother. So she nodded her head, and with as much enthusiasm as she could muster, "Oh, the ranch is great. This is a great idea you have here. Don't worry, I won't hold you responsible for our unexpected departure. E-mail me the answers as soon as you can. All's good."

Tori piped in saying, "Don't worry about the extra week I paid for. I had a lovely time. I just have to deal with an issue for my client."

Emma pursed her lips in displeasure. "Colt."

"Colt isn't my only client," Tori told her, "but for what it's worth, you're wrong about him."

With condescension dripping through her voice, Emma expressed her belief, "Thanks. But I think I know him better than you do. "

Tori nodded her head at Emma saying, "Exactly. Which is why I don't get why you abandoned him. That doesn't matter, though. We need to leave. It was nice meeting you and good luck with your new business."

Tori opened the passenger door and got inside. As she heard the door close, Ginnifer walked over to Emma and gave her a hug. "It was a pleasure meeting you. Please keep in touch."

Ginnifer walked over and got into the driver's side. She closed the door and started the engine. After her seat-belt was fastened, she quickly put it in gear and started to drive away from the ranch, away from the place that would always hold her heart. It was her deepest wish that Dallas got everything he wanted. Ginnifer had hoped for a brief moment he would want that with her. She had hoped he would be the one person meant for her. Her last first kiss and her only love.

"Are you going to be okay, Ginny?" Tori asked.

"I think so. I need time."

She could feel Tori's gaze on her as she drove. It was clear she wanted to say something, but she was holding it in for some reason. So Ginnifer asked, "What's on your mind?"

"I think you're wrong."

Wrong? What could she be wrong about? Ginnifer was confused. "I don't know what you're talking about."

Tori sighed. "Dallas. He does care about you. I saw how he looked at you. Running away isn't the answer this time."

Ginnifer shook her head in disagreement. "No. I hurt enough. I couldn't listen to him break things off with me. We weren't even really together. It was a fling. It had to end sometime. I did it on my own terms."

It was Tori's turn to disagree and shake her head. "That's just it, Ginny. It wasn't a fling as you called it. You fell in love with the man. That means something."

She couldn't believe that Tori was pushing the issue. She was the last person Ginnifer ever expected to endorse love or a relationship. She firmly believed all relationships were doomed to fail, so it was with surprise she asked, "Why does this matter to you? Not too long ago you told me men couldn't' be trusted. I didn't think you believed love was possible."

Tori snorted. "I never said I didn't believe in love. That was your interpretation. I don't have faith in a man's ability to commit. That's a different story altogether." Flipping her hair out of her eyes, she turned to look out of the window before continuing. "This is something different. You're throwing a chance away at something real. Just because it's rare for a man to be faithful doesn't mean it isn't possible. Dallas may want exactly what you want, and you didn't even give him a chance to tell you. You ran away like a scared rabbit."

Ginnifer squeezed the steering wheel, anger building up in her. "I thought you would support me on this."

Tori bit her lip. "I do. Always. No matter what, I have your back. But I have to be the voice of reason too. I'd hate for you to throw something good away because you're too scared to find out if it's real or not."

With a sigh Ginnifer had to admit that Tori might be right. It wouldn't be the first time she turned out to be her own worst enemy. She had been running away from relationships and commitment her whole life. Independence had been her objective in life. Ginnifer had accomplished all of her goals, but she was also alone. She didn't even have a pet at home to comfort her. She didn't like relying on anyone. The only person she remained close to was Tori, but only because she wouldn't have it any other way. Tori was a force to be reckoned with, and once she decided Ginnifer was her friend, she wouldn't allow her to put any distance between them.

Ginnifer whispered, "I don't know if I can let him in. I'm scared."

"All you can do is try. You could be right. Maybe he's relieved you left. I'm willing to bet, though, that he'll be pissed and come looking for you. That man doesn't seem like the type to give up."

Ginnifer sighed. "No, he is tenacious as hell."

"So the question of the day is, what are you going to do about it?" Tori asked.

With a smile on her face, Ginnifer kept staring ahead while she drove down the road, considering everything Tori had told her. She knew what she had to do. "Nothing."

Tori's face crinkled up in puzzlement. "Excuse me?"

Tori didn't know Dallas the way she did, but in some ways she had seen him more clearly. She hadn't been blinded by heartache and insecurity. Once the obvious had been pointed out, it was clear what her course of action should be. "If it's like you say and he wants me, he'll come looking for me. I just have to be in a place he can be sure to find me. That's the only way I'll know for sure it's me he wants."

Understanding finally, Tori smiled. "You're going back to New York?"

With a nod of her head, Ginnifer agreed, "Yes."

Tori let out a laugh of excitement. She began to rub her hands with glee. "You're evil. I like it."

"I'm not evil. But, yes, I'm testing him."

Tori sighed before saying, "I wish I could go back with you right away. Sadly, I have to stay back and deal with the Colt situation. You'll keep me informed on all of the details?"

With a smile forming on her lips for the first time that day, Ginnifer glanced quickly at Tori before saying, "You know it." She had to keep her eyes on the road and couldn't look at her for long. No reason to kill or maim them before she made it back to Seattle.

"Did you bother to think about a flight back?" Tori asked.

Ginnifer shook her head. "No, I thought I'd deal with it when I got to the airport."

"Do you want me to call and change your flight while we're on the way?" she asked.

"It might be a good idea. Less to deal with once I get there."

Tori took her phone out and dialed the airline. It didn't take her long to change Ginnifer's flight. She got lucky and a return flight was available right away. She would only be in Seattle for an hour before she boarded a plane for New York. Before she knew it, she would be back in her own bed with Dallas on the other side of the country. She hoped Tori was right and that Dallas did have feelings for her. More importantly she hoped she was right and he would actually come to New York to chase after her. How dumb would it be if he decided she wasn't worth the hassle and she threw her chance with him out of the window over her fears? Nothing to do now but to stay the course; there was no changing her mind now.

CHAPTER 23

*D*allas made his way back to the ranch along with Wes and the group of females. He ached all over and wanted to take a long hot shower. It was the first thing on his agenda before he had that long-awaited talk with Ginnifer. He was willing to give her a reprieve after being terrified by the rattler. They were going to talk and soon, but a shower was required first. He wanted to be able to give her his full attention and feeling cruddy would get in the way of that. Even before he took the shower, though, he had to deal with Melody. The woman needed to realize there wasn't a chance in hell they would ever get back together. He had no idea why she had even thought it was a possibility.

Melody was currently hanging all over him. He had tried to push her away several times, but she kept coming back and grabbing his arm. It was time to end the charade of niceness. "Melody, quit grabbing my arm. I'm tired and it's annoying me."

She looked up at him, her mouth forming into a pretty little pout before saying, "Why are you being so mean?"

Dallas stopped dead in his tracks, looking at her with a piercing gaze. "I don't have the patience to be nice to you anymore. What the fuck kind of game are you playing here?"

With a small whimper, she brought her hand up to her mouth as a slight tear fell from her left eye. In between sniffles she managed to say, "Well I thought it was obvious. I want us to be together again."

Dallas let out a breath of frustration before saying, "Not happening. So you can get that idea out of your pretty little head. Why'd you think I'd ever try anything with you again? You made it perfectly clear you didn't want to be a rancher's wife."

Big crocodile tears started to stream down her face. Between sobs, Melody said, "But you loved me."

Dallas shook his head in disbelief. His head was pounding at the frustration of having to deal with her. Trying to be as honest as he could, he expressed what he finally realized, "I thought I loved you. But even if I had, that's all in the past. You're not my future and never really were. You should go back to wherever you came from. You don't belong here, Melody."

He said all there was to say, so he turned to walk away from her. That was distasteful, but it had to be done. He thought he was done with her for good until he heard her say, "It's because of that awful Ginnifer woman, isn't it?"

Dallas turned back and asked her, "What does that matter?"

A sneer formed on her face. "I saw how you were with

her. In the barn when she visited the newborn foal and when that snake crawled on her leg. She probably did it all on purpose to get your attention. You deserve better than her. She'll never change her life for you."

Dallas stared at her with scorn. "Oh, you mean like you did? Oh that's right, you didn't. You broke up with me because Novak Springs seemed like more work than you were willing to do. I wasn't worth the effort of even trying. So how are you any different?"

"You're right. I bailed. I regret that, but I've changed. Please give me a chance," Melody begged him.

Dallas shook his head. "No. There's no us anymore, Melody. I doubt there ever was. Furthermore, you haven't changed at all. You are still the selfish, spiteful woman I knew back then, only I was too blind to see it when we were together. Pack your bags and leave Novak Springs. Don't ever return. I never want to lay eyes on you again."

"What's going on?" Dallas turned to find his sister Emma walking down the steps of the ranch. He hadn't realized they had stopped in front of the house. He was too busy trying to get Melody to leave him alone to take notice of his surroundings.

"Melody is leaving. I can't deal with her anymore," Dallas explained.

"But who's going to run the yoga program, then? I can't change things last minute. How do you expect me to run the program without the yoga instructor?" Emma asked.

Dallas shrugged his shoulders. "I don't care. Melody leaves today. Refund everyone's money if they complain."

Emma's voice was filled with fury, "You're trying to

make sure I fail at this, aren't you? I know you're the reason that Ginnifer left early. Admit it, you chased her away. Now you're trying to chase my yoga instructor off of the property. Why did you even let me try if you were going to sabotage me every step of the way?"

All Dallas heard in her rant was that Ginnifer was gone. So his own voice filled with anger. "What do you mean Gin left? How long has she been gone?"

Emma placed her hands on her hips and screamed back at him, "Does it matter? Why do you keep chasing everyone away?"

Dallas shook his head in denial. "I didn't. Get her to come back. I only want Melody gone." Had she really left? He thought she had understood they needed to talk. Apparently she had other things in mind when she agreed to talk to him the next day.

"Well it's a little too late for that now, isn't it? They left hours ago. I'm sure she is on a plane back to New York by now," Emma said. "That still doesn't explain why you want Melody to leave."

Pacing back and forth in front of the porch, he stopped long enough to look at his sister. "Because she's my ex-fiancée and I can't stand her."

Emma turned to Melody, anger spewing out of her mouth, "Is that true? You never once told me you knew my brother. I talked about him all the time. You knew everything about me. Did you help me plan my business model knowing it was a way to get close to him again?"

Melody started to stumble backward in an attempt to put distance between her and Emma. "Um, well yeah, I didn't think you'd be my friend if you realized what my former association with Dallas was…"

Emma stared straight at her, enunciating each word clearly and firmly so there was not any misinterpretation. "Right. Because then you'd never have been able to get on this ranch and get close to Dallas again. Go pack you things and leave. Never come back. Oh, and Melody, pack fast. If you're not gone in fifteen minutes, I'll forcibly remove you."

Dallas stood there watching the whole exchange, reeling from the fact that Gin was no longer on Novak Springs. At that point he didn't care where Melody was. His heart dropped in his chest as he realized he wouldn't be able to talk to Ginnifer like he had planned. Pissed wasn't an accurate description of how he felt. Well, if she thought she could escape him, she was dead wrong. Dallas had some planning to do before he could leave. But Gin better be prepared for a reckoning when he finally got to her.

Emma's voice brought him out of his thoughts. "I'm so sorry, Dallas. I didn't know."

Dallas was forced to admit, "It's partially my fault. I never told you her name. It would probably have helped you to know who she was. I'm sorry. I know I can be an ass at times. I need a favor from you, though."

Emma nodded her head at him. "Anything. Tell me what you need."

"Give me all the information you have on Gin. I'm flying to New York as soon as I can get things arranged here on the ranch."

With a jolt of surprise Emma asked, "Whatever for?

Why would you need to go to New York to see her? I thought you two didn't get along."

Dallas laughed at her surprise. She had no idea what happened between the magazine writer and him. "No, Gin and I have some unfinished business. It needs to be handled in person. For the record, I didn't set out to sabotage your business. I truly did want you to succeed. Will you get by okay without Melody to do the yoga classes?"

"Okay. I can get everything for you in a few minutes. When she said she never got her questions answered, I thought it was because you were being an ass. What really happened? And don't worry about Cowgirl Yoga. I took enough classes to run the class for now. Melody was going to be replaced after this session, anyway."

A small smile formed on his lips. "Good. I'm glad that it won't hurt things too much. As far as me and Ginnifer, well we got a little distracted. Let's just say we both forgot those questions ever existed."

A knowing smile formed on Emma's face. "Ah. So you know she e-mailed me her list of questions. Do you want to answer them or should I?"

An idea formed in his mind. He knew exactly what he was going to do with those questions, so he said, "How about you print those up and add them with her contact information. I think she needs those answered in person."

Emma nodded in agreement. "Consider it done. How long before you plan on leaving?"

"Tonight, after I pack and confer with Wes. He's going to have to take charge of the ranch while I'm gone. As soon as I'm packed, I'm leaving. I don't know for sure how long I'll be away. I'll keep in touch."

"That's fine. Go bring her back," Emma turned and walked back into the house.

Dallas pulled Gin's phone out of his pocket and rubbed his thumb over the screen. She was going to get it hand-delivered back whether she liked it or not. There wasn't any way he was going to allow her to walk away from him. Their relationship may have happened fast, but that didn't make it any less real. Dallas wasn't afraid to use any weapon in his cache to get his point across. Ginnifer was his, and it was time she accepted that. No matter what it took, he was going to make sure she would be in his life forever. He put the phone back in his pocket and sprinted into the house. He had a lot to do before he got on the road to Seattle. New York wasn't a far enough distance to escape him. He had a plan firmly in his mind as he walked into his bedroom to pack. Dallas hoped Ginnifer realized the mistake she made in running, because she was going to get one hell of a spanking thinking she could run away.

CHAPTER 24

*G*innifer had been wrong. Completely and utterly mistaken in her assumption Dallas would chase after her. She had been back in New York a week and hadn't heard a peep from him. She had remained at home for the remaining week of her vacation and thought for sure he would seek her out there. But she had remained miserable and alone. In fact, she hadn't heard from Emma, either. She thought for sure the e-mailed questions would have gotten answered. There was total radio silence, and to make things worse, she realized once she was on the plane that Dallas still had her phone. She didn't have it replaced because she had hoped he would bring it with him when he came to see her. It was starting to look like she needed to go to the store and buy a new phone after work. With a sigh, she got up from her desk and walked over to the window to look out at the New York skyline. At least she had work. It was something she had always relied on and stayed true no matter what. It was the most dependable thing in her life. Today was her first day back, and it was time to get back to the grind. She had an appointment in fifteen minutes that had been scheduled while she was on vacation. Her assistant had said it was an important story opportunity she couldn't afford to turn down.

A voice announced from behind her, "Miss. Zeiss, your appointment is here. Should I show him in?"

Ginnifer turned to find her assistant, Alison, standing in her office door. Well, no reason to put it off just because she was miserable. If work was the only thing she could depend on, it was time to give it her full attention. "Yes, but give me five minutes. Also, see if he wants anything to drink and bring it in after you show him in."

Her assistant nodded her head. "Okay. I will."

Ginnifer strolled over to her desk and pulled her chair out so she could sit. Once she was sitting, she scooted the chair closer to her desk and turned on her computer. When it was fully booted up, she entered her password and waited for her home screen to load. A picture of her and Tori came up on the computer's wallpaper. They had been so happy when the picture had been taken. Now Tori was still in Seattle dealing with the Colt Lewis drama. Ginnifer was in New York wallowing in her own misery. In time surely it would be easier and the pain would lessen. She was still staring at the computer when she heard a voice say, "Well, if it's that bad, you should probably change it."

With a start of surprise, she looked up to find Dallas standing in her office. He was holding a manila folder in one hand and a cup of coffee in the other. Ginnifer knew it was coffee because she could smell the heavenly brew from the short distance between them. Her mouth watered at the tantalizing scent. She hadn't bothered to get any that morning and never asked Alison to get her any. She was picky, and Alison never got it right. It was easier to get it herself. What Dallas was holding in his hand was either exactly what she'd drink or damned close.

Dallas continued to look at her saying nothing, forcing her to ask, "Why are you here?"

He walked farther into the room until he reached her desk. Dallas stopped once he reached the edge. "Well, there are many reasons. First though, I owe you a cup of coffee." He reached across her desk and handed it to her. She took it out of his hand and took a long sip. It was perfect. How could he have possibly known how she took her coffee? Ginnifer had never gotten the chance to tell him. After a long groan of pleasure, she said, "Oh God, that's good. How did you know how I like it?"

Dallas flashed his famous devilish smile. "I have my ways. Let's just say I made it my mission to learn everything I needed to know about you before this meeting."

Well, that was surprising. If he kept this up, she'd beg him to stay. Hell, who was she kidding? She was going to beg him regardless. She loved the blasted man, and now that he was here in New York, she wasn't going to let him go that easy. Deciding she needed to fight dirty, she leaned back in her chair and crossed her legs, her skirt raising a couple of inches up her thigh. "I see. Did you learn anything interesting?"

Dallas stared down at her exposed leg before he pulled

237

a chair out. "Oh, I learned a lot of interesting things, but that isn't why I'm here."

"Yeah and who helped you learn all those interesting details?" Ginnifer raised her eyebrow and asked, "Why are you here?"

"I had a lil chat with your bestie, Tori. I ran into her while waiting for my plane in Seattle. She was a font of information." Dallas set the manila folder on her desk. "As to why I'm here—a number of reasons really. First, you needed these. Emma asked me to give them to you…"

Why hadn't Tori told her she spoke with Dallas? The next time she spoke to her, she'd have a lot of explaining to do. Ginnifer picked up the manila folder and started to flip through it. It held the answers to her e-mailed questions. Well that explained why she hadn't received them yet; Dallas decided to deliver them personally. She turned to look at Dallas. He had made himself comfortable and leaned his elbows on her desk, watching her intently. His stare was unnerving, and she didn't know how to take it. So she looked into his eyes and asked, "What?"

Dallas kept looking at her with his face so serious it almost scared her. What could possibly be going through his mind? He had better start talking soon. The more he stared at her, the more nervous he made her.

After several minutes, he finally spoke, "There was another reason I came in to see you today. I have something that belongs to you."

She expected him to say her phone, but she still asked, "What's that?"

He surprised her by saying, "Me."

She sat forward with surprise. "Excuse me?"

He got up and started walking around the office. When he got to her window, he stopped and looked outside at the same view that Ginnifer had been admiring earlier. His arms twisted behind his back, he stared out the window for a long time not saying anything. It was starting to torture her. Here he was in her office and nothing was happening. Nothing was going the way she had imagined it. Dallas was making things more difficult and painful by not speaking to her. He said he belonged to her. She needed him to tell her why he believed that. She didn't understand any of this.

Dallas turned around and looked at her. A look of determination on his face, he gave her his full attention. "You heard me. I told you that we had unfinished business. You said you understood and you'd talk to me later. This is a hell of a lot later than I had planned, Gin. When I got back, I found you gone. Why'd you run away?"

She should have known he would want answers. Ginnifer had run away. There were so many ways she could have answered that question, but she chose the cowardly answer. "How's Melody?"

With a cocky smile, Dallas tilted his head. "I wouldn't know. I'm not her keeper."

Ginnifer looked up at him and raised one eyebrow. "Oh, it didn't look that way. Melody looked ready to dig her claws into you and never let you go."

Dallas looked pissed. "What Melody wanted is irrelevant. I wasn't going to fall in line with her plans. You should've talked to me before leaving."

Ginnifer shrugged her shoulders. "I didn't see the

point. We made no promises to each other. Tori had to leave, so I decided to go with her."

Dallas clenched his mouth together and glared at her. "Fuck if we didn't. They may not have been spoken out loud, but plenty of promises were made."

Ginnifer stood up and walked over to him. She looked him straight in the eye. "I'm sorry you feel that way, but I need words. I can't read your mind any more than you can read mine. If you wanted more from me, you should have asked."

"You never gave me a chance to. Before I had the opportunity, you were long gone."

"Well, you're here now. What do you want from me?" Ginnifer asked.

He stared deep into her eyes. "I want forever. Come home with me, Gin."

Ginnifer thought he might want her, but she didn't know exactly what he was asking of her, so she said, "You expect me to quit my job and move to Washington? Why should I do that?"

With a smile, Dallas grabbed her and pulled her into his arms. He leaned down and whispered in her ear, "Because it's where you belong."

Ginnifer shook her head and stated her concerns. "I don't know for sure if that's true. I need more, Dallas. I can't leave everything because you want me to."

"Please, Gin. Don't fight me. I need you with me. I haven't felt like this in a long time. There's no way I could handle it if you said no."

Ginnifer was confused again. Did he mean it would devastate him if she refused to move in with him? She tilted her head at him and asked, "What exactly are you asking me, Dallas? I need more in my life than a part-time lover. I already told you I can't read minds."

Dallas pulled her closer, hugging her tightly. "I don't want a part-time lover. I want a forever wife. Marry me, Gin. I love you."

Oh, thank God. She was beginning to think he didn't really love her. Ginnifer never doubted for a minute he wanted her. The sex had been really good between them, but that wasn't enough to build a relationship on. She smiled up at him and teased, "That's all? Here I thought you needed me there only to help birth all of the baby horses."

Dallas groaned. "You're slowly killing me, Gin. Are you going to come back with me?"

She stepped back and put a little distance between them. "No."

"Good...wait. What did you say?" Dallas said shock filling his voice.

"I can't leave yet, Dallas. I have responsibilities here. Don't look so upset."

With hope in his voice, he ventured, "You said yet, not never."

Ginnifer laughed and gave him a quick kiss. "Exactly, I love you too. I want to marry you and spend the rest of my life with you. Give me a little time to settle things here. Hopefully it won't take too long. I don't want to be separated from you for any longer than I have to be."

Relief filled Dallas's voice. "Oh, thank God. You scared me. I can't wait to have you in my bed every night. By the way, please tell me you still have that outfit you wore on the camping trip. I think I need you to put it on so I can slowly strip it off of you."

Ginnifer laughed with delight. "Of course I do. So you know, I learned some interesting things during Cowgirl Yoga that I'm dying to try."

Dallas raised his eyebrow inquisitively. "I hope it's not some new yoga moves. I'm not into that new-age stuff."

"Please. Give me a little credit here. This is something much more enjoyable," she mused. "Although it might be highly entertaining to see you do a few of those poses. It gives me something to think about."

"That's a bit scary. Let's work on one idea at a time. We have plenty of time to try out everything your imagination can think of."

"I'm glad you said that. I happen to have one of those items you mentioned earlier, right here in the office."

"Oh yeah? Which one? I'd ask you if you have that outfit, but I'd rather you be naked."

A wicked smile began to grow on Ginnifer's face. She walked over to her desk drawer and pulled out the lasso Tori had given her. The black silkiness rolled through her fingers. Her hips swayed with seductiveness as she sashayed over to his side again.

"Do you want to play a little game?" she asked.

"Does it involve you losing your clothes?"

"Maybe." Coyness wrapped around every nuance of the word.

"Then I'm all in, baby."

Ginnfer's smile took on a sinful gleam. She surveyed the room for the best spot to enact her pleasurable torture. She located the right area to tie him up and have her way with him. She crooked her finger at him to come forward. He took a moment to let his gaze trail from her from top to bottom. Heat filled his gaze as he stared into her eyes. A flutter of anticipation filled her deep inside as she waited for him to join her. Dallas sauntered over to her side and waited for her next instructions.

"Stand right there and put your hands over your head."

Ginnifer stood on the chair next to him and began to tie the lasso around his hands with the secure knot she learned at one of the lessons. With care she twisted and turned it around his wrists and secured him in front of her office window. The low ceiling hosted an overhanging hook screwed firmly near the side, and she trussed him there. Ginnifer didn't do voyeurism, but she thought the idea of pleasuring him next to the window was incredibly hot. Of course she was pretty high up in her building, and the chances of anyone actually seeing them through the window wasn't likely. The idea of it, though, turned her on.

"Now what are you going to do with me?" he asked.

"Oh I don't know. Maybe I'll leave you there for a while and enjoy the view."

"You wouldn't dare." Dallas glared.

Ginnifer's laughter floated around the room in response. She rolled her teeth over her bottom lip as her desire burned through her. Of course she dared. With Dallas she would do just about anything, but he was right in one respect. She had plans, and they didn't involve staring at him all day. Reaching down she began to undo his pants, and with a flick of her wrist, pushed them down. They fell down and rested at his ankles. Looking down at his hard shaft she began to lick her lips in anticipation. Ginnifer placed her hand on it and began to stroke him up and down in languid movements.

"Please" Dallas begged.

"Oh you're not enjoying this?"

"You know I am. I need more." A bright blue flame sizzled from his eyes. His need was blatant with each stroke of her fingers down the entire length his growing shaft.

Ginnifer decided to have mercy on him and dropped to her knees. She licked her lips and brought the head of his cock inside her mouth, running her tongue over the tip and nipping at it with her teeth. When she heard Dallas's intake of breath, she took it as encouragement and took him fully inside. With a stroke of her tongue down the side of his shaft, she could feel him begin to tremble. It made her feel powerful and in complete control. She wrapped her hand around his balls, massaging them, and began to roll her mouth over his shaft repeatedly; hitting the back of her throat as she sucked him in deep. Dallas began to rock his hips in sync with her movements. It took mere moments for his release to hit her tongue, and she tasted its saltiness. She licked the tip one more time and stood up to look into his passion-filled eyes.

"Are you going to untie me now?" he asked.

"I haven't decided yet."

"Oh I think you have. I can't return the favor if you don't."

"That's true, but this is a sight I'd like to savor for a while."

A half smile tilted in up the corner of his mouth. His eyes told her he enjoyed every ounce of attention she gave him. He only appeared content to wait for her to let him off the hook. She knew that once he was free he would have his way with her—and it would be amazing. As much as she enjoyed having him tied up and in her mercy, she really did want to explore other ideas rolling around her head. So she hopped back up on the chair and untied him. As she worked the knots free, he leaned forward and nipped at one of her breasts. The action almost caused her to topple off the chair, but she readjusted herself, instead falling forward into him. She wrapped her arms around his neck and kissed him.

"If you'd rather stay tied up, I don't mind."

"No I want to touch you."

"Then quit distracting me so I can loosen the lasso."

Ginnifer once again began to untie the knots of the lasso. Once he was free, he pulled up his pants and secured them. When he finished, he wrapped his arms firmly around her. Dallas pulled her closer and kissed her senseless. Nothing ever went as planned; in fact, sometimes they went a whole lot better. When Ginnifer left for vacation, she never would have expected to meet the only man she could ever love.

Dallas stopped kissing her and whispered in her ear, "Oh yeah, there's one other thing."

Ginnifer looked up at him, still giggling with pleasure. "What's that?"

He grabbed her hand and led her back toward her desk. He reached into his pocket and pulled out her phone and set it next to the folder on her desk. He sat down in the cushiony chair and gathered her into his lap. She wound her arms around his neck, leaning down to press her lips to his. "Oh, good. You brought me back my phone. Is that all, or is there something else? And does it really require us to be sitting? If so, it must be serious."

Dallas flashed a smile filled with pure sin. "Oh, it's very serious." He pulled Ginnifer's head down, turning it so his mouth caressed her cheek. Then with a hint of wickedness, he leaned in and whispered in her ear, "I do believe I owe you a spanking…"

EXCERPT: UNBRIDLED PURSUIT

NOVAK SPRINGS BOOK TWO

CHAPTER 1

*V*itoria's eyelids were narrowed into tiny slits, still heavy from sleep. The sun's bright rays bounced in a diagonal through the room and landed across Vitoria's face in sync with the shrill of her alarm clock. The screeching noise reverberated against the bedroom walls and recoiled throughout her eardrums. The light blinded her sleep-filled eyes. Reaching out her hand, she batted her alarm clock with more force than necessary to end the constant stream of annoyingness.

Mornings and she did not get along very well.

They were her least favorite part of the day, but time waited for no one. It kept beating steadily on whether she was ready for it or not. Sadly, Tori was almost never equipped to take on the infernal clock constantly counting down the seconds of her life. She had so many things to do in a single day it was next to impossible to accomplish it all.

Today she had a plane to catch, a flight scheduled to take her to the west coast—to be more specific, Seattle,

Washington. The state her best friend now called home. The past three months without her chipped away at Tori's thick shell.

Loneliness invaded her world in a way it hadn't in many years. Not since the days before she met Ginnifer Zeiss, or as she was often called, Ginny. Prior to meeting her best friend, she only existed and went through the motions of her day-to-day life. She gave the impression of happiness, but in reality, she was an empty shell. Without someone to shake up her world, she feared she would sink into oblivion.

She missed the ability to drop in on her at a moment's notice. Tori and Ginnifer didn't go a day without talking. The difference now was it almost always involved a telephone, whereas before she stopped by for an impromptu lunch or a nightly glass of wine. Ginny had to go and fall in love and ruin it all.

Her dearest friend was getting married. The wedding was several weeks away. Now Tori had to fly out to Seattle to help with some of the planning and of course check in with her growing clientele.

Her work was never done.

Vitoria owned and operated a public relations firm. She also handled some legal work for her clients. She had passed the bar in several states. It gave her the opportunity to negotiate contracts when they were up for renewal. Her business wasn't merely a public relations firm. It had been designed to meet any and all necessities that might arise. The sheer level of energy she required to get through her day took its toll. She wanted a change, and she missed her best friend terribly.

The distance between them was more difficult for her than anything else in her life. Tori needed to be near Ginnifer. So much so, she seriously considered a more permanent solution to her situation. While in Washington for this trip, she planned on scouting the area for a place to set up business. Thanks to her growing client base on the west coast, the transition should go smoothly. It made sense to move when the majority of her clients were on a different side of the country. The boon was her best friend lived there too. In her mind it was a win-win situation. So why did she have such a hard time making a decision?

Tori rolled out of bed and stumbled into her bathroom. She flicked on the light and rubbed her face. The lack of sleep played a toll on her normally gorgeous exterior. Her caramel-blonde hair could be compared to dried straw and her blue eyes were dull.

The constant back and forth had to stop. It didn't matter if everything was completely settled. When she arrived in Washington she required a change. So she made the decision to start arrangements for her move immediately.

Resolution made, she picked up her cell and scrolled through the contact list. After several rings someone answered with a muffled hello.

"Alison, good you're up."

"Damn it Tori, do you have any idea what time it is?" she asked.

"Of course I do. I figured you would already be awake and ready to start your day."

"If I had known how evil you were, I wouldn't have

taken a job with you after Ginnifer moved to Washington."

"Well, you came highly recommended, or I wouldn't have hired you at all. You should be thankful I gave you a job."

Vitoria stared at her fingernails. The nail polish had started to chip at the top and one of her nails had a ragged edge where it broke the day before. When she got to Seattle, at some point she would get a manicure.

"What do you need? I'd like to get some more sleep today. You do realize it's a Sunday, right? I don't work on the weekend," Alison mumbled.

"Well you do now. I have a job for you to start working on immediately."

Tori could hear the groans coming through the speaker of her phone. She probably should feel guilty, but she didn't really. Perhaps she did a little—she didn't like getting woken up and ordered around. It plain sucked. But Alison knew what her job would entail when she agreed to work with her. An early morning wakeup call shouldn't come as a surprise. Vitoria explained the possibility to her, and she knew a last minute assignment could pop up at any moment.

"I repeat, what do you need?" A growl came through loud and clear. Nope, Alison was far from happy. Tori didn't consider that her problem. She paid well and expected results.

"I'm going to move to Seattle. I want you to contact some movers. I want my entire apartment and office packed up in preparation for the move. I don't plan on coming back once I fly out there later this afternoon."

Tori rattled off her list. "I also would like you to contact every person on my east coast client list and inform them of my move. If they want to consider moving to a more locally-based agent, I'll allow them break their contract for a nominal fee, but please explain to them I am not coming back to New York unless it's an emergency. From now on they will have to meet with me in Seattle."

"What? So I'm going to be out of another job?" Alison asked.

"Only if you don't want to move to Seattle with me. I'll pay your moving expenses if you want to transfer out there. If not, I will give you a letter of recommendation."

Alison really was a good assistant. Plus Vitoria had already broken her in. All of her expectations were fully ingrained in her. She really didn't want to train someone new. Paying her to move out to Washington was a sound business decision. If Tori was lucky, and she didn't rely on luck very often, Alison would grab at the opportunity to relocate.

"I will have to think about it and let you know. Where's everything going to be sent to?" Alison asked.

"I'm not exactly sure. I'll call you in a few days with the information. It's going to take at least a week to pack both places up anyway. Make the other arrangements first."

"All right. I will call and see who is available. It's kind of last minute, and there might not be too many openings."

"Do the best you can. I have faith in your ability to make this happen. It's a good thing I'm not a coffee nut like Ginny. Everything else you do stupendously. That was her only complaint as to your skills."

"If you can keep a secret, I'll tell you why I failed miserably at that."

"Let me guess. You did it on purpose."

"How'd you guess?" Alison asked.

"It's what I'd do. No one wants to be that person. The one who fetches coffee repeatedly. If you show your ineptness for it, they'll quit asking."

"Exactly," Alison agreed.

"Anyway I have a few things I need to do before my flight. I'll be in touch with the rest of the details. I have an extra set of keys to my apartment in my office safe. You have the combination, so retrieve them when you need to let the movers into my apartment. I'll talk to you later."

Tori ended the call and got ready for her trip. She had packed the night before, but in light of her change of plans, she packed an extra bag with a few essential items. The additional cost of the baggage would be worth it to take everything she needed. With care, she folded more clothes and placed them in the large suitcase. Ginnifer often made fun of her over-packing, but she believed in being prepared for any scenario.

The one thing Vitoria hated more than anything was being blindsided.

In a lot of ways, she was a control freak. She hated giving anyone any kind of power over her. Her parents were tyrants and meticulously planned every part of her childhood. Their need to have successful, ambitious children led to her estrangement from her sister, Vivian. She hadn't seen Viv in over two years. The last time they saw each other the conversation had been stilted and heavy with tension.

The encounter happened purely by chance. They were almost like two ships passing in the night.

Her sister was walking into a lawyer's firm Vitoria had been leaving. At first seeing her sibling directly in front of her startled her. They normally kept a large distance between them. Vivian could be very coldblooded and distant. She developed her attitude as a coping mechanism. At times Tori wondered if she was actually sociopathic because of some of the things she did to get ahead in their parents' eyes. Nothing stood in her way, not even her own sister.

A high-pitched noise filled the room, and she looked over at her phone. She had tossed it on her bed as she began to pack. Vitoria reached for her cell and smiled when Ginnifer's name flashed across the screen.

"Hey, Ginny. You do know what time it is, right? I mean you are like three hours behind me, so is the sun even up there?"

"As a matter of fact, no, it isn't. Dallas starts chores quite early."

"And he wakes you up first? That brute! I will have a chat with him when I get there. Sleep is a sacred thing, and he shouldn't deprive you of yours."

Tori stopped and tapped her chin as a thought entered her mind. "Although I have to admit that is kind of brave of him. I'm aware of how perilous it is to wake you up before the sun comes up."

Ginnifer's laughter floated through the phone. "Oh

trust me. I don't mind. Everyone should experience our version of peril at least once in their lifetime."

"Have you been watching Monty Python?"

"Of course not. It was horrid enough the one time you made me watch it."

She could imagine Ginny's shudder as she said the words. She did every time Tori mentioned the one movie she actively despised. Of all the films Tori made her sit through, *Monty Python and the Holy Grail* left Ginnifer quivering with displeasure. It didn't take long for it to become her least favorite movie. Of course using favorite in any context was overstating it. Ginny hated that particular movie.

"It reminded me of the scene when Sir Galahad was in that castle full of women. Sir Lancelot said he was in peril."

"Oh, I think I do remember that. Seems like it had to do with his duty to experience such peril or a lot of peril. I don't remember exactly."

"Yes!" Tori shouted with excitement. "He said and I'm paraphrasing it here—*it is my duty as a knight to sample as much peril as I can.* You came pretty close to it with your comment about Dallas."

"Tori dear, you watch too many movies. You need to get a life."

"Hmmph, I have a great life, thank you very much. So back to you. Why are you calling me?"

"Oh, I wanted to double check to see what time your flight arrives today." Ginnifer asked.

"Why? I'm not going to be coming out to Novak

Springs until next week. I have a few things to take care of in Seattle first."

"I thought I'd arrange to meet you, and while we are there, we can get the fitting done on your bridesmaid dress. I also want you to see the dress I picked out and get your opinion."

"You finally found a dress?" Tori squealed. "I can't wait to see it."

"I figured you might."

"Hmm, my flight actually gets in kind of late. It might be best for you to come out tomorrow or the next day. I'm not so sure anything will be open when I get there."

What Tori didn't tell her was she had other plans once she arrived in Seattle. She needed to find an apartment and some office space. What she hoped was to be able to give her the good news about the move when she saw her. No way could she do that if she didn't have any time to scout out the area first. Her first stop, after she checked into her hotel, was with the real estate agent she set up an appointment with. She needed at least a half day to make some headway on her idea.

"Oh. Okay. I will plan on driving out tomorrow morning. Dallas wakes me up pretty early, so I should be able to get there by nine. We can shop and have lunch. Does that work for you?"

"Of course. I can't wait to see you. I'm excited."

"Good. I'm gonna hang up. Maybe I'll get some more sleep."

Tori could hear Ginnifer yawn. Dallas might have been very good at a morning wake-up, but that didn't change her best friend's sleeping habits. She would probably call it a power nap.

"All right. Bub-bye Ginny."

Tori hung up the phone and finished packing. The cab was scheduled to arrive in an hour, and she needed to get done before they arrived. After everything was packed, she zipped her suitcase and rolled it next to the other two in her living room. She only had twenty minutes to wait until her ride came to pick her up. With everything arranged and planned, Tori sat on a chair in her living room to relax. No reason to expend any unnecessary energy. She had a long day ahead of her.

CHAPTER 2

*T*he plane landed at Seattle's Sea-Tac airport on time. The problem didn't start until five minutes after Tori entered the airport terminal from the plane. The outside windows portrayed a torrential downpour of rain and hail the size of ping-pong balls. It pounded against the glass panes with a force leading her to believe they'd break at any moment.

This, of course, left her without much desire to actually leave the airport.

If it appeared this bad from the inside looking out, it had to be ten times worse to actually be underneath the wicked spray. Tori pulled her phone out of her purse and clicked the side button to check the time. The phone had already adjusted itself to the time difference between New York and Seattle. Her appointment with the realtor was in an hour. She needed to go check into her hotel and soon if she hoped to make the appointment on time.

With a sigh of resignation, Tori grabbed her carryon

bag and trekked through the terminal to baggage claim. She pulled her two suitcases off the conveyer and stacked her carryon bag on top of the smaller one. As she turned to go toward the rental car area, she walked right into a hard male chest.

"I'm so sorry. I didn't see you..." She gazed up into a pair of aquamarine eyes filled with hatred.

"No need to explain. I'm well-aware how self-absorbed you are."

The beginning of a sigh built up deep inside of Tori's chest. She squashed it before it could expel itself from her body. Wesley Novak, the bane of her existence. She wanted to avoid him on this trip. Apparently the fates had a different idea altogether. At any other moment in time, with any other male, she'd have enjoyed the encounter.

Especially a male as gorgeous as Wes.

His long hair was a beautiful, golden shade of blond, his eyes alternated between green and brown, and he had a rock-hard chest she was desperate to run her hands all over. Unfortunately for her, for reasons she didn't quite understand, the man loathed her.

"What are you doing here Wes?"

"I'm here to offer you a ride."

Well, wasn't that just peachy? By the expression on his face, he didn't want to extend the offer any more than she wanted to accept it. His eyebrows were so scrunched together, they threatened to form a uni-brow. Every time he glanced at her, his eyes shot daggers, ready to kill her on sight. She had to wonder whose bright idea it was to have him pick her up from the airport. Hell, who even knew she'd arrived to be picked up? She thought she had stalled Ginny earlier on the phone.

"I don't need a ride. I'm gonna walk on over there to get a rental car. I'm not about to rely on you for anything. I might end up in a body bag somewhere marked as a Jane Doe."

"You would be familiar with body bags seeing what you are responsible for."

What? That was a new one. She had nothing to do with body bags or dead bodies for that matter. Clearly Wes decided to take a trip off the deep end into loco town.

"I'm not even going to touch that one. Leave me be, Wes. I can take care of myself," Tori snidely remarked.

"I know. It's what you're good at. But I'm here anyway. Don't worry, it's not for you. I'm here 'cause Ginnifer worries about you. Only God knows why."

"Well you can go on back to the ranch and tell her you saw me and I'm fine. I'm going to check into my hotel. I have an appointment. I don't have all day to stand here and argue with you."

"Well then quit bitching, and do as you're told for once." Wes continued to glare at her in disapproval. If he kept it up, he was going to get some serious forehead wrinkles and some unflattering ones around the edges of his mouth.

He wrenched her largest bag from her hand and stomped out of the airport. His attitude suggested he expected her to follow in his footsteps. Vitoria stared down at her four-inch, fire-engine-red stilettos. She had no chance of catching up to him with them on. So she didn't even try. One thing was perfectly clear though—he took off with the bag housing most of her essential items in it.

She had two choices; either follow him, albeit a little slower, or let him keep the bag and get the rental car she intended.

After weighing both options with care, she decided on the rental car. Worst-case scenario, he would take her bag back to the ranch. It wasn't lost, only misplaced for a little while. If she was being honest with herself, she'd rather lose it than deal with Mr. Grumpy the rest of the day.

Body bag? Really? A new low for him. She sashayed over to the rental car counter pulling other two bags.

"Can I help you, miss?" A guy with white hair and dark-rimmed glasses stared back at her.

Tori saw a nametag displaying the name Pete in bold black letters on his blue button-up shirt. "Yes—Pete." She flashed him her most alluring smile and ran her fingers down his arm. "I'd like the most luxurious car you have available."

Tori was in the mood to be splashy and extravagant. Why not? She had the money to burn and it filled her with happiness. The trust fund her parents' set up left her quite wealthy. She hadn't seen them in years. After she left her parent's home and went away to college she saw no reason to visit—it really was best for her mental stability. Her parents didn't give off any warm and fuzzy feelings. The money though she utilized at every opportunity. It was hard earned living with two emotionless people who claimed to care about her. With the added profits from her business, Tori never needed to stress about money. She hoped they had a sports car, rare yes, but desired after dealing with Wes.

"I'm sorry, but we only have one vehicle left."

"I guess I'll be glad you have something at all. What kind is it?"

"It's a standard SUV, a Ford Edge," he explained.

"I'll take it."

Admittedly it was not a vehicle she preferred, but beggars couldn't be choosers when they wanted out of the airport as fast as possible. She didn't know if Wes planned on coming back and attempting to strong-arm her into going with him.

She located the yellow Ford Edge and clicked the remote on the keychain to unlock it. Luggage deposited in the rear hatch, she hastened to the driver's side. The little disagreement with Wes put her behind schedule, and the awful downpour of rain still battered the streets.

So instead of going to her hotel, she put the realtor's address into the GPS. Several minutes later she parked her vehicle and took a minute to relax while she plotted her next move. She needed to get inside without drenching herself from head to toe. If only she'd planned for the possibility of rain. Who went to Seattle and didn't bring anything to prevent the rain from soaking them to the skin?

Clearly her sleep-deprived mind didn't function well since she'd forgotten such an important accessory as an umbrella.

She gathered everything she needed and prepared to run as fast as possible in four-inch stilettos. She damn near skipped toward the office door as it opened to allow her inside.

"Quite the storm we are getting today." A cultured voice filled her ears, and she looked up to see a male with black curly hair and chocolate-brown eyes smile down at her. Dimples formed at the corners of his mouth, giving him a charming exterior. She found him incredibly sexy and a nice change after Wes's rude attitude.

"Yeah, it sure is. Not something I was expecting either."

"I can tell with your lack of umbrella." His dimples popped back out as he smiled.

"Thanks for getting the door for me." Lame response, but she lacked anything else to say. His male beauty stunned her into stupidity.

"It's always my pleasure to help a beautiful woman. I'm Miguel Santiago."

"Vitoria Miene." She held her hand out to shake his. Instead he pulled it up to his lips and kissed it. A small shiver traveled down her spine at the gesture.

"What are you doing in Seattle, Mrs. Miene?"

"It's just Miss. I'm not married. I'm hoping to relocate here from New York. Are you a real-estate agent, Mr. Santiago?"

"No, not at all. I do have several holdings, but I am a developer, not an agent. I'm leaving a meeting with my agent, Miss Dearborn."

"Funny you should mention her name. I am actually

supposed to meet with her in fifteen minutes to look over some possible office space. It's been nice meeting you, Mr. Santiago, but I'm afraid I must run."

"Miguel."

"What?" Tori stopped in her tracks, baffled.

"Please call me Miguel. I hate being so formal with such a lovely woman as yourself. Perhaps I can talk you into having dinner with me this evening?"

Smoothness, this man oozed it out and recycled it for future use.

"Oh, I don't know. I have quite a bit to do. I'll have to take a rain check." She waved her hands outside. "No pun intended."

Miguel chuckled. "I will hold you to it."

"I'm sure you will." Tori flashed him her most gamine smile.

"Until we meet again." Miguel nodded at her and exited the building with an open umbrella raised to the sky.

The things she learned and the people she met when she least expected it. He certainly dripped charm and charisma. Maybe she should have taken him up on his offer of dinner. She could use a good meal with a handsome man. Sadly, she had way too much to do before she could enjoy such things. Like finding a new office and a place to live. Those took precedence over drool-worthy and lickable men. Tori watched him stroll down the sidewalk until his black suit was no longer visible from the office window. She turned her attention back to the task at hand and went to check in with the receptionist.

"I'm here to meet with Miss Dearborn. I'm Vitoria Miene."

"I'll let her know you are here." The perky redhead got up and bounced over to Miss Dearborn's office. After delivering her news, she sat back down and typed at her computer, not glancing up once, even when Miss Dearborn finally exited her office to retrieve Tori for their meeting.

"Miss Miene?" she asked.

"Yes. That's me."

"If you follow me to my office, we can get started."

Vitoria got up and trailed after her. She entered a plush office with a color scheme of beige and cream. Vitoria sat down in a chair located near her desk and relaxed back into its cushiony comfort.

"I have a list of places that would be acceptable for what you require. Here is a mock-up of each office space and where they are located. It includes rental fees and what is expected in the lease."

Tori took the files and browsed through the materials. When she made the appointment, she detailed exactly what she would need in an office space and apartment to help expedite the process.

"What about apartments?"

"I have a separate folder for those, but I thought the office space was a more immediate need."

"Both are now equally important. I've had a change of plans. I'll look over the office file first though."

Tori went over each rental unit carefully and picked the one most suited for her needs. She needed a basic space for her office and her assistant. Only one fit her exact requirements.

"I want to sign a lease on this one today if possible after I view it in person. When will you be able to show it to me? If it fits my needs, after I sign the contract I will leave the deposit and first month's rent with you."

"We can go look at it right now if you have time." Tori nodded. Miss Dearborn continued, "I'll have Tabitha print out the contract for us to take with us. Look over the apartments, and I'll be back in a few minutes."

As Miss Dearborn left the office, Tori perused through the pictures of the apartments. She wasn't particular, but she wanted it to be comfortable. Maybe she shouldn't rush into a living space. A visit to each one was required before making a decision. There were at least two she desired a personal look at before she made a decision.

"Did you see anything you like?"

"Yes these two apartments might work. I'd like to arrange a viewing of each one."

"Certainly, that can be arranged. I'll call them and set up an appointment. Is there any specific time that works for you?"

"No, call me when it is all arranged." Vitoria shook her head. "Wait, I can't look at them tomorrow. I have other plans, but any other day will work. "

"If you're ready to view the property we can head over now. Would you like me to drive?"

Vitoria nodded. "Yes that works for me."

Miss Dearborn led them to her vehicle. Tori stepped into the passenger side and sat down. The location of the space for lease wasn't far from the real estate office.

Fifteen minutes later they were already inside looking over the floor plan.

"As you can see it meets all of your requirements."

The office space was located on the fifth floor of the building. She scanned the front area—the room was filled with natural light and a view of the Seattle skyline.

The walls were painted soft beige accented by chocolate-brown carpet. The windows were ceiling to floor with long sweeping venetian blinds the same color as the carpet.

Some new seating with a mix of the already existing colors in the room would look chic. The desk Alison already used would fit in nicely within the room. It had three rooms that could be used as separate offices and one large room that would make a nice conference room.

The largest space utilized for office space would be hers. It was a corner room with the same window design as the front entrance. All she needed was a small table for her personal office. A table along with some chairs and then she could set up her meeting with her client, Colt. She would order one from a furniture store to be delivered. This office space would work well with all of her plans and ideas.

"Yes it does. Do you have the contract?"

"Yes. Here it is."

Vitoria looked it over and made sure it all appeared to be in order. She didn't go to law school to get taken in by a real estate lease. Everything looked good so she signed it and wrote a check out for the rental fee and deposit.

"Do you have the keys or do I need to come back and pick them up?"

"I can give them to you when we return to the office."

"Thank you."

They left the building and went back to the real estate office. Tori was relieved to have at least one thing settled. It would be a lot better once she knew where she was going to live. In the meantime she could live out of a hotel room.

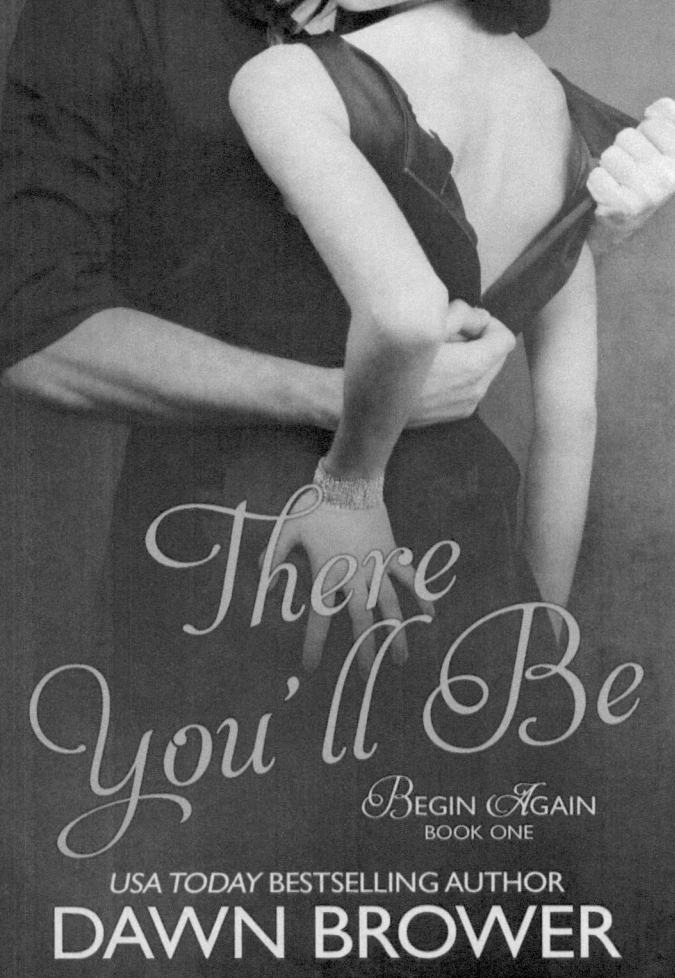

There You'll Be

Begin Again
BOOK ONE

USA TODAY BESTSELLING AUTHOR
DAWN BROWER

This book is for everyone who has adopted a pet and fallen in love instantly. My dog, Bella is a huge part of my family. One we never thought to have, but she is the brightest part of every day. It is amazing how much our fur babies become so integral to our lives. I am thankful each day she found a place in our hearts.

PROLOGUE

*C*arly Gallagher strolled into her office and tossed her phone on her desk. How could this have happened? The operation should not have gone down the way it had. Everything had been planned down to the last detail and yet... Images of an explosion flashed before her eyes. Logan was dead. There was no turning back time and saving him. Her misjudgment had cost him his life.

"Carly..."

She turned toward the sound of her name being called out and frowned. She didn't want to deal with him either —her partner, Phillip Morrison. He was tall, several inches above six feet, and his red-orange hair cropped short, military style. "Go away, Phil." His big beefy frame took up the entire expanse of the entrance to her office. He probably wanted to tell her it wasn't her fault, but she knew better. It had been her call to make, and at the time she'd believed it was the right one. How wrong she'd been...

"I'm not going to do that," he replied. "You're going to

shoulder the blame for this and we both know that nothing could've been done to prevent..."

She interrupted him and said forcefully, "Do we?" Carly stormed over to his side and glared up into his light blue eyes. "Are you sure about that? Because I'm not. There had to be something that we could've done to stop it from happening."

He pulled her into his arms and kissed the top of her head. A sign of affection that shouldn't be broadcast in the FBI offices, but Carly couldn't make herself care. It was a comforting gesture, nothing more. Phil would never make any actual advances on her. At one point in her life she had hoped he would—to no avail. She'd given up on a real relationship a long time ago.

"It was an accident," Phil said soothingly, his soft voice in direct contrast to his large size. Looking at him no one would be able to tell that he had a gentle side. Only Carly had the pleasure of seeing it. She wasn't entirely sure why he let his guard down around her, but in moments like this one she was grateful for it. "Once the investigation is done you'll see that."

She doubted she'd ever see it that way. Logan Crane was her best friend, and one hell of an operative. They'd gone through training together and he'd always had her back. It should've been a routine mission. She still couldn't figure out what had gone wrong. He'd gone into the building with his dog to search the perimeter. They were looking for a missing girl, and Logan's search dog, Spike, was one of the best. Spike was a beautiful golden retriever. Somehow the dog had survived the blast and had been transported to a nearby animal hospital for treatment. Carly had no idea what would happen to the dog. She hoped he survived its injuries. Logan had loved that animal and treated him like a part of the family.

The investigation would take a while. There was a lot of rubble to sift through and they still hadn't located Logan's body. The dog had come running out whimpering, but Logan had been nowhere to be found. Everyone assumed the explosion killed him. A part of Carly was hoping they were all wrong, but she couldn't see how he could have survived it. The dog only lived because he had run out before the explosion went off.

"The investigation will tell me exactly what I already know," she scoffed. "Logan is dead. The rest is just details." Information she'd demand on any other case. This one was different though. She should hand it off to another agent to take care of. "I can't do this right now."

She tried to push past him but there was no moving Phil when he was dead set on staying in one place. He was a boulder too heavy to lift and she was fighting a losing battle. Carly beat against his chest and he stood there taking each blow. He brought his hands up and captured her wrists with them. "Stop," he said quietly. "This isn't helping."

"Nothing I do will, so what difference does it make?"

"You're breaking my heart," he replied. "I want to do something to make it better."

"There's nothing that you could do that would ever make any of this all right. So do me a favor and don't even try." She blew out a breath. "Please let me by. I want to go check on Spike."

"They'll let you know what's going on with the dog,"

Phil said. "Why don't you go home and rest. It's the best thing you can do for yourself."

That was the last thing she wanted to do. If she went home she'd stare at the walls and drown in the silence. Home wasn't anything other than a place to lay her head down when she was weary. With the emotions currently running through her it would feel more like a tomb.

"No," she replied. "I'm going to the vet to check on Spike." Carly glared at him. "Don't try and stop me."

"I'll go with you," he volunteered. "You shouldn't be alone."

"That's sweet." She smiled at him reassuringly. "I'm fine. I don't need you hovering over me."

It would be nice if she could give into the urge to wrap her arms around him. Phil had been her partner at the FBI for several years. They'd been assigned together as a special team that investigated espionage. Through the years they'd brought down a lot of criminals. She suspected they'd do several more together too. They made a good team. Phil probably knew her better than most, but even he didn't have a clue what her deepest darkest secret was.

She loved him.

Her feelings for him had grown day by day until she couldn't deny them any longer. She kept them buried deep down inside of her because Phil wasn't free to love her. He was married to someone else and it was wrong of her to even think of him as something other than her partner. He'd be horrified if he knew how she truly felt about him. She was his friend and partner at work—

nothing more. So she couldn't drag him down the path she was currently going down full-throttle.

"Don't argue with me," he said gruffly. "I'm going with you and that's final."

"Go home to Addison," Carly said softly. "She's probably worried about you. The explosion has been all over the news all day. You can't tell me she hasn't called."

Addison Roberts Morrison was a prestigious psychologist. She was soft spoken, sweet, and the epitome of grace. Everyone that met her loved her. Well, except Carly. There was something off about her but Carly had never been able to pinpoint it. She wanted to like her and tried to. Maybe it was because Addison had the one thing Carly craved—Phil. At least that was what she kept telling herself. That had to be the reason Addison bothered her so much.

"Addison will be fine," Phil said. "She didn't have the shock of her life today."

Carly wanted to give in and allow him to come with her to the vet. It would be easier on a lot of levels if Phil was there with her. Spike would remind her of Logan and she'd break down. No, she wouldn't. Giving into emotions wouldn't bring Logan back. She'd stay strong and do her best to keep herself in check. Being the boss meant she had to put on a brave front and do her job. Something happened in that building and she owed it to Logan to figure out what it was. If Phil wanted to tag along and babysit her, then so be it.

"Fine," she said. "Let me know when you get bored. I'll let you off the hook so you can go home to your wife."

Phil frowned. "You don't have to do that."

What the hell was he talking about now? "Do what?"

"Pretend with me," he replied. "Logan was a friend to us both. So I understand how you feel."

Carly held back the urge to curse. Phil had been friends with Logan too. They'd all been close. It was inevitable working so close together. There had been some get-togethers outside of work. Well, when they had time to breathe anyway. That didn't happen too often. Carly didn't have any female friends and hadn't always gotten along with those of her sex. She did better with males. They, for her, were easier to understand. The cattiness that often erupted in female circles drove her insane. Pettiness and backstabbing wasn't something she handled well. Logan and Phil were the only two people she let get close. There were a few underlings that she had a cordial relationship with, but that was business. Personal relationships were harder for her to maintain. Without Logan all she really had was Phil, and even him she held at a distance.

"Don't psychoanalyze me," she retorted. "I don't have time for that bullshit."

"Carly..." He sighed. "Fine, but if you want to talk about any of it I'm here."

"Shut up and let's go," she said tossing him the keys to her SUV. "You can drive."

She didn't trust herself behind the wheel. It was probably good that Phil had insisted on coming with her to the vet. With her luck she'd cause an accident or some shit. Her hand shook as she brought it up to the passenger side of the vehicle and opened the door. That would be all she needed to fully crack—someone else's possible death on her shoulders.

Phil slid into the driver's seat and started the engine. It was perfectly normal for her to make him drive so he hadn't questioned it. Most of the time she hated being behind the wheel. Being the passenger gave her more freedom and flexibility. If she needed to take a call or do some quick research she could do so with ease. Phil, for his part, preferred driving. It was one of the reasons their relationship worked so well.

They drove in silence to the vet. Phil pulled into a nearby parking spot and turned the engine off. He turned to her and asked, "Are you sure you want to do this?"

What else could she do? The reports from the explosion wouldn't be in for days. She had to do something or she'd go stir crazy. "Don't start again," she warned. "Let's go check on Spike."

She didn't give him a chance to reply and slid out of the vehicle with practiced ease. After taking a reassuring breath she headed inside. The vet office was relatively quiet and empty. It was a little bit of a shock to her to find it that way. Was it not a busy day? Where was everyone?

"Can I help you?" An elderly gentleman stepped out from a back room. He had snow white hair and soft brown eyes.

"Yes," she replied. "I'm Special Agent Gallagher. One of our dogs was brought here for care. I want to check on his status."

"What is his name?"

The dog? He had to mean the dog. There was no way

he could know about Logan and how much she already missed him. "Spike," she offered. "He's a golden retriever."

A bell jingled in the background announcing Phil's arrival. Carly didn't turn to greet him. It was already hard enough to deal with Spike without Logan there.

"Ah, yes," the old man said. "He's a fine dog. The surgery went fine. We had to put a pin in his leg. The bone was too shattered to set."

"But he will be all right." Please say yes...

"Barring any unforeseen complications, yes, he will be." He smiled warmly. "Are you his handler?"

No. She closed her eyes and reminded herself to breathe. How many times a day would she have to do that before she'd do it automatically again? The pain shooting through her heart burned into a deep unending ache. "He doesn't have one any more. When will he be all right to go home?"

The doctor frowned. "Does he have a home?"

He did—with her. She hadn't realized she needed the dog until that moment. Spike would help her heal and in time she'd be able to handle Logan's loss better. Phil rested a hand against her back. He understood her better than anyone.

"He's coming home with me as soon as you allow it," Carly said.

"Good." The old man smiled. "He should be ready in a few days. I want to keep him here to monitor him. Would you like to see him?"

"Yes," Carly said stepping forward. She stopped and glanced at Phil. "Are you coming?"

He nodded and followed behind her. They stopped in

front of Spike's cage. His golden fur was shaved around his front leg and a stark white cast covered most of it. Carly leaned over and kissed his head. "Everything will be fine, I promise."

It was one she intended to keep. When she was done the person who murdered Logan would rue the day they'd been born. No one hurt someone she cared about and got away with it. With that resolve settling deep inside of her she was ready to move on and face the world. She stood up straight and nodded at Phil. "Let's go."

He didn't say a word the entire time. His silence was enough to tell her what he thought. Phil wouldn't push her—yet. When he believed the time was right he'd make her deal with her feelings. She couldn't allow those to come to the surface. Not until Logan's killer was brought to justice, and she would be the one to see it done.

CHAPTER 1

One year later...

Phil skipped the steps leading to Carly's condo. He promised to stop by and feed Spike for her and he was running late. On some levels he understood why she'd taken in the dog, and on the other hand he didn't. Carly had never been the pet owning type. She barely had time to take care of herself let alone an animal. If she'd been aiming for a companion of any sort a fish tank would've been a better option. Even with the aquatic creatures, he feared they might end up dead... She'd surprised him with Spike in more ways than one. They'd taken to each other and, in the process, Carly had a chance to heal. She'd taken Logan's death too hard and it pained him to see her hurting. He would've done anything to take the agony from her, but he realized that was an impossible task. No one could bear that kind of burden for another.

If they had captured Logan's killer things would've

been easier. As the days went by, catching them became a daunting task. After a while they had to set it aside. Leads were elusive and near nonexistent. The crime scene reports had come back with nothing. They hadn't even managed to locate Logan's body to bury. It was believed the explosion was so hot he incinerated on contact. That hadn't sat well with Carly either.

Phil paused, unlocked Carly's front door, and then stepped inside. Spike was used to his presence and didn't even flinch at Phil's arrival. The dog had healed well, but wasn't up to any active duty. The pin in his leg allowed him to walk, but too much strain and it might break down the muscles holding it together. It was good Carly had taken the dog in because he might not have found a home otherwise. Not too many people wanted to care for a lame dog.

"Hey buddy," he said as he brushed his hand over the dog's head. "How are you doing today?" Spike lifted his gaze upward but didn't move. "Are you hungry? Carly is busy in meetings all day…" As if the dog understood what he was saying. It seemed easier to carry on a conversation with him. It was better than the silence echoing through the condo.

Phil went to the cupboard and pulled out a can of dog food. He opened it up and dumped it into a bowl. It smelled disgusting, but Spike loved it. It turned Phil's stomach as he set it down on the floor. "Come and get it," he said energetically. Spike remained on the floor unmoving. Was something wrong with him? Should he call Carly? He'd hate to worry her for nothing.

"Come on Spike," he said pleadingly. "Have a heart. If

something happens to you Carly is going to nail my ass to the wall."

Spike stood up reluctantly and brushed past Phil. He sniffed the food and then licked it, testing it for lord knows what. Phil didn't want to hazard a guess. When the dog started eating more enthusiastically Phil let out a relieved breath. One last thing he'd have to stress over.

There was something much harder for him to deal with on his agenda. He glanced at his watch and sighed. He had thirty minutes to get to the court house. "All right, buddy. I hate to leave you but I've got to run." He leaned down and patted the dog's head. "Look after Carly for me won't you."

Phil rushed out of the condo and headed back to his vehicle. He pulled out of the parking lot as fast as possible and sped toward the courthouse. Going to court was never fun, but this particular time was one of the worst. He didn't look forward to what was about to happen. When he arrived he pulled his car into a parking slot and cut the engine. This was not going to be pleasurable. He stepped out of the vehicle and headed inside. Outside the courthouse doors Addison paced back and forth glancing at her watch repeatedly.

"You're late," she said.

He rolled his eyes. "No, I'm not."

There was no use arguing with her about it. Addison was always right and didn't bother to entertain anyone else's opinion. It had been endearing when they'd met, but now it grated on his nerves. Strange how things could change that way...

She pinched her lips together in displeasure. Her

hands rested on her hips as she tapped her foot. "I don't have time for your shenanigans today. I have a lot to do and I want this over with."

On that point Phil couldn't agree more. He didn't bother to reply to her, just headed into the court room and took a seat at his side of the room. He glanced over as Addison did the same. There was a time he'd never have imagined he'd be where he was at that moment. About to end his marriage to the woman he had believed he'd loved more than anything in the world. And he had when he married her, but he hadn't known her like he believed he had. Everything changed after the wedding and, in truth, their marriage had been all but over years ago. They'd stopped truly living as husband and wife almost immediately. He couldn't even remember the last time they'd made love. They should have divorced a long time ago. It had seemed easier and less embarrassing to pretend it was as perfect as everyone believed.

Until it hadn't...

He hadn't counted on falling in love with Carly. It had happened slowly until one day he opened his eyes and realized how much she meant to him. Carly didn't hold anything back. She was as real as any person could be. There wasn't a person alive he trusted more than her. But he couldn't act on those feelings. What right did he have to her when he wasn't truly free to love her? So he asked Addison for a divorce. It had been easy enough to give her a reason why. She'd been eager to end their farce and hadn't questioned him too much. His soon to be ex-wife didn't need to know that he'd fallen in love with his partner. That was his secret for now and when the time was right he'd tell Carly. For now, he'd settle with finally bringing his marriage to a close.

CARLY PACED her office frustrated at her impatience. Phil had left her a message letting her know he'd fed Spike and would be late returning. She needed him back and didn't understand what was so important he had to make a pit stop for it. She glanced at the clock on the wall and sighed for the hundredth time. *Damn it.*

She walked over to her desk and grabbed her phone and listened to his message again. *"Carly, Spike's eating like a champ. Be back later, something I have to do. Don't work too hard."* As if she needed to be reminded of something so silly.

There were no clues in the message indicating where he was going or what was so damned important. How was she going to get anything done if she kept pacing her office worrying about him? Sometimes loving another person just plain sucked. She slammed her phone on her desk and cringed. That was a little too hard—she picked it up and made sure she hadn't cracked the screen. There didn't appear to be any damage...

A knock echoed through the room and she turned at the sound. Phil stood in the doorway looking as right as could be. No, that wasn't entirely true. There was a little strain around his mouth. He'd tried to hide it but the muscles in his cheek twitched and there was a slight wrinkle in his forehead.

"What's wrong?" she asked immediately.

"Nothing you need to worry about," he replied. "Checking in with you to see how the meeting went."

"It didn't," she said. "They're all a bunch of bureaucratic assholes."

She'd wanted to keep Logan's case open a little bit longer. The leads weren't there to argue it though and, in the end, they'd told her to add it to the cold-case files. It wasn't officially closed, but it was no longer a priority. She hated that she hadn't found the person responsible for Logan's death.

"I'm sure you'll find the answers you need someday."

"But not today. Blah blah blah," she said as she waved her hand in the air. "I don't need to hear it from you too."

God she hated when people were condescending to her. As if being female made her more prone to melodrama. She was capable of making sound decisions and didn't fly off on tangents for no apparent reason. Something about Logan's case wasn't right… She'd figure it out eventually. In the meantime, she could harass Phil a little bit.

"Now tell me what is really going on with you. What was so important you had to take a sabbatical for the afternoon?"

"I believe I said it isn't anything you have to worry over. It didn't require your assistance." His lips formed a thin white line.

My, my, someone is a bit testy... She narrowed her eyes and said, "Now I have to know."

"I wish you wouldn't push," he said. "I don't particularly want to discuss it."

Carly frowned. What could have possibly happened

that had him so upset. She didn't like it one bit. Phil was usually more—congenial. He wanted to help others and didn't do anything outright mean. He was no nonsense and she loved him for it, or maybe it was in spite of it. She wasn't entirely sure but that didn't matter. What did was his apparent distress. Phil never was like that.

"Maybe you would be better if you went home. Talk to Addison if you can't talk to me." It irritated her to say that. She wanted him to confide in her. "If you're going to be so crabby—you're no use to me."

"I am not talking with Addison about a damn thing," he grunted out. "She's the last person I want to see right now."

Carly paused and stared at him. What the hell was that about? Was there trouble in paradise? Was it sad that actually made her happy? She shouldn't wish any kind of distress in his marriage, but she didn't like Addison. She'd tried to like her, truly she had. Addison was just—not friendly. It boggled her mind that two people as different as Phil and Addison had married in the first place.

"Are you and Addison fighting?" she asked gently, regret pooling in her gut as if she had eaten something rotten. "I'm sorry. I shouldn't have needled you."

"It's not that…" Phil stepped back and brought his hand to his mouth. He turned his back to her and bowed his head.

What wasn't she getting? None of it made sense. There hadn't ever been a time that Phil couldn't or wouldn't tell her something. Hell, he knew all of her secrets—save one. Maybe one day she'd tell him that she loved him, but now was not that time.

He didn't bother to face her as he spoke, "If you want to know where I was…"

"Only if you want to tell me," Carly interrupted. "It's none of my business if it was something personal."

He glanced over his shoulder and glared. "Will you let me get a word in?"

"I'm sorry," she replied remorsefully. "Please continue."

"I was in court." He sighed and turned fully around and met her gaze. "I finalized my divorce today."

She could not have heard him correctly. "Say what?"

Carly hadn't even realized there was any sort of discord in his relationship with Addison. Why in the hell would they have gotten a divorce? What had she missed?

"My marriage has been over for a while," Phil said without an ounce of emotion. "Despite appearances to the contrary."

That was…amazing. Leaping for joy was probably a very bad idea. She shouldn't be happy, but oh God was she. But for now she'd be the good friend and say the right things. "I'm sorry, so so sorry. Is there anything I can do for you?"

He shook his head. "I'm fine. Like I said, it's been over for a while."

With those words, he spun on his heels and stormed out of her office. He had left her with a lot to think about. The question was, what would her next move be?

CHAPTER 2

*E*arly ambled up the steps to her condominium a little too leisurely. Exhaustion was on the brink of setting in and she wanted to be settled inside her apartment before it overtook her, but she lacked the motivation to quicken her pace. When she finally reached her door, it was wide open. Adrenaline pumped through her quickly and she immediately went on high alert. She reached for her gun holster and unlatched it so she would have easier access if needed.

She remained as quiet as possible and kept her gaze peeled for any sudden movements. As she made progress through her home, she took note of everything and filed it in her mind to revisit later. The entire living area was total chaos. Her coffee table was overturned and her television lay on the floor with a smashed screen. Whoever had trashed her place had not been a thief. They had been searching for something, but she wasn't sure what. Who would have come into her home and turned it upside down? Then terror settled into her heart causing it to beat at a rapid pace.

Where was Spike?

Up until the moment she remembered the dog she'd been calm. Now worry swirled through her as she frantically searched for him. Where could he be? Did the intruder take him? Why would he do that? Panic filled her as she realized Spike was missing. She reached for her phone and called Phil.

He answered after one ring. "I don't want to discuss…"

"Shut up," Carly said. "I need you." Her voice shook as she spoke those words. She couldn't get anything else out. After Logan died, Spike was all she'd had to hold onto and now he was missing. She'd failed Spike in the same way she'd done with Logan. At the rate she was going no one would be safe around her. She fell to the ground and gave into tears she'd been holding in for over a year. Not once at Logan's memorial service had she given into her misery and through everything she had remained strong. Now with Spike missing it reared its ugly head and overtook her.

She was still in the same place when Phil came rushing through her front door. He kneeled down beside her and pulled her into his arms. "Shh," he whispered. "I've got you."

Carly wrapped her arms around him and let everything out. She laid her head on his shoulder and ugly cried. Sniffles overtook her and bless Phil for allowing her to mess up his fine shirt. After what seemed like forever she glanced up at him with a wobbly smile. "I'm sorry," she said. "You've had a bad day; you didn't need to deal with me."

"Now that you're coherent, how about you tell me what the fuck is going on," he ground out. "I didn't miss the condition of your place as I walked in."

Of course he'd thought of her first and the condo second. That was the type of person he was. He put other people first and that would not change because he was sad. "I don't know," she told him. "This is how I found things when I returned home. Nothing was amiss when you were here earlier?"

He shook his head. "Spike seemed a little depressed, but other than that things were fine. They were certainly not like this. I'd not have left it alone and I'd have told you immediately."

Wait a minute. "What do you mean? Spike was fine when I left this morning." She didn't really care about her things. Her dog was way more important. If she felt she needed to she could buy a new television. It wasn't as if she had much time to watch the damn thing.

"He wasn't his usual self. I thought perhaps he'd sensed my mood…" He frowned. "I had to coax him to eat. Now that I think about it, I should've let you know about that."

What could have made Spike react like that? He was usually friendly and eager to see the people who took care of him. That was usually either her or Phil. They had become Spike's family after Logan's death. Carly glanced up and smiled at Phil. "Don't be hard on yourself. It's been a stressful day all around, and you have a good excuse for being distracted."

She didn't have to like it, but he went through something tough earlier. It could not have been easy to put an end to his marriage. Even if he'd believed it had truly been over a long time ago.

"Where is Spike now?"

Carly shook her head. "I don't know. That's why I broke down."

He nodded. "I understand. Do you want me to look around outside to see if he is nearby?"

Why hadn't she thought to do that? He could be in the neighborhood wandering around. All she had done was fall into a heap of misery and given into the selfishness residing inside of her. Without Spike, she didn't have much to look forward to when she came home. He was the reason she had not given up and kept moving forward. It was hard to not give in to the loneliness that had become a permanent part of her life.

Carly wiped her face with her hands and nodded. "Could you please? I'll call the locals and have them come make a report."

"I'll be back soon," Phil said as he headed toward the open door. He paused and turned to glance back at her. "Will you be all right while I'm gone?"

If she were being honest, she didn't know if she'd ever be all right again. Her whole world was off balance. She kept her gaze steady as she stared at Phil. There were possibilities that had not been there before. The question was, would she be brave enough to reach out and take a chance? Phil could be hers one day if she remained patient enough and gave him time to heal. Would he even want her? There were so many questions and not enough answers. First though she had to find her dog and figure out what was going on with the mess in her condo. The rest could wait for another day.

"I'll be fine," she said reassuringly. "Go look for Spike."

Phil turned and left. Carly made the phone call to the local police and sat down to wait for them. It was going to be an even longer night than she'd planned.

WHERE COULD SPIKE HAVE GONE? Phil didn't want to entertain the idea that whoever had broken into Carly's place had taken him. Spike might be retired but he was a well-trained dog. He would have attempted to attack anyone who entered the condominium and trashed it. There must be a reason he was no longer around.

When he'd arrived at Carly's place and saw it trashed his heart had about leapt out of his chest. He had immediately scanned for her thinking the worst. After he located her on the floor crying his concern increased a thousand fold and his heart broke into a million tiny shards. He hadn't even thought about the dog at first. Carly was always his main concern and comforting her was his priority. Everything else would always take a back burner to what she needed. When the time was right, he would tell her he loved her and wanted a chance. He only prayed she did not think he was ridiculous when he laid it all out to her. That could wait for a better day. There were bigger things that they had to deal with. First, he had to find Spike and take him back to Carly. The rest would sort itself out when it was supposed to.

"Spike," he yelled. Phil wasn't sure if he'd come if he

called or not but he had to try something. Silence greeted him in response. It had been a long shot either way.

He turned the corner and headed toward a nearby park. Carly took the dog there as often as she could. It was one of Spike's favorite places. Phil walked through the park at a brisk pace and whistled. Dark was starting to settle in and the streetlights buzzed on illuminating a path for him. Even with the added brightness, he had trouble scanning his surroundings.

"Spike," he yelled again hoping this time he'd get a response. Nothing happened and he was starting to get discouraged. Phil was about to give up when he caught movement in the distance. A golden retriever was running toward him. Spike was heading straight for him at full speed. When the dog reached him he leapt up and knocked Phil to the ground. "Easy now," Phil laughed as the dog licked his face. "It's good to see you too."

Carly would be glad to know the dog was safe. There were still a lot of unanswered questions though. Like who the hell broke into the condo and why had Spike run out? "Come on boy," Phil said. "Let's go home. Carly is worried about you."

It was so easy to talk to a dog. They did not judge and showed affection with ease. If only it was that simple with people. His life would be a lot less difficult if he could approach it the way Spike did. They headed back to the condominium side by side. Spike did not need a leash; he just knew what he was supposed to do. They still used one on him when they normally went out to put others at ease though. Spike ran ahead of Phil and leapt up the steps toward Carly's place. Phil wasn't far behind him. They entered to find a local police officer taking notes and another taking several pictures.

"What did I miss?" he asked Carly. Her eyes seemed to brighten when she saw Spike by his side.

"You found him," she exclaimed as she knelt down to hug the dog. "Thank you so much. I owe you."

He frowned. "Don't be ridiculous."

Carly kissed Spike's head and hugged him again. Phil was starting to become jealous of the dog. If only she'd greeted him as enthusiastically.

"You found Spike," Carly said as she still held onto the dog. "There is nothing ridiculous in how I feel about that. I am so happy he is all right. I can't thank you enough."

Phil was right on the edge of begging her to love him. How pathetic was he? He was barely hanging on to his dignity. Instead of declaring his feelings, he focused on something else. "It's not safe here."

Carly stood up and met his gaze. "Because someone broke in and trashed the place?" She rolled her eyes. "I'm capable of taking care of myself. If someone is stupid enough to break in while I'm here they will regret it immediately."

Phil opened his mouth to argue with her and closed it immediately. He had to play this smart or she would dig in her heels. If he called her stupid or incapable in any way, she would be even more stubborn. Where he was standing there was only one solution to the problem—emotional blackmail.

"Carly, please have mercy on me."

She narrowed her gaze at him and frowned. "I don't understand."

"It's been a really long and miserable day," he said gravely. "Please don't argue with me about this. I realize you're a highly trained agent and quite capable of taking care of yourself, but I'd still worry about you all night. I'd like to relax knowing you're safe and not in a place that is so trashed you can't even see the floor." He met her gaze and said as easily as he could muster, "Come stay at my place for the night and I'll come back here tomorrow to clean up the mess. You'd be doing me a favor."

He hoped he had not played that last part too heavily. If she came back to his place, he would rest easier. There was a reason someone had broken into her condominium and until they knew what that was, she should not stay there.

"Fine," she said. "I wasn't actually looking forward to picking up this mess by myself. If it makes you feel better Spike and I will stay the night with you."

Words he never thought he would hear from her. If only it was something more like: *I love you and want to be with you forever.* Maybe one day he would hear them, but for now he'd take what he could get.

*P*hil pushed opened the front door to his apartment and gestured for Carly to enter. She strolled inside with Spike trailing behind her. It seemed perfectly natural for her to be inside his home. He allowed himself a moment to stare at her and take everything in. Her simple black dress hugged her at her waist and accentuated her breasts perfectly. She glanced back at him, her violet-blue eyes filled with what he interpreted as desire, and it was like a sucker punch to his gut. He wanted to cross over to her, unbind her dark black hair, and watch it fall down her back in waves. That couldn't be right—Carly would never look at him in that way.

He stepped inside carrying Carly's bag. The local police wanted to have longer than a day to examine her condo and allowed Carly to pack up some of her things for an extended stay at Phil's apartment. Spike stayed with him from time to time so he already had food and supplies for the dog. Carly had not been to his apartment though. It was invigorating to have her so close, and yet in contrast, an untenable distance bridged a wide gap between them.

"You can have the bedroom while you're here," he said. "I'll put this in there."

Sleeping on the couch would be uncomfortable at best, but he'd do anything for her. He wanted her to have a good night's rest. There wasn't a chance in hell he'd manage any sleep with her slumbering in his bed. So it didn't matter to him where he ended up. The more time he spent in her company the harder it was to hold his feelings in.

"Don't be silly," Carly called out. "You'll be miserable out here."

Phil paused at the entrance to his bedroom and glanced back at her. "Don't argue with me. I'm not in the mood."

He went inside and set her bag down against the wall. Carly wasn't going to make any of it easy and he was at a loss on how to handle it. Everything inside of him screamed to pull her in his arms and kiss her the way he'd been imagining for so long. There wasn't anything except his own sense of decency holding him back. Freedom was finally his and he wanted to embrace it fully. Soon he'd do that, but he wasn't an asshole. Carly deserved better than to have him leap at her like a dog in heat.

"Phil," Carly said bringing her hand up against his back. He closed his eyes and took a deep breath. He loved having her hand on him but she didn't realize she was poking the beast. "Look at me."

"There are towels in the closet outside the bathroom if you want to take a shower," he said instead. He hadn't managed to rein in his desire enough to look at her yet. "If you're hungry I can order a pizza. I'm afraid rations are a tad low as I don't often eat here."

"I don't care about food," she said exasperated. "Why won't you look at me?"

He clenched his hands into fists at his side. She didn't understand and he couldn't explain it to her. His desire licked at him like a fire on the edge of exploding. She was what fueled it and the closer she was the hotter it burned. There wasn't much breathing room between his desire and good intentions. It wouldn't be long before the flames burned through his resolve and he gave in.

Slowly he turned and glanced down at her. Immediately his focus went to her full lips. The need to taste them ignited sending a new wave of heat flaring through him. Carly opened her mouth and swiped her tongue across her lips. Phil barely restrained a groan. He had to put himself out of his misery. Maybe a cold shower would help…

"If you're not going to use the shower, I'm going to." Phil stepped past her and headed toward the closet to grab a towel. He whipped open the door and grabbed the first one his hand landed on, then stepped into the bathroom. Just as he was about to shut the door Carly lifted her hand to stop him.

"What is going on with you?" She tilted her head and studied him.

He didn't want her too close to him or he might do something foolish. A cold shower would help him gain control of his need for her. At least he hoped so. The idea of her being hurt put him on edge and it was harder for him to control what he wanted. She was all he thought about every second of the day. When he looked into her eyes he saw his future and the hope for happiness. He didn't want to use her body to sate his needs—he wanted it all with her—love, family, and the promise of forever.

"I'm fine," he said as reassuringly as he could muster. "It's been a long day."

Fuck. That was an understatement. It was possibly the longest day of his entire life. When it started he'd never imagined it would end as it had. Would it be so much to ask that it didn't cave in completely before it was fully done? At least everything had gone as planned in court. Everything else had been chaos he couldn't control.

"I'm sorry," she said and glanced down. "I shouldn't be bothering you. But Phil…" She looked back up at him. "I can't take your bedroom."

Why did she have to be so difficult? "Carly you're driving my patience down a very thin line. I'll discuss this with you after my shower." He pushed her lightly out of the room and shut the door with a soft click, then rested his forehead against it. After several slow breaths he started the shower, stepped inside, and let the frigid water cool his heated skin. It was agonizing and exactly what he needed. Maybe, just maybe, he'd be able to spend an evening with Carly without giving into his need to kiss her, touch her, and show her how much he loved her.

CARLY WASN'T sure what was going on with Phil. He was acting rather strange and she didn't have a clue how to approach him. Ever since he'd come to her condo to check on her it had been as if he'd become a different person entirely. No, that wasn't exactly true. He was the same person he always was, but the way he looked at her. That was what was different. There was something there she couldn't identify and wasn't sure what to make of it. Had she done something he didn't approve of, or was it something else entirely?

Spike came up to her side and rubbed his head on her leg. She laughed and patted him on the head. "What do you need?" He barked in response as if she understood dog speak. "Are you hungry? Do you need some doggy food?" He barked two more times and his tail started to wag rapidly. "All right, let's see what Phil has stashed here for you."

Carly wandered into the kitchen with Spike trailing behind her. She started opening cupboards and frowned. "He wasn't lying, was he? There isn't much of anything in here." Finally she opened a cupboard and found a stash of dog food. "At least he has provisions for you," she said glancing down at Spike. "The man has strange priorities."

He may not have been living in the apartment long enough to fully stock it. The house he'd shared with Addison probably had more stuff in it than anyone could use in a lifetime. His now ex-wife seemed like the type to go overboard. Carly had only been to his house once and it was enough for her to never go back. It was pristine and unwelcoming. There wasn't a thing out of place and it didn't have that lived-in feel to it. She didn't understand how anyone could live like that. When he wasn't so crabby she'd have to ask him how long he'd been living in this apartment. In some ways it suited him more. It was—comfortable. He might be lacking such amenities as food, but there was a homier feel to the place.

Carly opened up a can of dog food and dumped it into a bowl, then placed it on the floor for Spike. He dove in immediately and ate with gusto. At least she was able to please one of the males in her life. Spike was easier to understand than Phil was. Why was he insisting she take the bed anyway? He had to realize he'd be uncomfortable on the couch. He was huge and that couch would barely be big enough for her small frame.

She left Spike to enjoy his food and headed back to the living room to wait for Phil to finish his shower. It turned out to be a short wait. He entered the hallway joining the rooms the same time she did wearing only a towel wrapped around his waist. Small drops of water trailed down his broad chest down to his belly. Carly couldn't help herself—her gaze followed one as it made a path toward the towel. She glanced back up and sucked in a breath when saw the look in Phil's eyes. There was definitely heat reflecting back at her. He wanted her.

She stepped forward not able to stop herself from closing the gap between them. If he desired her even a small amount she wanted to explore it. To finally know what it was like to kiss him, touch him, have him for herself as she'd always imagined. Perhaps it was wrong—no, it was definitely wrong. His divorce was only finalized earlier that day. He was probably vulnerable and going to him in that kind of state was taking advantage of his emotional chaos. Carly stopped in front of him and looked up at him. He was staring down at her intently.

"What are you doing?" he asked hoarsely.

She didn't say a word, not trusting herself to speak. It was almost magical, this pull she felt toward him. In response to his question she lifted her hand and skimmed it across his bare chest. He sucked in a breath with each stroke of her fingers across his skin.

"Carly?" He groaned. "If you keep doing that I'll lose control."

"Sounds promising," she retorted. "Why don't we find out how wild you can be?"

Who was this person talking to him that way? Carly didn't recognize her, but she wanted to let her out to play. It was everything she'd held inside for too long, and finally allowed the freedom of her darkest desires.

The muscles in Phil's cheeks twitched. He was still fighting to remain in control. He needed more incentive to lose it and, lucky for him, Carly was willing to step things up enough to help him fall over the edge. It didn't matter what was right or wrong anymore. All that mattered was him, and her, and what they could do for each other—there was no room for possible regrets. She took a step closer and pressed her lips to his chest, then licked one of the drops of water. Phil hissed and wrapped his arms around her holding her against his tightness. His hard cock pressed into her belly through the towel. That was all that stood between him and total nakedness. Carly couldn't wait for it to fall to the floor and give her the one view she'd been craving for so long.

She glanced up at him and demanded, "Kiss me."

Phil didn't need any more encouragement. He leaned down and pressed his lips to hers. The kiss was everything she'd ever imagined it could be—wild, passionate, and demanding. His kiss didn't stop at her lips ether. He trailed his lips over her cheeks, down her neck, and across the top of her breasts. She wanted to feel his hot mouth over her nipples, but the dress she was wearing prevented it. The darn thing had to go. Carly had a need to feel his skin against hers.

"Unzip my dress," she ordered.

"Not yet," he said.

Damn him. She had needs. Carly tried to spin out of his arms to remove it herself but he held her in place. "So bossy," he said. "God I love that about you. But tonight I'm in control."

"No," she said. "I…" She didn't get a chance to say anything other than that as his mouth crashed down on hers again. It was a different kind of kiss than the first one. This one was a battle of wills and the winner would steer the rest of their night. In the end they'd both win though. Phil pushed her against the wall and held her hands in place as he ravished her mouth. Carly whimpered with each thrust of his tongue against hers. She was a quivering mess of need. After several moments he lifted his mouth and stared down at her. "Are you ready?"

She wasn't sure if she'd ever be fully prepared for the onslaught of desire he brought out of her. The raging emotions rolling through her body was almost too much to bear. Carly didn't respond verbally, instead she met his gaze as boldly as possible and licked her lips.

Phil picked her up and carried her into the bedroom. He set her down and spun her around to slowly unzip her dress. It fell to the floor in a pool around her feet. He brought his hands up to cup her breasts through the lace of her bra, slid them around and swiftly unlatched it letting it join her dress on the floor. Wetness pooled between her thighs, dampening her panties even more.

"I've been waiting so long to touch you," he breathed. "It's so much more than I could've imagined."

Wait... He'd what? Later she'd make him tell her what he meant by that statement. For now she had bigger demands. "Fuck me," she ordered.

"Patience," he said softly. "There is so much I want to do to you first."

She'd never survive it. "Please," she begged.

Phil picked her up and set her on the bed, then slid her panties down her legs. He let the towel fall to the floor giving her the view she'd wanted the moment he'd stepped out of the bathroom. She reached up and wrapped one of her hands around his thick length. He moaned deeply as she stroked him with her fingers.

"Stop," he groaned out. "or this will be over before it starts."

"Never," she said. She loved having control.

Phil brought his hand up and wrapped it around her wrist again and pinned it together with her other one. He held both together above her head as he stared down at her. "So beautiful," he said. "Need you." He brought his free hand up to his dick and stroked it.

Carly groaned and lifted her legs to wrap them around his waist. "Please now."

He pressed his cock against her wetness. She moaned in anticipation. Phil didn't push into her as she'd hoped, but did something even better. He rubbed himself against her clit until she was squirming against him. She was so close to climax. It didn't take long for her screams to fill the room. As the waves of her release started to ebb, he pushed himself into her. Each stroke was an intense pleasure that bordered on pain.

"More," Carly said. "Faster."

After she muttered those words he lost all control and rocked into her hard and swift. Stars exploded behind her eyelids as she hit her second release, and Phil followed shortly after. It was even more amazing then she'd dreamed it could be. It was perfect because it was real.

Phil rolled off of her and pulled the covers down on the bed. He tucked her underneath them and then joined her pulling her into his arms. They would have to talk about it, but she wasn't ready for that. Thank God he didn't push.

"Sleep," he said. "Tomorrow will be here soon enough."

Carly did as he suggested and let herself fall into oblivion.

CHAPTER 4

*P*hil rolled over and found the bed beside him empty. Had last night actually happened? In some ways, it seemed like a dream—one he never wanted to wake up from. After his shower, he had realized he hadn't brought anything with him to change into, but figured it was not a big deal. He could walk across to his bedroom quick and dress. When he spotted Carly as he walked out his whole body had hardened in response—so much for a cold shower to cool his desire. One glance from her and he was a goner.

Where was she?

He rolled out of bed and threw on some clothes to go search for her. First he checked the kitchen, and then the living room. After a quick perusal through the entire apartment, he had to accept she was gone. Had he scared her away last night? Did he read it wrong? No, if she hadn't wanted him she'd have kneed him in the balls. Carly didn't do anything she didn't want to do. However, it might not have meant the same to her as it did to him.

For Phil it had been making love to the woman he had loved silently for months. Carly might have just needed someone and he was readily available.

The previous night had been amazing. Loving her had been something he had hoped to have, and had not expected it to happen so soon. What if he'd made a mistake by falling into bed with her the very day of his divorce? What must she think of him? Phil wandered over to the couch and fell into it. Despair filled him at the idea he could have ruined any chance he had with her. When she returned, he would have a long talk with her and explain how he felt. It was the only option he had if he wanted a chance at a real relationship with her. It was time for him to take a risk and put it all on the line. If he loved her, he had to fight for her.

She'd probably taken Spike for a walk. The dog needed regular exercise and he'd pointed out a park near his apartment when he'd driven them over the night before. That had to be where she'd gone, and perhaps instead of sitting in his apartment thinking the worst he should go looking for her.

Phil grinned like an idiot at the idea of seeing her again. God he loved her and he even liked Spike. They could be together and he'd do whatever it took to convince her of it. He wasn't sure what was going through her mind, but he knew what he wanted and there wasn't a thing he'd not do to keep her in his life.

Resolved, he stood up and headed to his bedroom to make himself more presentable to the world because once he located her he planned on making a play at forever. He should try to look his best if he wanted to convince her that was a good idea. It wouldn't hurt to make himself more appealing when laying his heart at the feet of the woman who owned it.

~

CARLY WALKED Spike through the park and thought about the night before. She had made a complete fool of herself and she could not bring herself to care. That wasn't entirely true. She cared way too much. What must he think of her? When he stepped out of the bathroom wearing only a towel... She'd lost her damned mind and practically threw herself at him. The pleasure of being in his arms had undone her. If she had her way, she would be in his bed holding him close every night.

She hoped he did not think badly of her for any of it. He had just gotten divorced earlier that day, and the first chance she had found she'd leaped on him like a starving animal. It was an apt description actually. She had been dying to taste him, kiss him, and truly touch him for too long. The only way she would find out what he thought or believed was to have a conversation with him. As much as it pained her to admit it, it was time to own up to her feelings for him and finally tell him she loved him. It might not be an ideal situation but it was her only choice. If she wanted a chance at a real relationship with him, she would have to lay it all on the line. Waiting for a better time would have been more ideal, but they were past that. They had already taken a step they couldn't undo.

Spike started pulling hard on the leash trying to run in the direction of some trees. He stuck his nose in the air and sniffed, then yanked hard again. "What are you doing?" Carly tightened her grip on the handle. "There is nothing in those trees for you."

Spike barked louder and jerked Carly forward. She lost her balance, hit the ground hard, and lost her hold on the leash. The dog took advantage of her disarray and took off on a dead run toward the trees. Carly rolled to her knees and yelled, "Spike, no!" She jumped to her feet and took off after him.

What the hell was in those freaking trees that the dog found so interesting? Was it a squirrel? If it was, she was going to smack that dog in the nose the first chance she got. This was ridiculous. She had to go back to the apartment and have a talk with Phil.

Tree branches smacked her in the cheek as she ran through the mini forest in the park. Spike had gotten an enormous lead and she was having trouble keeping him in her sight. It appeared as if there was a clearing up ahead. Carly followed Spike into it and halted beside him. "What is it boy?" There was a small building that had security cameras on every corner of it. Whatever was inside the owners thought it was really important. It was not her place to decide if it was or not. She had to get Spike to turn around and head back to Phil's apartment.

Before she had a chance to grab Spike's leash, he took off on a run again. He hit a nearby door hard and bounced off of it. What the damnation was wrong with the stupid dog? Spike leapt to his feet and sniffed the door. There was something or someone in there that interested him. She feared the only way he would leave willingly is if she found a way to show him there was nothing there for him to be concerned about.

She walked over to the dog and picked up his leash. "I don't know what you smell, dude, but this is getting a tad ridiculous. The owners of this building are not going to be happy you're making it a priority." She studied the door and tried to make a decision. It would be easy enough to break into it. There were not any complicated locks on it. It was weird actually. There was a hinge with a padlock on it instead of on the door handle. Every bit of her FBI training screamed to leave it be. It was wrong to go inside the building, and even worse to unlawfully enter, but she decided to go against those instincts. She pulled a bobby pin from her hair and straightened it to use as a pick, then slid it into the padlock. After a few clicks in the chamber it slid open. Carly pulled it off the door and slid it into her pocket, then turned the door handle and pushed it open. Spike yanked on the leash and it slid from her hand once again and ran inside. She was a bad dog owner.

"What the hell are you doing here?"

She had been so engrossed in her lock picking she had not heard anyone approach. Shit. Carly slowly turned around and her mouth almost fell open in shock at who was standing behind her—Addison. Her blonde hair was pinned up in a tight chignon and her brown eyes were narrowed into a hateful glare. What held Carly's attention though was the pistol she had aimed at her.

She raised her hands slowly to let her see she was unarmed. Perhaps she did not take it too kindly when someone broke into her, well, whatever the building was to her. Carly was not sure what the hell it was, and didn't particularly want to know either. "No need to hold me at gunpoint," she said reassuringly. "I don't mean anyone harm." Not to mention she was completely unarmed and could not hurt anyone if she tried. She was well trained but even her abilities were limited. A gun trumped just about anything in this sort of standoff.

"You've already seen too much," Addison said. "I can't let anyone know my plans yet." She gestured toward the door and ordered, "Go inside."

Was Phil's ex-wife Looney tunes? Was that why they had divorced? Had Phil realized she was crazy and got out while the getting was good? No, Phil would not do that. If she were sick, he would have stayed by her side no matter what. There was something else going on and Carly was certain she was not going to like it.

"I said go inside," Addison shouted. "Don't make me shoot you. I abhor bloodshed."

Good to know. She might be able to use that to her advantage later. Carly turned and walked inside the building slowly, unsure what she might find.

"Why are you doing this?" Maybe if Addison started talking Carly could reason with her. "You don't have to keep me here."

"Shut up," Addison said. "I never liked you. I may not like the idea of blood but I'm not afraid to take a life if need be."

Carly reminded herself to breathe. Addison was definitely nuts as nuts could be. How had Phil stayed married to her when she was clearly insane? More importantly how had she hidden this side of her psyche from him?

"I rather like living," Carly said. "No need to kill me."

Spike's bark echoed through the building. "You have the dog with you," she said and grinned. "Good. That saves me the trouble of grabbing him later. The men I hired failed to find him last night."

"Wait," Carly said and turned to face her. "You're the one that broke into my house? Why would you do something like that?" Why did she want Spike?

"You already know too much," she said and pushed her into a dark room. "At least he will have you to keep him company before you both die." The door banged shut and a lock clicked in place. A tiny window let a small amount of light into the room, but it was still so dark she had trouble seeing a foot in front of her.

"Spike, what kind of mess did you get me into?"

"I'm afraid it's my fault," a male said.

Carly spun around at the sound of that voice. She recognized it immediately. Tears formed in the corners of her eyes and she stumbled toward the direction the sound had come from. Her voice wavered as she said, "Logan?"

"I'm afraid so, honey," he said sadly. "Spike must have caught my scent and led you here. If I could've prevented this I would have."

She brought her hands up to her mouth as tears fell freely. "How is this possible?"

"It's a long story and I promise I'll explain it later," he promised. "But for now, do you think you could untie me? We have to find a way to escape and I'm no use to you this way."

Carly didn't think twice. She fell to the floor and started to work on the ropes around his wrists, and then his ankles. Once he was free she wrapped her arms around him and hugged him tight. "I thought you were dead."

"For a while there I thought I was going to die. She has her reasons for keeping me alive," he explained. "None of them are good."

She frowned. "She's crazy."

"You have no idea," he said with a sigh. "The things I could tell you..." He let out a breath. "There isn't a lot of time to go over it all. You're going to have to trust me."

"Always," she promised. Spike barked in response adding his own two cents. Carly laughed and brushed her hand over his head.

Spike leaped onto Logan and licked his face. "I missed you too," he said, pulling the dog into his arms. "Now comes the hard part, well at least the first one—finding a way out of this room."

Carly was afraid that might prove to be impossible.

I t was a beautiful day for a walk in the park—at least that is what Phil told himself as he searched for Spike and Carly. He was about to give up and go back to his apartment when a movement caught his attention. A flash of tan followed by green... He turned toward it and saw Spike run into a bunch of trees followed shortly by Carly. A laugh escaped from deep inside of him as Carly bolted after the dog. He must have caught the scent of a squirrel again and decided to chase it. Poor Carly.

Phil headed in the direction they had gone into the woods. He couldn't wait to hold her in his arms again. Yeah, they had a lot to talk about but he didn't believe for a minute she had no feelings for him. The night before had been too intense to believe otherwise. Finally, things were headed in a direction he could hold onto. She was his everything.

"Spike," he heard Carly shout. The dog was determined to get that damn squirrel, wasn't he? He did not understand the fascination with the small furry creature but he would not hold it against Spike. Joy came from the small things in life.

He strolled leisurely through the trail of chaos Spike and Carly had left in their wake. Fallen branches and leaves littered the ground. Branches cracked in half as he stepped on them. He pushed past some lower ones that Carly and Spike probably were able to run under. As he walked into the clearing, he stopped short when he heard a voice he'd hoped to avoid for the rest of his life. Clearly, he'd pissed someone off in a former life because his ex-wife was less than three feet away. She had her phone held up to her ear and her back was turned to him.

"Did you bring it?" she asked. "I have him locked inside. We've run into a small complication." She paused and listened to the response before answering. "Don't worry, I've handled it and she won't be a problem for long. The dog is here too. They're secure. Don't keep me waiting."

Phil stood frozen as he stared at Addison. What was she talking about? Who was locked up and why did she feel the need to secure anyone? He should do something. Carly... Addison had to be talking about her and Spike. If they were locked up he had to find a way to free them. First he should do the proper thing and call for backup. Only a fool rushed in alone. But fuck—it killed him to step back into the trees for cover and wait. He reached into his pocket and pulled out his phone.

After three rings someone answered, "Name and Credentials."

"This is Agent Morrison, Phillip," he replied matter-offactly and shot off the necessary information to go along with it. "I need backup on the other side of the woods adjacent to Crescent Park. There is a building locked tight, unknown number of suspects within. They are holding Agent Gallagher, Carly hostage."

"Affirmative Agent Morrison," the person said. "Backup will arrive in fifteen. Wait for arrival before proceeding."

Like hell he would. He hung up the phone and scanned the area. Carly was in there and he was not going to leave her there. Backup could assist when they arrived. Addison must have gone back inside. He wished he'd thought to bring his gun because he feared he might need it. Addison may, or may not, be alone. She must have an advantage over Carly if she was able to lock her up. Was it Spike? Carly would do anything for the dog, but Phil hoped she would not put her life above the dog's.

The area appeared to be clear so he jogged quickly to the side of the building. He kept close to the side and eased his way to the entrance. The door was wide open so Carly and Spike must be locked up somewhere inside. It was dark and hard to see inside but he did not let that deter him. Phil slid inside as quietly as possible and made his way down a long hallway. At the sound of Addison's voice he halted and waited.

"What have you two been doing while I've been busy?" Addison asked.

"Did you think we'd lie down like cowards and let you win?" Carly laughed. "You don't know me very well if you believed that."

"As if I want to crawl around inside your head,"

Addison scoffed. "I wouldn't lower myself that far. You're nothing and will die as such."

Not if Phil had anything to say about it. How long had Addison been so hateful? He had stopped paying attention to her so long ago. Was she always like this and he dismissed it as nothing? It really didn't matter—what did matter was Carly and Spike. He would not allow Addison to harm them.

"Addy," he said softly. She turned toward him immediately, a gun in her hand.

"I should have known you would show up. Wherever she is you're following behind her like a trained puppy."

"What are you doing?" he asked. "This isn't you."

She laughed maniacally. "As if you ever truly knew me. You're an idiot, but you served your purpose."

He flinched at her words. What the hell did that mean? "Put the gun away. You don't want to hurt anyone." Phil inched forward closing the distance between them. If he could wrench the gun from her he'd be able stop anyone from getting hurt.

"As if I'd care if anyone was hurt," she said derisively. "As far as I'm concerned you all could die right now. The dog is all that matters."

"Why do you want Spike?"

Addison hated dogs. He had wanted to get one a while ago and she had thrown a fit. When Carly had taken Spike in he'd thought she was crazy because Addison had him convinced someone in their line of work did not have the time for a dog. Carly had proven him wrong. Sure, there were times she couldn't be there for the dog, but she'd made arrangements to see to his care.

"That dog has a computer chip imbedded in him," Addison explained. "It has all the information I need to make millions. It holds the key to accessing the nuclear missile codes. When I auction it off to the highest bidder, I'll be set for life and no one will see me again."

He stared at Addison through the darkness trying to make out her features. When had she lost her mind, but more importantly when had she decided being a traitor to their country trumped everything else? Addison was right, he had never truly known her and now he wasn't so sure he wanted to.

"Ouch," Addison screeched and fell to the ground. "You bitch."

"And darn proud of it," Carly said, then turned toward Phil brandishing the gun she'd taken from Addison. "Thanks for keeping her occupied."

He wanted to take credit for doing something good, but it wasn't as simple as that. Listening to Addison had been earth shattering. He'd been damn near useless through the whole exchange. He realized in those moments he was a poor judge of character and didn't know what to make of anything anymore.

"Yeah," he said absentmindedly. "Where's Spike?"

"Inside the room keeping Logan company. He wanted to help, but he's not in the best condition."

"Logan?" he had to have heard her wrong. Logan was dead.

"Yeah," she said. "I was as surprised as you are."

That was... How was he supposed to process any of this? Logan was alive? The very Logan that Carly had mourned so hard? She loved him. Had he lost her before he'd ever even had a real chance with her? Fate fucking hated him.

She'll never love him the way she loved Logan. He'd lost and he'd never recover from it.

"Go outside and wait for backup. They should be arriving soon. I'll make sure Addison doesn't go anywhere."

"Backup is coming?" she asked, surprise filling her voice. "I don't understand how you knew to come here and have backup follow you, but I'm grateful. I don't think Logan would survive in there much longer. He's so weak."

Logan. Logan. Logan. He shouldn't be jealous but he couldn't help how he felt. The man had probably been through hell and all Phil could think about was how he'd lost Carly.

"Go outside," he said again. "I'm just doing my job and it's not finished yet."

She nodded and did as he suggested. He kept his emotions in check because he did have a job to do. His ex-wife would pay for the tragedy she'd caused him. It was all her fault that he lost everything—if not for her scheming he'd never have believed he had a chance at happiness.

He kept his focus on her the entire time. Not once did he think to check on Logan or Spike. The rage burrowing inside of him had one thing to hold onto and there wasn't a chance in hell he was going to let that go. Addison, the bitch, would pay.

"Phil," Logan croaked out.

He was torn between helping him and keeping vigil over Addison.

"He doesn't sound too good," Addison mocked. "You don't want him to die now, do you?"

Phil ignored her as heartache burrowed deep into his soul. No, he didn't want Logan to die. He would help him at the expense of his own life. Nevertheless, he would have to make sure Addison could not escape before he did anything else. "Addy," he said with false sincerity. "Your kindness knows no bounds."

"Sarcasm doesn't suit you," she said evilly. "Though in time it could."

"Don't listen to her," Logan said. "She's an evil bitch."

Tell him something he did not know. He didn't reply to Logan because he didn't trust himself to not say something stupid. "You'll have plenty of time to hone your skills when you're locked up in a federal penitentiary. I'm sure you'll be fabulous at it too."

Footsteps echoed through the building as several men headed in their direction. Soon several agents were inside and taking charge of the situation. Phil left them in control and headed outside. Sunlight blinded him when he stepped out of the building. When his vision cleared, he searched for Carly. He found her talking to another agent animatedly. Her hands were flying in all directions. He headed toward her to make sure she was as unharmed as she appeared to be. Afterwards he'd go into the office and file paperwork to be transferred. He couldn't be near her and not be able to claim her. It would be too hard on him to watch her with Logan.

"The bat thought Spike had some computer chip in him. She'd been torturing Logan for a year trying to find it and finally he broke and told her it had been in his dog.

He thought Spike died in the blast or he'd never had told her that. She had someone break into my apartment to try to steal him. Spike somehow evaded them. It was pure luck we stumbled on the location she was holding Logan today. He's going to need a lot of medical care."

Phil swallowed a lump in his throat. He'd been married to her and he'd been blind to who she was and what she was capable of. Somehow this all seemed like his fault. How would he ever make it up to Carly and Logan? The agent Carly had been talking to nodded and walked off. She turned toward Phil and grinned, then launched herself into his arms. He caught her on instinct and breathed in her scent mentally memorizing it. Soon he wouldn't have the luxury of it surrounding him and he wanted to remember every part of her.

"I'm so glad you came," she wrapped her arms tightly around his neck. "I kept thinking that there was no hope and then like a miracle I heard your voice. You are my saving grace, you know that? Whatever trouble I find or somehow finds me I can count on you to see me through it. When I start to lose all hope I remind myself it isn't as bad as I thought because all I have to do is close my eyes and there'll you be. The one man who's been by my side through everything." She leaned back and met his gaze. "I love you."

It slammed through him like a boulder smashing over his entire body. "Could you repeat that? I don't think I heard you right."

She pressed her lips to his with a quick kiss. "It's not the best timing, but I can't keep it inside any longer. I've loved you for so long but I thought it was a lost cause.

Last night..." A blush stained her cheeks and she glanced down briefly. "It changed things. I had to tell you how I feel and I hope in time you can love me too."

Mere moments ago he had been making plans to leave and never look back. He had falsely believed she loved Logan. How had he read everything so wrong? Phil was seriously starting to doubt his observation skills, but he wasn't going to walk away from her. She said she loved him and he was not going to allow her to take that back.

His lips tilted upward. "I don't know," he said with amusement. "That's a huge thing to hope for. You're a lot of work..."

She tilted her head and studied him. "Are you messing with me?"

"Only a little bit," he replied and leaned down to whisper in her ear, "I love you more than I ever thought possible. Things happened so fast I'm afraid they could fall apart."

"We can make it work," she said. "Don't give up before we have had a chance."

He was so scared of losing her. If he did, he wasn't sure how he'd react. "All I can promise is that I'll love you through it all and beg you to have patience with me."

She smiled. "Those are reasonable terms. I accept."

Spike came running out of the building and circled around them. Carly laughed and picked up the leash still attached to his collar. "Let's take Spike home."

Those were the sweetest words he'd heard next to her admitting she loved him. The day was starting to look better and better, and if he was lucky enough their future would be even better.

"Sounds like a plan," he agreed. "Then we can go to the hospital to check on Logan. You're not going to rest until you do."

Her lips tilted upward. "You know me so well. It's going to be hard to let him out of my sight. It hurt so much when I believed he died."

He kissed her forehead. Not too long ago that would have hurt to hear, but now he knew she loved him, not Logan. What she felt for Logan was something entirely different. He's been so jealous he'd not recognized the friendship they shared for what it was. What a fool he'd been.

"Now you have him back. He's not going anywhere and neither am I."

Carly hugged him tighter. "You better not or I promise you'll regret it."

Phil chuckled lightly. That was his Carly—fierce to the bitter end. He could not have loved her more if he'd tried. How had he managed to get so lucky to fall in love with such an amazing woman? It was best not to question it and accept the gift he'd been given. Something Phil had every intention of doing for the rest of his life.

EPILOGUE

One year later...

"Carly," her sister, Harper, said exasperated. "I didn't go through the trouble of obtaining leave so I could watch you pace around the dressing room."

"The Navy can do without you for a day or two," Carly snapped. She might give her sister a hard time, but Carly was proud of her. She had climbed through the ranks of the Navy with sheer grit and determination.

"Shows what you know," her sister retorted. "If it wasn't classified I'd lay it all out and shove your face in it."

As an intelligence officer her sister's job was so super secret no one even knew it existed. All Harper had been able to tell her was that she'd been selected for the intelligence program. A part of her had been dying to say something teasing to that announcement, but she had held back.

"My apologies Captain," Carly saluted. "Forgive me for questioning your importance. Now stop harassing me and fix this," she demanded. She yanked on the back of her dress. A piece of lace was tangling by a thread. Harper rolled her eyes and pulled out a pair of scissors clipping it off. Carly glared up at her. "That was not what I meant and you know it."

The dress was supposed to be, well perfect. Slicing off a piece of it didn't make it that way. At least that particular area of the dress looked fine without the extra adornment. Carly glanced at herself in the floor length mirror admiring the dress. The skirt had sheer tulle panels with a white floral appliqué up to the bodice, surrounding a plunging vee neckline. The soft ivory accentuated her skin nicely.

"You'll be fine," she said. "You're perfect. Nothing else is going to go wrong."

It was her wedding day. In less than ten minutes, she would walk down the aisle and marry the man she loved. They had a rocky start but everything had improved after Addison had been taken into custody. Logan had healed, but he was so sad all the time. He was not the same man, and Carly feared he never would be. Something or someone would have to snap him out of it. Spike continued to live with Carly but Logan insisted on visitation rights. Carly gave them to him quite willingly.

Perhaps she was starting to turn into a monster. The only thing that truly mattered was Phil, and he would not care if there was a small piece missing from her dress. She would be willing to bet he wouldn't even notice it was gone. Especially as he hadn't even laid eyes on the dress yet.

A knock echoed through the room. Logan stepped

inside. A smile pasted on his face. "Look at you all dolled up. I never thought I'd see the day you willingly tied yourself to another man."

Carly hugged him tight, so glad to have him back in her life. "Shut up," she told him. "You're the one person who's always known how I felt about that man. You shouldn't be surprised."

"I'm not," he said. "Can't I mess with my best girl?"

He let her go and took a step back. He glanced at her and then slid his attention to Harper. "You both look lovely. Are you ready to do this? The natives are getting restless out there." Logan shoved his hands into his pockets, but not before Carly had seen them shaking. After being held hostage for over a year, he had been having trouble acclimating to society again. People in general made him nervous and crowds were even worse. She had kept the guest list small hoping to ease some of his discomfort. It would probably take a lot for him to start to be at ease around others. Having him at her wedding had been important to her. Phil knew how much Logan meant to her and asked him to be his best man. That way Carly could have her two favorite people, well besides Phil, standing by her side as she said her vows. It meant the world to her that both Harper and Logan were able to be in her wedding. "Unless you've changed your mind," he joked. "Say the word and I'll clear the church in a heartbeat."

Carly answered him with a huge grin. She had never been more ready for something in her entire life. When the day was done, she would be Mrs. Phillip Morrison. Well, she was not taking his last name, but he did not need to know that yet. She doubted he would argue too much about it anyway.

"We're ready," Carly said. "Tell them to get this show on the road."

He nodded and left the room. Harper's gaze had not left him the entire time he had been in the room. When she had a free moment she would question her sister about it, but she had more important things on her mind at the moment.

They exited the room and headed toward the chapel. Spike waited for them in the alcove. A basket laid next to him with a pillow nestled inside and two rings tied to it— he was the official ring bearer. He barked when he saw them. "Are you ready to do your part?" Carly leaned over and patted him on the head. When music filled the church, she kissed his golden fur and said, "You're up, Spike. Go do us proud."

He lifted the basket and trotted down the aisle. Carly laughed as she watched him wag his tail rapidly. When he reached the end Logan lifted the rings off the pillow and set the basket aside. Spike sat next to him and turned toward the aisle. Harper walked down, and then Carly followed behind her. Her gaze never left Phil's the entire time she strolled down the aisle.

This what she'd been wanting for so long—to belong to him. He was where she always needed him to be. Now she did not have to close her eyes to picture their happiness together. Now all she had to do was lift her gaze and there he'd be waiting for her with open arms. There was nothing more perfect than the love they shared.

One Heart
to Give

Heart's Intent
Book One

Dawn Brower

EXCERPT: BETTER AS A MEMORY

BEGIN AGAIN BOOK TWO

PROLOGUE

*B*elle brushed her hand down the skirt of her black cocktail dress. The ballroom of the hotel where the fundraiser was being held was decorated in high style. She hated these events her parents insisted she attend. Her father, Wentworth Brennan, was a United States senator. She'd gotten used to attending the tedious events early on in her life. That didn't mean she'd ever grown to like them. This one would be no different than any of the others.

"Hello, dear." Her mother, Adria Brennan, leaned down and kissed her cheek. "I'm glad you were able to attend tonight. Has work been keeping you too busy to pay us a visit?"

She grimaced at her mother's condescending tone. Adria didn't approve of her occupation. Belle worked as an emergency room doctor at the local hospital in Castle-berry. It kept her busy and she loved the constant adrenaline rush involved. She couldn't imagine doing anything else. Her mother thought it was beneath her. It wasn't being a doctor she objected to. It was not having a prestigious doctor in the family. Belle had a lowly position at the hospital without any real ambition to climb to a higher one. A different specialty would have been better, anything other than a general surgeon. It was, in her mother's mind, uncouth. Her daughter should rise higher and do better. She came from one of the best families, and there were expectations.

"Everything is fine at work, and yes I've been busy." Belle glanced around the room and spotted a gorgeous man sipping a glass of champagne. His dark hair curled around his ears enticingly, and his gaze left her breathless. He was staring at her, and her mother. At least it appeared as if he was. She could be wrong. With a quick glance she surveyed her surroundings. No, there wasn't anyone else near enough for it to be anyone else. Who was he?

"Are you listening to me?" her mother demanded.

"Hmm?" she said absentmindedly. The man called to her on a level she didn't understand, and wasn't sure if she wanted to. He might make this evening worthwhile after all. She'd have to introduce herself later, after she made sure to speak to both her parents. "I think I'll go say hello to father."

After she hugged her mother she turned on her heels to leave. She didn't want to give her mother any reason to keep talking. Belle had heard it all before. Why should she listen to her tirade any longer? It had been old before and now it was ridiculous. She loved her mother, but that didn't mean she had to follow a path of her design. This was her life and she'd live it as she chose, not how her mother wanted her to.

Belle strolled over to her father's side and waited for him to quit speaking. He turned toward her and smiled. "I didn't see you come in. Have you been here long?"

"No. I arrived a short time ago." She gestured to the room in general. "This is a huge turnout. What's the cause this time?"

Her father was as far from a corrupt politician as one could get. He supported a lot of liberal causes that put the conservatives on edge. He was big on preserving the environment and cutting down this generation's carbon footprint. It was one of the things that appealed to the voters. He was charismatic and had big ideas. Those ideas kept him in office, and they evolved with whatever he deemed necessary to the preservation of the country he loved. Sometimes she wondered what her parent's saw in each other. They were two totally different people.

"This one is to raise awareness to a number of environmental concerns. There is also a few endangered species I want to bring attention to." He grinned. "If you get me going on this topic you won't be able to shut me up."

"You're enthusiastic about it." She smiled back at him. "I see nothing wrong with that."

Her father was amazing, but he never had a lot of time for her. His causes always pulled him way from the family. She rarely saw her parents when she was growing up. It wasn't a bad childhood. Belle had everything she could possibly want or need. Except attention from the two people who had brought her into the world. She'd accepted it, mostly. They meant well and they loved her in their own way. That was all that counted.

"Pardon me, Senator Brennan," a man interrupted. He was glancing around the room with agitation. "I was wondering if you had a moment to speak privately."

"I'm sorry this isn't a good time," her father stated. "Please set up an appointment and I'll gladly speak with you in my office."

The man sighed and shook his head. "I've already tried that. Your secretary said you don't have any immediate openings. Please, sir, it's important."

Her father nodded, resigned, to dealing with him. "I'm sorry, dear. We'll catch up later."

"Don't worry about it. I know how to entertain myself." Belle sadly, did. This sort of thing happened more often than not. Perhaps she should seek out the gentleman who'd been staring at her earlier. His gaze had promised entertainment. She could use a diversion. After scanning the room and being unable to locate him she became resigned to another boring evening.

Why did she even come to these functions anymore? She should go home and kick her shoes off. Days off didn't come around often enough for her to enjoy as it was. She'd already handled all the niceties by speaking with both her parents. In all honesty she could leave and call it good. They'd not bother her any more that evening. An appearance was all that was required of her. She grabbed a glass of champagne off the tray of a nearby waiter and downed it. She set it on a different waiter's tray passing by, and grabbed another. She sent up a silent thanks for her parents' belief in having plenty of wait staff on hand for their fundraisers. One was always nearby when a drink was needed.

"What are we drinking to?"

Belle turned toward the man she'd been thinking of a few moments prior. Damn he was sneaky and quiet. Where had he come from? "My freedom for the evening. You?"

"I'm not much for drinking."

She wanted to call bullshit, but refrained. It hadn't been her imagination that he'd been nursing his own glass of champagne earlier. Though she supposed he could have not finished it. Maybe he'd grabbed a glass for show. These events could be rather tedious and boring. Sometimes it helped to have something to hold onto.

"Your loss." She grinned. "I rather enjoy a good glass of champagne every now and then."

He lifted it from her hands and set it aside. "Why drink when you can do other things to make you feel just as pleasurable."

Belle shivered at his words. More pleasurable indeed—what did he have in mind? *Down girl—you don't even know his name.* "I agree." She licked her lips. "However I don't have anything else to elicit such feelings so I'm opting for a known quantity."

Let's see what he takes from that. She itched to pick her champagne glass back up and take a sip. She resisted, but only because what she really wanted was to put her hands on his chest and see if he felt as good as he looked. When had she turned into a wanton? What was it about this man that made her want to throw all caution to the wind and take a chance? This was not her, and yet she liked it.

His steel grey eyes filled with something she couldn't quite identify. Desire? Interest? Whatever it was it made

341

her tingle from the inside out. "Maybe I can help you with that."

She bet he could. He was so damn delectable. "Why sir I'm not that kind of lady." She leaned into him and ran her hand across his jacket. "At least not without a proper introduction first."

"What's the fun in that?" He leaned down and whispered in her ear. His hot breath caressed her cheek. "Don't you like a little mystery?"

Ah hell. He was smooth. "Does this usually work for you?"

He chuckled lightly. "Yes, actually it does."

Belle believed him. She was about to throw herself into his arms and beg him to take her in front of everyone. Her body lit up hotter and brighter than a firework on the 4th of July. What would it hurt to give in and take what she wanted? His words promised they could enjoy each other and leave any and all expectations behind. Could she do it? She might need a little more liquid courage to throw away all her inhibitions. She glanced up and was mesmerized once again by the gray pools of his eyes. All she had to do was reach up and she could run her fingers through his dark tresses. Would he let her? Ah, yes, he would. He wanted her to give in and take what he was offering.

"Your offer does sound—intriguing," she replied. "I'm not sure it's for me though."

"Oh sweetheart," he said huskily. "You're the only one it could ever be for. Don't think, just feel."

He leaned down and brushed his lips across hers. A rush of tingles spread throughout her entire body. The jolt pushed her forward and she gave in. She wrapped her arms around him and allowed herself to become lost in his kiss. Working in the hospital drained her and left her without any motivation to do anything other than crash in her bed. This man did things to her that she'd never experienced before. She wanted all of it.

The kiss ended as abruptly as it began. He stepped back and lifted his hand to caress her cheek. "Let's get out of here."

She should say no. It wasn't a wise choice to leave with a man she didn't know. "Where would we go?"

His lips twitched into a smile. "As luck would have it I have a room here. Say the word and I'll take you there." He leaned down, his nose touching hers. "I promise you won't regret it."

That showed how little he knew her. She'd regret it, dissect it, and question every part of it. It would bother her until the day she died. The very fact she was contemplating going through with it was so out of character for her she might as well be someone else entirely. He was so enticing, and out of her league. His touch was magic and she wanted to drown herself in it.

Was she really going to do this? Yes, absolutely she was. For once she'd take something she wanted and the consequences be damned. "Lead the way, Mr. Mysterious." She promised herself she wouldn't think to hard about what she was about to do. If she did she'd back out of it. So she focused on what she wanted. One night where she'd have all of him, and he'd have all of her. Tomorrow wasn't always promised after all. So she'd take it and keep it as a treasured memory.

"Thank Heavens."

He didn't wait for her to change her mind. The enigmatic man pulled her hand into his and led her away from the ball room. The time for conversation had ended and the promise of something wonderful awaited her on the horizon. They rushed to his room. He caressed her every step of the way. In the elevator he kissed her breathless. In the hall outside his room he pushed her against the wall and ran his hands up the skirt of her dress. Her body was alight with sensation. It took a long time for them to even make it into his room and make good use of the bed inside. It was wild, thrilling, and more than she could have ever imagined.

Every part, every inch, and every single touch was perfect.

It truly was. That night was one she'd never forget. He kept every one of those promises he made and then some. She was loved in so many different ways she'd lost count. Her body ached in a good way. He was an amazing lover, and he ruined her for all other men.

Somewhere in the aftermath of passion and the contentment only found after truly unforgettable loving she'd thought she heard him whisper, "I'm better as a memory than as your man…"

Then he left without a word. It broke her heart into a million pieces. He promised she wouldn't regret the night in his arms. In a way he was right. She'd not have traded it for anything in the world, but she did regret one thing.

Belle never did get his name.

CHAPTER 1

*C*ain Dempsey studied the scene in front of him. His partner at the FBI laid sprawled out on the office floor. Blood oozed from a bullet wound to the head and pooled around him. Fuck. It was a damn mess. They'd been deep undercover in a covert mission, and apparently their cover had been blown. The members of the Garcia syndicate had to be hunting for him. Steve's death was a clear indication of trouble waiting for him. How could he have allowed this to happen? He was usually so careful. There was no helping it. There was only one choice he had left. It was time to bail and take cover. If he couldn't get away from Carlos Garcia's home he'd be a dead man.

He eased his way down the hallway making sure to make as little sound as possible. When he arrived at the end he stopped and listened. There were voices in the distance. Each step would take him away from danger, but it was fraught with it as he continued on. Which way to go? The voices seemed to be moving away. He breathed a sigh of relief and turned the corner. He made it to the patio door and slid it open, exiting quickly. The night sky was dark the only light that shown was from the moon. He'd be able to get clear and disappear into the night.

"Well, look what I found." Bruno Santiago whistled. "Boss's looking for you. He has a few questions."

Cain stilled at Bruno's voice. He'd been close to escaping damn it. "Oh?" He turned toward him with a raised eyebrow. "What's he want to talk about."

If he had to hazard a guess it probably had something to do with Steve's dead body and his connections to the FBI. Either way Cain wasn't about to stick around and find out—he rather enjoyed breathing. There was no way around it. He'd have to disable Bruno and make his way to the boat house and grab a speed boat. The fastest way to escape was across Lake Ryn. Once he was on the other side he could make his way to his hidey hole to grab his gear.

"It's not your place to ask the questions." Bruno glared at him. "Come with me and you'll find out all you want to know."

Nope. Not happening. He'd be dead before he had a chance to do anything. Bruno was not forcing him back into the house. If he went inside he'd not be coming back out. Ever. "Do we have to do this now? I have an appointment in town."

"I bet you do." Bruno sneered. "I'm afraid you won't be making it."

Yup. If there was any doubts that his cover was blown Bruno's attitude made it crystal clear. What had tipped the crime lord off? There had to have been some sort of slip up for them to have been made. Whatever it was Cain would have to figure it out later. He had to get away and report to his superiors about all of it, not to mention Steve's death.

"I'd rather not. It's important."

"That's too bad." Bruno pulled out a gun and pointed it at Cain. "Start moving."

"Is the gun really necessary?" Cain froze and studied Bruno for a few quick seconds. He could disable him if he played it right. First he'd have to get the gun from him. After that he could knock him out and make a break for the boat house. He took a step toward Bruno, and put more distance between him and the house.

"Yes it is, and I believe you're well aware why."

Cain took another step forward. If he kept him talking he might not realize what he was up to. Bruno wasn't the brightest person to begin with. He could use that to his advantage. "I'm clueless actually. Why don't you explain it to me?" He took another step.

"What are you doing?" Bruno asked. "I told you to get moving." He gestured toward the house.

"I am moving." Cain smiled menacingly. "In the direction of my choosing."

He acted with swift precise movements. His hand wrapped around Bruno's wrist and yanked. The gun went off, a bullet hitting him in his side. The pain burned through him, but he fought through it. The fight was quicker than it seemed. Bruno was sprawled out on the back yard unconscious. His gun laid firmly in Cain's grip.

Cain glanced around the yard quickly and then bolted toward the boat house. The gunshot would alert everyone and they'd come running soon to see what the commotion was about. He couldn't be there when they arrived. He rushed to the nearby speed boat and started it. He saw movements from behind him, but he was already well on his way across the lake before they could reach him. Gunfire could be heard in the distance. They were trying to shoot him, or the boat, he couldn't be sure. Either way it was a near thing.

He was already bleeding from the wound he received fighting with Bruno. Cain couldn't afford any more wounds. It was a battle to stay focused on his escape. If he lost consciousness he was a dead man—a sitting duck for Carlos Garcia to swoop in and take back to torture for information. He refused to give the bastard any kind of leverage, and allow the man to murder another innocent.

Not that Cain was innocent. He'd done a lot in his life he wished he'd done different. A flash of dark hair burnished with caramel highlights, and ocean blue eyes flashed before him. Why was he thinking about her now? She was never far from his thoughts. He wanted her more than he wanted anything. He'd had one night with her, and in truth it would never be enough. It had to be though. She deserved more than what he had to offer.

His life was wrought with danger and he refused to bring it to her door. No, she was far better off not knowing who he was and how much he'd grown to care for her in a short time. One night and she'd become more essential to him than his own life. It's why he left without a word. She might not see it that way, but he'd been protecting her. What she didn't know wouldn't hurt her.

Cain steered the boat toward the dock. He stopped beside it and killed the engine. He tied the rope around the post and hopped out. The pack he hid with his gear was by a nearby lake house. He didn't know who the house belonged to. He knew it was rarely used. That was what made it a good place to stash it. He checked his surroundings making sure there would be no surprises. There was nothing and no one around the lake. The summer season was ending and most of the houses were closing up for winter. That would make things easier for him. No one around to report his whereabouts and he could get out of town without incident.

His breathing became more ragged with each step he took. "Fuck and Damnation," he swore. "I have to keep moving."

The house was a few more yards up the hill. He cleared the hill and leaned against a tree to catch his breath. He turned and froze. There was a light on in the house. No one came to the lake house this time of the year. Who could be occupying it? This would complicate things. He didn't have time to wait for them to go to bed for the night. He had to leave the area right then. There was no choice. He had to try to be as quiet as possible and grab his bag without them noticing. Easier said than done. Cain hobbled toward the back porch. The back pack was stashed underneath it. He pushed a board aside and reached in to pull it out. The pain from the actions sent him reeling backward. He hit his head against the porch as the back pack came forward with him.

The ground spun underneath him. He'd been doing so well up until that point. Now he couldn't see two steps in front of him. Hell, he might actually pass out. Breathe

Cain, breathe. The ground kept moving no matter what he did and he fell fully to the ground.

A door creaked open and thuds filled the air as the occupant of the house stepped down the porch. "Who's out there?"

Shit. He knew that voice. Maybe he was hallucinating. He glanced up and met her gaze in the moonlight. "Are you real?" He winced with pain and clutched his arm around his waist. The wound may be worse than he'd thought it was.

His dream woman froze and stared down at him. She frowned as she studied him. "You're hurt." No shit. She was observant. *Not her fault, don't take it out on her.* She leaned over him and brushed the back of her hand over his forehead. "And you're burning up. Come on let's get you inside."

"You and who else is going to make that happen? I don't think I can move."

He'd come this far, and he should be more willing to aide her in her plan to help him inside, but he didn't want to endanger her. If he stayed by her side he'd be doing that. He left her three months ago to save her from a situation like this one. What kind of hypocrite would he be to put her right in the middle of it all now? Cain was human enough to admit he was glad to see her. He'd never thought to lay eyes on her again. Now she was here before him and just as beautiful as he remembered.

"Quit being a baby and stand up." She shook her head. "You can do it."

Well when she put it like that... Cain stood up and wobbled on his feet. She stepped beside him and braced him as he walked up the steps. They made it inside and to the living room before he fell again. This time at least he landed on the couch.

"What happened to you?" she asked.

Blood stained his shirt. Not that he could tell it was blood against his dark blue shirt, but he knew he'd been shot and the dark stain was clearly a result. "Nothing I can't handle. The pack outside go get it. I have a phone inside. I need to contact someone for an extraction."

She put her hands on her hip and glared to him. "I'm not here for you to order me around. How are you hurt? I can help."

She probably could. Except he didn't want her to. He'd researched her and had extensive knowledge of her credentials as a doctor. She was one of the best emergency doctors in the country. He could trust her with his life. The problem was he didn't trust her in his general vicinity. "I need one thing from you. Go get my pack."

"You're an asshole." She rolled her eyes. "If it's so important to you get it yourself."

He leaned forward and winced as the pain shot through him again. He fell back against the couch. If she didn't get his pack he was stuck in the lake house with her. There had to be a way to make her see reason. "I think I liked you better before."

"Ditto." She glared at him. "You were much more fun when you weren't being a dick."

His lips twitched into a smile. He adored her. "Please get my pack."

"No."

"Why the hell not?" His mouth fell open in shock. "I asked nicely."

She sighed. "You're not going anywhere. It's clear you're injured." She rushed to the other side of the room and grabbed a bag. "Take your shirt off." She came back to his side and set the bag down.

"As much as I'd love to get naked with you—" He couldn't resist teasing her. Cain knew she had something else in mind, but she looked so damn beautiful when she blushed, in pleasure and in anger. He wanted to see her cheeks stained a pretty pink "—I'm not in any condition for that kind of fun."

She didn't say a word, only glared until he complied. So she was going for the no nonsense approach. Cain could appreciate it. His injury was smarting, and a doctor should look at it. He reached down to pull his shirt up, but couldn't get it past his chest. The pain coursed through him and he slumped back from the exertion.

"Here let me."

She pulled out a pair of angled scissors and cut the shirt away. He stared down at his ruined shirt and frowned. "Well that's one way of handling it."

"It's efficient." She stared at the bullet wound in his side. "The good news is the bullet went clean through, and the injury isn't serious. It's more or less a flesh wound. I'm going to have to dress and clean it though to prevent infection."

"Are you now?" He raised an eyebrow. "You see gunshot wounds often?" Of course she'd have to have seen some—an E.R. doctor had to deal with numerous situations. She didn't even flinch at the sight of the hole in his side.

She pulled out items from her bag and set them aside. "More than I'd like." She worked in silence after that until his wound was cleaned and covered. "You're going to need something else to wear. I will grab one of my father's shirts for you. He keeps some things here. I'm also going to get a glass of water and then I want you to take these." She pulled out a bottle of pills and set them on the table. "You're burning up and I'm afraid the wound might get infected. Your fever needs to be managed. If it worsens you'll need antibiotics and I didn't come prepared to handle anything serious."

He hoped it wouldn't come to that, but he planned on being gone before she had to worry about his condition. She left the room before he could say another word. When she came back she had his pack, a black t-shirt, and a glass of water. She held the water in front of him and said, "Here drink this." Cain set the water on a nearby table, taking the pills could wait until later.

Belle set the pack on the other side of the room out of his reach. "You can have this tomorrow after you're rested. Here put this on." She tossed the shirt next to him on the couch. He lifted it and slowly pulled it over his head. Cain winced with pain, but managed to get his arms through the sleeves and smooth the shirt over his stomach.

"When did you become so bossy?" he asked. "I don't remember that about you."

"You don't know me. How could you?" She raised an

eyebrow. "We had one night and we didn't exactly exchange information."

They hadn't, but he knew who she was, Belle Brennan. The daughter of Senator Brennan, and the one woman he'd thought about laying it all on the line for. "I knew enough." At least he thought he had.

"Really?" She snorted. "You must not need to know much before taking a woman to bed. I'll leave you to rest." She turned to leave.

"Only with you," he replied. "Don't go, Belle."

She stopped in her tracks. "How is it you know my name, but never felt the need to share yours with me? Mr. Mysterious, it doesn't exactly seem fair."

Cain was drifting off. He was having a hard time fighting it. The pain and the excursion to escape was taking its toll. "Better that way. Protects you."

"Bullshit," she said. "But I won't fight you on it now. Get some rest. You'll need it if you're going to heal."

She spun on her heels and left him alone. He wanted to call her back, but it was for the best she left. If he stayed around she'd be in danger. With her out of the room he could get to his pack and make the call for someone to come get him. In a matter of hours he'd be out of her life again.

ONE HEART TO GIVE

USA *TODAY* BESTSELLING AUTHOR
DAWN BROWER

ACKNOWLEDGMENTS

This book wouldn't be what it is without my fabulous editor. Big thanks to Victoria for helping me create a better story.

Thanks to Elizabeth for being my awesome proof-reader. I appreciate all you do for me.

In life we are faced with many choices. One of the best choices I made was starting to write. Above that the only thing that tops it is my two boys. Luke and Nathan I love you so much and you are truly the biggest blessing and best thing to come into my life. This book, more than any I've written, holds a piece of me in it. We all have that one person we let get away. This story is for those that play the what if game and wonder what might have happen if they'd taken a different path.

ONE HEART TO GIVE

When tragedy strikes Dani's business partner it brings Ren back into her life. She'd thought she moved past her feelings for him, but one glance and they come flooding back.

Growing up as an orphan, Daniella Brosen has trouble connecting with other people. She has no room for anyone in her life, except her best friend, Rendall Sousa. He is the only male she's ever loved or will love. Circumstances beyond her control tear them apart, and she has no choice but to leave him behind.

When Daniella left without a word it broke Ren's heart. If she'd given him a chance he'd have told her how much he loved her. Dani was everything to him, but she made her choice. There was only one course of action left to him—move on without her.

As their lives become intertwined again, can Ren convince her he's always loved her or will she push him away forever?

PROLOGUE

Ten years earlier

*D*aniella spun around in her prom dress. The dark green gown shimmered in the sunlight streaming through her bedroom window. She didn't have a date. It should bother her, but it didn't. There was one boy she wanted to go with: her best friend, Rendell Sousa. Ren was so handsome, strong, and perfect in every way. The only downside was he had a girlfriend. She hated Jessica Clarke. The girl owned a part of him Dani never would.

She'd planned on skipping prom, but Ren had talked her into going. He said he could have two dates. It would have been easier to say no... He made it impossible to turn him down, stating he couldn't go to prom without both his girls. Jessica wouldn't be happy at the idea of sharing Ren, and Dani didn't want to upset her by going along with his plan. She told him no until he agreed to arrange for a group of friends to join them. Even with that idea, Dani decline anyway. Ren was insistent and too persuasive for her to resist. Not having a dress wouldn't even be a deterrent.

He'd talked Sarah, another friend of theirs, into taking her shopping. Dani had dipped into her savings, using the money meant for college to pay for it. Her foster family didn't help her with anything they didn't deem necessary. A prom dress was not high on that list, like most things Dani may want or even need. It was why she worked after school most days.

Now she stood in front of her bedroom mirror, admiring the green satin dress. It was worth it. The dress was amazing and it made her feel like a fairytale princess. She glanced at the clock and hurried to finish the last minute preparations. Ren would be by to pick her up at any moment.

"Dani," her foster mother yelled. "Ren is here."

"Time to face the music." She ran her hands over her dress to ease her nerves. Would he like what he saw? It wouldn't matter. She couldn't let it because Ren had a girlfriend. She started down the stairs and stopped at the bottom. Ren looked gorgeous in his tux. He'd opted for a white jacket with a black tie. It wasn't the usual black penguin suit almost every other boy would no doubt choose to wear. He looked amazing and absolutely gorgeous. His rich golden brown hair was brushed back and his wicked grin made him even more devastating.

"Are you ready?" he asked. "Jessica's already in the car."

She nodded and let him lead her out the door. This was foolish. Dani hated being the third wheel on his date. It didn't matter that a group of friends were going together. She would end up between Ren and Jessica in some way. He wouldn't allow her to essentially be a wall-flower. He had always been protective of her. She should have said no. It would have been better for them both if she had. Why had she let him talk her into this? Jessica would do something to make her miserable. Ren didn't see her the way Dani did. Her viperous tongue only came out when Ren wasn't around to hear it. Jessica made sure they were in private when her worst came out to play.

"Are you excited?" Stupid question. Why would he be?

"I'm looking forward to dancing with you later." He smiled softly. "And with Jessica too."

Dani frowned. Why did he feel the need to add that part in? Of course he would look forward to dancing with his girlfriend. He didn't need to remind her of that. Tiny pinpricks of pain shot through her heart. She couldn't let him know how much it hurt her to see him with Jessica. He deserved to be happy. She chose this path. He was her best friend, and she wanted him to be happy. She'd smile and fake it as long as she could. Ren didn't need to know she'd fallen in love with him. The burden was hers and hers alone.

He opened the door to the limo. She peeked inside and let out a relieved breath. A group of their friends were already inside. Most of them were also dateless. At least she didn't have to suffer in awkward silence while they picked everyone up. Ren must have saved her for last. She waved at them and hopped in. She sat across from Ren and Jessica next to another male friend of theirs. It didn't take long for the car to get to their destination. Prom was being held at the Tempest Ballroom on the opposite side of town. It was where it was always held. Ren was the first out of the limo and helping all the girls out.

"I forgot to tell you how pretty you look," he said as he held his hand out to her. "You're going to break some hearts in there."

She laughed. "I doubt it."

His gaze seemed to go unfocused for a second before he shook his head. Something bothered him; whatever it was he was holding it inside. "Trust me on this."

She wouldn't push. The night was supposed to be fun. If he wanted to tell her he would. For now, they would go inside and enjoy the evening. "If you say so." She shrugged. "I'm not holding my breath."

"Can we go inside now?" Jessica whined. "You're supposed to be my date." She glared at Dani, letting her gaze roll over her as if she'd witnessed something disgusting.

Ren turned to her and pulled her into his arms. He placed a quick kiss on her lips. "And that I am. Let's go see what the fuss is all about." He held out his arm to Dani. "You coming?"

She shook her head. "Give me a minute. I'll be in later. Take Jessica inside."

He frowned. "Are you sure?"

She didn't want to explain that she needed time to build up her strength. It would take all she had to get through the evening of their lovey dovey affection. She couldn't stand Jessica, and that wasn't only because the other girl had something she wanted. Jessica was mean and spiteful. For the life of her, Dani couldn't figure out what Ren saw in her.

"Go." She pushed at him. "I'll be fine. Promise."

He stared at her for a few seconds and then nodded in agreement. Dani breathed a sigh of relief as she watched them go.

"Why aren't you going inside?" Brian asked. He was one of the friends who'd traveled with them in the limo. "Something preventing you from entering? Did Cinderella already lose her shoe?"

"Ha. Ha," Dani mocked. "I'm far from the unwanted stepsister." No she was plain unwanted. Her mother had tossed her aside when she was a little girl, left her on a church doorstep for someone to find. She'd never know who her real parents were. They probably had been teenagers with no ability to care for her.

"Why don't you push her out of the way and claim your prince," Brian asked. "You know you want to."

She scrunched up her nose and winced. "Ren is not my prince." He never would be.

"Maybe not. But don't you think it's time to admit that there's more than friendship between the two of you?"

Was Brian drunk? There was, and always would be, nothing but friendship between her and Ren. She was all right with that. Honestly she was. *Yeah, keep saying that Dani, maybe one day you will convince yourself it's true.* She loved him. Unfortunately, he loved Jessica. Maybe it was time she put some distance between her and Ren. Being around him hurt too damn much, and she wasn't strong enough to handle it. Graduation loomed on the horizon. She'd make a break for it and not look back.

"Deny it all you want. It's not my place to convince you. Come on, let's go inside."

Nothing would persuade her. Ren loved Jessica. Dani wouldn't get between them. She followed Brian inside and steeled herself to pretend to be happy.

REN WATCHED for her to enter. He didn't know why she refused to come inside with him and Jessica, but he worried. If she didn't show up soon he'd go look for her. The dress she'd chosen was sinful on her perfect body. The shimmering green matched her eyes, and her dark midnight tresses fell down her shoulder in curls. He wanted to run his hands through her hair and feel the silky softness. Why couldn't he feel that way about Jessica? She was nice enough, and lovely to look at. He'd started dating her to try to take his mind off the one he wanted, his best friend. Dani had said over and over how much she appreciated him. She was glad they were friends and she could rely on him—how lost she'd be without their friendship. It grated on his nerves every time those words came out of her mouth. Didn't she see how much he wanted her? Dani owned his heart. If only she wanted to be more than friends...

But she didn't, and why not date Jessica? At least she saw him as boyfriend material. Sometimes he regretted that choice. All right, most days he did, and he'd almost broken up with her several times. Then Dani would repeat her friendship tirade. Nothing pissed him off more and made him dig his feet in with innate stubbornness than listening to that. He shouldn't let it bother him, but he couldn't help what he felt. In truth, he wasn't doing himself, Jessica, or Dani any favors by denying them. Both girls deserved better, and soon he'd own up to everything. When the time was right he'd break up with Jessica and be honest with Dani. Prom night wasn't the night for shattering hearts and confessions.

Ren frowned as she walked in with Brian. Were they seeing each other? He'd thought they were friends, but he could be wrong. Jealousy welled up inside of him. He clenched his fists at his side. He would not make a scene. If Brian was the one Dani wanted, he wouldn't get in her way. He had a girlfriend, and he shouldn't be mooning over his best friend. She would be the first to tell him that.

"Come on, let's dance." Jessica pulled him toward the dance floor.

He allowed it and did the best he could to pretend Dani wasn't staring at another boy. He wanted her, always had. It hurt to watch her with someone else, especially since she'd never seemed interested in someone else. She didn't date, said it was a waste of her time. She had plans and a boyfriend would deter them. Dani worked hard at everything so she could leave their small town behind and never look back. Had she changed her mind? Did she consider dating an option now? Maybe he could finally convince her they should be more than friends. He gulped back the lump in his throat and glanced down at Jessica. She seemed so happy and carefree. The strands of music ended and everyone broke apart. Ren didn't want to dance any longer. He had to find Dani. It was an impulse he couldn't resist. She was on the other side of the room laughing with Brian. He headed toward them, Jessica close behind.

"I see you made it inside," he said.

Dani smiled. "Did you think I'd get lost?"

He pasted a happy expression on his face. She didn't need to know he'd worried. "Of course not."

"They have some awful punch and snacks set out." Brian gestured toward a table nearby. "I damn near spit the crap out. I barely managed to swallow it, and choked it down. Dani thought it was hilarious."

"Oh, come on." She laughed again. "It couldn't be that bad."

Ren gritted his teeth together. He had to do something to stop this…whatever it was between Brian and Dani. He couldn't take it. It was time to stop fooling himself. He wanted to step back and let her be happy with someone else, but in reality it was impossible. The strands of a slow song started to fill his ears. He held his hand out to his best friend. "Come dance with me."

She nodded and placed her hand in his. "Oh yes, please, I love this song."

He didn't stop to look at anyone. His gaze was locked firmly on Dani's face. He didn't care if Brian was mad he'd usurped his time with her. Jessica knew Dani was his best friend. This wasn't the first time they'd danced, and she'd understand. Well, as much as any girl would he supposed. Ren couldn't make himself care. This was what he wanted and the rest of them be damned. He glanced across the room and noticed there were a lot of people dancing with someone they'd not arrived with. It was perfectly normal for him to enjoy a dance with someone other than Jessica. It was high school and prom was supposed to be fun—a memory they'd keep forever.

Let me love you... He wanted to say that to her. The song wasn't a perfect fit. But he wanted to say some of those very words to her. She deserved to be cherished. They swayed to the music. She glanced up at him and stole his breath. For a moment, he could pretend they were together and had a future together. He wanted to give her everything, show her the way love was supposed to be. He wanted to hold her as more than a friend.

The music ended and they stood there, staring at each other. Everything else ceased to exist. It was just the two of them locked in beautiful moment he wanted to burn in his memory. Her full sultry lips tilted into a brilliant smile, and her gaze radiated happiness. It left him with a warm and fuzzy glow spreading through his whole body. Until the spell was broken by his actual girlfriend—Jessica always did have the worst timing.

"It's my turn," Jessica demanded and pushed Dani aside.

For a brief moment, everything had been so perfect. The smile on Dani's face fell before she turned to head off the dance floor. He reached for her, but Jessica demanded his attention. Dani was all the way across the room before he could do anything to stop her. The dance had been worth every second of the clinginess he was about to endure from his girlfriend. She said she understood his friendship with Dani, but if he paid any amount of attention to her, Jessica ultimately became jealous.

He understood it, even as it irritated him. He couldn't blame her. They were dating, but he wouldn't stop being Dani's friend, even if it tore at him in every possible way. Ren glanced across the room and located Dani. He couldn't go after her to see what was wrong, at least not yet. He would later when he could shake Jessica for a few minutes.

"Finally," Jessica complained. "I thought that song would never end. I don't know why you feel as if you need to placate her."

Ren clenched his hand into a fist at his side and reminded himself Jessica didn't understand. She didn't realize he loved Dani in a way he could never love her. It was time to break up with her. Not at the dance, but definitely before graduation in a couple weeks. He'd tell Dani how much he loved her. It was time to man up and own his feelings.

DANI PUSHED her way into the girl's restroom and sighed in relief when she found it empty. She needed a breather from the hot dance floor and Jessica's glaring eyes. Every time she looked over at Ren, she would meet Jessica's gaze. The girl had every right to hate her. Ren tended to drop everything if Dani needed him for any reason. That's what friends did for each other. Dani didn't want to make him stop either, and yes, she depended on him. He was the only one she let get even remotely close to her.

She loved him.

The dance had been perfect. For a small moment in time she could pretend they were more than friends. That she allowed him to be hers in every way she wanted him to be. It had all come to a screeching halt when Jessica stormed over to them at the end. The spell had been broken and she had to go back to being his best friend.

Dani headed over to the sink, turned it on, allowing the cool water to run over her fingers. She splashed a little on her heated cheeks. It felt amazing washing over her warm skin. She turned the water off, grabbed a paper towel to dry her hands, and then tossed it in a nearby trash can. It was time to go back to the dance and pretend everything was all right.

"I saw you come in here, and I think it's time you and I have a little talk."

Dani spun around and met Jessica's gaze. She wanted to groan, but repressed it. At some point she should have known Jessica would confront her. She always did. Ren's girlfriend would spout out her demands to leave him alone and then drive home the final point—*she* was his girlfriend, not Dani. As if Dani needed the reminder. Maybe she did on some level. She hated sharing him. It grated on her in so many ways. She made her choices though, and now had the pleasure of living with them. Dani grimaced as she swallowed down that bitter pill. Pleasure? It was far from it.

"I think you've said everything you need to say to me." Dani turned away from her. "You say it so often I could repeat it verbatim."

"No. I haven't said all there is to say." Jessica pushed Dani's shoulder. "Look at me."

Dani rolled her eyes and turned back to Jessica. What did she want now? Did she really feel the need to mark her territory again? And yeah, in Jessica's mind Ren was hers to mark. He couldn't be friends with Dani while he dated her. Yes, Dani loved him, but she never made a move on him. She kept things strictly platonic. That was the whole meaning of friendship after all. Anything else would muddy the waters, and she could lose what little she did have with him forever. It was why she insisted at the beginning they be just friends. Friendships lasted far longer than any other relationship.

"What do you want?" Dani folded her arms across her chest. "I would like to get back to the dance."

"Why?" She raised an eyebrow. "So you can insinuate yourself further into Ren's life?"

She wasn't having this argument with Jessica. "I don't know how many times I have to tell you that Ren and I are *friends*." She glared at her. The more Jessica said the more pissed off she was becoming. She got it. Honestly she did, but she was sick of listening to it. Nothing she said to Jessica would make her feel better. "There is nothing other than that going on between us."

"I have eyes, you know." Jessica took a step closer. "I can see how you look at him. I know you want to be more than friends. I'm not going to stand here and let you come between us. I'm done with you and your neediness."

"I don't know what to tell you." Dani sighed and shook her head. "I'm not going to stop being Ren's friend to make you feel secure in your relationship." She couldn't imagine a life without Ren in it. He was the one person she could always depend on when everything seemed to be falling apart. Every one needed at least one person they could rely on. For Dani, it had always been Ren.

"Do you even know how he really feels about you?" Jessica sneered and took a step closer to Dani. There was barely any room between them as she angrily retorted, "Because let me tell you, he's not as happy as he seems when having to constantly run whenever you need him."

She was lying. Ren wouldn't talk badly about her. Would he? He always seemed happy to help her. He was the one who'd talked her into going to prom. It was his idea for them all to come together. Jessica was pissed because Ren danced with her. That was all this was about, and she wouldn't let her get to her. "Ren is a big boy. He can make decisions for himself. He doesn't need you to fight his battles for him." If he was annoyed with Dani for any reason, he'd tell her himself. It'd never stopped him in the past. Ren was the most vocal person she knew.

Jessica lifted her hands and pushed Dani hard, taking her by surprise. Pain shot through her backside as it met the floor with a hard thump. She wanted to jump to her feet and punch Jessica's perfect face, but it wouldn't do any good. The girl wanted to fight. Dani wouldn't humor her. Ren would be in the middle of it all, and Dani wanted to do what was best for her friend. Fighting with his girlfriend wasn't going to make things easier on any of them. She took a deep breath and prepared to reason with the girl. "Go back to the dance." Dani said calmly. "I don't want to do this with you."

"Too bad. It's time we settled things once and for all. I'm tired of you getting in the middle of my relationship. School is almost over, and Ren and I have plans. They don't include you."

Dani knew what Ren's plans were. Where he was going to college, what medical school he hoped to get into, and his need to help others. Jessica should know he would share that with her. "I don't have time for your histrionics." Dani got to her feet and brushed down her skirt. "I won't mention any of this to Ren." She walked past Jessica and headed to the exit.

"Not so fast." Jessica grabbed her arm preventing her from leaving. "I'm not done. You don't leave until I have my say."

She gritted her teeth together. Jessica was so damn demanding. Dani couldn't believe she called her the needy one. The girl insisted on getting her way far too often. This was the last time she gave in and conceded. "You always have something you have to say. What is it this time?" Dani raised an eyebrow mockingly. "Ren actually hates me? He only puts up with me out of a habit? I've heard it all from you. What makes this any different?"

Jessica raised her hand and slapped her. The sting spread across her cheek in tiny pinpricks. Dani rubbed her hand over her face and glared at the other girl. "I'm done with you. Don't corner me again. If you leave me alone, I'll do the same."

"No. I'm not going to step aside and let you ruin my relationship with him. I'm tired of him always running to do something for you. Find your own boyfriend. Ren is mine."

Dani stepped close to Jessica and stared into her eyes. "Ren is my friend. Get used to it. I will always be a part of his life." Even when it hurt too much to be around him... It was the path she chose. "Now I'm going to go back to the dance and try to enjoy what's left of it. I'll do you a solid and not mention this to Ren because I'm not the vindictive bitch you seem to think I am."

Dani turned to leave once again but stopped short when she heard Jessica say, "I'm pregnant."

Dani closed her eyes as her words washed over her. They froze her heart. Any hope she'd thought she had with Ren evaporated. He would never abandon Jessica and his child. She turned toward Jessica. Tears were falling down her cheeks. She was fighting to hold onto Ren. It didn't matter how Dani felt about the girl. She was going to have Ren's baby. There was only one decision she could make.

"Does Ren know?"

She shook her head. "I haven't told him yet."

"Why are you telling me?" She should be having this conversation with Ren. "You should tell him." What game was Jessica playing? There had to be a reason she was dropping this particular bomb on Dani.

"I want you to leave us alone. We don't stand a chance with you constantly around us. We deserve to have the best possible start. Our child needs both parents to be completely devoted to it."

She was right. Dani knew it. She was done fighting fate. Ren couldn't even be her friend anymore. He wouldn't be solely focused on his family if he was always hanging around with her. If she needed him, he'd come running. For his sake, and his child's, she would have to disappear and allow him the chance to be happy.

She nodded. "You win. You have until graduation to tell Ren. If you don't, I will." Dani turned and left the room. The roles had reversed, and now she was the one fighting tears. She'd lost something significant to her, and there wasn't a damn thing she could do about it. She left the dance and walked the entire way home. It gave her time to work out what had to be done. There wasn't much of a choice left. She had to leave, and the sooner the better.

REN NEVER GOT the chance to tell Dani he loved her. She ran away before graduation. He'd been blindsided by her choice, and beyond pissed off. What had he ever done to her to deserve such little regard? He searched for her. She'd hidden herself too well. If she really didn't want him in her life any longer, he'd respect her wishes. Ren always did what Dani wanted. Probably always would. They'd set that pattern up early on in their relationship. "Friends forever," she'd said. How wrong she'd been; how pitiful he was. He'd been a fool to believe they could have anything...

"Damn you, Dani," he shouted. Tears fell from his eyes. How was he supposed to let her go? She'd been a part of his life for as long as he could remember. Now he was alone. A piece of him would always be missing without her in his life. What if he never loved again? He doubted he truly could. He only had one heart to give—and Dani owned it. She left him with a hole in his chest and nothing to fill the void.

Jessica had become more attentive. He'd allowed her to somewhat fill what was missing, even though a part of him screamed in protest. What else was he to do? There wasn't much choice left to him. Dani had taken all of them away. He wanted to hate her for it, and maybe he even did on a small level. One day maybe they would see each other again, and he'd be able to ask her why. Until then he was left with so many questions, and absolutely no answers.

He always came back to one thing. Why. Why had she left? He should have known something was wrong. She'd been so weird at prom—after they danced. He'd meant to ask her what was bothering her, but she'd disappeared before it ended. Brian had been no help, when he'd asked him about Dani. No one had seen her or noticed when she'd left. The next day she'd been gone. All her foster parents were able to tell him was she had decided to leave for college early.

So much for confessing he'd love her forever.

He was a damned idiot. The biggest and most moronic fool alive—how could he have believed he could have it all? Some things were not meant to be. Sadly he couldn't do anything to change the feelings rolling through his heart. He'd always love her, nothing, and no one would ever change that. His heart would be hers, and anyone else who came into his life wouldn't compare.

No, this couldn't be the end. He wouldn't accept that. Someday, he promised himself, if he found Dani again he'd make sure she stayed around long enough to realize what she meant to him. What they'd lost by her actions. It was the only thing he could hold onto. When he saw her again, and he fully believed he would, there would be nothing to stand in his way—even Dani herself.

"One day, Dani, love." He stared up at the sky. "I will find you, and if we're both lucky enough we will find a way to be together." Ren rubbed his chest trying to erase the ache that filled his heart. "Nothing will be the same until that day, but I promise we can make it right if we fight hard enough."

She was worth fighting for. The best things in life were. It might just take longer than he'd like to make his promise a reality. As time went by, he'd do everything in his power to hold on to hope. It was the only thing he had left. If he lost it, then all would be lost. There would never be a Dani and Ren. There would be nothingness.

"I'll do my best," he whispered. "But I'm far from perfect."

And there was Jessica. She wanted more than he'd been willing to give. It was a temptation he was finding harder and harder to resist. In time he was afraid he'd give in. Life had a funny way of throwing a wrench in even the best laid plans. There was no telling what his future had in store for him, but he had hopes, dreams, and wishes he hoped to one day see fulfilled. Dani was one part of that bigger picture. If he couldn't have her, at least he could have the rest. He'd work hard and achieve what he could. Maybe, somewhere along the way, he'd discover that he could live without her.

He snorted. "Not likely."

But he'd attempt to. Oh he'd try; he had no choice after all.

CHAPTER 1

"*E*xcuse me, Ms. Brosen," Claire said as she knocked on the door. "You have a call on line one. It sounds important."

Dani sighed and set down the motion she was reading over. She didn't have time for interruptions. Her partner, Matthew Price, had been a no-show at the office. The case they were working on was both high profile and potentially career making. It could make or break their practice. He knew how important the motion was. He was late. It both irritated and worried her. Matt was usually reliable.

She lifted the receiver and placed it against her ear, and then pressed the button for line one. "Daniella Brosen, how can I help you?"

"This is Lana Kelly. I'm calling from Envill East."

"Yes?" Why was someone from the hospital calling her? They didn't deal with Malpractice cases…

"Matthew Price was brought in. You're listed as his emergency contact. Could you come to the hospital?"

Panic seized her heart. Matthew was her only friend

and if something had happened to him... How would she go on without him? He'd been her rock for so long. This couldn't be happening. She'd finally managed to feel safe and content with her lot in life. Without Matt, it might fall apart all over again. She reminded herself to breathe. It'd do no good to suspect the worst before she had all the information. The hard question needed to be asked, even if she was afraid of the answer.

"Is he..."

Lana interrupted her, "He's fine—or well—as okay as he's going to be for now. The doctor can explain more when you get here."

Dani gulped. She could handle this. She dealt with more complicated problems in court. Her friend needed her and she would go to him. The case could wait. It was minor in comparison. She wasn't about to lose another friend. Leaving her best friend behind in high school had devastated her. An image of him floated through her mind, and she brushed it away. Thinking about him would only make things worse. She couldn't let her old doubts fill her now. Matt's condition was an immediate concern. The things she couldn't change had to stay firmly where they belonged...in the past.

She shook her head clear and focused on the call. "I'll be there shortly."

"Come in through the emergency room. They can direct you where to go. Mr. Price isn't in a room yet."

"Who should I ask for?" She hated to go into a situation with little to no details. The least she could do was figure out who to direct her questions to. This woman wasn't being forthcoming at all. Dani was on the brink of becoming pissed off.

"Ask to be taken to Mr. Price. When the doctor has time, he'll come by and speak with you," she replied briskly.

Dani reluctantly agreed and set the phone back down on the receiver. She stood and realized she forgot to ask who Matt's doctor was. She would have to remember to do so when she arrived at the hospital. Information was power, something she learned the hard way in law school. The more she had, the better equipped she was to handle a situation. If she was going to take care of Matt, she had to learn everything she could about his circumstances.

"Claire, hold all my calls and reschedule any appointments for either Matt or myself for next week." She paused and revised her statement, "Wait, for Matt don't reschedule at all. Cancel them and let them know we will call them back when we are able to reschedule."

She lifted her head to meet Dani's gaze. "Is everything all right?"

"I'm not sure." Dani bit her lip. A rush of anxiety filled her. "Something happened to Matt. I don't have the facts yet. When I know more, I will let you know. I'm heading to the hospital now."

Claire nodded. "I will handle the office. Please tell Matt…" She frowned and shook her head, appearing to rethink her words. "Call me when you get a handle on the situation."

Dani didn't have time to figure out what that little slip meant. Claire seemed to be even more anxious than she was. What was going on between Claire and Matt? When she had the chance she'd have to ask him. It could be her imagination.

It took her twenty achingly long minutes to get to the hospital. She ran into the emergency room after she parked her car. Tears burned at the corners of her eyes, threatening to spill freely. She fought them. They were a sign of weakness and she refused to give into them. Matt would be fine. He *would*. If she kept telling herself that she might actually believe it.

"I got a call from a..." What was that woman's name? Damn it, she forgot. The woman hadn't been helpful, and she had a name that wasn't easy to remember too. "It started with an L. Lisa... Laura..." She was usually much better with details. Dani waved her hand. "It doesn't matter. Matthew Price was brought in. I'm his emergency contact."

The nurse handling admittance in the emergency room typed away at her computer. She was probably used to frantic people in search of their loved ones. She didn't appear fazed at Dani's inability to remember the other woman's name.

She stood up and gestured. "Follow me. I will take you to Mr. Price."

Dani trailed behind her until they reached a set of double doors. The nurse lifted her identification card and held it against an electronic panel. The doors slid open to let them on the other side. Dani followed her down a few halls and into an exam room. Loud steady beeps from monitors filled the entire area. Matt lay upon the bed, still and silent. What was visible of his body appeared to be an immense bruise of various shades of purple and blue. His eyes and the entire top of his head were covered with white gauze, and his left arm was splinted and wrapped.

"What happened?" Dani turned to the nurse. It hurt to look at him. She swallowed the lump forming in her throat and asked, "What's wrong with him?"

The nurse shook her head. Her mouth was set into a firm line. "I'm not at liberty to say. I'll let the doctor know you've arrived."

She hated not having answers. It was a simple question. The nurse should be able to tell her what happened to him. She might not be able to disclose his exact condition, but surely she knew how he came to be injured in the first place. Dani reined in her frustration. It wouldn't do any good to interrogate the nurse. The answers would be given to her as soon as the doctor came to see her. Until then, she would remain patient.

"Will Matt regain consciousness?" Dani could feel tears threatening to fall again. "He looks so...is he in pain?"

"He is sedated and has been given something for the pain. He's comfortable." The nurse shook her head again. "I can't give you any more details. I promise I'll let the doctor know you're here. He can explain it in more detail and tell you what we need from you."

Dani grabbed a chair and pulled it up to his bedside. She lifted his uninjured hand into hers and held it against her cheek. "Please have the doctor come in as soon as possible. I need to know what is wrong with my friend."

The nurse nodded and left the room.

"What's going on Matt?" She rubbed his hand with

hers. She wanted to hug him tight against her and not let go. "What mess did you get yourself into?"

Matt had been her friend since the early days of college. They even went to the same law school together. After leaving her hometown of Hope Beach, and a foster family she'd been happy to forget, Matt had been a breath of life she'd not realized she needed. She'd been so lonely until she met him. He'd been her rock, the center she'd been craving to keep her balanced. Dani had grown up in a series of foster homes and never had a stable home life. Her last set of foster parents were not the loving sort, and she'd been ready to run as soon as she graduated. Only one person would have kept her in town, and he'd found someone else to build a family with.

It was her fault. She'd loved him and gave him her heart the moment she laid eyes on him. He was kind, generous, and oh so handsome. He was her first friend and the only man she would ever love. But he wasn't hers. Not anymore, and never in the way she'd dreamed of. It was her fault. If she hadn't been afraid to lose him… In the end she lost him anyway. She thought if she had him as a friend it would be enough.

Until he fell in love with someone else…

Dani hadn't factored that part in. How could she remain friends with him and get in the way of his relationship. It was clear the other woman in his life didn't like or trust her. A part of Dani didn't blame her. It had to have been obvious how much she loved Ren. If their roles had been in reverse, she'd have acted the same way. So, for him, she left. She never looked back and wished him all the happiness in the world. He was nothing but a memory now, albeit a painful one.

Matt was her present. A friend she didn't fear losing her heart to. It had been given away to someone she never planned on seeing again. Matt had a much more stable and special place in her life. "Please be all right," she whispered. She loved Matt, but not as a woman loved a man. He was the one person she cared about, and she would move Heaven and Earth to make sure he would pull through the hell he now found himself in. Matt was all that mattered. Sometimes she wished she still had a heart to give him. Loving Matt could be so easy if she didn't still love another man.

The man who would always be in her heart, the one she'd love until the day she died. Dani believed soul mate's existed. There were different kinds for different reasons. She met the love of her life when she was a teenager. In a different time or place maybe they would have had a chance. Circumstances and her bad decisions separated them forever. She was lonely until she met Matt. He was another version of her soul mate. The true best friend she could lean on. She loved him in a different way, but never in the romantic sense.

"So the nurse tells me you're Mr. Price's emergency contact."

A voice filled the room. It was as familiar as breathing. She would have known it anywhere. It haunted her dreams and sneaked into her thoughts when she least expected it. For a brief moment she thought she might be hearing things. Had she conjured up his voice because she'd been thinking of him earlier? No, that was silly.

There was no way he could actually be behind her. Dani turned slowly and blinked several times. She could feel the color draining from her cheeks. This couldn't be happening to her. "Ren?"

"Dr. Sousa, I forgot to give you Mr. Price's chart." A nurse with dark auburn hair and soft brown eyes bustled in and handed him a file.

Ren stared at Dani and didn't say a word for several seconds. He studied her in awkward silence. He was almost exactly as she remembered him. His hair was a bit shorter, and his blue eyes stole her breath. It was Ren. Having him near always had that effect on her. He turned toward the nurse, took the file out of her hand, and dismissed her with a nod. "Thank you, Lana."

Lana...that was the woman who'd called her office. Dani filed her name away for future reference. She was pretty, petite, and had a no-nonsense attitude. Something Dani appreciated. The nurse nodded and left the room. Leaving Ren alone with her. He set the file down and walked over to her side. The silence in the room was palpable. She had no idea what to say to him and still wasn't completely convinced he was real. Hallucinations had never plagued her before, but there was always a first time for everything...

"Dani, I didn't realize...I should have asked Lana for a name."

Real. Definitely real. She gulped down a lump in her throat. Hell how was she supposed to deal with Ren, and Matt's situation at the same time? This was an over-whelming emotional circumstance, and she wasn't entirely sure she was up to dealing with it. She sent up a silent prayer for strength.

She shook her head. "There was no way for you to know." This was all too much. Matt was hurt and Ren was his doctor. How could life have set her on this path? Her two best friends—one's life depended on the other.

Was this the fate's way of making her face her past?

She cleared her throat and turned away from him. It hurt to look at him. He looked as amazing as she remembered. A golden-brown haired god with ocean blue eyes, pain stabbed in tiny pinpricks against her already aching heart.

"What do you need from me?"

Ren didn't answer her. Had he remained in the room with her? She didn't want to turn around and look, but he was forcing her to face him. Why did she have to deal with this? Normally she could handle anything... This was too much in one breath of time for her. The tears she'd been holding back were about to come crashing forward.

Her breath hitched as she turned to look at him. All the love she had been carrying around for him—it was still there. He was a walking reminder of what she didn't have. His gaze held such concern for her.

"Dani, perhaps we should go to my office to discuss this."

Hearing her name spoken in his voice was almost her undoing. They'd stepped into an easy pattern of familiarity, but they knew next to nothing about each other anymore. They had a past. That was it.

"Does it matter where we talk about Matt?" She looked

down at her friend. "The nurse said he was sedated. I doubt he will hear any of it."

What she didn't say was she needed the buffer. She didn't know what she would say or do if she was completely alone with him. Sure Matt wasn't about to jump into the conversation, but he was better than talking about the elephant in the room. Her feelings for Ren, his lack of them for her, and the fact she'd disappeared from his life so many years ago. She hadn't even said goodbye. It would have been too difficult to face him and explain why she couldn't be in his life anymore. Jessica needed him to devote all his attention to her. Dani would have been in the way. Leaving was the only decision she could have made.

"I think you will be more comfortable there discussing his condition," he replied softly. "I have a lot to go over with you."

Ren had always been kind. This wasn't about her. Matt's condition had to be more important. It was time for her to suck it up and deal with her emotional overload. Ren wasn't going to bite her head off. It wasn't who he was.

"Fine, lead the way, Dr. Sousa."

Dani had to put up barriers and ignore her rampant emotions. He couldn't be Ren anymore. He was Matt's doctor and nothing more. Her feelings on the matter were irrelevant.

CHAPTER 2

*R*endell Sousa fought the need to pull Daniella into his arms and breathe in her scent. It was hard for him to believe she was real, in front of him, and looking as beautiful as he remembered. He'd lost her once, and he wasn't about to do it a second time. She didn't know it yet, but he was a permanent fixture in her life.

He led her to his office and held the door open for her. What they had to discuss wasn't meant for anyone's ears. She came in for Matthew Price, but they had a lot of other unfinished business. Her disappearance had hit him hard. Not once had he thought she'd leave him and never speak to him again. If he had—he'd have done something, anything, to stop her.

"Please have a seat." He gestured toward the chair in front of his desk. He set the file on Matthew Price down and sat. Ren rested his elbows on his desk and stared across at her. He would never get enough of the sight of her. Her beautiful midnight tresses were pulled up in a knot behind her head, and her soft green eyes were filled with worry and something he couldn't identify. She didn't seem to want to look him in the eyes. *Are you feeling guilty for not saying goodbye?* "I think we should get right to the heart of the matter."

Tell me why you left me...

She nodded. "I agree. Explain Matt's condition to me."

"Who is he to you?" He shouldn't ask. Never would he have asked another patient's friend or family member to clarify their relationship. Dani was different. He had to know. Ren cleared his throat. "What is your connection to Mr. Price?"

She tilted her head and studied him, not saying a word. Lana had mentioned Matthew Price's emergency contact was his partner in a law firm. He could see how she might make a witness uncomfortable with that stare. He had the bug-under-a-microscope feeling crawling all over him.

"Does it matter?"

"I'm trying to figure out the best way to approach this." He leaned back in his chair and tapped his fingers together. "To tell you how to proceed once he's released."

She ignored his first question. "Start at the beginning."

What beginning? Their past or Matt's injuries? He wished for a brief moment he could forget the reason that brought her back into his life. Ren was horrifyingly thankful for it. He might never have found her again without her friend's accident. He looked for her when she left, but she'd done a good job of covering her tracks. After a while he had to face the fact she didn't want him in her life, and reluctantly let go, moved on with his life the best he could.

"Several hours ago, Mr. Price was brought into the emergency room after being involved in a multi-vehicle accident. His injuries were extensive and we were able to stabilize him."

If he stuck to the facts he might make it through their meeting. Mr. Price had to come first. After that—he wouldn't hold back. Ren needed Daniella in his life.

"I saw that." She pursed her lips together as she stared at him. "What are you not telling me?"

"His brain is swelling, but we've already taken measures to reduce it." He paused and thought about his next words. "It's his eyes we're concerned about. There is a surgery that can help him, but it's risky. If he doesn't have it, he will be blind for the rest of his life—even if he does, he might still be."

Dani stayed quiet. She always remained silent after hearing something she didn't like. She weighed the options and processed the information. It was one of her quirks and one he'd always appreciated. Dani was one of the most rational females he had ever known. It could be disconcerting. She was almost too practical. Deep down she was a well of barely contained emotions. What was on the surface scarcely touched the core of who she really was.

She tilted her head and studied him, her hands folded neatly in her lap. Dani showed almost no emotion as she spoke, "What are the risks, other than permanent blindness? It appears that's on the table regardless of what we decide."

Her mouth was in a firm tight line. Ren knew what she was doing. She was fighting tears. She cared about this man. He found it bothered him more than perhaps it should. Dani hadn't been a part of his life for some time. She would have moved on and found someone else to love. Lord knew she never claimed to love him. It was why he started dating Jessica—what a colossal mistake that turned out to be.

"He could end up paralyzed, and death is always a risk in any surgery."

How much did she care about him? Did Ren even have a chance? Was he an ass to even consider pursuing her when he knew how much she was about to deal with? He'd played the part of a good guy and where had it left him? With a harpy for a wife who hadn't blinked an eye about cheating on him, and a former best friend who exited his life without so much as a by-your-leave. No, she hadn't needed his permission to do anything, but she could have at least told him what she'd planned. He'd missed her so much. When she'd disappeared, she took his heart with her. He was an empty shell without her. She was his light and his strength, and he'd never loved anyone the way he did her.

All she'd wanted from him was friendship. He swore it would be enough, but it never was. He ached for her. How had she not see it written all over his face? So she would never know the depth of his love, he'd started seeing Jessica and devoted all his pent up feelings on her. He got to be pretty good at faking something with her. Maybe Jessica had known somehow and that's why she sought out another man. Ren didn't really know. When he walked in on her with a fellow colleague it had been a relief. He no longer had to pretend to love her. It was a blessing to file for divorce and move on with his life. There had only been one thing missing—Daniella.

Even if Dani had never loved him the way he loved her, he wasn't going to let her disappear on him again. Ren wanted to be there for her in all the ways she might need him, and it would be enough. He didn't need a repeat of his ex-wife. Dani may never love him the way he loved her. He hoped she would allow him to be a part of her life again.

"You recommend this surgery?" She stared into his eyes. They were so full of faith in him. He almost didn't feel worthy.

"I do," he said firmly. It was the best chance Matthew Price had.

"Will you be performing it?"

He shook his head. "No, but I will assist." He swallowed down the bile threatening to come out of his mouth. As much as he hated Preston West, he was a damn good doctor. It was wives he couldn't be trusted with. "There is another surgeon with more skill and experience in this type of case who'll do the bulk of the surgery."

She bit her lip and a tear finally escaped from the corner of one of her eyes. Dani buried her face in her hands and they flowed free. Ren never could stand to see her cry. She did it so little; she must be in enormous pain to give into them. Dani believed tears showed weakness, and she learned early on the fragile people of the world got stomped on. The pain she suffered as a child had made her who she was. She'd been in several bad foster homes until she ended up in a fairly descent one. She'd explained once that one of her foster mothers would punish her if she showed any sign of tears. He'd seen Dani struggle not to cry more than he liked. It broke his heart she'd had to fight so much to survive. He wanted to protect her from all of the world's hurts.

He stood up and pulled her into his arms. Dani leaned into him and let him comfort her. To have her in his arms again, he had no words to describe how good it felt. If he could, he'd have stood there forever basking in her warmth. He was more than aware they couldn't. Reality had a bad way of shaking apart the good things in life.

Some strands of her hair had fallen loose and wrapped around her face. Ren lifted his hand and caressed her soft curls and whispered soothing words. Whatever would help her and calm her down. "I promise I will do everything in my power to help him. I can see how much he means to you."

She took a step back out of his arms. He wanted to howl in protest. Ren barely held in the frenzy rushing through him. He kept his hands at his sides to prevent himself from pulling her back into his arms. If he didn't take things slowly, she would bolt right back out of his life. Patience was the only way to make sure she didn't act on her impulse.

"Matt does mean a lot to me. He helped me a lot, and if not for him I might not have made it through law school. He's the best friend I have."

He tried not to wince at her words. They were as painful as a knife in the chest. Did that mean he wasn't a good friend to her? Is that why she left and didn't look back?

"You're a good friend too, Ren." Her gaze locked with his. "Matt is my present, but you're my past."

"I don't want to be your past," he replied harshly. "If you hadn't disappeared you would know that."

Her head whipped back as if he'd slapped her. "Maybe this isn't the best time to discuss this. I can come back later."

Dani turned to leave his office. Before she could open the door he reached above her and held the door closed. "Your friend doesn't have time for you to have a hissy fit." His words came out sharper than he meant them to, but he couldn't let her run away from the problem. He was being an ass, but couldn't seem to stop the words from spilling out of his mouth. He was one big mess of bitterness. Most of it surrounded her and what could have been —if he hadn't been too afraid to speak up and tell her how much he loved and needed her. Now it was too late, and he would have to live with those choices.

She spun around and looked up at him. "What do you want from me?"

He wanted her to tell him she loved him. It was all he'd ever wanted from her. No that wasn't true... It was the first item he wanted in a long list of things he'd hoped they could have. A life together, a family, and so much love it would sustain them through whatever life threw at them.

He stared down at her and thought about saying the words aloud. Finally telling her she owned his heart.

Instead, he decided to take the coward's way, again. "You need to sign some forms consenting to the surgery."

"I can do that? I'm his emergency contact. I thought a family member had to make those decisions."

Ren shook his head. "He left you in control of his medical power of attorney, including what was to be done if he was ever on life support. He filed them with the hospital. It was how they knew to contact you."

She let out a harsh breath. "He never told me…"

Ren turned his gaze away from hers. He didn't want to have any insight into her relationship with Matthew Price. A part of him hated the man for taking his place in Dani's life. He should have been by her side through every single one of her achievements. He hadn't spoken to her or even seen her in ten years. She was supposed to be his, but he messed up. It was his mistake and his to rectify. If Matthew was her friend, it meant she had a place for him in her life. Ren could be her lover and the only man in her heart. The one she loved and came home to every night. It wasn't too late for them. They could have it all. He had to be honest with her for once.

"I'm sure he had his reasons."

"You're right. If you give me the consent form, I'll sign it."

Ren walked back to his desk and picked up the file. He opened it up and removed the form and set it on the desk with a pen. Dani signed it with her usual flare and pushed it over to him.

"I'm going to go back to Matt's room. If you need anything else, you can find me there." She didn't give him a chance to respond. Dani flew out of the office as if the hounds of hell chased her.

"You can run, Dani love, but you can't hide. I found you again. It's time we faced what is between us." And Ren didn't doubt for a minute she felt more than she realized or admitted to herself. Why else would she run? First, he would make sure Matthew Price was taken care of. His health had to take precedence. Afterward though—there would be no holds barred. He would win the woman he loved and no one would stop him, not even Dani herself.

*D*ani filled out the stack of paperwork required for Matt to be moved to a private room when he came out of surgery. It would be pricey and their practice would cover whatever the insurance plan didn't. They just wouldn't be doing any of the expansion they had planned over the next year. They had hoped to hire a couple of associates to take some of their more tedious cases. That meant moving to a bigger location and paying for a more expensive lease.

"Ms. Brosen."

Dani had taken up residence in a waiting room. She didn't think anyone would know where to find her. So she was surprised to see her assistant, Claire, walking toward her.

"Is something wrong at the office?"

Claire handed her a file. "It has to do with the Nettles' development project. The building permits you filed for them weren't approved. Mr. Nettles is livid and is insisting on speaking to Mr. Price. I tried to tell him it wasn't possible, but he wouldn't listen to me."

The Nettles family was difficult to manage. She didn't blame Claire. "I will call him and handle it."

Dani chewed on her lip and shook her head. If she were honest with herself she'd admit she didn't want to deal with anything pertaining to work. All she really wanted to do was pack a bag and disappear from life. Deep down she accepted that it wasn't possible. She was an adult with real world problems. Running away wouldn't solve any of them. So instead of giving into the urge to take an impromptu and permanent vacation she took a reaffirming breath and continued to fill in the paperwork for the hospital.

"How is he?" Claire asked, her voice barely above a whisper.

Dani filled in the last box on the paper and signed her name at the bottom of the page, then looked up at Claire. It was then she saw the worry etched on her face. Claire twisted her fingers in front of her. Her blonde hair was a tangled mess.

"Sit down." Dani gestured to a seat near her. "I'm sorry I didn't think to update you."

"I know you're busy." Claire plopped down near her.

It was then, staring at her assistant, that everything became crystal clear. Claire was in love with Matt. She'd bet everything she owned he wasn't aware of the woman's feelings. She hadn't seen it herself, and Matt was even more oblivious than she was. How selfish she'd been to not think of Claire and her feelings. Even if she wasn't in love with Matt, she cared about both of them. She remembered their birthdays, bought them gifts on every holiday, and made sure their day was generally better.

"I should have called you sooner," Dani said. "I apologize for not thinking of it."

"I don't want you to feel bad. Please tell me what is going on with him. How serious is it?" Claire leaned back and waited for Dani to start speaking.

"He sustained injuries when he lost control of his car and went into oncoming traffic. A large truck smashed into the side of his vehicle. He's lucky he wasn't killed on impact." None of their lives would have been the same if he'd died. Dani didn't want to think about it. She pushed the dark thoughts from her mind and continued, "His arm is broken in three different spots. They splinted it and he will get a better cast after surgery. His head's hurt the worst with the swelling and a threat of a brain bleed. His eyes were damaged, and he could lose his eyesight. He's in surgery now."

Her lips wobbled. "What does that mean?"

Dani had to be strong. At least she was used to it. The only time she let her guard down was around Matt...and Ren. She'd lost it a little with Ren. Something she could be excused for doing. Her friend was close to death and seeing Ren tore at the edges of her carefully built walls. After Matt was taken care of she would have to figure out how to put some distance between her and Ren. It would be easier to do once Matt was released from the hospital. Her heart would hurt too much to see him every day. She would do her best to keep their interactions to business only. If he required her to sign something to aid in Matt's recovery she would. But she wouldn't break down again and let him comfort her. It would make things too hard on both of them to try and be in each other's lives again.

As far as she knew, he was still happily married to Jessica. She'd kept tabs on him long enough to see their wedding announcement in the Hope Beach daily paper. She wondered for a brief moment why it had taken so long for them to get married, but had brushed it away. There had been no announcement of the birth of a child. Maybe they hadn't decided to tell the world about their bundle of joy. It wasn't her place to judge what they decided to share. The wedding announcement had been enough for her to finally let go. After that, she couldn't look in on him. She'd refused to have her heart break all over again with each update of his happy life.

It was selfish. She was more than aware of that, and as much as she wished him happiness, she couldn't live it and remain sane. So she took the final step and cut the cord. Never had she pictured meeting him again and in a new town. She expected him to build his happily ever after in a big city or, at the very least, their hometown. Not a small town on the other side of the state. For now, she would deal with Claire and her concerns for Matt. It gave her something other than her problems to concentrate on. Thank God for small favors...

"It means if it goes well he'll be the Matt we know and love—" She paused and stared into Claire's eyes. "—but if it doesn't, he'll never be the same again. He'll have to learn how to get by without the use of his eyes. Everything he knows will be turned upside down. It'll leave him cranky and pissed off. Hell, we should expect that regardless." She smiled reassuringly. "It'll be up to us to make sure he has someone to lean on and keep him on the path to recovery. Do you think you can do that?"

She nodded.

"Good. Now can you do me a favor?"

Dani handled problems better when she had something to focus her energy on. Somehow, she believed Claire would too. She dealt with her and Matt on a daily basis. She probably thrived on a similar energy.

"Anything"

She lifted the stack of papers she'd filled out. "Take these to the administration office. Let them know to contact me with any questions they have."

"I can do that." She took the papers and stood up. "Don't forget to call Mr. Nettles."

"Who is Mr. Nettles?" Ren asked as he walked in.

Dani stood and crossed the distance of the waiting room to stand in front of him. She searched his face for answers, but it remained passive. Damn it, she couldn't tell anything from his blank expression. "How'd it go?"

"Relax." He lifted his hand and rubbed her shoulder in an attempt to soothe her. "It went well and we're hopeful. We won't know if it was successful yet. He needs time to heal before we can remove the bandages."

He wrapped his arms around her and rubbed her back with small soothing movements. Dani leaned into him and took the comfort he offered before she realized what she was doing. She jerked back once her brain caught up with her body's instincts.

"Can I see him?"

"In a little while," he replied. His eyes squinted down at

her with displeasure. "He's in recovery. I'll have a nurse let you know when he's been moved to his room."

He spun on his heels and stormed out of the waiting room.

What had she done? Whatever it was, she wanted to take it back. The way Ren was looking at her—it did funny things to her heart. The look of disappointment devastated her. She should be happy. Earlier she had been thinking about ways of distancing herself. Why did she have to have all these confusing and mixed feelings?

"Do you know Dr. Hottie?" Claire asked with a raised eyebrow.

Dani sighed. "We used to be friends."

At one time she'd hoped they could be more than friends. Until she got scared. She watched relationships start and end badly while they were in high school. It ruined a lot of friendships. Dani had thought she was doing the right thing. A friend was forever. A boyfriend, lover, or husband wasn't guaranteed. She could keep Ren in her life if she kept her feelings in check. Dani wasn't sure if they could have ever been more than friends. It was her belief that a friendship would last and the other options would only lead to her losing him. She never once thought what it might do to her to watch him with another woman. Then Jessica had dumped her pregnancy on him and all of her insecurities no longer mattered. There was no decision to make, it's been made for her.

If she could go back she might change things, before it'd been too late to do anything about it. And at least try and see if they had what it took to make it as a couple. She'd do it if it might make a difference. Sadly she didn't think it would. What ifs didn't change the outcome. All that mattered was what happened, there was no changing the past. The truth was that her plan to keep him in her life had backfired and she lost him anyway. He married Jessica and started a family with her. She didn't have his friendship. It had been her choice. All of it had. She didn't regret leaving without saying goodbye. Ren wouldn't have allowed her to put distance between them any other way.

Their time had passed, and she couldn't get it back. No amount of wishing would make it so. But the things she still remembered—watching him play baseball, the laughs around the bonfire, playing card at his parent's house— those memories would always haunt her. Reflecting on how things could have been wouldn't do her any good. She'd made her choices.

"It seems like you were more than friends."

Dani's gaze flew toward Claire's. "You're wrong. We were never more than the best of friends. I haven't seen Ren since high school. We went our separate ways. He married his high school sweetheart and I met Matt."

"But you and Matt really *are* just friends." Claire placed her hand on Dani's shoulder. "I recognize how a woman looks at a man she loves. I look at Matt the same way every day and he doesn't see it. That's how you look at the doctor."

"Am I that obvious?" She'd thought she hid her feelings better.

Claire frowned. "Only to a woman who's in a similar situation. If it helps, I didn't see a wedding band on his finger. Are you sure he's married?"

"No, and I'm not going to ask him."

It'd be tantamount to asking him if he wanted to be with her. Dani wasn't ready to open herself up to that kind of pain. Her heart was beginning to wake up, and her walls wanted to tumble down. One little push from him and they would crash around her. Until then, she would hold on tight to the edges and hope she survived this encounter.

"If you want my advice…"

"I don't," Dani interrupted her.

She laughed lightly. "You're going to get it anyway."

Dani rolled her eyes. Her assistant was getting cheeky. She didn't say a word that would be encouraging, and it was the last thing she wanted to do.

"Matt's in there fighting for his life. He could've died today." Claire's voice cracked as she spoke. "I'd have lost the chance to tell him how I feel about him. I've been foolish, and I'm not going to keep making the same mistakes."

Claire *should* tell Matt she loved him. "You're right. He needs to know."

"Ren does too. The way he looked at you…" She paused and took a deep breath. "If Matt had just once stared at me with such intensity I never would've held in how I feel. That sexy doctor wants you. He may even need you. I don't know what happened between you two, but you need to fix it."

She was wrong, Ren didn't want her, and never had. He might need her though. They were the best of friends once; maybe she should set her feelings aside and go to him. Whatever was going on in his life she could at the very least be his friend again. It wasn't his fault she stupidly fell in love with him.

"I don't think Ren wants me in the way you think." Dani shrugged. "But I will think about what you said. I won't make any rash decisions. In the meantime, go drop off that paperwork. I'll call Mr. Nettles in the morning."

Claire nodded. "Don't avoid him. This is a mistake you can rectify if you let go of your fears. Trust me. I have them in spades myself." She turned and left the room, leaving Dani with much to think about.

Who knew her assistant was so insightful? It was time to let go of all of her insecurities. She thought she had a long time ago. How wrong she'd been. One look from Ren and they came flooding back. Dani couldn't admit how much she'd loved him or that he'd owned her heart, but she could once again be a friend he could lean on. She missed him so much over the years. It'd be good for her too to accept him as part of her life again.

*R*en set the files down he'd been studying and rubbed his hands over his face. The current lab reports on Matthew Price's condition didn't look promising. The surgery had gone well. He'd had high hopes for a complete recovery, but the lab reports suggested otherwise. It didn't look like he would ever regain his vision. He dreaded giving the news to the patient, and to Dani. She'd appeared to have grown close to Matt over the years. The stream of jealousy flowing through his veins didn't sit well with him. He had to set it aside and do what was best for his patient.

"Are you busy?"

Ren glanced up and groaned. The last thing he needed was to deal with his ex-wife. He preferred to never see her again. Unfortunately, she volunteered at the hospital on a regular basis. He was forced to see her every time she came for her scheduled shift. Not once had she thought to skip stopping by his office. When would she ever get the hint that he wanted nothing to do with her?

"I don't have a lot of time, Jessica."

"I understand," she replied. She breezed into the office before he could object to her joining him. She sat down on the edge of his desk and leaned into him, lifting her hand to caress his cheek. "I know how busy you are. You can spare a few minutes for me though."

He wanted to push her off his desk and watch her fine ass hit the floor. Jessica's audacity knew no bounds. Their divorce was finalized over three months ago, their marriage over several months before that. She still believed she could win him back. Ren was done with her and her machinations.

"What do you want?"

"You know what I want." Her lips formed a sultry pout. "That hasn't changed. Not once."

Yeah, he did know what her game was. She was upfront about her desire for them to rekindle their romance. He mentally snorted. What romance? They hadn't had much of a relationship since she miscarried their child two years ago. Jessica had claimed she needed time to mourn the loss. Whenever he touched her she'd flinch. So he respected her wishes and buried himself in his work.

"That didn't stop you from crawling into bed with Preston."

His wife couldn't stand his touch, but she had no problem sleeping with his friend and colleague. Make that his former friend. He hadn't spoken to Preston since he found him fucking Jessica—in the bed Ren shared with her. At first Ren had stood there stunned, and then he couldn't do anything but walk away. Jessica had made her intentions clear. He wasn't good enough for her. She didn't want him to even touch her. Preston was her choice now, and if Ren were to be honest he'd been relieved. It gave him permission to give up on his marriage. He'd been miserable too long. Preston was another story though. *A friend doesn't screw around with your wife.* How could he ever trust him again?

"It was the one time. I was lonely." Her eyes welled up with tears. She always could get them to fall on demand. He was aware of all her tricks. "You worked so much. What did you expect me to do?"

As if Preston didn't work as much as he did. Ren rolled his eyes. None of her excuses were worth a damn. Why couldn't she see that?

"I expected you to be faithful and respect your wedding vows." Why did he bother? Did this even matter anymore? "Please leave. I'm not rehashing this with you again. If you wanted me, you never would have pushed me away, and you sure as hell would never have had sex with my friend."

"Don't be cruel." Tears fell down her cheeks. "You know what I was going through. When I lost…" Sobs spilled loudly from her mouth.

Ren cursed. She wouldn't leave quietly. When had she ever? The only solution he had left was to comfort her or she'd never leave. It was all part of her plan to get him back. He knew it, she knew it, and yet they continued to play the game. He couldn't see any way out. With a heavy sigh he stood up and pulled her into his arms.

"Losing the baby was hard on us both, but that isn't an excuse to blow up our marriage and the life we built together." He rubbed her back attempting to soothe her. Mustering up feelings of sympathy was the problem. He had none for her any longer. "It's time to let it go and move on. You burned those bridges."

She glanced up at him. Tears were no longer spilling down her cheeks. "I don't believe that. Love doesn't go away. It's always there if you open yourself up to it."

Jessica wound her arms around his neck and pulled his head down. Her lips were on his before he had a chance to stop it. She ran her tongue across his lips to encourage him to open his mouth. He kept it firmly closed. Maybe she would get the hint. Who was he kidding? She didn't take hints. The kiss didn't inspire any passion in him. All he could see was her and Preston in bed. It was something he would never forget. One day Jessica would accept their marriage had imploded.

The soft click of heels on the linoleum floor filled his ears. The noise stopped right outside his office. "Ren, do you..."

He pushed Jessica aside and stared at Dani in the entrance to his office. She had stopped short of actually stepping inside. Her hand stood frozen in place as she'd been about to knock on the door frame. Her beautiful dark hair flowed around her shoulders and pain seemed to pour out of her eyes. He wanted to wrap her in his arms and comfort her. Her pain was real. Jessica's, on the other hand, was as feigned as a shark's disinterest in swallowing its dinner whole.

"I'm sorry. I shouldn't have interrupted." She turned to leave.

Wonderful. He felt like a school boy caught with his

pants down. This was the last thing he wanted her to witness.

"Dani, wait," Ren called out.

Jessica grabbed his arm. "Let her go."

He glared down at her. How dare she prevent him from going after Dani. "Remove your hand from my arm before I force you to."

She gasped. "Why are you being so mean?"

He was done. It was time to rip the Band-Aid off once and for all. He'd been as nice as possible with her up until this point. She wasn't getting the message. Instead, she bulldozed through his life on a regular basis. It didn't appear to sink in that the day she decided to betray him was the day their marriage ceased to mean anything to him. *She* didn't mean anything to him. What little respect he gave her was to preserve his dignity, not hers. If he wanted a chance with Dani, provided she wanted one with him, he had to make it completely clear that there was no marriage to save. The divorce was final for a reason.

"We're divorced." He ground the words out. "Do me a favor and remember that before you think you have the right to question anything I do. I don't owe you a damn thing. Do *not* come to see me. Do *not* ever try to kiss me again. If you have a problem with that—too fucking bad. I don't give a damn. Would you please leave now?"

She stepped back as if he'd slapped her. Something he wished sometimes he could do. He knew better than to act on the impulse. Jessica pushed his buttons like no one could. Sometimes he wondered why he ever married her in the first place.

"Is this because of her?" She motioned toward the door. "When did she pop back into your life? I was so thankful when she'd disappeared. You always went running to her if she called. She couldn't do anything without involving you."

Dani had been everything to him. If she'd not put him firmly in the friend zone, he'd have tried for more with her long before she disappeared on him. So, yeah, he answered her calls. He would do anything for her. It had devastated him when she ran away. Ren still didn't understand why. All he knew was she'd broken his heart into a million pieces. Dani made it clear she'd wanted space, and he respected her wishes even though it killed him. Now she was back in his life. He'd not let her disappear again. She would explain why she vanished from his life—it was time to get to the truth. As far as Jessica... She could go find someone else to bother.

"I don't have to enlighten you on the details of my life." He grabbed her arm and led her to the door. "Need I remind you—again—that we're divorced? I want nothing to do with you. Stop coming by to see me. I can't stand these little visits of yours."

"You don't mean that." She pouted. "You still love me. I know you do."

Ren took a deep calming breath. He had to or he'd strangle her. A doctor didn't kill people. He closed his eyes and sent a silent prayer for patience. His ex-wife was pushing him over the edge. She needed to leave and fast. As soon as he got rid of her he could go find Dani. She came to his office for a reason, and he wanted to find out what it was. It was about damn time she sought him out for a change. Yet, he'd chase after her over and over again if it would get him what he wanted most—her in his arms. His deepest desire was for her to love him as much as he'd always loved her. First he had to remove the trash from his life. Then he could go to Dani with a clean slate. Jessica and her insistent demands would stop. He'd been placating her for too long.

"I'm going to say this one more time, so listen." He lifted his hand and grabbed her chin making her look him in the eyes. "We're done. We've been done for a very long time. Getting in bed with Preston was the final nail in the coffin of our relationship. We are *never* getting back together, and I do *not* love you. Whatever feelings I had for you died a slow death when you pushed me away, accept it and move on with your life."

"You're making a mistake." She pulled away from him. "One day you'll wake up and realize it. If you're lucky, I'll forgive you and take you back."

He laughed and shook his head. "I'll take my chances."

"You're a fool if you think Dani wants you. She never saw you as more than a friend. Why do you keep chasing after someone who doesn't see you the same way?"

Her jab was on point. It hit a wound that continued to fester. She was right. Dani didn't want him as more than a friend, never had. Why couldn't he let her go? Maybe if he tried to be more than friends he'd have a chance. He never once pressured her for more, and instead let her set the parameters of their relationship. Dani didn't know how he felt because he never told her. If she knew, maybe it would make a difference.

"You'll excuse me if I don't let your poison infect me."

He pushed her out of his office and closed the door. "I have other priorities. Go find someone else to harass."

He walked away from her and didn't look back. Dani was probably with her friend. He would go find her and tell her what was going on with him and Jessica. She might not realize they were no longer together. How would she know? They hadn't had any contact in years. Whatever choices they'd made in their lives was a mystery to them both. This was an opportunity to get to know each other all over again. They would make different choices this time. This was too important to him to do anything less. Ren wouldn't let her go so easily this time.

CHAPTER 5

*D*ani rushed away from Ren's office. She'd gone there searching for her friend again. To see what had put sadness into his eyes. Something was wrong in his life, and she sought to ease his pain. She could always tell when something was bothering him. He didn't always share his demons with her, but she could at least make him smile through them.

It wasn't her place to ease them anymore. She couldn't be what he needed, no matter how much she longed to be. He'd made his choice long ago, and it hadn't been her. Jessica gave him what he needed. He'd married her. He loved her. All Dani had been was his best friend. It should have been enough. It pained her to walk away from him. She wondered what happened to the child Jessica had been carrying. Did they have a son or a daughter? Did they have a child at all? Seeing him with Jessica in his arms... She had so many questions, but she was afraid to find out the answers.

It shouldn't bother her, yet it did. He had every right to

kiss his own wife. Stupid, plain out right stupid, that's what she was. Her heart had seized tight inside her chest when she'd seen them, it always had. Nothing had changed, it was like a decade hadn't gone by, and she was that lonely girl again on the outside looking in.

It seemed like she was constantly the third wheel in Ren and Jessica's relationship. It'd been painful to see then, and still was. Why did she think it would be any different. Her feelings hadn't gone away when she disappeared from Ren's life. She'd left because of Jessica's pregnancy. If not for that, she might have broken down and told Ren how much she loved him. It may or may not have made a difference; something she'd never know one way or the other. Since it was a moot point, she shouldn't expect to find anything other than what she walked in on. Ren had a family, and she was not a part of it. For her own peace of mind, she had to put some distance between them.

She stopped outside of Matt's room and took a deep breath. He didn't need to know about her internal struggle. Her friend had his own issues to deal with. She pushed open the door and headed to his bedside. His breathing was deep and even. He was sleeping peacefully —she pulled a chair closer to his side and laid her head down next to his hand.

Why did bad things happen to good people? Matt didn't deserve this fate. What would he do if he was permanently blind? The things he would have to relearn and readjust himself to. It would be a long uphill battle. She had faith her friend would come out all right and make it to the other side of that journey. He was strong-willed and one of the best people she knew.

"Dani?" Matt's voice was hoarse and cracked as he spoke.

She lifted her head and glanced over at him. "Yes. It's me."

He lifted his hands, and ran them over the bandages covering his head and across his eyes. "What happened to me?"

She had a lump in her throat. It was so good to finally hear his voice again. The worry festered inside of her. If she had lost him… No, she wouldn't think about that. He was alive and wasn't going anywhere. Matt needed her to be strong.

"You were in an accident."

Matt didn't respond to her words. She couldn't tell if he'd fallen back asleep or if he was silently processing her words. Dani lifted her hand and placed it on his chest. "Matt?"

"Why is my head covered in bandages? What's wrong with me? What are you not telling me?"

"I…" How could she tell him about the damage the accident had wrought on his body. That he might never see again. She wasn't ready to impart that bit of news. He had a lot of healing to do yet. She cleared her throat. "You had an operation. The accident did a lot of damage, and you hit your head hard. The bandages are covering some pretty serious wounds."

"You're holding back, Brosen. I know you." Matt turned his head toward her. "Don't start lying to me now."

Tears welled up in her eyes. She wiped them away

quickly. Crying never solved any problems. It wouldn't do Matt any good for her to give into the urge now. "I don't know everything. It's best you wait for the doctor to explain it to you."

A soft knocking sound filled the room. Dani turned her head and met Ren's gaze. Jessica must have left for him to have time to come check on Matt. His presence had nothing to do with her. He had patients to take care of, and Matt was one of them. She looked away. It hurt too much and she kept seeing Jessica in his arms. She had exorcised that vision a long time ago and now it was forefront in her mind once again. It would take a long time for it to go away. She knew from before, and yet it still haunted her every day. It might not pop up as often, but it lingered; otherwise, it wouldn't hurt so damn much.

"I believe that's my cue." Ren strolled into the room. "I'm Dr. Sousa. Whatever questions you have can be directed at me."

"I can leave you to explain." Dani got up to leave.

"Don't go." Matt latched his hand onto her wrist holding her in place. "I need you."

"Yes, of course." She sat down. She kept her gaze focused on Matt. Dani didn't want Ren to see how much his presence shook her. The pain in her eyes would be a dead giveaway. "Anything for you."

"Tell me what my prognosis is, Doc." Matt cracked a wobbly smile. "Am I going to live?"

His humor was his defense. Matt was putting up walls, preparing for the worst. She wished she could protect him from what Ren was about to say, but there was no sheltering him from the upcoming pain.

"I'm afraid it doesn't look good. The blunt force trauma damaged your sight. Dr. West and I attempted to repair it with surgery. Time will tell if we were successful."

Matt's smile fell from his face. "I'm blind?"

"For now, yes." Ren didn't pull any punches. "I believe in time your vision will improve. Chances of it being fully restored though are slim. When the swelling goes down and as you heal, some of it should return. It's going to be an uphill battle to get to the end."

Dani glanced up and met Ren's gaze. As he talked to Matt, he stared at her. She could almost feel his stare burning into her. He was holding something back. What it was she didn't know, but she intended to find out. What wasn't he saying?

"How long?" Matt asked.

"I'm sorry," Ren replied. "How long for what?"

Dani frowned. What was Matt asking?

He pounded his fists on the bed. Anger appeared to seep out of him. "Until you know if I'm permanently blind."

It was sinking in. The possibility of never being able to see again—Dani didn't know what to do to help him. "Matt you shouldn't worry about that now. Time will…"

"No," he interrupted her. "I need answers. It's how I work. I have to plan and make sure I cover all my bases.

She acceded his point. He did work that way. "I know. I'm sorry." She turned to Ren. "What do you think, in your expert opinion, his prognosis will be and when will we have more answers."

Ren nodded to her. "I wish I could tell you what you

want to hear. All the tests have been inconclusive up to this point. All we can do now is wait. Try to be patient."

"Patience isn't one of my strong suits." Matt frowned. "How about you tell me how long I'll be stuck in this bed."

"For longer than you'll like." Ren folded his arms across his chest. "A week at minimum, maybe longer."

"You're chalk full of bad news, Doc." Matt shook his head. "I hate this."

Dani patted his hand. "I know. Please don't do anything that'll impede your progress."

He sighed. "This has to be a nightmare I'm trapped in. This sucks donkey balls."

Dani smiled at his words. "I wish it was. I hate that you're going through this, but I'll be here with you every step of the way."

It was a promise she fully intended to keep. If Claire had her way she'd be with him too.

"I won't do anything stupid," Matt agreed.

"Don't say that to placate me. I know you. Now promise me you won't leave this bed without medical permission."

He remained silent for a few moments. No doubt trying to figure out a workaround that would get him what he wanted. She couldn't allow him to find some loophole that would harm him further.

"Don't even think about it," she said in a steely voice.

"What?" he asked, the epitome of innocence. "I don't have a clue what you're referring to."

"Don't overthink this. Promise me you're not going to do anything infernally stupid."

He smiled. It was disconcerting with all the bandages

covering his face, but it was also a relief he could find something worth grinning over in his current condition. "Yes, counselor."

Ren cleared his throat. "She's right. Make sure you listen to her."

She didn't need Ren backing her up. Why did he feel like it was his place to interfere with her and Matt's relationship? "Did you have anything else to add, doctor?"

"Not about Matt's condition, but if you have a moment I'd like to speak with you."

Dani wasn't ready for that conversation. If she had her way, she'd continue to avoid it for the foreseeable future. "Now?" She raised an eyebrow. "I don't want to leave Matt."

"Don't think you need to keep vigil at my bedside. Go see what the doctor has to talk to you about. I'm not going anywhere any time soon."

Damn Matt. She didn't want to have a private conversation with Ren.

"Dani, please," Ren begged. "Give me five minutes."

She glanced down at Matt and considered her options. "Fine, but not now. I have a couple things to discuss with Matt before he rests. I'll meet you in your office in a half hour."

"Very well. I'll see you soon."

Ren turned and left the room. She breathed a sigh of relief as she watched him leave. It was a short reprieve, but she needed it. Maybe when she saw him again she'd be able to handle her raging emotions better. She needed ice to flow through her veins to deal with Ren one on one again. Her luck, Jessica would return and then where would that leave her? It killed her to see them together. She couldn't handle it.

"Want to tell me what that's all about?" Matt asked.

"Not really." She fidgeted and looked down at the floor. Matt knew about her former best friend. She'd told him everything on a drunken night during law school. She never told him Ren's name though. He wouldn't put two and two together unless she enlightened him. Maybe she should. It would help to get some of it off her chest. It was weighing down on her pretty heavily, making breathing almost impossible.

"I know something's going on. I hear it in your voice. Tell me," he urged.

"Do you remember why I ran away from my hometown?"

He nodded. "I do. What does that have to do with the doctor?" His mouth fell open. "Oh, I think I understand. He's the man, the best friend."

She nodded, and then remembered he couldn't see her. Damn, she was a bumbling mess. "Yes. Dr. Rendell Sousa. The only man I ever loved and also unequivocally unavailable."

"What's he want to talk to you about?"

She was sure there was a long list of things she had to answer to him for. Dani wasn't ready to face even one of them. "I'm sure he wants answers. I didn't leave him with any when I disappeared."

"Let me guess. You're doing what you do best— avoiding the situation until you have no choice but to face him. Are you even going to meet him in his office?"

"Didn't plan on it, actually. I have to go back to work."

She patted his arm. "Since you're awake and I can quit hovering at your side, I'm going to leave. Someone has to keep the day to day things running. Claire can only do so much to keep the clients at bay."

"Is there anything I need to worry about?"

She would not add to his stress. He had other things he needed to concentrate on. "Nothing major. The Nettles family is up to their usual tricks. I can handle it. Get some rest. I'll come back tomorrow to see how you're doing."

"Avoiding him won't work, you know."

"I do. I need a little more time." She leaned down and kissed his forehead. "Take care."

She left the room and glanced up and down the hallway. Ren was nowhere to be seen. Good. He'd taken her at her word and went to his office. She had a clean escape and a reprieve—at least for one more day. Ren would seek her out now that he knew where to find her. When he did she'd deal with it. In the meantime, she'd do what she did best...run away.

*R*en lifted his hand and ran his fingers through his hair. He'd waited for Dani to come see him in his office. After a half hour, he decided to go looking for her. He couldn't wait too long. His break was short as he had other patients to look in on. Dani couldn't take up all of his time even if he wanted to devote it all to her. Before he saw to his other duties, he stopped in to visit Matt's room to see if she was still there. It was then he realized she'd never intended to come to his office. Spikes of anger shot through him. Why did she keep running away from him? What did he do to her to make her want to get as far away from him as possible? It was bullshit, and he was going to make her talk to him.

Unfortunately, he had no clue where she lived and it had been too late to go to her office in search of her. So he'd been forced to wait. It grated on him to have to give in to her penchant for running even a second longer than necessary. As soon as possible, he intended to hunt her down and make her face him. The only problem was he had his own responsibilities and patients that needed him. So the confrontation was put on hold for two days before he found a break in his schedule. He'd been told she visited Matt every day, but he kept missing her. She was getting far too adept at avoiding him. Dani never came at the same time, so he couldn't even begin to guess when she'd come by the hospital to check in on her friend.

He stood in front of her office building and stared at it, mentally preparing for dealing with his wayward friend. Ren took a deep breath and ambled inside. He tried to remain calm and carefree on the outside. On the inside, he was a tornado of emotions he couldn't rein in. A state he'd constantly been in around Dani. He suspected he would always be where she was concerned. He pushed the door closed with a soft *click*.

A pretty blonde woman glanced up at him. She held up a finger and muttered, "I'll be with you in one moment." She wrote some notes on a piece of paper that didn't look like more than scribbles to him and then glanced up at him with a stunning smile. "What can I do for you?"

"I need to speak to Daniella Brosen." He figured it would be best to remain professional. This was her place of business. Ren couldn't very well barge in and demand to see her. Even though that was exactly what he wanted to do.

She scrunched up her eyebrows and studied the computer on her desk. "Do you have an appointment?"

He frowned. No he didn't. If he'd gone so far as to schedule one, it would have given Dani a warning to expect him. The element of surprise would work better in their situation. "This is an impromptu visit. Is she available?"

"Amy, has Mr. Nettles called?" The blonde woman who Ren had seen with Dani before came rushing into the reception area. She stopped short at the sight of him standing in the office. Her breath hitched and her eyes widened. "Is something wrong with Matt?"

He didn't think. Of course they'd jump to the wrong conclusion. Maybe he should have called first. No, Dani wouldn't have seen him. "Mr. Price is fine. Recovering slowly, but there are no new developments. I need to speak to Dani."

She nodded. Relief appeared to pour off of her. "Good." A wobbly smile filled her face. "I'm Claire—Matt and Dani's legal assistant. Dani isn't in the office yet, but I expect her to come in soon. If you want, you can wait in her office."

That would be perfect. He could surprise her in her own surroundings. "Yes, please."

She nodded, and then turned to the receptionist. "Amy, do *not* disturb Ms. Brosen with anything while she's meeting with Dr. Sousa. Send all calls to me." She gestured to Ren. "Follow me. I will show you to her office."

Claire led him down a hall and stopped by a door, waiting for him to catch up. She entered the office and showed him where he could sit. "Would you like something to drink?"

He shook his head. "I'll be fine. Do you know how long it'll be before she arrives?" Ren was anxious to see her.

"Any moment." Claire folded her arms across her

chest. "I didn't want to say anything in front of Amy, but I have to ask you something."

What could Dani's assistant know? Her stare was piercing as she looked at him. Ren would bet everything he had she'd learned that from Dani. He had the bug-under-a-microscope feeling spreading throughout. The only person who'd ever made him feel that way was Dani, and now Claire. He didn't like it one bit.

He raised an eyebrow. "What do you want to know?"

"What can you tell me about Matt's condition?"

Ren suppressed a grin. This had nothing to do with Dani. She wanted to know about Matthew Price. He tilted his head and studied her. Was there something going on between her and the other man? If Dani had been the one injured he'd be demanding some answers too. Unfortunately, he couldn't tell her much.

"What information do you already have?"

She bit her lip and fidgeted. "Not much. I know it's serious. Dani gave me the facts, but I want your honest opinion. Is he going to see again?"

He couldn't give her the answers she wanted. Ren didn't know. "Every case is different. There's only so much we can do. The rest is up to the healing process, the person's will, and fate. Some fair better than others. I wish I could give you absolutes, but unfortunately it's not in my hands."

Claire nodded. "I understand. It's well…" She sighed. "I was hoping for something to hold on to and work toward. You're not telling me anything I didn't know or suspect."

Ren's heart hurt for her. He couldn't imagine being in her shoes. To want so much for a better outcome for someone he loved. "I can tell you one thing. He's going to be surly and try his best to push you away. Don't let him." Ren would do the same. He'd not want to burden the woman he loved with his problems. "He's needs support from those that love him. His recovery is going to be strenuous and exhausting. That'll hold true no matter what."

"Claire, did Mr. Nettles call? We've been playing phone tag for two days." Dani rushed into the office, speaking at a rapid pace. She stopped short when her gaze fell on him. "Have Amy hold all my calls."

"All ready taken care of," Claire replied. "I'll leave you two to talk." She turned to Ren. "Thanks for listening." She spun on her heels and exited Dani's office closing the door behind her.

Dani stared at her closed door. She cleared her throat and turned to Ren. "Why are you here? Is there something wrong with Matt?"

Ren smiled. Claire and Dani both jumped to the wrong erroneous conclusion to him coming by. He sauntered closer to her side and reached for her. The desire to touch her was too much for him. Giving into it was the only option. He leaned over and briefly stroked his finger on hers. She snatched her hand away before he could do anything else. It would have to do for now. He wanted so much more, but recognized he had to go slow. She was already too skittish.

"Matt's the same. No changes."

She breathed a sigh of relief. "Why are you here, Ren?"

"You didn't come by my office," he accused. "Why are you avoiding me?"

She turned her back to him and paced in the small room. He let her work through her thoughts and waited as patiently as possible. It was killing him to watch her as if the walls were closing in on them both. Why was she so nervous?

"I'm sorry. That couldn't be helped." She stopped and stared up at him. "I had to leave."

He didn't doubt that. Why she felt she had to was the reason he was standing before her. She didn't offer up any excuses. Stated it plainly and offered it up to him to accept or not. Well, he didn't accept it. Dani damn well was going to quit running from him.

"I see." He tilted his head. "I'm here now, so we can talk about a few things."

Ren had a lot to say to her. The problem was he had no clue where to begin. Did he start at the beginning—when she'd run away the first time—or did he start now in their present? He glanced at her and he could see a hint of fear on her face. Her eyes widened and her mouth fell open. He wished he could allow her to retreat. Hurting her had always pained him, but he was tired of the ache that filled him.

"I fail to see what we could possibly have to discuss." She glared at him. "If this doesn't concern Matt, we don't have any business with each other."

She was trying to compartmentalize him. Pushing him into a box of things to avoid forever and only take out when necessary. He'd be damned if he'd allow it. They were more than acquaintances. He stalked forward and stopped directly in front of her. There was no space separating them. All he would have to do was reach out and pull her into his arms. Ren doubted she'd fight him. "There's *plenty* we need to discuss." He let his gaze roam hotly over her face and rest on her lips. He raised his hand and skimmed it down her arm. She shivered under his touch. What would she do if he kissed her? "Why don't we start with this."

He leaned down and pressed his lips to hers. A spark of heat rushed through him. Dani leaned into him, giving him permission to pull her into his embrace. Ren wrapped his arms around her and deepened the kiss. Their tongues touched lightly. A rush of desire flooded him. He couldn't get enough of her sweet taste. Why had he put this off? Kissing Dani was everything he'd ever imagined it to be. Ren never wanted to stop.

Dani pulled back and stared into his eyes. "You shouldn't have done that."

He disagreed. The kiss was long overdue. "I should have done it ten years ago."

She shook her head and took a step back. "The past needs to stay there. Don't bring up things we can't change."

He hadn't imagined her reaction. She'd wanted that kiss as much as he had. Why did she keep pushing him away? There was an undeniable attraction between them. Maybe she didn't love him, but at least now he had something to work with. She could try to put him into a neat box. Ren wouldn't fit in it, and he'd do everything in his power to make her finally see him and what he really wanted from her. He loved her and wanted a chance to have more. To learn who she'd become over the past ten years and build a life together.

"You're right," he agreed. "We can't go back and change our past mistakes. All we can do is move forward from this point and see where it leads us."

She frowned. "What do you want from me?"

He wanted it all. Everything she had to offer and then some. Mostly he wanted her. "I think that's pretty obvious."

She closed her eyes and took two deep breaths. When she opened them she said, "I don't know what to say to you. Nothing is apparent or understood."

Ren studied her. Was she that oblivious to the feelings pouring out of him? How much clearer did she want him to be? "How can I make you see?" He took a step toward her. Ren lifted his hand and caressed her cheek. "I want to explore what this is. It's past time to see if there's more between us. We were friends once. I want more than that."

She shook her head. "What about Jessica? Don't you have a family? Kids?"

What about her? She was nothing to him and there were no kids. There might have been if Jessica hadn't lost the baby. Maybe that was fate's why of ending things cleanly between them. Dani thought there was something that would hold him back. That he had something more with his ex-wife. And why shouldn't she believe that? After what she walked in on... "Jessica and I are not together."

Her eyebrows puzzled up. Confusion filled her gaze. "But I saw..."

He interrupted her, "Forget what you saw. That was Jessica up to her old games. We've been over for a while now. She refuses to accept it." Ren stared into Dani's eyes. "Trust me. I don't want anything to do with her."

Dani gulped and glanced down. Did he get through to her? He hoped so.

"You don't have any children?" Dani scrunched up her eyebrows as she stared up at him with a perplexed expression on her face.

"No. Jessica was pregnant, but she miscarried a couple years ago." He'd wanted kids, and at the time it had upset him. After their marriage imploded he'd been glad they hadn't brought any children into their mess. "At the time it was painful for us both."

"I don't understand." She paced the room, and then stopped suddenly. "It doesn't matter. Not anymore."

"What doesn't?" Ren tilted his head and studied her. He was missing something, but he wasn't sure what. Why was this important to her? "Tell me what's bothering you."

She shook her head. "I don't want to talk about this anymore."

Ren wouldn't push. She'd tell him everything in time. For now, he was happy they were finally talking. The rest would come over time. He could be patient as long as she allowed him to be a part of his life.

"When you're ready I'm here. You know you can tell me anything right?" He stepped closer to her and brushed her cheek with the back of his hand. "I want nothing more than to be a part of your life again."

"I don't know if I can do what you want," she whispered. "I hurt."

He pulled her into his arms and held her close. "I hurt too. We can figure it out together."

It was the only way. He would accept nothing less. Once and for all he would make sure of it. This was the beginning they should have had years ago. Sometimes things happened for a reason. Ren had to believe their separation needed to happen for them to appreciate each other in ways they never would have otherwise.

She sighed. "I don't know if I can do that."

"Don't say no," he begged. "Try to consider the possibilities."

"Ren…"

He put a finger over her lips. "Don't say it."

She stayed silent. He sent up a silent prayer that she'd see reason over time. Dani was too important to him. Ren had to convince her to try.

"I have tickets to a fundraiser for the hospital. I'd like you to go with me."

She shook her head. "It's not a good idea."

He wouldn't let her say no. "Think about it. It's in a few days. I'll call you and ask again later."

Ren rushed out of the office before she could say no. Dani would be a tough nut to crack, but he was up for the challenge. If he left her alone to think things over she might come around. If she required time, he could give it to her. He'd waited this long, so he could hold out for a little while longer. She was worth it.

*D*ani studied the legal documents sitting on her desk. How was she supposed to think after what happened with Ren? He'd left her a bumbling mess of emotions. The kiss... Oh hell, Ren kissed her, really did, not something she'd imagined. She lifted her hand and ran her fingers across her lips. This was uncharted territory. Something she'd never in a million years believed would happen. The next move was hers, and she had no clue what it should be. He left the ball in her court and waited for her to decide if she wanted him.

Oh lord, did she ever...

She'd wanted him her whole life. Now that she had a chance, she was afraid she'd fuck it up. The idea of having something more with Ren terrified her in ways nothing else had. If it didn't last and it ruined something between them—she shook her head. That was her old way of thinking. When they were teenagers, she refused to be anything but friends with him for that very reason. The thought of losing him scared her. So she put up those walls to protect herself. It was too easy to fall back into that line of thought.

The reality of losing Ren was something she was painfully familiar with. She'd walked away and didn't look back. A life without him was her new normal. So she had to ask herself what she was really afraid of. She'd left him behind a long time ago, and she could live without him in her day to day life. Dani had managed to do it fairly well over the past decade. If she had to, she could go on and be all right without him, but she didn't want to. She never had.

Jessica had either lied to her or she'd miscarried and never told Ren. If she had to choose between those two options, she'd pick lied. It didn't seem likely she'd have been pregnant and miscarried. Ren had only mentioned the one pregnancy which didn't line up with what Jessica claimed back in high school. That was ten years ago, not two. She'd been jealous of Dani's relationship with Ren. Jessica saw a way to get her out of the way and took it. When she got the chance she was going to confront the other woman. She wanted answers, and she deserved to know the truth. She'd left on the assumption Ren and Jessica were about to become parents. She hadn't wanted to distract Ren from his new responsibilities. If she'd been a fool—well there was no turning back. There was no undoing the past. It would help her make a decision about her future though. She might be able to have it all if she wasn't too afraid to reach out and take it. The hard truth smacked her in the face. It wasn't losing him that scared her anymore. It was having him; all the promises of a wonderful future, and then having it ripped away from her. If she opened her heart to that possibility only to lose it—what if those dreams didn't live up to her expectations? What if the reality was subpar to her fantasies? Would Ren be enough then?

Dani dropped her head into the palm of her hands and sighed. The bigger question was, what the hell was wrong with her? Why did she have to overthink every little detail in her life? For once, why couldn't she take a chance and see how something went. Because this was one of the biggest decisions she'd ever have to make in her life. Allowing herself to openly love Ren and accept she could be happy with him...that was daunting. If they failed, it would break her, but if they didn't—pure bliss would be the beginning of something more wonderful than she could ever imagine.

She took a deep breath and pushed her worries out of her mind. A decision didn't need to be made yet. Ren told her to keep an open mind. He wanted to get to know her all over again. Maybe she could do that and see where it led them. She did want to know him again and discover how he might have changed over the years. He was far from the boy she remembered. Still handsome, only he had the ability to turn her insides to mush.

"Ms. Brosen?"

Dani lifted her head from her hands and stared into Claire's eyes. "Yes?"

"Sorry to interrupt you, but Mr. Nettles is on line one."

Finally. The phone tag they'd been playing had become rather tedious. She had to put the man at ease. She had no idea why their permits were being blocked, but she intended to find out why. Mr. Nettles had some of the pertinent information she needed to figure everything out. She couldn't proceed until they had a conversation.

She picked up the phone and clicked the button for line one. With the receiver nestled between her shoulder and ear she said, "This is Ms. Brosen."

"It's about damn time. What kind of shady business are you running over there? You should've gotten back to me days ago."

Dani gritted her teeth. Mr. Nettles had always been an ass, but this was an all new level of assery, even for him. She silently reminded herself he was one of their most important clients. His business helped keep the firm afloat. She couldn't afford to piss him off.

"I apologize for not handling your concerns sooner. It's been crazy here for a few days. I'm not sure you're aware that Mr. Price was in an accident and was hospitalized." She didn't think for one moment Mr. Nettles would care, but had to give him something. "I'm going to take over your case until he's well enough to do so. Could you fill me in on what's happening?" Matt usually handled Mr. Nettles. He was a misogynistic pig and didn't think females had enough brains to take care of anything important.

"That's unacceptable," he shouted through the receiver. "When is he going to be out of the hospital? I don't have time for you to mess up while he's laid up."

Someone needed to punch the man in the face. Why someone hadn't already done so was a mystery to her. She took a deep breath and reminded herself they needed his business. Especially with Matt's medical bills to consider

—they'd never be able to afford them if they lost the Nettles account.

"Again, I'm sorry," she said firmly. "Mr. Price will be unavailable for the unforeseeable future. I assure you I'm more than qualified to handle your account. So, please, tell me what the issue is exactly so I can begin working on it."

She prayed he'd quit being difficult. His stubbornness might be his undoing. How Matt was able to deal with him on a regular basis, she didn't know. She'd have to get him an extra big Christmas present for this alone.

"*Hmmph.*" A sound filled her ears. "We'll see how much you think you can do. If you fail, I'm going to have to seek out another attorney."

Thank heavens. He was going to see reason. "Thank you for the opportunity," she said sweetly, swallowing back a gag. *Prick.* "Now, if you'll explain what the issue is?"

"It's that damn Sullivan Brady," he cursed. "He can't mind his own fucking business. The bastard has too much time on his hands if he can snoop into my life as much as he does. You have to put an injunction or something on him. He's the one blocking my permits."

Sullivan Brady? Who the hell was that? She'd never heard of him. "Why do you believe that?"

The more information she had, the more she'd have to work with. Since Mr. Nettles had no problems complaining about the man he believed responsible, she'd let him ramble on.

"He hates me. Always has. I don't know why."

She almost snorted. Did he not realize what a cantankerous dick he was? When she was bitchy, she was all too aware of it. The problem was she was unable to stop herself from spilling the poisonous babble from her mouth. Mr. Nettles must not be in tune with his own inner demons not to realize it. Dani was grateful she didn't work under similar illusions. She had plenty of demons as it was.

"There must be something you can think of." *Did you offend him by opening your mouth and speaking?* "How long have you known him?"

"None of that matters. Do what I asked and get him to stop blocking the damn permits. Do the job I hired you to do."

Money. Need money, she reminded herself. She took a deep breath. "Without more information, I don't have much to go on. I'll do my best and handle it."

She sure hoped she'd be able to do as she told him. They needed his account. How she was going to obtain the information needed she didn't know, but she had faith she'd find a way. She always managed to. It was a matter of knowing the right people.

"You better. Don't call me until you have good news."

A dial tone filled her ear. She breathed a sigh of relief the call was over. If she'd stayed on the phone with him even a moment longer she may have said something she'd come to regret. Mr. Nettles was a jerk. Dani hated dealing with him.

She picked up the phone again and dialed Claire's line.

"Yes, Ms. Brosen?" Claire's voice filled her ears.

"Come to my office please. Bring the Nettles file."

"Give me a moment and I'll be right there."

Dani set the phone down and waited for Claire to

arrive. She had a special job for her assistant. Maybe even Amy could help with it. The best assistants knew their bosses' schedules. She needed as much information she could get on both Mr. Nettles and this Sullivan Brady. He was an unknown element. Mr. Nettles, she at least had something to go on. Almost everyone knew how difficult he was.

"I have the file. What do you need me to do?" Claire asked as she bustled into the room.

"Have a seat. There are several things I need you to work on."

Claire sat down. Dani filled her in on the details of her phone call with Mr. Nettles.

"Did you say Sullivan Brady?"

Dani frowned. "Yes, are you familiar with him?"

How could her assistant know who he was and she didn't? What was she missing?

"The question is how could you *not* know who he is? He's a billionaire, drop dead gorgeous, and his pretty face graces the society pages on a regular basis."

Well, that explained it. She couldn't be bothered with high society. They were all a bunch of hypocritical snobs in her opinion. There were more important things to do than show up to charity events and be seen by the world. That's why most of them went. They only wanted to show their money off to the world. *"Look at all these good deeds I'm participating in."*

"A billionaire you said. What does he do?" That was information she could use. "Is he a businessman of some sort?"

"His family is old money. They own Brady-Blue International."

Dani had heard of that particular company. She'd hadn't made the connection. Brady was a rather common name. How was she to know he was part of the famous family chock full of philanthropists and do-gooders?

"Hmm." She glanced up at Claire. "How do you feel about digging up some details on Mr. Brady?"

Claire grinned. "Please tell me you want me to go out on a date with him." She fanned herself. "That man has pure sin pouring off his face. I bet he's amazing in bed."

Dani's mouth dropped open. "I thought you were in love with Matt!"

"Oh, I am, but Sullivan Brady's so pretty. A girl can have a crush can't she?" She sighed. "I wouldn't mind having him for one night. You know, to remember when I'm old and gray."

Dani shook her head and smiled. There was only one man she'd had such a crush on. She could relate on a small level. "I don't know what he looks like, so I don't know if I agree with your assessment."

Claire studied Dani. She tilted her head and frowned. "Actually, you kind of look similar to him." She held up a hand. "I'm not saying you look masculine. But you have similar coloring. His hair is almost the exact shade as yours, pitch black and slightly curly. It's the eyes though that are the most comparable. I've never seen a shade of green so eerily alike. It's too bad you're not part of that family. They're so rich they probably don't know what to do with all that money."

Dani frowned. Claire didn't know she was an orphan.

Well, she liked to think herself as one. She didn't know who her biological parents were. She'd been dropped off at a church on the other side of the state. It was as far away from Envill as possible. It was a nice thought, but she wasn't related to anyone in the Brady family. She didn't belong anywhere. At first it had bothered her, but she'd grown used to it over the years. It'd made her strong and resilient. Dani was independent and glad for it. Yes, she had Matt if she needed someone, but it was nice to not have to rely on anyone if she didn't have to.

She smiled. "Go get cozy with someone who'll know Sullivan Brady's social schedule. I'd like to arrange an informal meeting. Enlist Amy's help if you need it. I want to know as much as possible before I act."

"I'm on it. I'll come by to fill you in after I gather the information. I can tell you one thing now though."

Dani raised an eyebrow. "What?"

Claire reached under her files and pulled out a newspaper. She flipped through it until she found what she was looking for and handed her the society section of the Envill Post. "I was taking a break and looking at the paper before you called me to your office. I like to see what's going on in our community." A picture of one of the most gorgeous men she'd ever seen graced the top of the page. Her assistant had been right. Sullivan Brady was indeed beautiful. Underneath it was an article about a charity event his family was hosting. It was for the new pediatric wing of Envill East.

"You can find him here if you're willing to go to one of those tedious fundraising events you hate so much."

Claire smiled. "You might even know a handsome doctor willing to take you."

Damn it, Ren had mentioned a fundraiser. It had to be the same event. She would have to call him and agree to go. She sighed. He'd take it to mean more than she was willing to accede to. If she played it right, she might still be able to get him to go slow. Dani wasn't ready to jump into anything yet.

"I'll give Ren a call." She frowned.

The more information she gathered, the more her anxiety level rose. It was proving to be colossal level chaos. In her gut, she knew it was all going to blow up in her face.

CHAPTER 8

*D*ani put off calling Ren. She was being ridiculous and knew it. Why did she keep putting off the inevitable? Instead, she headed for the hospital to check on Matt. If she ran into Ren, she'd talk to him then. It gave her a reprieve of sorts. She had to talk to him at some point, but she wasn't ready to. She'd never be at the rate she was going.

She strolled through the hallways of the hospital until she reached Matt's room. She pushed the door open and breathed a sigh of relief. There wasn't anyone else in the room. It would give her some time to visit with her friend and pull herself together. Ren hadn't called her either, he'd said he would. Why did her insecurities have to rear their ugly head? For the most part she was a strong independent woman. She took the world by storm. When it came to Ren, she was the little girl whose parents abandoned her. Her self worth took a hit every time. She wasn't good enough to keep, so why would anyone else want her. The yo-yo emotions had to stop. Avoiding Ren wasn't the way to get anything done. She'd go see him after her visit with Matt. It was time to face her fears and set them aside. She was acting like a silly school girl and it was plain stupid.

"How's my favorite person in the world doing today?" she asked as she entered the room.

"I've had better days," he replied. "Where have you been hiding yourself?"

The sight of him laying damn near helpless in the bed was hard to see. She'd never get used to it. He was usually so strong and steady. A rock when she was on the verge of falling apart. Now she had to be the glue to hold it all together. For Matt, she'd try. She owed him that much.

"Someone has to keep the office running." She sat in a chair by his bed. "If you hadn't decided to take this impromptu vacation I'd have more time to dote on you."

She was attempting to keep things as light and carefree as possible. He didn't need to know they were on the verge of losing one of the firm's important clients. He had more important things to worry about. Matt's convalesce was essential to the healing process. If he had a chance of getting better, he had to take the time to recover properly.

"Hardee har har," he said. "Best vacation ever. Don't knock it 'til you've tried it."

"I'll take your word for it." She patted his hand. "Now, seriously, tell me how you're doing."

He was quiet for a moment. Was something wrong? They hadn't removed the bandages around his eyes yet. They were going to do it the day before he was scheduled to be released. Dani wasn't sure when exactly that was. She'd have to ask the nurse before she left. There were arrangements that needed to be made before Matt could go back to his house and live.

"I did get some good news today," he said quietly. "I'm not sure how I feel about it."

That didn't sound good at all. What could have him so down? She didn't like the path they were headed down. Matt was falling head first down depression lane.

"Why don't you tell me what's bothering you and let me decide if it's as good as you believe it is."

"They're taking the bandages off today." He frowned. "I'm glad you're here. Can you stick around until they're off? I'm afraid…"

Matt scared? No. He was more fearless than anyone she knew. Of course she'd stay by his side. "I'm here for you. Always."

"I'm not invincible." He clenched his fists. "I lived each day as if I was. Take a look at me now. I'm laid up and possibly blind for the rest of my life."

This was a side of Matt she'd never seen before. She wasn't sure if she liked it. He sounded so—defeated. "Don't borrow trouble. Let's take it one step at a time."

"Claire came to see me yesterday."

He didn't elaborate. Had their assistant opened up to him? She'd said she wanted to tell him how she felt. Did that have something to do with Matt's attitude? Was he questioning every choice he'd ever made? Dani could relate to that. She was doing something similar. After Ren kissed her, she'd had to reevaluate every life choice she'd made. The mistakes she'd made in the past decade were coming back to haunt her. She'd run away instead of staying and fighting for what she wanted. Now she was on the verge of repeating those mistakes. Ren was hers for the taking. She just had to reach out and take what he offered. If only she was brave enough to do it.

"That was nice of her. Did she stay long?"

She wouldn't come out and ask what she wanted to know. Claire may not have said anything, and it wasn't her place to tell Matt the other woman was in love with him. If she hadn't told him, she had her reasons. When the time was right they'd share their feelings.

"I was a bit of an ass."

"You?" She mocked, holding her hand to her chest. He'd laugh if he could see her. "Never. You're the epitome of all that's fabulous in this world. Why ever would you be a jerk?"

"No," he said solemnly. "I'm a dick, plain and simple. I can't seem to stop myself from spouting pure venom. The things I said to her..." He rubbed his free hand over his chest. "I don't know how she'll ever forgive me."

Dani didn't doubt Claire would forgive him anything. That was what you did for those you cared about. Otherwise, Ren would have run screaming at the sight of her. She didn't doubt she hurt him deeply when she'd run away from him years ago. Now he was holding his arms out to her and asking for more than she'd thought possible. Ren was willing to forgive her without knowing all the details. She'd explain it all to him once she fully understood what had happened. She thought she'd had it all figured out. Now she questioned everything. She may have sacrificed their friendship for no reason.

"I suspect Claire'll go easy on you. She realizes you're going through quite a lot right now." She chuckled. "I'm sure there's no real damage done. You're human, and what we know of you, you're not a monster."

He snorted. "Debatable. But I'm not up to it now. The doctor should be by soon to see how much of a monster I am."

Matt was in a mood, and not a good one. Dani didn't have a clue how to snap him out of it. Maybe a better person would be capable of it. She'd never claimed to be one. She sighed. "I think you're being a tad overdramatic now. You're acting as if the doctor is about to unwrap your bandages and reveal Frankenstein's monster."

He chuckled. "Close enough."

"He's...He's...alive," she said dramatically. "Relax, and you're worrying yourself into a tizzy."

Matt sighed. "It's hard. Lying here all day with my thoughts to keep me company. It's enough to drive a person crazy."

Dani understood that better than most. She didn't have to be idle for her demons to stomp through her thoughts. All she had to do was breathe, and *poof,* there they were, ready to impart their evil wisdom on her unsuspecting brain.

"Please," she mocked, "you can't go crazy when you're already there." Dani was doing her best to lighten his mood. "You'd have to be to put up with me every day."

Matt smiled. "You do have a valid point." His smile fell slightly. "Thank you, Dani. I didn't realize how much I needed you here until you stopped in."

Tears threatened to fall. Didn't he understand she'd do anything for him? "It's nothing. If you have doubts again, call me. I'll set you straight." Dani pushed the chair forward and leaned her head on his shoulder. "There's nothing I wouldn't do for you."

The door opened and Ren stepped inside. "Are you ready to remove your bandages?"

Dani lifted her head; her gaze met Ren's. *Shit.* He looked pissed. What had she done?

DAMN IT. Ren mentally cursed. Why did she have to appear so comfortable with Matthew Price? He clenched his fists at his side. He didn't like the beast that was welling up inside of him. It wasn't pretty, and it wanted to be unleashed. Ren curbed his instincts. He had a job to do. It didn't have anything to do with pounding his chest, and claiming the woman he loved, as much as he wanted to. Dani almost appeared—afraid. What did she see when she looked at him? He took a deep breath and stepped fully into the room.

"I'm not sure how ready I am," Matt replied. "But I suppose now's as good a time as any."

Ren wrenched his gaze from Dani's and let it settle on Matt. She couldn't be his sole focus. His patient required his attention too. "Lana will be here in a moment with the supplies we need and then we can get started."

"I'm here now, Dr. Sousa." Lana rushed into the room. "Sorry I'm behind."

The petite red-head walked to the other side of Matt's bed and set up on the tray. As far as nurses went, she was one of the best he'd ever worked with. It's why he chose her whenever possible. She was efficient and practical.

Not once had she tried to hit on him. Unfortunately, there were some single women in the hospital who'd tried once they realized he'd filed for divorce. Lana was different. She came to the hospital to work and nothing else.

"I'm ready whenever you are." She turned to him.

"Do you need me to step out?" Dani asked.

"No, don't go," Matt begged.

Ren clenched his teeth. He hated how he felt seeing Dani with her friend. She'd been his best friend once. He'd wanted more than that then, and sure as hell did now. Jealousy wasn't a good feeling to have sitting in the bottom of his gut. Now wasn't the time to let it find a grip in him. Brushing past it, he joined Lana on the other side of Matt's bed.

"Hand me the scissors so I can begin."

Lana brought him the instrument and he started the slow process of removing the bandages around Matt's eyes. He peeled all the layers away and dropped them onto the tray Lana held. After most of them were off, only two squares remained covering each eye. They'd have to replace the ones over the incision on his head to prevent infection, but the removal of his dressing was to test the viability of his vision.

"I'm going to remove the gauze covering your eyes," Ren explained. "Keep your eyes closed. Don't open them until I tell you to."

The silence was eerie in the room. No one said a peep while he worked. Ren was thankful for it. He worked better when it was quiet, allowing him to concentrate. He removed the final two bandages and placed them on the tray. Now it was time to find out if the surgery worked.

"All right," he began, "open your eyes slowly. Blink a few times before you try to focus."

Matt did as he asked. They all waited on bated breath. After he blinked a few times, Matt shook his head. "It's blurry."

Ren smiled. That was actually good news. "Blurry is good. It means you see something."

Matt frowned. "I can't make out anything. How's that a good thing?"

Dani placed her hand over Matt's. "It means you're recovering. If I understand correctly, your eyes still have a lot of healing to do."

Ren appreciated her perceptiveness. As much as he hated seeing them together, Matt needed her support. It would be a long road to recovery. "She's correct. It's going to take a while for you to heal. Your vision might not become fully restored, but I'm hopeful. This is a good sign. Be happy."

Matt smiled. "I'll try. Does this mean I can get out of here?"

"Yes." He grinned back. "Lana, can you start the process to have Mr. Price released tomorrow?"

Lana finished putting new bandages over Matt's incision. "Yes, doctor." She threw away the old bandages in the biohazard waste. "I'll take care of it now." The nurse spun on her heals and exited the room. The woman could almost be considered too efficient, taking all the extra items with her as she left.

"If you don't have any more questions, I'll leave you two to your visit."

"I'm good," Matt said. "You've given me a lot to think

about, and I have the benefit of finally leaving this place soon."

"Then I'll go. Don't be afraid to ask anything. I'm a phone call away."

Ren turned to leave. He wanted to stay, but it wasn't a good time to do it. He'd corner Dani later. Interrupting her time with Matt wasn't the place to push himself on her.

"Ren, wait," she called out.

He closed his eyes and steeled himself for her refusal. Whenever she saw him she either pushed him away or ran as far as possible. Neither one worked for him. "Yes?" he said, turning back to her.

"If you have a moment, I'd like to speak to you before you leave."

This had the possibility of being either good or bad. *Please let it be good.* "I have a few moments before I have to see my next patient."

"Don't let me stop you," Matt said. "I'm going to take a nap. Come back and bother me later."

Dani smiled. "You can count on it." She glanced at Ren. "I'll walk out with you."

Ren didn't know what to make of her. She kept him on his toes. He stayed silent as they exited the room. Leaving it to her to tell him what she wanted to say. He grabbed her arm and led her toward his office. She bit her lip and allowed him to.

"We don't need to go to your office. What I have to say won't take long."

He didn't reply. Ren feared if he opened his mouth the jealousy would come spilling out. The privacy his office offered would give him more control. When they reached it, he pushed the door open and pulled her inside. The door shut with a soft *click*. Dani leaned back against it. Ren stalked forward placing his hands above her shoulders against the door. Their gazes locked.

She gulped. "Ren?"

The need to kiss her filled him. All he wanted was to feel her lips on his again. The beast inside him told him to take what he wanted. She belonged to him as much as he belonged to her. He leaned down and placed his lips on hers. A fire ignited as soon as his heat fueled hers. She wrapped her arms around his waist and pulled him against her. It was all the permission he needed to deepen the kiss. He touched a part of heaven he'd been denied for too long. It was coming home and finding the piece of himself he'd been missing. Dani was everything.

He stepped back and glanced down at her. Her full pouty lips were even fuller and appeared stung from their kisses. The desire filling her eyes was almost too hard to resist, but somehow he managed it. Their breathing was haggard as they fought for control.

"You wanted to talk?" he said.

She flashed him a sultry smile, and breathlessly said, "I like what you had in mind better."

Maybe he should listen to his gut instincts more often. He raised an eyebrow. "I did too."

She lifted both hands and ran them across his chest. "If I had more time I'd see what other things you had in mind."

He groaned. She had no idea. He'd had years of imagination to make up for. "What did you need?"

Ren braced himself for something he didn't want to hear. He hoped the kiss they shared would soften her toward him. If his luck held out it would, and what she said next would lead them in the direction he wanted.

Dani glanced up at him, and winked. "Text me the details on the fundraiser." She tucked a piece of paper in his coat pocket. "I do believe it'll be a night to remember." Then she turned around and left him in his office.

What the hell had happened? Ren let happiness fill him for the first time since he'd found her again. It appeared like he might be finally getting through to her.

"Dani, I do believe you're right. It'll be one I certainly won't forget."

Plans had to me made. He intended for it not only to be a night to remember, but one that Dani wouldn't be able to run away from. This was his chance to get through to her once and for all. One he didn't intend to waste.

*M*att was getting released from the hospital. She had to make plans to get him settled in at his home. There were so many things to arrange. Until he could function on his own, he needed someone with him around the clock. His vision was getting better, but it was nowhere near where it needed to be. He'd hate it, but he needed some live-in help. She was happy that the surgery appeared to work, and over time his vision should return. Blurry was better than total blackness any day.

Dani pushed open the door to her office building. Amy was sitting at the reception desk typing something on the computer. She glanced up at the sound of bells filling the room.

"You're back," she said. "Mr. Nettles called again. He wants to know if you've made any progress."

Damn that man. He had absolutely no patience. It'd been less than twenty-four hours since she'd talked to him. Did he expect her to work miracles? She mentally snorted. No, it was worse than that. The blasted man was anticipating her failure and wanted to find out if she had already. Well, she had news for him. She didn't fail and wasn't about to start to prove him right in his own idiotic misconceptions.

"I'm not prepared to talk to Mr. Nettles yet. If he calls back again, take a message." She'd deal with him after she had her spontaneous meeting with Sullivan Brady. After that, she'd make plans on how to proceed. "I have something in the works, but it's going to take time to get started. I can't have that arrogant man preventing me from gathering information."

She opened her mouth and closed it again. Amy winced and then said what was on her mind. "I don't like him. Every time he calls he's so condescending."

Dani rolled her eyes. She wished she could tell him to find a different firm to represent him. He was truly despicable. "I'm sorry he's being difficult. Let me know if it's too much to deal with."

Amy nodded. "It's frustrating, but overall he's harmless."

She hoped he stayed that way. Dani suspected if he didn't get his way he'd become a problem rather fast. "Is Claire in?"

Claire often ran errands and filed paperwork with the court. She hoped the other woman was available. Her visit to Matt hadn't come up when she spoke to her previously. Dani wanted to make sure she was all right and run a few things by her.

"She's in her office."

"Thank you. Hold all my calls for the rest of the day."

Dani headed to Claire's office. She was hunched over her desk reading a document. Her brows were bunched together in concentration. She didn't appear to be bothered by anything in particular, but Dani knew looks could be deceiving. With a shake of her head she brushed her own worries away and raised her hand to knock on the door frame. When the sound reverberated through the room, Claire glanced up and met her gaze.

"I'm sorry. I was so absorbed in proofreading this motion. How long have you been standing there?"

"It's only been a couple seconds." Dani pointed to the motion. "Is there anything I need to take a look at?" Claire was thorough when she wrote a motion. But since she didn't have a law degree, either Matt or she had to look over them before they could be filed.

"No." She furrowed her brow. "I'm making sure I've covered everything and there are no errors." Claire set the document down. "How's Matt?"

Dani walked fully inside and sat in front of her desk. They had much to discuss, and she needed Claire on board with what she had planned. Matt would be pissed, but Dani believed she was doing the right thing.

"I have some news." Dani smiled. "They took the bandages off his eyes today."

Claire sat up straighter. Her face was devoid of all emotion. "And?"

"The bad news is he can't see." She held up her hand when Claire opened her mouth to interrupt. "Let me finish. He can't see anything but a blur. But he *can* see."

A relieved breath fell from Claire's mouth. "Thank God."

Dani could appreciate her concern. She'd been on pins and needles waiting for the bandages to come off. When Matt had announced everything was blurry, her heart had skipped a beat. He might not have thought so at first, but it had been a good sign.

"He does have a long road toward recovery. He's going to need a lot of help to get to where he needs to be."

Claire nodded. "What do you need from me?"

Dani took a deep breath. She figured Claire would want to help. But how much was she willing to do to help Matt recover? "I have an idea, and I'm not sure you're going to want to do it or not."

"The only way you're going to know is if you ask." Claire sat back in her chair and folded her hands in her lap. "You're aware of how I feel about Matt."

"I am." She studied her assistant. "I also know you went to see him and he was, for lack of a better word, an ass."

Claire didn't say a word. She stared at Dani for several minutes. She leaned forward and set her elbows on her desk. "I gave him allowances for having a bad couple of days. I decided to give him some room to breathe and think about what a dick he was. I assume he said something to you?"

Matt was lucky Claire understood what he was going through. Not everyone would be so forgiving if he bit their head off on a regular basis. "He was regretful. I take it you didn't open a vein and bleed out your feelings for him?'

"No." Claire's lips tilted into a half-smile. "I deduced it wouldn't be a good idea to dump my emotions on him when he already had so much to deal with. In time I will though. I can be patient a little while longer."

"Good, now to my idea." She leaned forward and stared into Claire's eyes. "Matt's going to need round the clock care for a while."

She tilted her head and considered Dani's words. "I can see how that would be necessary. He isn't equipped to dealing with anything right now. He'd have to relearn where everything in his apartment is. Not to mention cooking, cleaning, and the day to day necessities."

Her friend had one hell of an uphill battle to the end of recovery. She didn't envy him that task. With her and Claire's help, he could make it to the other side. Unfortunately, she could already see how difficult he was going to make it for them. It was their job to suck it up and make it as easy as possible for him. They would also be there to remind him when he was being a jerk. More importantly, they would be able to tell him they had faith in him and he could make it.

"I want to hire a nurse to come in and check on him each day, and a therapist to help him to acclimate to his new surroundings, but someone needs to stay after they leave," Dani paused. "That's where you come in."

"Do you want me to research individuals to see who's available and qualified to do what you need?"

"That would be a good start." Dani frowned. "It's last minute. I should have started looking into this sooner, but it didn't occur to me until earlier today. We're going to need someone to start almost immediately. Matt's being released tomorrow afternoon."

Claire sat back. Her mouth fell open with surprise. "So soon?"

A part of Dani wanted to keep him in the hospital where he would get constant care, but he had to be going stir-crazy stuck in bed all day. For his own peace of mind, he had to go home. "He insisted, and I understand why."

Claire nodded. "Matt doesn't like being cooped up. He's still going to go crazy in his own home. I don't think he fully comprehends the ramifications of his injury. Does he know you're arranging for care?"

Dani smiled. Claire understood Matt as well as she did. If she agreed to stay with him when Dani couldn't, then it would all work out. They could take shifts making sure someone was with him. They wouldn't have to hire a stranger to see to his needs. Though Matt might actually prefer that to them hovering. She'd have to play it by ear and see how it went.

"For at least the beginning, I don't think we should have anyone staying overnight with him that doesn't know him or what makes him tick," she explained. "I haven't discussed it with him, but I don't think he should get much of a choice at first. He's going to argue regardless."

Claire tapped her fingers lightly on the desk. "You want me to stay with him, don't you?"

Her assistant was perceptive. It's one of the reasons she had been hired. "Not every night. I can take some too."

Her laughter filled the room. "Matt's going to be livid."

No doubt she was right. He hated having to be taken care of. It was his job to take care of those around him. It was part of who he was. Now he had to sit back and allow them to take care of him. He'd have to suck it up and deal with it.

"At first," Dani agreed. "After he gets done yelling at us." She tilted her head. "And pouting. He'll see reason."

"You are right." She grinned. "It's going to be fun to watch him go through all those stages too."

Dani shook her head. Claire had a perverse side she'd not noticed previously. Where had she been hiding it? It looked good on her, and she'd need it to deal with Matt. Her lips quirked up in amusement before she replied, "So you're willing to help me?"

"I will do you one better. I'm going to let you fully off the hook." She lifted her hands and steepled them together. "I'm going to interview nurses and therapists. Set up a schedule. And move into Matt's house later today. When he gets home tomorrow all his wants, needs, and desires will be met."

She had an almost wicked gleam in her eye. No doubt she was still pissed at Matt's attitude. Dani almost felt sorry for her friend, but Claire wouldn't do anything to truly harm him. He might actually require a bit of tough love. Claire wouldn't hold back anything. She'd see he'd have all the things that would necessitate his recovery.

"All right," Dani agreed. "I will allow you to handle everything as you see fit. If you need any help, don't hesitate to ask."

"Don't worry, I can handle Mr. Price, but if something comes up you'll be the first person I call." She smirked. "But I don't think I will find the need to. Go play with your doctor man. Don't you have a fundraiser to get ready for?"

She did, and she rather looked forward to her evening with Ren. The last kiss was even better than the first. Dani couldn't wait to see if they would improve each time. The more she felt his lips on hers, the more she wanted from him. Her desire had reached all new heights. When they were teens, she'd thought she wanted Ren, but she had no clue how much until now. He made her feel things she never imagined.

"I actually do have a lot to do. A dress is at the top of my list." She planned on finding one that would knock his socks off. He thought he was making all the plans. Ren had no clue what she had in store for him. "Since I trust you to see to Matt, I will gladly go shopping for something extra special for my night with Ren."

Claire winked. "Go get 'em tiger."

Oh, Dani intended to.

*D*ani strolled into her bedroom and yanked her closet door open. She reached across the rack and pulled out a garment bag. She lifted it and carried it over to her bed and set it down. Dani unzipped the bag and stared at what laid inside. She'd bought the dress as soon as she'd laid eyes on it. It was the prettiest dress she'd ever seen, and she'd had to have it. The cocktail dress was a bright pomegranate chiffon with a sweetheart neckline.

She skimmed her fingers over the soft material and sighed. It was perfect, and she couldn't wait to wear it for Ren. He'd arrive soon to pick her up. She sat at her vanity and dried her hair into soft ebony waves. Then slowly applied eyeliner and mascara, and then, with a quick swipe of lip gloss across her lips, she was good to go. The only thing left was to get dressed and wait for Ren to pick her up. She opened a drawer and pulled out the sexiest lingerie she owned and slid them on. It was all black silk and lace, a strapless bra with matching panties. Dani felt sexy having the material slide over her bare skin. The chiffon dress hugged all her curves and showed them off to perfection. She slid on a pair of black heels and headed down the stairs. The doorbell chimed as she arrived at the bottom.

Dani strolled to the door and then opened it. Her gaze met Ren's and she sucked in a breath. He was even more devastating in a tuxedo than he had been at their high school prom. He'd stolen her breath away then too. This time was singular and magical. He was her date, not some else's. A rush of nerves flowed through her. What had she gotten herself into?

"You're beautiful." His gaze roamed over her from the bottom and back up to stare into her eyes. Heat spread through her, covering over her anxiety in a different way. He held his hand out to her. "If we don't leave now, we never will."

"I don't know about you, but I'm rather looking forward to this event. I heard it's the place to be." She reached out and ran her hands over his chest. "I might be convinced to stay in another time though."

He leaned down and placed a soft kiss on her cheek. "I've been wanting to be with you for so long this almost seems surreal."

She had to agree with him. This was a fantasy come to life. There was a time she'd never have imagined this could ever be real. Her insecurities always stood in their way. In all honesty, they might still be a hindrance if she didn't need a valid reason to go to the fundraiser. Sullivan

Brady was attending, and she needed a way to meet him in an innocuous way. Was it a benefit to be on the arms of the only man she'd ever loved? In more ways than one—but she couldn't let Ren distract her from her main purpose.

"Let's not examine it too closely." She wound her arm through his. "We have a lot of history to wade through before we can move forward. This is one step in a million to arrive at our destination. Tonight, let's enjoy each other's company and see where it leads us."

He nodded. "I can do that as long as you make me a promise."

Dani was almost afraid to find out what he wanted to secure from her. He made her nervous on a good day. Today? When she agreed to spend an evening in his company and resist every urge she had to run… She didn't know how much she could guarantee.

"It depends on what you want."

"I want a lot." He grinned wickedly and leaned in to whisper into her ear. "And, in time, I intend to have it all. But for tonight I want one thing."

"What?" she asked eagerly.

His breath was hot on her neck. It sent shivers down her spine. The desire to pull him inside her home and do naughty things to him grated through her. The impulse was almost too great to resist. He didn't kiss her. He didn't even lean in more to initiate closer contact. No, instead he took a step back and stared her in the eyes. His mouth straightened into a firm line. This was serious. He was done playing. Disappointment filled her.

"Don't run away from me." His voice was raw with emotion. "Not now or ever again. I promise you won't get far, and when I find you it won't be pretty."

Dani gulped down a lump in her throat. She glanced away. What she saw in his eyes… There was so much hurt reflecting back at her. She'd done that. It may not have been her intention to do it, but she was responsible for his unhappiness. It didn't sit well with her. Maybe it was time to see her actions for what they were. Cowardice. She'd run from him to protect herself and didn't once think about how they'd damage the one person who'd meant the world to her.

Ren had been her best friend, the one man she'd loved, and she'd spit on him like he was trash. She was wrong. The least she could've done was say goodbye. Pretend that they'd keep in touch and slowly let communication fall away. She'd cut him off and didn't look back. Sure, she'd checked on him a few times without him knowing, but once he married Jessica she didn't look again. One glimpse of his apparent happy life and she'd concluded her decision had been for the best. What had she known?

"The only promise I can make you is I won't disappear without explanation ever again."

She still didn't know what their future held or if they even had one, but she could do better by him. He deserved more from her, and she could give him better consideration.

"I can work with that." He smiled. "Now let's go to this fundraiser. I haven't danced with you in over ten years, and I'm itching to do it again."

Dani had a small flash to prom. The one and only time

they'd danced. It had been perfect. Until it wasn't. At least there wouldn't be a Jessica to steamroll through it this time. Dani pulled her door closed and locked it. She looped her arm through Ren's and let him lead her to his vehicle.

"So tell me what this fundraiser is all about?"

Ren held the passenger door open for her and she slid inside. Once he was seated on the driver's side he answered her. "The Brady-Blue foundation set it up to design a new pediatric wing at the hospital. They want to update the NICU and provide care for families of children in long term care. They want to ensure that all children get the care they need regardless of the family's ability to pay. It's more than designing a state of the art facility."

The more she learned about the Brady family the more she liked them. What would they have against the Nettles family? There had to be more than old man Nettles was saying.

"They seem like a philanthropistic group." Dani frowned. "Do they want to do good for show, or do they truly believe in the cause they stand for?"

Ren maneuvered the car through traffic. He kept his focus on the road but continued their conversation as he drove. "I've had several conversations with the head of the foundation. He has many reasons for this particular project. He lost a sister when she was a two years old. His family has never been the same since. The new wing is to be named in her honor."

That was interesting. She wondered what his sister's

name was. "That's sad. Do you know what happened to her?"

"No, he never said, and I didn't ask. It's not my place to pry."

Dani crunched her eyebrows together. She wanted to know more. Her curious nature was about to push her to places she shouldn't go. "So what's the wing going to be called?" If she couldn't find out the reason the sister had died, at least she could find out a name to do research with later.

"I don't know."

Damn. She almost blurted out something she shouldn't. Instead of saying he wasn't any help, she bit her tongue and held it in. After a minute of reflection, she said, "That's strange."

It really was. She was riveted and couldn't find more. A mystery had always appealed to her. This one was full of details without any real answers. Before the night was over she'd have some of those blanks filled in.

"Not really. They wanted to wait to unveil it until it was built. When it's completed, there will be a ceremony with the name announced."

Was this how Alice ended up falling down that blasted rabbit hole? Her curiosity led her to a strange land, and Dani was starting to understand her fascination. She'd have happily followed that damn white rabbit for answers too. There was a story here, and she intended to uncover it.

"You really have no clue?" she had to ask. "You said you talked to him. Surely he mentioned it to you."

He remained silent. His lips pressed together tightly.

"You do know!" She turned to him and shouted. "Spill it, Sousa."

He shook his head. "It's not my place to say."

How could she get him to tell her? She was dying to know. "Ren, please tell me. I won't tell anyone else."

Damn man. Why did he have to keep this one secret from her? There'd been a time when he told her everything. At least she'd believed he did. She was starting to believe she didn't know as much as she thought about her friend. The way he acted, he'd always wanted her and she'd never seen it. Had she been that blind? Not to see what was right in front of her all that time. He'd played the part well. Dating Jessica was a big obstacle, and if he'd wanted her why bother with another girl? None of it made sense, and she was tired of trying to figure it all out. That was a mystery that would unfold when she was ready to see the truth. This was different and safer. It wouldn't lead her to pain.

"You know you want to tell me."

"What will you give me if I tell you?" His lips twitched. The jerk was trying not to smile.

This was something she could work with. "What do you want?"

His face finally lit up with a bright, wicked smile. It didn't bode well, but she was willing to give in to find out what the wing would be called. For some reason she needed to know it. She wouldn't be able to explain it if she tried.

"How about a boon of my choosing when I decide to claim it."

"Hmmm…" That could be dangerous, much more than she thought it would be. "I'm not sure."

"I guess you don't want the name as much as you insisted."

Hell. He knew her too well. She'd played right into his hands. If she hadn't been too eager she might have gotten it for nothing. Now she'd have to damn near sell her soul to get him to give it up.

"All right," she begrudgingly agreed. "You have a deal."

He pulled into the front of the hotel hosting the event and parked in front of the valet. Ren stepped out of the car and handed the attendant his keys. Once he pocketed his receipt he opened her door and helped her out. When was he going to tell her? Her patience was running thin.

"I'm glad you decided to accept my terms." He wrapped his arm around her waist leading her inside. "We're going to have so much fun tonight."

She furrowed her eyebrows. "Not until you fulfill your end of the bargain."

"You're right. A deal's a deal." He leaned in and whispered in her ear. "Ella's Haven."

Dani heart skipped a beat. Ella's Haven—it had a nice ring to it. She'd have given anything to have something resembling that when she was little. She envied Ella Brady and longed to belong to a family. She couldn't help but wonder what happened to her. Maybe one day she'd find out. It was a weird fascination she couldn't quite explain. A shiver ran down her spine and a coldness set in. A sense of dread filled her. She shook it away as foolishness. It was nothing. She'd let it go; the chance of something bad happening was next to zero.

As far as Ella Brady's situation—it didn't concern her. She was a girl she'd never met and never would. It was nice she'd be remembered. The Brady family must have loved her a great deal for them to do so much in her name. Jealousy over a lost little girl was a new low, even for her. She shouldn't long for something she'd never had.

CHAPTER 11

*R*en led Dani into the banquet hall. Sparkling lights were strung up throughout the room giving it a fairy tale appearance. It had a romantic feel that filled her with giddiness. She'd always balked at fundraisers and had no clue how to act at them. It hadn't occurred to her to do any research. She'd jumped in head first and had no choice but to follow Ren's lead.

Dani leaned into Ren and asked, "What exactly can I expect from this evening?"

"There will be lots of alcohol offered in an attempt to loosen the attendees' grips on their wallets." The tips of his fingers brushed over her hand softly as he held it in his grasp. "There's also dancing, a silent auction, and h'orderves being passed about."

She scanned the room. There wasn't a person in the room she recognized. At least she had Ren. It didn't matter if she was familiar with anyone else. Meeting Sullivan Brady and spending the evening with Ren were her purposes for attending.

"Come dance with me," Ren demanded.

She laughed. "Don't you want to mingle first?"

He shook his head. "Not at all. You're the only person here that matters to me."

She hugged him close. "Then let's dance."

A flash of their first dance floated through her mind. The one time he'd held her close and made her feel like a princess. She'd imagined, for a brief moment, he'd loved her and no one else was in his life. Of course, back then, he'd had a girlfriend. Now he was free and all hers. All she had to do was reach out and claim him. The opening strands of an old country song filled the room. One that invoked even more memories within her, it was magical. The tiny lights were like blinking stars on the night sky. She floated in Ren's arms as they spun around the dance floor. The rest of the world disappeared, and for a few minutes all the world was right. If it all ended tomorrow, she'd have this one moment in time to hold on to. It was all worth it to experience the whirl of dancing in Ren's arms. Magic had nothing on the feeling that overtook her. Dani wouldn't have missed it for anything. When she glanced up and met Ren's gaze his own happiness reflected back at her.

"This is how it always should've been." He pulled her closer. The heat from his hands on her back burned through her. She wanted to get lost in his touch and forget about all the problems of the world. "If only I'd been braver."

She took in his words, shocked at his own admission. They'd both had their own demons to work through. Fear held them both in check. Had he been equally afraid to lose her as she'd been of losing him? What they had here was a failure to communicate. If they had any chance of going forward, they'd have to break down that wall. It was funny how in hindsight she could pinpoint where she'd gone wrong. Dancing in his arms, she could clearly see the moment of no return. When she'd decided they'd be better off as friends. That was a decision that had altered their course irrevocably.

"I don't think you're alone in that feeling." She reached up and wound her arms around his neck, pulling him down to place a soft kiss on his lips. "You followed my lead. I'm the real coward. All we can do is see where we go from here."

She swallowed back her urge to run away again. Nothing terrified her more. Opening her heart to the possibility of a future with Ren petrified her. The pain of losing him would be too much. Over time, she hoped it would ease as she became more comfortable with the idea of having his love focused on her. Something she'd never dared to imagine. The strands of the music died. It was as if they were at the prom all over again. They were lost in each other and no one else mattered. This time there was no Jessica to break the spell.

"I suppose we should move off the dance floor," he whispered in her ear. "I rather enjoy holding you."

She laughed lightly. "You don't have to let me go once we move away. Dancing isn't the only reason to keep me close."

They headed toward the other end of the ballroom. A waiter stopped and offered them champagne. Ren grabbed two glasses and handed one to her. She took a sip. The bubbles tickled her nose and made her feel giddy, or maybe it was the joy she couldn't restrain. Ren gave her a reason to let go and enjoy what life had to offer. A weight she hadn't realized she carried was suddenly lifted off her shoulder. They could do this. All she had to do was keep the past where it belonged. If she didn't look back or question anything, she could have it all.

"It's good to see you outside of the hospital," the nurse with striking auburn hair said as she approached them.

What was her name again? Why did she have such a hard time remembering it? Dani was almost positive it was the same woman who'd called her about Matt's accident. She hadn't been able to recall it that day either. She was around all the time and damn near blended into her surroundings. The woman was one of Matt's nurses, so Dani should be able to recall her damn name.

"Hello, Lana," Ren replied. "Are you having a good time?"

That's it! *Thank you, Ren.* Dani filed away her name. She'd not forget it again.

The young nurse smiled. "I haven't been to one of these functions in years. It's for a good cause, and I had to come to support it."

Ren nodded. "It is. I wasn't aware you'd be here tonight."

Lana grabbed a glass of champagne from a waiter as he passed by. She took a drink before she spoke. "It's hard to not know what this is all for. I know they say it's to support the hospital and give the pediatric wing some much needed funding, but it's more than that. The Brady family went through a lot when Ella went missing. No one understands that more than I do."

Dani perked up at her pronouncement. Did she know what happened to the little girl? Maybe she could grill Lana for more information. Ren didn't seem to know any more than he'd told her. The mystery was so intriguing. It might also give her more to go on concerning her annoying client, Mr. Nettles. She didn't understand what he had against females.

"Do you know the family well?" Dani couldn't hold the question in. She had to know more. "I've not met any of them."

Lana turned to her, a puzzled expression on her face. "I'm sorry. I should know you. You seem familiar."

"Dani's Matthew Price's friend," Ren offered.

"No, that's not it." She scrunched her nose up. "But now that you mention it, I do recall seeing you in his room."

Dani decided Lana was odd. She seemed nice enough, but easily distracted. She shrugged. "I am unre-markable."

"If you say so," Lana reluctantly agreed. "To answer your question, I grew up in their household. My mother is their housekeeper. Most of the family is nice enough. I lived in the main residence when Ella went missing. It's not something I'm likely to forget."

Dani restrained from shouting out. She wanted to do a jig. This is what she needed. A source to pump for more information, if she could hold back the need to press deeper for information she might get Lana to spill everything.

"It must have been devastating for the family. Do you know what happened?"

She'd wanted to forget about the little girl, but she couldn't seem to let it go. It might be silly, but she was intrigued. Deep down Dani realized the little girl's disappearance wouldn't help her with Mr. Nettle's case though.

She shook her head. "It's not my place to say."

Damn. Stonewalled again. How was she going to get any details on the family if no one would open up? Instead of pushing her, she nodded her agreement. "I understand. I can be morbidly curious."

"If you don't mind me asking—where do you come from?" Lana asked.

"Excellent question," a deep baritone agreed. "I haven't had the pleasure of meeting you. Lana, please introduce us."

Lana frowned. "Go away, Sullivan. We're having a grown up conversation. You weren't invited."

He chuckled lightly. Dani glanced up at him. He was even more gorgeous in person. The pictures in the paper hadn't done him justice. His hair was a rich ebony, slightly long, with curls hugging the edge of his ears. His deep green eyes *were* the exact same shade as hers. Claire hadn't been wrong on that account. Sullivan Brady was breathtaking to behold, and Lana appeared to be more annoyed than entranced by him.

"I beg to differ," his reply rolled of his tongue. "I'm the host. I don't need an invitation. It's implied."

The prim and proper Lana did something Dani wouldn't have expected. She glanced over her shoulder and stuck her tongue out at him. Dani's mouth fell open with shock. They were almost—playful. Lana said she'd grown up in the Brady household. Did that mean they were childhood friends? Their actions certainly implied as much.

"Doesn't give you leave to be rude." She rolled her eyes. "I was having a nice conversation with Dr. Sousa and his date. You had no right to impose yourself on our conversation."

He held his hand against his chest and turned to her and Ren. "I apologize. I didn't realize my behavior was untoward. Please forgive me" He held his hand out to Ren. "Dr. Sousa, it's good to see you again. Thank you for coming tonight."

"The pleasure is all mine." Ren shook Sullivan's hand. "It's a good cause."

Sullivan nodded. "My family certainly thinks so." His gaze focused on Dani's face. Sullivan's scrutiny was akin to studying a bug under a microscope. She squirmed under his thorough examination. "I don't believe we've met. I'm Sullivan Brady."

"See, you're capable of introducing yourself. I'm going in search of better company," Lana paused. "I don't mean you, Ren." Then she spun on her heels and left.

"I'm going to check on her." Ren leaned down and kissed Dani's cheek. "I'll be back in a few minutes." He followed after Lana. Dani pushed down the rush of jealousy. Lana was a friend and colleague. It was perfectly fine for Ren to make sure she was all right. It was in his nature to look after those he cared for.

Sullivan shook his head. "I apologize. We tend to needle each other whenever we cross paths. It's the result of growing up together, I'm afraid. We know too many of each other's secrets and faults."

"That's not always a bad thing."

"No." He smiled down at her. "It isn't. So are you going to keep me in the dark forever?"

"What?" She furrowed her eyebrows in confusion.

"Your name," he stated plainly. "I've never seen you before. The first time I met Ren he was married to a blonde harpy."

Dani smiled at his description of Jessica. "An apt description if I've ever heard one." She liked him. He was easy to be around, and there was something comforting in his demeanor. "I'm Daniella Brosen."

He nodded. "A pleasure to meet you, Ms. Brosen. Have you known the good doctor long?"

"Most of my life. We were best friends in high school."

Why were details spilling out of her without much thought? She didn't usually open up to people she barely knew. This was supposed to be her inquisition. If she wanted to gain control of their conversation, she'd have to turn things around, and fast.

"Hmm." His gaze went unfocused. "So were you child-hood sweethearts as well?"

She shook her head. "Why are you so curious?"

He was silent for a brief moment. A flicker of some-thing flashed in his eyes before he pushed it back. What-ever it was, he'd suppressed it before it could surface. It made Dani a little uneasy. What was Sullivan Brady after?

"You remind me of someone."

That seemed to be the standard answer lately. What was going on with him? He acted like he knew her at a glance. She didn't like it one bit. The familiarity wasn't settling well with her. She'd found him comforting at first —now she wanted to put some distance between them. He was freaking her out.

"If you say so." Dani shrugged. As far as she knew, she didn't resemble anyone. They did say everyone had a twin of some sort in the world. Maybe she did look like someone he'd met before. Claire said Dani's coloring was similar to the Sullivans'. It wasn't beyond the realm of possibility she could look like someone he was acquainted with. "I wouldn't have a clue about anyone you know."

He raised an eyebrow. "I don't suppose you would." His lips quirked upward. "I'd like to know you better."

"I promise I'm not interesting enough to bother with." She waved a hand. "I bet you live a fascinating life though. Tell me about yourself."

Dani attempted to change the subject. She didn't like the path it had gone down. Whatever Sullivan wanted to know, she wasn't so sure she wanted him to find out. He was charming and smooth. If she allowed it, he'd have intimate knowledge of every one of her secrets before she knew what she was saying.

"I'm not all that intriguing. I promise." He shrugged. He flashed her one of his charming smiles that almost caught her off guard again. "So you grew up with Ren in Hope Beach on the other side of the state."

Damn, he was good. She almost didn't catch it. He was so subtle. Digging for answers when it was clear he wanted more information on her. Did he think he was protecting Ren from another harpy? Maybe if she gave him enough details, he'd leave them alone.

"Not entirely. I didn't get transferred to a foster home there until I was at the end of eighth grade. Before that, I'd been in so many different places I don't remember them all."

He stilled. All emotion fell from his face. "You were in foster care?" His voice was pure steel. Why did it bother him so much?

She nodded carefully. "For as long as I remember. My parents abandoned me. I was found asleep on a church steps in a town near Hope Beach. I don't know who my family is."

He reached out for her. She jerked her hand out of his grasp before she realized what she was doing. Something in his face scared her. She stepped back, away from his grasp. "What are you doing?"

"I'm sorry." He shook his head. "No one should go through that. I wasn't thinking—it's…" He paused and scrubbed his face with his hands. "I hate to think of any child suffering. It's part of the reason my family set up this foundation. We want to help all children. If you understood what happened to my sister…"

She nodded. He wasn't reacting to her, but what happened to Ella Brady. She could forgive him his reaction. Unfortunately, it didn't stop her from shaking. "I'm sorry your family went through such a terrible ordeal. You have my sympathies." She brushed her hand nervously over her dress and downed the rest of her champagne. "If you'll excuse me. I'm going to join Ren. Have a good night."

She set her empty glass on a nearby table and escaped as quickly as her feet could move in three-inch heels.

When she reached Ren's side, she was able to breathe a sigh of relief.

"What's wrong?" he asked.

"Nothing," she attempted to reassure him. "I missed you."

He stared off in the distance. "Was Sullivan bothering you?"

"Of course not." She shook her head. "He's harmless."

Ren was silent. He stared across the room. She turned to see what held his attention. Sullivan Brady was leaving the ballroom, exiting by a side door. Their conversation must have bothered him more than she realized.

"Sullivan can be—intense, but he is a good guy," Ren said. "This fundraiser means a lot to him and his family. It's hard on them, but they want to make a difference where they can."

She shrugged. "I don't have any family, so I don't have any experience to fall back on. I would hate to go through what they have." She didn't experience what the Brady's had when Ella went missing. The whole thing would be more than she could handle. She would much rather think of pleasant things. "Let's focus on what we came here for." She leaned into him and let her hands skim across his chest. "Dance with me again."

Ren let her pull him back on the dance floor. After a while, the weird actions of Sullivan Brady appeared to slide where it belonged—in the back of her mind. Later, when she had a clear head, she'd re-examine it all and figure out what was going on. For now, she'd enjoy her night with Ren fully.

Sullivan hadn't come back to the ballroom since he'd exited. Ren glanced at his watch. He'd been gone over twenty minutes. He'd hoped to have a conversation with him while Dani went to use the restroom. He'd have to catch him another time.

"Ren, it's nice to see you."

He looked up at Preston West and scowled. "What do you want?"

"I was hoping we could talk."

It was the last thing Ren wanted to do. Preston had damaged their friendship when he'd taken his ex-wife to bed. They had a working relationship, nothing more. "I think we've covered every subject we would ever have to discuss outside of the hospital. There's nothing you could possibly say that would make things any different between the two of us."

Preston closed his eyes and took a deep breath. "Please listen to me. Give me five minutes."

Ren tightened his hand into a fist and held it close to

his side. Dani would come back from her trip to the ladies' room any moment. He wanted Preston gone before she did. "You have less than that. Say what you need to and leave me alone."

"I wanted to talk to you about Jessica."

"As far as I'm concerned, whatever is going on between you and my ex-wife can stay between the two of you. I don't figure into that equation any longer." He stared into Preston's eyes and hammered home his point. "I divorced her for a reason. You were only one part of it. I've moved on and don't give a damn what you two decide to do."

Preston nodded. "I saw you with your date. You look happy."

How long had Preston been watching them? He shook the thought away. It didn't matter. Nothing Preston did concerned him. All he wanted was for the other doctor to leave him in peace. "Did you have a point?"

"I wanted you to know that I didn't do what I did with Jessica to hurt you. I fell in love with her." He paused and then said, "I wish I'd done things differently. I miss having you as a friend. Is there any way you can forgive me?"

Oh, hell. Ren didn't want to deal with any of this nonsense. "I doubt it." He loved Jessica, so that made it all right? What world did he live in? He was supposed to be his friend, but he didn't really fault him for falling in love with Jessica. It was the betrayal that soured his stomach. "You made your choice. Go make nice with Jessica and make sure she leaves me alone too. I'm tired of dealing with the both of you. If it isn't a professional issue, don't bother talking to me."

Ren spun on his heels and left his former friend behind. He'd go look for Dani himself. He was ready to leave the fundraiser. It had been one conundrum on top of another. It was time to move on to phase two of their evening. He leaned against the wall near the restroom and waited for her to exit. She did less than a minute later. Dani stopped short when she saw him waiting.

"I wasn't in there that long was I?"

"Not at all." He grinned. "I was getting anxious to see you again."

She laughed. "It was five minutes, Ren."

He pulled her into his arms and said, "Five minutes is forever to be separated from you. Let's get out of here."

She gazed up at him with a soft, dreamy smile. "I'm ready if you are."

He wrapped an arm around her waist and led her out of the ballroom. When they got outside, he handed his receipt to the valet. While they waited for him to retrieve Ren's car, he decided to further his agenda. He lifted his hand and ran his finger through her dark curls. They were silky soft. He trailed his fingers up her arm lightly. Her breath hitched with each movement he made. Dani's mouth fell open and her eyes drifted closed. Ren took advantage and leaned down and placed his lips on hers. A light kiss at first, followed by a deeper, needier one as she leaned into him pulling him flush against her. Ren wanted to take her home and love her properly.

"Ahem, pardon me," a man said from behind him. "Here's your car." He dangled his keys in front of Ren.

"Thanks." He grabbed them and led Dani to his car.

They both got inside and he started the drive to her home. "Did you have a good time?"

Will you let me inside when we get to your place? That was the question he really wanted to ask, but could wait a little longer to get the answer he desired. He'd waited this long, so he could wait fifteen more minutes. She was his. They both knew they belonged together. It had taken longer for them both to come around to the same conclusion, but they had and that was all that mattered to him.

"I did. It was a wonderful, albeit strange, evening. But I'm glad I went."

Ren was pleased. The drive to her house flew by. Before he knew it, he was pulling into her driveway and shutting the engine off on his car. He hopped out and opened her door. She placed her hand in his. When she was out of the vehicle, he pulled her into his arms and kissed her again. She lifted her arms and wound them around his neck. He kissed her as he led her to her front door. Their lips barely leaving each other's with each step they took. Ren would never get enough of her. She was perfect for him.

"I should go inside." She was breathless, leaning against her front door. "But I'm enjoying this too much to let you go."

"Then don't." He kissed her bare shoulder, trailing his lips lightly up her neck. He stopped to whisper in her ear, "We can go inside and do a whole lot more."

He waited for her to say yes. It wasn't a given, but he expected her to agree. They both wanted more. Ren wanted it all, and this was only the beginning.

"I don't know."

Not a yes, but definitely not a no. He could work with that. "Let everything else fade away. Open the door so we can get lost in each other."

"Yes," she agreed.

She searched through her purse for her keys. When she found them, they fumbled in her hands and fell to the ground. Ren picked them up and pushed the house key into the lock. He turned the key and pushed the door open. "After you." He gestured for her to enter. He closed the door behind him.

Dani turned to him. Her gaze didn't leave his as her purse hit the floor. He stalked forward, pulling her into his arms. "You're so beautiful."

"Love me, Ren."

"Always," he agreed. He leaned down and captured her lips in his. With careful precision, he lifted his hands and slowly slid the zipper of her dress down. It fell at her feet in a pool of satin. She took a step back and stood before him in her panties, bra, and killer shoes. For a brief moment, he forgot how to breathe. The silk and lace barely covered her, and all he wanted to do was tear it off her. The desire to taste every inch of her was too strong to ignore. She went to kick off her shoes and he held up a hand to stop her.

"Leave them."

He moved toward her and lifted her in his arms. "Bedroom?"

"Up the stairs."

"Too far," he said, and carried her into her living room. "We'll go there later."

Ren laid her gently down on the sofa. She was flushed

a pretty pink. His desire rocketed through him. Her lingerie, while pretty, had to go. With quick movements her bra was unfastened and tossed over his shoulder. Ren sucked in a deep breath as he gazed down at her. Slow and steady, he reminded himself. He leaned down and sucked one of her breasts into his mouth. She moaned in pleasure. He slid one of his hands down her belly and then underneath her panties. He trailed a finger over her swollen clit. Her moans grew louder.

"Breathe, baby," he said as he pushed a finger into her wet channel. He pumped his finger inside her as his thumb rubbed over her sensitive nub. Her breathing became more ragged. Ren increased the pressure as he sucked on her other breast. She screamed as her climax hit her.

"Ren!"

It was music to his ears. The desire to be buried deep inside her over took him. He stood up and stripped all his clothes off. He grabbed a condom from his pocket. It paid to be prepared as he slid it over his hard cock. Dani lay on the couch, blissfully content from her orgasm. Ren intended to bring her to ecstasy again and again before the night was over. He slid her panties down her legs and tossed them. He lifted her legs and prepared to slide into her.

"Are you ready, baby?"

She nodded. Ren slowly entered her hot channel. He groaned in pleasure as she clenched around him. He pushed all the way into her, stopping to let her adjust to him. Her breath became ragged again.

"More, Ren," she begged. "I need."

"All you had to do was ask."

Hell, she didn't even have to ask. He'd give her anything whether she knew she needed it or not. His love for her knew no bounds. Ren rocked back and forth inside of her. He set up a rhythm and pace that brought more deep moans from her. He kissed her neck and relished in the pleasure surrounding him. Nothing had prepared him for the joy of being with Dani. It was everything he'd ever imagined and more. His need grew, and he pumped faster inside of her. Her nails raked against his back as she once again found her climax. She screamed his name and wrapped her legs tightly around him. He lost it as his own orgasm exploded from deep inside of him. Stars flashed behind his eyes. It was a million times more pleasurable than he'd thought it would be. Reluctantly, he pulled out of her. The loss of her warmth was overbearing. Ren drew her back into his arms and rolled them to their sides, holding her tight against him.

"Is that how it's supposed to be?" she asked.

He always knew it would be like this between them, perfect in every way. Emotions made sex so much better. It was the way love was supposed to be. He could feel her breathing. She drew a heart on his back with the tip of her finger, contentment filled him.

"Yeah, when you love someone it's pure magic."

"Yes," she whispered. "I could stay wrapped up in your arms forever, and it wouldn't be long enough."

Ren couldn't agree more. They stepped into the fire and melted into each other. He'd never loved anyone the way he did Dani. She was his everything. Sex was only one way of showing her how much he adored her. He intended to do it as often as she allowed him.

"Holding you in my arms is a pleasure," he replied. "As much as I hate to say it, I think we should move. I'm sure your bed's a million times more comfortable."

"You're right." She lifted her arm and cupped his cheek. "You always are. I should listen to you more often."

"I'll have to remind you of that fact every time you're being stubborn." He laughed. "We both know you're going to dig your feet in when you're not caught up in pleasure."

"And I'll hold you to that." She wrapped her arms around his neck and said. "Now shut up and kiss me."

A command he wouldn't—no couldn't ignore. It was a desire equally held between them. He kissed her lightly and slid off the couch. Ren held his hand out to her and helped her to her feet. He lifted her into his arms and carried her up to her bedroom. Once he had her settled on her bed he started to love her all over again. They had a lot of time to make up for.

*D*ani strolled into her office with a smile on her face. That was her normal state after her evening with Ren over a week ago. She couldn't have had a better night if she wished for it. Everything had gone so well she kept waiting for something to go wrong. Whenever she started to feel happy, something always came crashing through it. Whenever doubts crept into her thoughts, she reminded herself there was nothing to worry about.

"You look happy," Amy said.

"I am." It was surreal how much she was. "Do I have any messages?"

Amy handed her a couple slips of paper. She perused them and frowned when she read the one from Mr. Nettles. In the bliss of her week of joy with Ren she'd forgotten about him. Sullivan Brady had thrown her for a loop when she met him. She'd pushed him out of her mind as well. Whatever was going on between those two, she wasn't sure she wanted to get in the middle of it. Even though the firm needed money to function, dealing with Mr. Nettles wasn't worth it. She'd call him and tell him she could no longer represent his interests. Matt would understand. He hated the unreasonable man too. They didn't need the stress of dealing with him on a daily basis. There were more important things they had to deal with.

"There was a delivery too. I placed it on your desk."

"Thank you," Dani said and headed to her office. She wasn't expecting anything. Amy hadn't mentioned what it was. It couldn't be too important. When she saw the bouquet of flowers, the smile returned to her face in full force. A vase filled with roses in every color imaginable sat there waiting for her to admire them. It was like having a rainbow of happiness displayed only for her. She picked up the card and read the note.

Dani-

I have one heart to give. Lucky for us both, I was smart enough to give it to you years ago. It always leads me back to you. I never got over you, and I never will. Keep my heart with you forever, and wherever you are it will fill you with all my love.

Eternally yours,

Ren

"That must be some note to put such a glowing smile on your face."

Dani spun around and faced Sullivan Brady. Had she conjured him up with her thoughts of him earlier? Why was he in her office? More importantly, why hadn't Amy warned her he was on his way back to her work area? She'd have to talk to her receptionist later.

"What can I do for you, Mr. Brady?"

"Who are the flowers from?" He pointed to her bouquet of roses. "They're from Ren, aren't they?"

She frowned. He seemed too comfortable invading her space. Dani didn't like it one bit. "What are you doing here?"

His gaze met hers. There was something she wasn't following. The one and only time she'd met him he'd acted odd. He was even more so on their second encounter. He lifted his hand and tapped at his jacket. "I have something to discuss with you. Actually, I have a lot to say. We should perhaps sit down for this. It might take a while." He gestured toward her chair.

She sighed and sat as he'd suggested. He followed suit. "I don't have a lot of time. I have a full schedule today." Not a total lie, but she did have a lot of work to do. The sooner she got him out of her office, the better she'd feel. "Let's get this done quickly."

"First, I want to apologize for my behavior when we met. I don't usually behave in such a manner." He attempted to appear chagrined. He crossed his legs and leaned back in his seat. "You took me by surprise."

She raised an eyebrow. "How so?" Dani didn't comprehend how she'd managed to do something she'd not intended to do. "I assure you I didn't do anything to cause any such reaction."

"I am aware of that. Your intentions have nothing to do with my reaction." He nodded at her and began speaking, "You have to understand something. My family is close, and when my sister was kidnapped..."

"Wait," she interrupted. "First, I don't know anything about your sister or what happened to her years ago.

Don't feel like you need to tell me anything." What did his sister have to do with her? She didn't need the long explanation.

"Please, listen to me. Everything will make sense when I'm finished."

She pursed her lips in displeasure. He wasn't going to make any of this easy on her. The only solution she had was to listen to his lengthy discourse and then see him out. "Fine. Please proceed."

"As I was saying, when Ella was kidnapped it put us all into a tailspin. I was four years old, and even I understood what it meant. Our lives were torn apart, and my parents were never the same again."

He was already telling her details she had no business knowing and didn't want to either. Why did he insist on going through all of it with her? Dani sighed. "What does any of that have to do with me?"

He reached inside his jacket and pulled out a couple items. One was a photograph. He handed it to her. She glanced down at a lovely family portrait. There were four individuals, two parents and two small children. The older man had dark black hair and brilliant green eyes. Both children had the same hair and eyes. The woman had hair the shade of burnt chestnuts; her lips were full and wide as she grinned at the camera. Except for the differences in their coloring it was almost as if she were looking at a picture of herself. She shook as she stared at the picture. Her stomach tingled and alarm washed over her. "Who are these people?" Dani was afraid of the answer. She knew what he was going to say before the words left his mouth.

"Those are my parents, Malachi and Siobhan Brady." He tapped them off on the picture. "The little boy is, of course, me. The little girl is you."

She sat back stunned. When she saw her resemblance to the woman she knew he'd claim she was his sister. It was a lie. It had to be. There was no way she was Ella Brady.

"You're wrong," she denied vehemently. "I'm not that little girl. Don't try to make me into something I'm not."

He remained quiet as he studied her. What he hoped to ascertain by his perusal, Dani didn't have a clue—but it was disconcerting. Ren often remarked on her ability to make a person squirm with a look. This man had that affect on her. She found she didn't like experiencing it from the other side. Sullivan Brady's silence was horrible to sit through. It made her uneasy. She didn't like it one bit. He had to go before she lost it.

"Do you think I'd come here if I wasn't sure?" he asked. "I have proof. If the picture isn't enough for you—I ran a DNA test."

Dani stood up and paced around the room. She clenched her fists at her side. Sullivan Brady was wrong. She didn't care how many tests he ran. Oh, hell. That was why he'd been acting so weird at the benefit. He'd suspected she was his sister, and he'd somehow obtained the means to attain the answer.

"How did you manage to get your DNA proof?"

He blanched at her question. "You're not going to like it."

Sullivan was stalling. She didn't know why, but it was obvious. "Spill it. I don't have time for your shenanigans."

He smiled. It was an easy lift of his lips that spread his amusement across his features. She wanted to slap it off his pretty face. "I did what any self-respecting brother would do."

"An assumption. I'm still not sure we're related." Although the more he spoke, she could see the connection. That didn't mean she believed it or even wanted to. "What did you do?"

"It was simple." He shrugged. "I snatched your champagne glass after you set it down. It was easy enough to pull your DNA from it and have it tested against mine, and my parents. It was a match."

"It was that easy?" She snapped her fingers. "I somehow doubt it was."

"It was the only way to make sure. I hope you understand." He gestured his hand, pleading with her. "There are no doubts you are a part of my family."

Hell and damnation, she wanted to scream. Things were already complicated in her life. She didn't want to add another one onto the ever growing pile. "I don't recognize your proof." She couldn't deal with any of this. Her heart raced against her chest. What did he expect her to do? Run into his arms and thank him for welcoming her into his family? "It's not valid without my consent, and you could have used any DNA to test it with."

"I also tested it against the DNA we had on file for my sister. The others were for confirmation." He stood up and walked over to her. Sullivan reached up and lifted her chin with his hand. "I realize this can't be easy for you, but please accept what I already know is the truth. You're a Brady. The one we lost and have been searching for."

Dani stepped back out of his reach. She put some distance between them and lifted her chin defiantly. "I don't have to accept anything. You're a stranger to me." She was grasping at straws, and she knew it. He knew it. In a matter of time the world would know it. The Brady family wasn't going to leave her in peace. She lifted her shaky hand and clenched her stomach. Trouble always seemed to find her. Why couldn't the fates let her be happy? She'd finally found a little bit with Ren.

"We can run as many tests as you want. What will it take for you to believe me?"

The problem was a part of her believed him, had known when she met him. They shared an undeniable connection. She'd been comfortable around him. That didn't make any of his news an easy pill to swallow. She wasn't ready for a readymade family. They would smother her. The little she knew about the Brady family told her that much. She was their long lost daughter. They'd want to wrap her in cotton and keep her safe. Dani would die before she let them do that to her.

"I can't do this right now." She shook harder. "You need to leave."

A full panic sent in. Her breaths became shallow and heavy. She fought to get air into her lungs. Dani waved her hand and tears fell from her eyes. *No, no, no.* The mantra kept playing on a loop inside her head.

Sullivan crossed the distance of the room and pulled her into his arms. "Breathe, it's going to be all right." He rubbed her back and cooed soothingly.

Dani hiccupped. Why did he have to be so damn nice? She stepped back.

"I don't handle surprise well."

"I can see that." He lifted his hand and wiped a tear from her cheek. "We don't bite, Ella. Come home to your family."

"That's not my name." She stepped back, needing the space to think. His presence muddled everything.

Sullivan smiled. "Your full name is actually Daniella Haven Brady. Father refused to call you Dani. He said it was a boy's name and you were his fairy princess. So you've always been Ella to us. I doubt they're going to call you anything different."

Dani straightened. "They can think and do whatever they want, but I'm Daniella Brosen, Dani to my friends. I don't know you, and I sure as hell don't know them."

He sighed. "I haven't told them about you yet. I wanted to come see you first."

She didn't know what to make of that pronouncement. Did he want to get her measure before exposing his precious parents—her parents—to her crudeness? She still couldn't wrap her head around that little tidbit. She'd been on her own for so long. Now she had a whole family. Accepting Ren back into her life had been a big step for her. This? It was beyond her comprehension. She'd longed for a family years ago. Back then it would have mattered more to her. Now? She wasn't so sure she was cut out for one. She was far too independent. Ren knew more than anyone her penchant for running away from things that terrified her. Facing Malachi and Siobhan Brady not only topped that list, they were the epitome of it.

"Well, perhaps we should keep this to ourselves." She

ran her hands over her skirt to smooth out wrinkles it didn't have. "No reason to bother them with it."

Dani didn't look at Sullivan. She didn't want to see disappoint reflecting back at her from him. No doubt this wasn't going the way he'd envisioned when he marched into her office. Ren could have warned him how surly she could be.

"Why, don't you want to meet them?"

She turned to him and shrugged. "I've been on my own for years. Don't see any reason to change that now."

"You'd rather be alone when you have a family that wants you?" He tilted his head. "I'm not sure I understand why you'd choose to ignore us."

Dani didn't know how to illuminate him on her damaged psyche. How did you explain the defense mechanisms you built over the years? She had walls in place for a reason. The things she went through going from foster home to foster home... Well she would rather forget them. The walls allowed her that luxury.

"I'm damaged, Sullivan." She glanced at him. "There's no reason to cause them the pain of knowing who their daughter has become."

"At least you're admitting who you are. That's a start." He smiled. "It's something I can work with."

"Don't get false hope." She shook her head. "I'm intelligent enough to recognize the truth when I see it. Do me a favor and do the same."

He studied her in silence. "We've been looking for you for too long. They never gave up hope they'd find you. It would be wrong to not tell them I have and chose not to enlighten them to that fact."

Damn him and his integrity. "You'd cause them unnecessary pain?"

"I don't see it the same way you do. You're not damaged." He smiled softly. "They will see what I do. You're a strong, independent, and successful young woman. One who fought against all odds to make something of yourself. You're so far beyond broken it's ridiculous you see yourself that way."

Dani frowned. What would it take to get through to him? Maybe it would be enough to beg for time. She'd need it to process the bombshell he'd dropped on her.

"Think what you want. You don't know who I am or what I've gone through any more than I know you. We might share some common DNA, but that doesn't make a family."

Sullivan sighed. "I will give you some time to consider everything. Before I go, I want you to know we love you. The person who stole you from us will pay for taking you away."

She frowned. "You act as if you know who it was."

A look came over his face; it sent shivers down her spine. "Oh, we've always known. We couldn't prove it."

"Who?"

She wanted to know who to destroy for ruining her life. She should have grown up with a loving family and no worries. Instead, she'd been tossed around as if she were garbage.

"I will tell you everything the next time I see you. I've already given you much to think about. Next time we meet, I'll take you to meet our parents."

Sullivan spun on his heels and exited her office.

"Don't leave now." She picked up a book on her desk and heaved it at him. He ducked out of the way and laughed as he kept walking.

"*Ohhhhh.*" He was so damn frustrating. Why did the Fates bless her with such an irritating brother? "The next time I see you, be prepared to explain everything to me, Sullivan Brady," she shouted.

In the meantime, she'd do some of her own research. The answers she sought might be in the local paper. A trip to the local library suddenly took precedence on her schedule. Dani never could wait around for someone to do something she could do herself. So she was Daniella Brady. Time to learn some more about who she was and the family she descended from. With steely determination, she breezed out of her office with a new mission.

CHAPTER 14

"*Y*ou're not going to believe the day I've had." Dani rushed into Ren's office and sat in front of his desk. "*Poof!*" She threw up her hands in demonstration. "My life has gone up in smoke. Obliterated in to nothingness."

Ren frowned. What the hell happened? The day had started out well. He'd woken up with Dani in his arms. Even remembered to send her some flowers to remind her how much he loved her. This was not the reaction he'd expected from her when he saw her.

"I'm sure it isn't as bad as you think."

She shook her head. "Oh, I'm sure it is. In fact, I'd say it's a bazillion times worse." She rubbed her forehead with the tips of her fingers. "I have the worst headache."

Ren loved her. He did. Sometimes, though, she made no sense and drove him crazy. "Why don't you start at the beginning." He was lost. It'd only been a few hours since he'd seen her last. What disaster could have arisen in such a short span of time. "Is it something to do with work?"

She glanced at him and smiled. "First, let me tell you I loved the flowers. They're beautiful. Thank you for sending them to me."

Good, at least one thing had gone right. He breathed a sigh of relief. She wasn't upset with something he'd done at least. This was an entirely new problem. "I'm glad you liked them." They were on a good path. The path they should have always been on. He'd go insane if they took a few steps back. "So tell me about your day."

Dani closed her eyes and took a deep breath. "Sullivan Brady stopped by unannounced."

He tilted his head and studied her. Sullivan Brady was a good guy. Him stopping by to see her shouldn't have been a bad thing. Still, Ren didn't like it. What business would Sullivan have with Dani? None that he could think of. He'd have to speak to the man when he next had the chance. "What did he come to see you about?"

"It's rather a long story." She bit her lip. "I'm not sure how I feel about any of this."

Ren leaned back in his chair and studied her. He took in all the little nuances. She fidgeted in her chair, and tapped on the arms with her fingers. Her cheek twitched every now and then. When it did, her fingers tapped faster in succession with it. Whatever Sullivan told her bothered her more than she wanted to say. He knew Dani, perhaps more than anyone did. Whatever news had been dropped on her must be intensely unnerving.

"If you don't want to tell me, you don't have to." She would when she was ready. If he pushed, her stubborn streak would make her run instead of leaning on him.

"But I think you might need someone to help you get through whatever's bothering you. It's why you're here."

"You're right." She nodded. "It's putting a voice to it that's making me pause." Dani clenched the arm of the chair. Her knuckles turned white. "As I was growing up, I never thought much about my name. I'm Dani. Always have been. It didn't ever occur to me to ask if or why Daniella Brosen was bestowed upon me. I think I assumed they somehow knew who I was but didn't want to tell me."

Where was she going with all of this? What did her name have to do with Sullivan Brady? One of Dani's triggers was the feeling of abandonment she'd grown up with. So her nervous twitch made more sense to him with the little she'd told him. Her meeting with Sullivan to her lost family—a revelation flashed through his mind. He saw Dani differently. Was she? No it wasn't possible. Was it?

"Dani?"

She rambled on. "I remember someone asking my name. Daniella was so hard to say. But they somehow understood. But my last name... I couldn't remember it. The *Brrrr* came out." Her gaze met his. "I was so little. They took what little information they knew and put me into foster care. Did they even check to see if my actual family missed me? Why was it all overlooked?"

"Oh, sweetheart." He stood up and rounded the desk. Ren lifted her into his arms and held her. Her body shook harder as he held on tight. "Shh. I have you."

"My life could have been so different. What am I supposed to do with all this information? I don't know how to think of myself as someone's beloved daughter. I want answers, and I intend to find out what happened. Sullivan claims he knows who is responsible, and he's going to tell me all later. Whoever it was is going to pay for what they did to me."

Ren ran his hand through her dark curls. He tried everything he could to soothe her. "Sometimes things happen for a reason. We don't always understand what it is." He stared into her eyes. "In time, maybe you will come to terms with it. I know how much you wanted to be a part of family. Now you have one. Don't throw it away because you're terrified of what it means."

Her lips wobbled. A small tear slid down her cheek. Ren reached up and wiped it away. "What did I do to deserve you?" she asked. Dani wound her arms around him and hugged him tight. "This's why I'm here. After Sullivan left, I went to do some research. I read everything I could about Ella Brady's disappearance—my kidnapping—the more I read, the more it all made sense. Then I had a flash of memory. A kind woman asking me my name, she gave me a lollipop."

"Do you think she's the one that found you?"

"I don't know. Maybe. Why don't I remember my family?"

Ren didn't know what to say to her. "You were two. Don't be so hard on yourself." His heart broke at the idea of a young Dani lost and alone. But he was also uneasy. If she'd never been taken, he might not have met her. It was wrong of him to go down that path, but he couldn't help but be glad she'd been a part of his life. Even with the ten year separation. When he said sometimes things happen for a reason he'd meant it. Her kidnapping was a horrible thing, but it brought her to him. He couldn't be sad about that happenstance. Dani was his entire world.

"You're right." She smiled. "You usually are. I'm glad I came to see you."

Ren kissed her lightly. "Remember that when you're ready to argue with me about something. Keep that mantra rolling through your mind. Ren's right, give in and make things easy for both of us."

She laughed. "I doubt I will remember that in the heat of the moment."

"I had to try." He lifted his hand and ran it through her curls. "What are you going to do now."

"I suppose I will have to go see Sullivan." She frowned. "Who's by far the most irritating man I've ever met. That's saying something."

"I've always thought so." Lana said as she entered Ren's office. "At least you didn't have to grow up with him. He was so mean."

Dani's smile faltered. Ren could almost guess what she was thinking. She should have grown up with him. Sullivan was her older brother. He leaned down and whispered I her ear, "Don't go down that dark path."

She nodded. "I have a meeting in an hour with Mr. Nettles. I'll go see Sullivan later." Dani hugged him again. "Will I see you this evening?"

"You can count on it." He kissed her quick.

Dani turned to Lana. "How's Matt doing?"

She rolled her eyes. "He's almost as bad as Sullivan, but not quite. That Claire has a backbone of steel. I don't envy her the task of dealing with him every day. I have to check in on him a few times a week."

"He's not happy at his progress. He wants to be healed and independent again." Dani frowned. "I will stop in and see him soon and talk him off the ledge. Maybe it will make things easier for the two of you. We only want what's best for him"

She nodded. "Good luck, you're going to need it."

"Don't worry, I know how to handle him. You both have a good meeting. I have to go meet with a different beast." Dani exited his office.

Ren watched her leave. He ached for her. She was a mess of emotions. When she met with Sullivan later she'd have a better handle on them. This was her meltdown. The safe place she could go to and let it all out. Ren was happy to be that person for her. He'd do anything for her.

"I don't envy her that meeting," Lana muttered.

"What?" Ren turned to her. "Which one? Sullivan or Mr. Nettles?"

"Both," she replied. "But Nettles mostly. He's evil."

Ren glanced at her, startled. He didn't know Dani's client. She complained about him often. Said he was a cantankerous old bastard. "Why do you say that?"

"Because it's the truth." She shrugged. Then tilted her head to study him. "I forget sometimes you're not from around here. I was privy to a lot of the details growing up because I lived with the Brady family. They were close to the Nettleses. Dani's Mr. Nettles was the prodigal son. His father believed he could do no wrong. Until he fell off that pedestal and couldn't climb back up."

Ren didn't like what he was hearing. He itched to go

after Dani and make sure she'd be all right in the man's company. He held in the urge because she would be okay. Nettles wouldn't do anything to her outright. At least he hoped he wouldn't.

"What did he do?"

"He was embezzling from the family company. His father caught him and cut him out of everything. Even went so far as to leave it to his goddaughter in his will."

"I'm sure he wasn't happy about that. If all that happened, how did he end up in control?" He had to have some pull if he ran the family business now. Dani mentioned it was a family owned corporation.

"The goddaughter went missing."

He jerked his head up and met her gaze. "Went missing?"

Ren had a bad feeling. He knew the name she was going to say before it came out of her mouth.

"Ella Brady was kidnapped before Charleston Nettles died."

Ren closed his eyes and took a deep breath. "Tell me everything you know."

She studied him. Something in his face must have told her how important the information was. Lana started talking. She filled him in on all the details she'd been privy to growing up in the Brady household. "Ella Brady is, or rather *was*, supposed to be the majority stockholder in Nettles Unlimited. Charleston Nettles was her godfather. He left her all of his shares in the company. They only went to his son, Anderson Nettles, in the event of her death, as long as her passing happened before Charleston died. Ella disappeared mere days before he took his last breath. He'd been sick for over a month. The doctors were baffled at what was causing his illness. It all appeared rather shady, especially after Ella disappeared. The Brady family believed Anderson somehow had a hand in it."

It was everything he feared. Dani couldn't meet with Anderson Nettles. He might not realize who she was, but it wouldn't take long before he figured it out. The Brady family had found their long lost daughter. They'd want to announce it to the world. If she was to inherit the majority of the stock in Nettles Unlimited, he'd want to remove her from the equation. It would have to happen before she was accepted back into the family fold. Right now, she was merely Daniella Brosen. As Daniella Brady she held too much power and was a huge risk to Anderson Nettle's bottom line.

"Thank you for telling me." He grabbed his keys and turned to leave.

"Wait." Lana stepped in front of him. "Why's this important?"

"I don't have time to explain it."

She shook her head. "You can't leave without telling me something. I broke a confidence by telling you some of that."

He clenched his hands into fists. Ren didn't have time for this. "Dani is Ella. That's why she had to go meet Brady later. He came to see her earlier to talk about it, and she pushed him away."

Her hand flew to her mouth. Shock filled her eyes. She shook her head. "Oh god. She can't meet with that man. He will hurt her. Go to her now. I'll call Sullivan."

Ren rushed out the door. He had to get to Dani. She

was his only concern. He didn't care if Sullivan knew one way or the other. Sullivan Brady wasn't Ren's priority. Dani was and always would be.

CHAPTER 15

*D*ani rushed into her office. She had a few things to do before the meeting with Anderson Nettles. The sooner it was over with, the better she'd feel. The money he brought to the firm was nice, but she couldn't stand him. She'd never actually met him, only talked a few times with him on the phone, and had seen him leaving Matt's office. She avoided him because of the awful conversations she'd had with him. When Matt agreed to take on his case and leave her out of it, she'd been relieved. Now she wanted the man out of all their lives. He made her feel icky, and she couldn't explain why.

"Do I have any messages?"

"No," her receptionist shook her head. "It's been quiet since you left earlier."

"Good. When Mr. Nettles arrives send him directly to my office. Then you can go ahead and leave for the day."

Dani left Amy to her tasks and headed to her office. She snatched the Nettles file off her desk. She decided to make a clean break with him. That meant handing him the final bill and not expecting to see a dime from the old man. No doubt he'd refuse to pay on the grounds of her lack of a penis. She sat down and reviewed Matt's notes. His chicken scratch was hard to decipher at the best of times. Claire usually typed up his notes to make it easier to do a quick read. Without him around and Claire picking up the slack in other areas, she'd not gotten to the file. She sighed and closed the folder. It didn't matter. Mr. Nettles would no longer be their client after their meeting. Whatever Matt had planned could be sent to the shredder for all she cared.

"Mr. Nettles to see you," Amy lead the man into her office. "If you don't need anything, I'm going to head home now."

"Have a good evening. I will see you in the morning," she replied to Amy. "Please come in." Dani stood up to greet Mr. Nettles. She gestured toward a chair in front of her desk. "Have a seat and we can get started."

"I'll stand, thank you. This won't take long."

Dani frowned. Fine, she was all for a short meeting. She had other things that she had to take care of. After this meeting she'd call Sullivan and actually listen to what he had to say. Mr. Nettles was a nuisance she'd like to put out of her mind.

"All right," Dani agreed. "We can make this short." She walked over to the file on her desk and opened it again. She pulled out the final bill and headed back to Mr. Nettle's side. "As of this moment, Price and Brosen can no longer represent you. Here's your final bill."

His face turned beet red. He took the document out of her hand and crunched it up into a ball. When he'd stomped it as much as he could between his hands he forcibly threw it in a nearby trash can. "Don't think you can dismiss me so easily, missy. I know who you are."

Dani took a step back. She'd thought him irritating, but harmless. With the evil sneer directed her way she had to reassess her opinion of him. What the fuck was going on? This was supposed to be a simple meeting to end their working relationship. She didn't know him, and as far as she was concerned never wanted to.

"Mr. Nettles. I don't know who you think I am or what I did to offend you, but this does conclude our business. I must insist you leave now."

She hadn't expected he'd pay the damn bill. Him throwing it in the trash hadn't surprised her one iota. The anger spilling off of him was palpable. Did he hate women that much? He should go live in the Dark Ages. This was a modern world and women worked in it regularly. She wouldn't apologize for having a brain and knowing how to use it.

"You don't fool me. I know what game you're playing." He stalked forward. "It's not going to work. We are settling this tonight."

Dani took several steps back and swallowed the lump in her throat. Her heart raced in her chest and her hands shook. Why, oh why, did she have to meet with him in person? She could have ended their involvement over the phone. Mental note: never ever invite sketchy people into her office to be alone with her again.

"You're right. This is settled. Forget about the bill. We will write it off as a loss." She took another step back. "Let's end this amicably."

"Oh, we're going to end it, but there will be nothing friendly about it." He sneered. "You should be dead. This is what happens when you delegate. Let that be a lesson to you. Don't trust others to do a job you can do better yourself." He kept moving toward her with purpose. "The person I hired couldn't stomach killing a little girl. So they paid someone to make you disappear into the foster system. I found out when he confessed all to me a few hours ago. He claimed it was the only way to ensure the Brady family never found you. He figured it was a win-win situation. I got what I wanted and you would be allowed to live out your life. No one should have been able to figure it out. The stupid man didn't count on your resemblance to your mother. To think you've been under my nose all this time." He laughed evilly. "If I'd met you sooner it would have been clear to me. Instead, I insisted on dealing with your partner. It's rather ironic when you think about it."

He pulled out a gun from his jacket and pointed it at her. She froze in place. What the holy hell was going on? Why did he want to kill her? Even if she was the missing Ella Brady that didn't make sense. At least he couldn't claim this was all because he believed she'd done a shoddy job on his case. Damn Sullivan for not telling her everything. If he'd warned her who was responsible for her kidnapping maybe she'd have been prepared for this. Anderson Nettles had her at a disadvantage. He knew everything, and she had a limited amount of information to go on.

"Violence never solved anything. Put the gun away

before someone gets hurt." She held her hands up. "I'm begging you. Please."

"Violence can solve a lot if you do it right." He laughed. "You had to know you couldn't hide forever, Ella."

What did he gain from her death? She'd only found out she was Ella Brady earlier today. How had he gotten the information so fast? It wasn't common knowledge. She was left with one option. Stall—and for as long as possible. It was the one thing she could do. Maybe if she got lucky she'd find a way out of the mess she found herself in. When she saw Sullivan again she planned on screaming at him and punching him in the face. She blamed him for the situation. Why had he run away without telling her all she needed to know? His reason had been he'd dumped enough on her. Surely he'd have realized at some point Anderson Nettles might realize who she was and act on it.

"I don't know what you're talking about." *Play dumb, Dani. He might believe you're clueless. He doesn't have a lot of faith in female's intelligence.* "I'm Dani Brosen."

If she'd had more time, she might have been able to do something to avoid this situation. Now all she could do was pray she could talk him out of murder. What were her chances of that happening? They didn't look good with her staring down the barrel of a gun. One click on the trigger from Mr. Nettles and there would be no more Dani Brosen left in the world. She wouldn't have a chance to meet her family. There would be no deciding if she wanted to know them. He'd take that all from her. He'd already done it once. She'd not allow him to do it again.

"Drop the act. I know Sullivan Brady came to see you

early. If that hadn't sent up red flags, my spy in the Brady household sure did." He kept moving toward her. The distance was closing between them, and before she knew it he was a mere two feet in front of her. "Are you ready to die?"

She took a calming breath. If she kept him talking long enough maybe she could find a way out of the situation. "Even if I am Ella Brady, why would you want to kill me?"

"Because he's going to lose everything he owns to you." Sullivan breezed into her office. "And now he's going to prison."

Anderson Nettles froze. "I should have known you'd show up. You're always dogging my heels. But you're too late. Your sister's going to die, and there's nothing you can do to stop me. At least you get a front row seat to see her end. When I'm done with her, I'll take care of you."

"No, don't hurt him." She may not know Sullivan, but she didn't want to see him wounded either. There had to be a way to get through to Anderson Nettles. "I will sign anything you want. You can have whatever it is I'm supposed to be taking from you. I don't want it."

"I don't need anything from you. As long as you die, it's mine. You're not officially Ella Brady. When you die, you'll be Daniella Brosen, attorney at law. The Brady family hasn't had time to resurrect you from the dead. With your demise, I keep my company and can forget you ever existed."

Oh shit. She was supposed to inherit Nettles Unlimited? That was almost as shocking as having a gun pointed at her. No, the gun was worse. Still she could do without both. All she wanted was to live a normal live and continue to love Ren. Was that too much to ask?

"As if I'd want your company," she scoffed. "It has been run by you. It has to be tainted by your evil."

"Then it's good you'll never have it." He cocked the gun and raised it. "Time to say goodbye to your sister, Sullivan."

Sullivan had been inching closer to Anderson. But he wasn't close enough to stop him from pulling the trigger. A loud *boom* filled the room, followed by a burning pain in her chest. Dani glanced down as blood spread over her white blouse, turning it a dark red. Her hands were shaky as she touched the crimson stain. It was surreal as she stared down at the red liquid on the tips of her fingers.

Dani hit the ground before she knew she was falling.

"Noooo," Sullivan yelled and jumped Anderson. He punched him in the face, knocking him to the ground. That didn't stop him from pummeling him even more. He kept beating him over and over again. His face was tinged with red as his fists hit Anderson until he knocked him out.

"Stop," Dani managed to croak out the word. It was barely above a whisper. Sullivan didn't seem to hear her. She tried it again. "Stop. Sull…" She couldn't voice his full name. Dani choked over it as she spit out the liquid pooling in her mouth.

"Oh my God," he rushed over to her side and kneeled before her. "Hang on, Dani. We will get you help. Don't die on me." He pulled his phone out of his pocket at hit something on the screen. She assumed he was calling for help. "Yes I need an ambulance as soon as possible. My sister's been shot. Her attacker is unconscious too. Please hurry." He set the phone down and stared down at her. There was so much worry etched on his face. If Dani had the strength, she'd comfort him. She was losing all feeling in her body; it almost felt like she was floating. His hand shook as he brushed it over her hair. "I'm so sorry I couldn't stop this."

I'm sorry too, Sullivan. She couldn't say anything. Strength was draining from her. She'd finally found love. Ren was everything and more. Then she'd found out who her family was. Of course her life would have to fall apart. She was feeling way to damn good for something not to go wrong. A tear fell from her eye and trailed down her cheek. Why hadn't she told Ren how much she loved him? What'd she been afraid of? Now she might never get a chance to tell him. If she had one regret, it was not opening up fully to him. If she made it through this horrible ordeal, the first thing she'd do was kiss him and tell him how much she loved him. *God, please, don't let me die.*

"Dani," Ren shouted and ran to her side. "What happened," he turned toward Sullivan and demanded. "I tried calling several times. No one is answering the phones around this place. Dani's cell went right to voice-mail." He ran his fingers through his hair. "I've been going crazy trying to reach her."

Sullivan sat back and let his head fall into his hands. "The bastard shot her. I wasn't fast enough to stop it."

Ren shook as he ripped open her blouse. "The bullet's still lodged inside her. She's losing too much blood. I don't like her color. I need something to put pressure on the wound."

"I will see what I can find." Sullivan stood up and exited her office.

The pain was lessening. Probably because she was dying, or maybe it was the shock. Dani had no idea what was going on. It all was surreal to her. This wasn't really happening. Any moment, and she'd wake up from the nightmare she found herself in. She wasn't really watching her brother and the man she loved talk about her. Nope. She'd wake up, any minute now. Why wasn't she waking up from this damned awful dream already?

"Can you talk?" Ren lifted his hand and cupped her cheek. "No, don't try. I'm going to do everything I can for you. Don't do something stupid and leave me now. I've finally found you again, and I'm not losing you now."

I love you too, Ren. If only she could say the word aloud one time. Then she could die in peace. *Welcome to my shitty life.* This is where every decision she made led her. If she hadn't second guessed everything and trusted her instincts she'd not be lying on her office floor in a pool of her own blood. She might even be happy and have a family with Ren.

"I found these hand towels. They will have to do until the paramedics arrive." Sullivan kneeled back down beside her. "Hang on, squirt. Mom and Dad will never make it through losing you again."

Way to put the pressure on, Sullivan. Now she had to worry about hurting two people she didn't remember. Ren was all that mattered. Parents whom she didn't know would have to take a back burner.

"Shut up," Ren said with vehemence. "Don't add any stress on her." He glanced down at Dani. "I'm going to put pressure on your wound. It's going to hurt."

She wanted to tell him she no longer felt any pain and to do his worst. But when he pressed down, gurgling screams echoed through the room. How wrong she'd been. The pain was so bad it swallowed her whole, until she saw nothing but blackness...

CHAPTER 16

"I'm sorry, baby. So sorry," Ren whispered as Dani lost consciousness.

Her pulse was weak, but her breathing evened out. When he'd rushed into her office to find her bleeding from a gunshot wound, fear had seized him. He couldn't lose her. His medical training kicked in and he focused on saving her. It was a relief to be able to do something to save her, and he would. She wasn't going to leave him again. He needed her too much.

"The paramedics are here," Sullivan said.

"Good, we need to get her to the hospital fast." His gaze never left her. He monitored her closely, checking for any signs of distress. So far it looked good, but he couldn't help but worry. Anything could happen, and it often did when least expected. "I have done all I can here. She'd going to need surgery to remove the bullet."

Sullivan's gaze fell to Dani's unconscious body. Worry lines furrowed above his brows. He lifted his hand and rubbed his mouth. His eyes were watery, and if Ren were to guess, the other man was fighting tears. He could relate. All he wanted to do was give into his worry. Break down and let the misery run free, but he couldn't do that. Dani needed him to be strong.

The paramedics rushed into the room. They kneeled down to check Dani. Ren kept his hand pressed against the white towel stained with her blood. Keeping pressure on the wound to stem the flow was imperative. He let them work and waited for them to start asking questions.

"How long has she been unconscious?"

"Less than five minutes," Ren replied. "I've done a cursory exam. We need to move her now and get her to the hospital. The angle of the bullet went down through her lungs. I suspect she has a collapsed lung and fear the bullet may be lodged near her spine."

Before she passed out, her breathing had been ragged. The gurgling sound was a clear indicator something was wrong with her lungs. When he checked the injury, and realized there wasn't an exit wound he feared where the bullet landed inside of her. He kept focused and made sure she didn't suffer because of his anxiety. She came first. Always.

The paramedic nodded. "You're probably right. Let's get her on the gurney." They worked together to keep her stabilized and lift her onto the stretcher. Once she was secured, they rolled her out of the office.

"I'm going with her," Sullivan announced.

"Like hell you are. Stay here and deal with the authorities, and then follow in your own vehicle to the hospital. I'm going with her."

Sullivan clenched his fists at his sides. "She's my sister. I'm family."

God save him from idiots. Ren shook his head. Instead of giving into the instinct to hit Sullivan Brady, he took a deep breath and reasoned with him instead. He wouldn't back down without solid grounds for doing so. This was not the time to get into a punching match with Dani's newfound brother.

"I don't give a damn what you are to her. She doesn't know you." Ren glared at him. "Besides that fact, I'm a doctor and her best chance of making it to the hospital. I'm going with her. Do her a favor and pull your head out of your ass. Think about what she needs, not what you do."

Sullivan frowned and ran his fingers through his dark hair. It was a disheveled mess. Ren was afraid they both had lost years off their life watching Dani bleed out. "You're right. Intellectually I know that…" He glanced over Ren's shoulder. "It's hard for me to let go. I protect those I care about, and I did a horrible job of it today. It's my guilt coming out. Go with her. I will wrap things up here and call my parents. They need to know what's going on. When I'm done I will head to the hospital," he paused and stared Ren directly in his eyes. "Don't mess up, Sousa. I'm counting on you to make sure my sister survives this."

Ren nodded. He didn't need a warning from Dani's newfound older brother. This was by far the most important thing he'd ever do, if he accomplished nothing else for the rest of his life, he'd make sure Dani survived. "Do your job and I'll do mine." He spun on his heels and headed toward the ambulance. He couldn't think about

Sullivan or Dani's parents. They didn't figure into anything as far as he was concerned. Not at that moment in time anyway. Dani's family would eventually be important to her, but she would have to live to make that determination. Ren hopped into the ambulance and took a seat next to the stretcher.

One of the paramedics tapped the driver seat and said, "Let's go."

The trip to the hospital seemed to take forever before they pulled in front of the emergency room doors. Ren hopped out of the ambulance first and headed in as the paramedics rolled Dani inside. He barked orders and everyone started moving. They all gathered supplies and met in one of the exam rooms.

"Ren, you can't work on her." Lana placed her hand on his shoulder. "You're too emotionally invested."

Hell, he knew she was right, but he didn't want to admit it. His love for her was the reason he wanted to be the one to help her. He had to make sure she survived. Ren pushed her hand off his shoulder and went to Dani's side. "I have to do something."

"Be reasonable. She will get the best possible care. You know it," she pleaded.

He didn't look up at her. Dani might die. Couldn't she see why he had to stay by her side. What if the last thing she remembered was him causing her further pain? She had to make it. Ren had to be the one to make sure she did. He owed it to her. "She needs me," he whispered.

Lana pulled at his arm. "Let go. I will stay with her for every step."

He closed his eyes and took a deep breath. Fighting to

be in the operating room wouldn't help Dani. He had to do what was best for her. Hadn't he said something similar to Sullivan? It was time to let go of his need to control the situation and have someone else take care of Dani. As much as he hated to admit it, there was one person he could count on to perform the procedure. "Call Dr. West. Have him come in to do the surgery. She's going to need the best, and he's the only one I trust to help her."

She nodded. "I'll make the call, but you need to go now. Let everyone do their job."

Ren clenched his hands into tight fists and nodded. He couldn't trust himself to speak. The urge to break down was too close to the surface. Without a word he spun on his heels and exited the room. He headed to his office. When he got there he was stunned to find Jessica waiting for him.

"What do you want?" He spat the words at her. The last thing he needed was to deal with his ex-wife. "I don't have time for you today. Go away."

"Please, don't push me away," she pleaded. "I'm not here to bother you. I want to help. I heard about Dani."

He ignored her and pushed past her, heading to his desk. Ren sat and sighed as the weight of all that worried him descended upon him. He'd come to his office for peace and quiet. To have privacy for when he lost it—now he'd have to hold it in longer to deal with Jessica. Damn it. She always turned up at the worst times.

"I don't need your false pretense of sympathy." He glared at her. "I know you hated her—hate her." He caught himself. Referring of Jessica's dislike of Dani in the past tense wasn't a good sign. She'd pull through the surgery. Ren refused to believe anything less.

"My feelings for Dani don't matter. Yours do. You've always loved her." Her gaze didn't waver as she stared at him. "You didn't think I knew that, did you? I'm not an idiot. She was always there and you dropped everything for her. Your supposed best friend." She snorted. "What fantasy world did you live in? If she hadn't left, we never would have made it past senior year together. I should have ended things between us as soon as I realized it, but I'd fallen in love with you. If you'd looked at me once the way you did her things could have been so different between us."

"I'm sorry. I shouldn't have put you through that. You did deserve better." Even if she had cheated on him, Ren realized he wasn't innocent in the dissolution of their marriage. He never loved Jessica the way he loved Dani. "If we'd talked about this years ago, we could have saved each other a lot of unnecessary hurt."

She smiled softly. "It's part of growing up. We have to learn from our mistakes. I'm finally starting to under-stand that myself. I've done a lot of introspection lately. I've not liked what I've seen." She frowned. "But that's not why I'm here. I will work through my own issues later and focus on liking who I am. Right now I want to be here for you." She stared down at her hands and fidgeted. "I have a confession to make, and you're not going to like it. I did something…" She paused and took a deep breath. "This is probably not the best time to dump it on you, but I wanted to let it all out once and for all. It's time to make peace and move on."

Ren stared at her and braced himself for whatever she wanted to unburden on him. She was right; it wasn't the time or place to talk about things that couldn't be changed. It might give him something else to focus his energy on. At least she wasn't being the harpy she was known for. Maybe this was what he needed. It was closure for them. They had a lot of years together and they'd been through a lot. Jessica had been a part of his life for a long time. It might not have ended great between them, but it hadn't all been bad.

"Whatever it is, it doesn't matter." He ran his hand through his hair and stared past her at the wall. His medical degree stood out against the stark whiteness. He'd worked so hard to get it. Now it didn't seem to matter when he couldn't use it to save the one person he wanted to. He turned to Jessica and asked, "How did you hear about Dani?"

"Let me tell you what I have on my mind. If you want me to leave after that I will." She glanced away. "I was with Preston when he got the call to come in. We were in his office talking. He was one stop on my path toward forgiveness. I didn't do right by him either."

The old irritation he'd felt when he heard about her and Preston didn't hit him. It was progress. It appeared as if Jessica was doing her best to change. He wished her well with her endeavor. "Is he with Dani now?"

"He headed to see her immediately." She nodded. "You can trust him to take care of her."

Of course he could. Preston may have betrayed their friendship, but that didn't reflect on his ability as a doctor. It's why he demanded he do her surgery. If anyone could save her, it was Preston West. "I'm counting on it."

"What I have to tell you…" Jessica blew out a breath. "It has to do with Dani."

Ren perked up at her words and his gaze flew to hers. "What about her?" Had she done something, or did she know more than she was letting on? "What did you do?"

She waved her hands. "Relax. It has nothing to do with what she's going through now. It's more part of why she disappeared."

He relaxed back in his chair and as relief overflowed through him. "The past doesn't matter right now. I'm more concerned about our future."

"Nevertheless, I have to say my piece. Will you let me get it all out before you lose it?"

"I can't make any promises, but I'll try." He leaned forward. "Go ahead and tell me what you had to do with Dani leaving."

She bit her lip and twisted her fingers together. "I lied to her."

He closed his eyes and shook his head. "Don't stall any more. What did you say to her?" It had to be something big to get Dani to run away from him. They'd been too close for her to do it for no reason. She hadn't told him why she left. He figured she would tell him when she came to terms with it. Ren could be patient when the ends justified the means. Dani was his everything and worth the wait.

"I told her I was pregnant." A tear fell down her cheek as she spoke the words. "I was desperate, and the words were out of my mouth before I realized what I was saying. She was as shocked by them as I was."

"She believed you?" His mouth fell open. Ren couldn't have been more baffled by Jessica's confession. They'd never been intimate in high school. He'd been too wrapped up in his feelings for Dani to even consider it. "It wasn't possible for you to be pregnant, but of course Dani wouldn't have known that."

"No, she did what I knew she would." She wiped the tears from her cheek. "She loved you too much to stand in the way of your happiness. So she agreed to leave and not speak to you again. I could see it on her face—how much it hurt her to put that distance between you, but I couldn't back down. I loved you too much to let her have you. I was so young and stupid."

Ren scrunched up his eyebrows puzzled by her words. "Dani has always cared about me. We were best friends. She would want what was best for me. But I don't understand why she thought she had to leave."

None of it made sense. It was even more confusing knowing what happened. Dani left because she'd believed Jessica was pregnant with his child. It was so far from the truth it was ridiculous. If she'd only said something to him he could have prevented it all. Why couldn't she have come to him? They could have been in each other's lives this entire time.

"I told you. *She loved you.* Do you think she could watch you with someone else knowing she could never have that family with you? Better yet, do you think you could have stayed away from her even if you had a family with someone else?" She shook her head. "You two were so stupid over each other. Anyone who looked at you would have known how you felt about each other."

"You're wrong." She couldn't be right. It was such a waste if it was. "Dani loved me as a friend, nothing more."

"No, Ren," Jessica said sadly. "She loved you for more reasons than that. It may have started as friendship, but it grew to be much more. I think she was on the brink of telling you. It's why I did what I did. I know it was wrong, but I can't change it now."

If what she said was true... He couldn't wait to have a conversation with Dani. They had a lot to discus. Jessica was right. Dani would have done everything she could to ensure Ren's happiness, even at the expense of her own.

"Thank you for telling me. It gives me a lot to think about."

"I hope it helps you. I never meant to hurt either one of you. It was selfish of me, but I as a teenager who didn't think beyond that day." She reached to him and placed her hand on his. "Please forgive me."

"I think it's time we moved on with our lives. There is much we have to live for." He stared into her eyes. "You don't need my forgiveness, but if you want it you have it."

"Thank you. I appreciate it."

"Good." He nodded. "Now all we can do is wait."

"If you're not averse to me waiting with you, I can stay and keep you company."

A part of Ren wanted to say no. He'd longed for solitude to think about all she'd had to confess. But the other part of him didn't want to be alone. Who would he lean on if he didn't take her up on her offer? He'd be alone in his office with only his thoughts to see him through the long hours of surgery.

"If you can suffer through my company. I can suffer through yours." He nodded. "Stay if you want."

She sat in front of his desk. He leaned his head into the palm of his hands. They sat in silence. Neither having much to say, and so they waited letting the quiet wrap around them. Ren waited for the news that the woman he loved would live, and she waited to be there for him if she didn't. It wasn't something talking about would help.

REN'S HEAD lay on his folded arms on top of his desk. Somehow he'd managed to fall asleep. Exhaustion had taken over. He'd needed the rest, but it bothered him that he'd managed to sleep when Dani was in a life or death surgery. He bolted up and found Jessica also asleep in an awkward position. Apparently they'd both needed rest.

He was about to wake her when Preston walked into his office. Ren stared at him, waiting for him to tell him what he wanted to hear. The other man remained silent. A wrenching pain filled his stomach and tightened into a tight knot.

"She isn't…"

He shook his head. "She's fine."

A *whoosh* of relief flooded him as the tense ball of worry inside of him eased. Then he realized there was something Preston wasn't saying. He seemed so foreboding when he walked in. "What is it?"

Preston frowned. "She made it through the surgery. I'm worried about what happens when she wakes up."

His heart fluttered, missing a beat at his words. "What happened?"

Preston pushed into the room and yanked his surgical cap of his head. He crunched it between his fingers. "You were right in your assessment. The bullet did lodge near her spine. I removed it and repaired the damage as best I could. We won't know how extensive it was until she wakes up and we can test her reflexes."

Ren frowned. It wasn't anything he hadn't heard before. This was the normal outcome from a risky surgery. Why was Preston so worried? "I don't understand. What's bothering you?"

"You love her."

"I do." Ren nodded. "That doesn't have anything to do with your skills as a surgeon."

Preston remained quiet. His gaze falling on Jessica's sleeping form. "I wanted to do more. To show you," he paused. "I know I damaged our friendship. This is purely selfish of me, but I wanted to prove to you that you could depend on me."

Ren understood. It all finally made sense to him. Dani was the love of his life. He'd done Jessica a disservice by ignoring that. He'd thought he could make his ex-wife happy, and maybe for a while he had. But it wasn't enough. Preston really did love her. He couldn't fault his friend for doing something he failed to do. Could they have handled it better? Yes, but it didn't negate his part in their downfall. Ren was as responsible as both Jessica and Preston. "You did your job. You saved her. The rest is up to Dani. You don't owe me anything," he paused and stared his friend in the eyes. "I do know I can depend on you. You're the first person I asked for when I knew it couldn't be me to save her. No one else could have done it. Only you."

Preston nodded. "She's in recovery. I know you're itching to go check on her. Go to your woman, and I'll see to mine. Even if she doesn't want me to."

Ren nodded. Preston was in for a battle to win Jessica. She didn't seem to want anyone anymore. The little he understood from their conversation told him that. Jessica was ready to move on with her life. If that was with Preston, time would tell.

"We will talk later," he said and then rushed out of the room.

He had to see for himself if Dani was all right. Preston and Jessica could deal with their problems without his supervision. He had more important things on his mind.

*D*ani's eyes fluttered open. At first, a blurry mess of colors assaulted her vision. She blinked several times to gain her focus. *Where am I?* She scanned her surroundings. The first thing she came across was Ren's face, his eyes closed. She lifted her hand and ran her fingers through his golden brown hair. His eyes flew open and met her gaze.

"Hello, sleepy head." Her throat was raw and she couldn't manage more than a whisper. "What happened?"

He leaned down and kissed her forehead. "Do you remember your meeting with Anderson Nettles?"

A flash filled her mind. The stupid old man shot her. She scooted her hand across her stomach and over the bandages underneath her hospital gown. "Well, it appears like he didn't manage to kill me as he planned." Dani laughed lightly. "Rat bastard. I hope he rots in prison."

"Don't even joke about that. I don't think I could handle losing you." He frowned. "I've never been so scared in my life."

Dani didn't want to think about her possible death. She was alive. The rest was all minor details. There was one thing she wanted to say. She'd feared she wouldn't ever get the chance. She'd not pass up the opportunity now that she had it. "I love you."

His gaze softened. "I love you too."

"I know. I think I always did. I'm my own worst enemy." She let her gaze fall. This was the hard part. "I know there are no guarantees in life. I was doing my best to ensure nothing would ever hurt me. By putting walls between us I was trying to avoid pain, and in the end I caused us a million times more. If not for my own hang-ups, things might have gone differently. Can you ever forgive me for my stupidity?"

"Don't you know by now I'd forgive you anything? You're my world." Ren reached up and ran his hand over her hair. "Besides, there's nothing to forgive. I'm as much at fault as you are. I knew what you were doing and allowed it. I had an interesting conversation with Jessica earlier, and it put it all into perspective for me."

"Yeah?" Dani raised an eyebrow. Her voice clearing up the more she talked. It was a little rusty, but she managed to force the words out. "What did you talk about?"

"It's a long story. But the short end of it is we all make mistakes." He lifted her hand and kissed her palm. "Turns out Jessica had a lot to say about what happened ten years ago. She admitted she lied to you about being pregnant."

"Wait, what? She actually admitted it? I suspected, but…" Dani remembered when Jessica dropped that bomb on her at prom. "Why would she lie?"

"Because she saw what we didn't."

"What was that?" Dani frowned. Jessica had seemed unreasonably jealous all those years ago. Was that what had made her lie? "It had to be major for her to fake a pregnancy."

"I have loved you since I met you. I may not have realized what it was at first, but it became clear to me not long after. But you insisted I was your best friend, and you didn't ever want to do anything to ruin that. So I humored you." Ren stared into her eyes. "I stayed your friend and dated Jessica. It was a stupid mistake I wish, sometimes, I could undo. Jessica claims you loved me as much as I loved you, but we were too blind to see it."

She'd not have thought Jessica was an insightful individual, and she was partly right. Dani had loved Ren, and always would, but she was well aware of it the entire time. It was her fear that kept her from admitting it. If she'd let it all go they may have been able to skip the hardships they'd endured since. It was beyond time to set it all aside and tell Ren the truth.

"She's right. I loved you more than I have ever loved anyone. I still do." She sighed. "It's why I left when she told me she was expecting your child. I believed it was the best choice I could make for you. Your happiness was all I ever wanted."

"I'm glad she told me the truth. We should have talked about all of this years ago."

She nodded. "We can't go back and change anything. It is what it is. All we can do now is figure out where we go from here."

"I agree," he said. "Sometimes we have to burn all our bridges before we see what they are. It's part of life. It's who we are. Whether we learn from them and make changes is up to us."

He made sense. It was similar to the conclusions she'd come to herself. Jessica wasn't to blame for the choices Dani made and vice versa. She couldn't hold it against the other woman for trying to hold on to Ren. She might have done the same in her position. It was time to let go of all her preconceived notions and open her eyes to the truth. She'd made mistakes, and no one was to blame for them. Yes, Jessica's lies drove her away, but the other woman hadn't made her leave. She could have talked to Ren and figured things out for herself.

"I agree." She nodded. "While I was lying on my office floor it made me take a hard look at my life." She stared at Ren resolved with how things needed to be. He was her future and she wouldn't throw away the love of her life ever again. "I've made up my mind. I'm not looking back. From this point on we're moving forward and making decisions together. No more pushing and running from our fears, or rather I'm not going to. You've always run toward me. You had more faith in us than I did."

"So we're in agreement. You're going to stay with me." He raised an eyebrow. "You know what that means, don't you?"

"What?" she asked, confused. Had she missed something? Maybe the drugs were still making things a little fuzzy. "I'm not following you."

"You pretty much agreed to marry me without me asking."

"That's not how I heard it. Let her recover before you start forcing wedding plans down my sister's throat."

Dani turned her head and met Sullivan's gaze. "Stay out of it. This doesn't concern you."

"I beg to differ." He shook his head. "You're a very wealthy woman. You have a family now. No need to rush into the first bloke's arms you meet."

"Go away, Sullivan." She glared. "I don't need your assistance. I am capable of making up my own mind."

She focused on Ren. "I would like nothing more than to be your wife. As soon as I'm able to, we can see about a wedding."

"I hope we're invited." A booming male voice filled the room. "I'd like to give my daughter away.

Dani closed her eyes and took a deep breath. She didn't want to face them now. Why hadn't someone warned her they were coming? She turned her gaze to Sullivan and glared at him. If she could have felled him with a look she would have. No doubt he knew they were coming in behind him and failed to mention it.

"You're getting married," a female said. "We only found out you were alive a few hours ago, and now you're leaving us already."

"Get out," Dani demanded. "I am not asking anyone's permission for anything. I don't know you."

She turned away from them and focused on Ren. Why were they intruding on her when she had no means of escape? Her breathing became ragged. Tears fell down her cheek.

"Sweetheart," Ren said. He lifted his hand and wiped the tears away. "Don't push them away. They are your family. Remember what we just discussed? No more running."

She closed her eyes and prayed for strength. He was right. Damn it, why did he always have to be? She rolled her head to stare at them. It didn't surprise her they hadn't done as she asked. All three of them flanked the other side of her bed. Hell. Why had she wanted a family again? So far, hers had become nothing but a nuisance.

"You're not getting rid of us that easily." Her father pronounced. Hell, yeah, he was her father. She couldn't wrap her head around that fact still. The woman next to him had to be her mother. "You're our daughter. We don't abandon family."

She sighed. "Fine. But now's not the time to push your will on me. We can make plans and learn about each other at a pace of my choosing." She lifted her hand and pointed at them. "You do not get to make decisions for me. Ren and I are getting married. Accept it or leave. He's the best man I know, and I don't need or want your approval."

Sullivan chuckled. "If you doubted you were a Brady, that little announcement told us all we needed to know. No one pushes us around." He leaned down and kissed her cheek. "Get well, little sister. It's going to be fun having you around."

"Hmmph. Go find someone else to bother." Big brothers were a pain in the behind. "I don't need your sage advice."

"Listen to her. She is wise for her years." Lana walked in. She winked at Dani. "I need to ask you all to leave. I need to examine her, and Dr. West will be here soon to see how she's healing."

"No," her mother said. "I don't want to leave her."

Dani recognized the look on her face. Siobhan Brady

541

was afraid if she left, Dani wouldn't be there when she got back. "I'm not going anywhere. Come by and see me later. This is all overwhelming."

Her mother nodded. "All right. I," she paused. A tear trailed down her cheek. "We never gave up hope. It's hard to leave you now that we've found you again."

"Come, dear. We can come see Ella later," Malachi Brady said to his wife.

"Dani."

He turned toward her and said, "Excuse me?"

"My name is Dani. I don't remember being your Ella. I couldn't be now if I tried."

Malachi Brady opened his mouth to argue with her. He stared down at her and closed his mouth, appearing to rethink it. "You're right. We will get to know you and who you've become. It will be an adjustment for us all."

Dani smiled. "I look forward to it."

Her parents nodded at her and left the room.

"You too, Sullivan. I don't need a babysitter."

He pouted. "You're not kicking him out." Sullivan pointed at Ren.

"I like him. The jury's still out on you."

Lana laughed. Dani decided she liked the other woman. The fact she sassed Sullivan on a regular basis endeared the nurse to her. She wanted to get to know them all. It was nice to have a family and friends to lean on. Why she'd ever pushed all the people in her life away, she'd never understand.

"Fine. I will come by and check on you later." He turned toward Lana. "Don't kill her while I'm gone."

"Oh my, what would I do without you threatening me

into submission." She held her hand over her chest and glared at him. "Find someone else to harass."

Sullivan shook his head and left the room.

Dani was amused. This was the most entertainment she'd had in a long time. If only it didn't have to happen with her chained to a hospital bed. She sighed, all's well that ends well, she supposed. Too bad it'd taken a bullet to wake her up and accept the people around her.

"How's our patient doing?" Preston West asked. "I heard you were awake."

Dani studied the doctor. He was Ren's friend, or former friend. She couldn't keep up with everything. Ren had to trust him on some level if he allowed the other man to treat her. So she'd remain open to him.

"I'm doing fabulous considering," Dani said. "When can I break out of this joint?"

She was beginning to understand Matt's reluctance to stay in the hospital. It was stifling her. The urge to leave and go home was great.

"Not today," was all he said. "Let's look you over." He lifted the blanket over her feet. "Can you wiggle your toes for me?"

She didn't know why he wanted her to, but she'd humor him. Her toes moved on cue. "Good. That's good." He wrote something down in her chart and turned to Lana. "Continue with the treatment in her chart." Preston West was a man of few words. He didn't say one more than necessary. After he gave Lana those instructions he turned and left the room.

"So did I pass a test or something?" she asked.

"Every one, baby," Ren said and kissed her cheek. "The rest will be cake."

Her stomach growled. "Speaking of cake…I wouldn't mind a slice about now. Who's a girl have to kill to get food in here."

Lana laughed. "I will have a tray sent up from the cafeteria. Something light. Sorry, doctor's orders."

"Fine." Dani sighed. "Starve me then."

Her laugher echoed through the room long after she was gone. Lana had a strange sense of humor. Dani rather liked it. It was nice to laugh and joke. For a brief moment in time, she'd thought she'd never have this. That she'd tossed her chance at happiness aside. Dani promised she'd never make that mistake again. A person's choices didn't have to define who they were or who they'd become. A course could be changed and adapted to set a new path. This was her opportunity to forge ahead in a new direction. Her gaze fell on Ren. He was her everything too. There was nothing she wouldn't do for him. He was the love of her life and her best friend. She couldn't ask for anything more.

"I promise you all the cake you want at our wedding," he said. "I'm thinking next week. Your stomach should be able to handle it by then."

This was what happiness was. Family, friends, and the one person you loved more than life itself. She thanked the heavens for giving her another chance. Never would she take anything for granted again. Every day for the rest of her life she'd make sure those she cared about knew how much she loved them. Starting with the one man she'd given her heart to over a decade ago.

"I will be there with bells on." Dani laughed.

"As long as you're there, nothing else matters." He kissed her lightly. "You're my best friend, the love of my life, and I couldn't ask for more."

Dani couldn't have said better if she tried. With Ren at her side she was a better person, one she was always meant to be. His love allowed her to open herself up to more possibilities. She was finally happy and free. It was beautiful and oh so amazing.

A part of her would always remain with Ren. He owned her heart after all.

EPILOGUE

*D*ani stared out the window as Ren drove to her parent's house. She still had trouble wrapping her mind around the fact she had not only two parents, but an irritating brother as well. Sullivan visited her as much as she would allow. He was being pushier than either of her parents were. They'd respected her wishes for space and agreed to let her come to them. The time to give in and allow them into her life had arrived. Sullivan insisted she attend a family gathering. It was a good way for her to visit with them and still have enough space to not feel claustrophobic. They'd all been wonderful, and it was silly of her to keep putting them at a safe distance.

"They're not going to bite you know," Ren reminded her. "They want the chance to know who you have become."

Damn had he been hanging out with her brother? Seems like Sullivan had uttered that phrase before... She wasn't sure if she was amused or scared how much her newfound sibling was insinuating himself into her life.

"I know. It's not easy for me to let anyone in. It terrifies me."

"Take it one day at a time. Don't over think it." He pulled the car into the long driveway on the Brady estate. It stopped in front of a house and looped around a massive fountain. It was amazing to look at. That was what it must be like to have money. The water sprayed up and fell into the pool.

"How rich are my parents, anyway?"

"I don't know." Ren laughed and opened his car door. He walked around and opened the passenger side for her. "Maybe you should ask them."

"I don't think so. That's a rude thing to ask." She scrunched up her nose and stepped out of the car. "What if they think I'm after what they can give me financially?"

"Seems like that doesn't matter. You're rather rich in your own right after all the paperwork is sorted out with your identity and inheritance."

Damn if he didn't have a point. Why did he have to bring that up? It was the reason she'd spent so much time in the hospital of late. Damn Anderson Nettles for putting a bullet in her. He was sitting in a jail cell awaiting trial. His bail had been denied. Sullivan explained how her family had rallied for that outcome. They didn't want to give him another chance to murder her. The judge, thank God, had agreed. She didn't want to face him with another gun flashing in front of her. The next time she laid eyes on Nettles would be when she had to testify, and at his sentencing. She had no desire to sit in court each day and watch his trial unfold. She'd be there when it was necessary.

"Don't remind me. I think I might become a philanthropist like my family. A lot of that money is going to charity to help underprivileged kids. I want to help some of them as much as I can. I know what it's like to be where they are."

Her family didn't like to think about her in foster care. Whenever she brought it up to Sullivan he changed the subject, but she couldn't ignore it. Growing up without a family is what made her who she was. She had to accept it and move on. It was one of the things she worked on each day now. It had been a month since Anderson Nettles had shot her. It'd changed all of her priorities. Ren was at the top of that list. They walked up to the front door, and Dani hit the door bell.

"Hello. Can I help you?" A middle-aged woman with red hair streaked with gray filled the door way.

"That's Dani and Ren, mom. Let them in." Lana stepped up behind the woman. "The Brady's would have your head if you didn't let their daughter through the door."

"I'm so sorry." She held her hand over her chest. "I should've seen the resemblance. You're the spitting image of your mother."

"Don't stress about it. I'm still acclimating myself to the idea. No reason you should've realized who I was in an instant. Where is my family located in this mausoleum?"

Anxiety pooled in her stomach. She wanted to become more acquainted with them, but couldn't help being nervous at the prospect. This was only one part of a huge endeavor. They had time to figure it all out. At least that was what she kept reminding herself.

"They are in the family room. I will show you the way," Lana said. "Mom, go gather some refreshments. Mrs. Brady is going to want something."

The housekeeper nodded her head and wandered away. She appeared happy to be given a task. Dani could relate. She wished she had something to do to avoid the upcoming meeting.

"Your mom seems nice." Dani attempted to make small talk. "How long did you say she worked here?"

"My whole life." Lana led them through a long winding hallway and stopped in front of a set of mahogany double doors. She pushed them open wide and entered. "I've brought you a couple of guests."

Siobhan Brady stood as they entered the room. "I'm so glad you were able to come."

Dani fidgeted and reached for Ren's hand. She didn't know what to say to this woman who was her mother. Ren squeezed her hand, reminding her he was there for her.

"I think it's time to start getting to know who my family is." She glanced between her mother, father, and brother. "If you're willing to put up with me."

"We would do anything for you." Her father's voice was husky with emotion. "All you have to do is ask."

The knot forming in her stomach eased at his words. They never meant for her to be abandoned. That wasn't their doing. They were good people, and she needed to stop blaming them for the trouble she endured growing up. If they could change any of it, they would. There was no use looking back and wishing. It wouldn't do any of them any good. All they could do was move forward. Ren was constantly reminding her of that fact.

"Good. We have news and we'd like to share it with you." Dani gestured toward Ren. "We set a wedding date, and we'd love it if you all would be a part of it."

"Of course we want to be part of it," he father replied. "We'll even pay for it. It's tradition after all that the bride's family take care of the wedding costs."

That wasn't what she'd been aiming for. They didn't have to anything so extravagant for her. All she wanted was to get to know her family. The wedding was the begging of allowing them to be a part of her life.

"I couldn't allow that." Dani frowned. "I haven't been a part of your family very long. I refuse to take advantage of your generosity."

"You've always been a part of this family." Sullivan replied defiantly. "You may have just returned, but don't believe for one minute we think any less of you. That was none of your fault. You should have grown up here. It's your birthright don't, deny it."

"Listen to your brother. It's how we all feel," her mother said softly.

Was she being too difficult? She thought she was being reasonable. They were her family and they wanted what was best for her. Would it really be too much to let them help with her wedding?

"I still say it's too much." Dani shook her head. "Can't we reach a happy medium?"

Ren lifted her hand and kissed it. "I have a suggestion."

She looked up at him and asked, "What?"

"Why don't we have the wedding here? It could cut down costs, and give your family the opportunity to show you the home you were denied."

"Oh that's a lovely idea," her mother exclaimed. "Everything can take place here and it will give us more time together before the wedding.' She glanced over at Dani and asked, "What day have you picked dear?" Siobhan Brady raised her hand to her chest and sighed. "We'd love nothing more than to be a part of your big day. If you'll allow it, I would love to help you plan it."

"Three months from today," Dani added. "We don't want to wait too long to begin our lives together as husband and wife. We've waited enough."

"Be careful what you agree to." Sullivan smiled at her. "She's been secretly planning your wedding since the day you were born."

"Oh, stop." Her mother smacked Sullivan in the chest. "You'll scare her away."

"If Sully hasn't scared her away already, nothing will," Lana piped in. "He is annoying enough for the whole family."

"I'm on my best behavior, I'll have you know. I only irritate you these days."

Dani laughed at their exchange. This was what having a family was like. They laughed, teased, and embraced every part of her. She'd missed so much not having them in their life. Why had she kept her distance this long? She should have given in sooner and allowed them in. It was a mistake she intended to rectify. Her wedding was only the beginning.

"Ha. I knew you did it all on purpose. Don't worry, I

can and will get even." Lana glared at Sullivan. "You wait, when you least expect it I'll pounce." She waved her fist at him. "For now I will go see if my mother needs help gathering refreshments." She exited the room shaking her head as she went.

Lana knew Dani's family better than she ever would. It saddened her in some ways. Still, she looked forward to learning everything about them all.

"I want you all to take part in the wedding. Ren and I agreed it is a good way for us to begin again. A way for us to become the family that we were denied so many years ago—a new start. If you're willing, I am."

"We're more than willing," her father said. "Anything you want, I will make it happen."

"All I want is for my mother, father, and brother to be at my wedding. I want to celebrate with the only other people besides Ren who mean anything to me." She gazed at each one of them. "In time we will become close. For now, I'm happy to have you here and willing to put up with my idiosyncrasies."

Malachi Brady pulled her into a bear hug. "You're my daughter. It's my job to protect you. I failed you once, and I won't do it again."

"I don't blame you," she whispered. "I know whose fault it is. Don't worry about me. I have everything I need."

She did. Ren was there for her every day, and now she had a family she could lean on if necessary. There wasn't anything else she could possibly ask for. One day she'd have children of her own. She wanted them to know her uncle and grandparents.

Her father let her go. "I know. But I have a hard time letting go of my perceived guilt. It might take me—us—a while to realize your safe and happy. I have to ask you to be patient with us, as we are with you."

Dani smiled. "I think it runs in the family. We are all a little hard headed."

"Move away old man. It's my turn to grab a hug." Sullivan pushed his way past their father and wrapped his arms around her. "I'm so glad you're finally here."

"Me too," Dani sighed with contentment. "We all have so much to be thankful for."

"That we do, little sister. Welcome home." He let her go, glancing down at her with a soft smile.

"I'm exactly where I've always wanted to be. When I was little, I'd stare up at the sky and wished I had a family who loved me. I didn't know then I was lucky enough to already have one." She glanced at each one of them. "All my wishes have come true. Thank you for loving me."

"It's our pleasure," her mother said as she wiped a tear from the corner of her eye.

The housekeeper rolled in a tray filled with little sandwiches, cakes, cookies, and a pitcher of iced tea. She set it up on a nearby table and then turned toward them. "If you need anything else, let me know." She exited the room as fast as she'd come in.

"I think we need to toast to Dani and Ren's upcoming wedding," Sullivan stated. "Too bad we don't have something stronger than tea, but it will have to do." He poured a glass for everyone and handed them out. Then he lifted his glass. "To my long lost little sister and the lucky bastard who won her heart. May they forever be happy and know love that will stand the test of time."

They all lifted their glasses and drank to Ren and Dani's happiness. Dani glowed with pleasure as she glanced at them all. They were everything she'd always wanted, Ren more than anything. She'd taken a long, hard path to arrive in the spot she found herself in. Even though it had been difficult, she wouldn't change any of it. Her struggles made her who she was. Now she had a family and the love of her life. What more could she possibly ask for.

"Are you happy?" Ren asked.

"Blissfully so."

He leaned down and kissed her lightly. This was worth fighting for. She'd demolish anyone who tried to take it away from her. She'd already lost too much in her life to do anything less. She'd been her own worst enemy in the past, but she wouldn't make that mistake ever again. These people were more important than she could ever explain with mere words. Yes, she'd put them at a distance at first. Now though, they were, and always would be, a priority for her. It'd taken her too long to come to that realization.

"Me too," he said. "If this is a dream, don't ever wake me up."

"My dreams are never this good." She laughed. "I promise nothing could ever be as perfect as our reality."

EXCERPT: UNVEILED HEARTS

HEART'S INTENT BOOK TWO

UNVEILED
HEARTS

♥Heart's Intent

DAWN BROWER

USA TODAY BESTSELLING AUTHOR

CHAPTER 1

a soft breeze fell over Matthew Price's face as he lounged on his backyard deck. The constant beeping from a car horn beeped sharply in the distance. One of his neighbors must be displeased to pound on it with such vigor. The taste of bile rising in his throat was becoming equally hard to ignore. He clenched his fist and allowed his nails to bite into his palms. All of his senses worked as they should. He counted them off each day as a reminder he hadn't lost everything. It was his sight that continued to elude him. Dr. Sousa told him to be patient, that his vision wouldn't return overnight, but he'd been hopeful. It'd been foolish and a complete waste of his time.

He'd been released from the hospital a mere two weeks ago, and he still couldn't see more than a blur. He managed all right moving around the safety of his home, but with anything else he was completely dependent on others. For someone who'd prided himself on his independence, it'd brought him down to the lowest of levels.

As far as he was concerned there was no reason to keep trying. What was the point? He was resigned to the circumstances life dealt him. This was who he was. The blind man—a lawyer who couldn't even read the law briefs he'd written. Research? It would be nearly impossible to complete now. What kind of lawyer—or man—would he be without one of the most basic of human abilities?

"Are you ready to go inside now, Matt?"

Claire Jackson—his babysitter, and the woman he desired beyond reason. At least until he had the misfortune of losing his capability to look at her. Hell, who was he kidding? He still wanted her. It was doing something about it that baffled him. Like everything in his life after the accident, this was a change he hated. He couldn't be the man she needed, and now she was something neither one of them anticipated she'd be. She was his constant companion. When she wasn't at work she was with him, a continuous nag and voice of reason. Between her and the medical personnel that came by weekly to check in on him he'd never been alone. All he wanted was for them to leave and give him time to breathe.

"Go away," Matt barked. "Can't you leave me alone for five minutes?"

"You've been out here an hour now. It's starting to get chilly." Her voice was calm and soothing. "I can make you some lunch if you're hungry."

Didn't she understand? Of course she didn't. How could she when he didn't fully get it himself? There was no reason to do anything anymore. He had no purpose in life and he was struggling to find his place in the world.

The car accident that blinded him had taken far more than his sight from him. It erased who he saw himself as. So what if it was chilly out and he'd been sitting in his backyard staring at nothing? It wasn't as if he could actually see what was in front of him. It took the phrase staring blindly to a whole new level.

"I don't want food." He clenched his fists. "I don't want a damn thing except for you to leave."

There was a time he'd have loved having her in his home. An all too brief moment when he'd imagined her with him, loving her in every possible way. He'd been an idiot to ignore his feelings for her. Now he didn't think he could have her the way he'd always wanted. His short-sightedness had cost him a lot. The opportunity to be the man in Claire's life was one of them. He'd thought he had time, sweet time, but what a joke. If he could go back he'd make so many changes. She wouldn't be his nursemaid, but his lover. How could he even begin to think he could be more than someone she'd have to take care of? Seduction? That was laughable. He'd grope her all right—but not in any romantic way. He'd latch on to her as his guide to make sure he didn't walk into a wall or trip over his own feet. The helplessness he experienced every day didn't make him feel suave or romantic.

"I'm not going anywhere." She sighed. "You need to realize that and accept it. Yelling at me isn't going to achieve the results you're hoping for."

What would? She was as unflappable as he remembered. He yelled at her every day—hell, several times if he was being truthful—and she still came back. She remained calm and steady. The picture of her as he remembered flashed through his mind, long golden blonde hair and warm brown eyes. She was so beautiful, caring, and independent. There wasn't anything she couldn't do. Claire was perfect, at least to him. "I don't understand why you're here. Find someone else to stay with me." He waved at her dismissively. "I don't want you around."

It was a lie, but maybe if he said it often enough she'd finally understand and leave. He couldn't handle her being around him every day. Not when it seemed as if he'd never see properly again. This was what he needed to get through his ordeal. She had to go, and fast. Someone else could do what she did every day. Claire deserved better than what he had to offer.

Claire stared at him for several beats of his heart. The harshness of her silence churned through him, drawing out the ache of never having her. When she finally spoke, he almost breathed a sigh of relief. He'd never been able to handle her silences. "I care about you. No one else, save Dani, would have your best interests at heart. She has her own problems and healing to do." She lifted his hand in hers and rubbed it. "Be reasonable."

"Why?" He yanked his hand from hers. "As far as I can tell, this is how I'm going to be for the rest of my life. I think I'm being perfectly rational." He clenched his jaw tight. "Let's quit pretending this is going to get better. I am blind. You're the one not accepting things that aren't going to change."

"Matt...I..." Clare's voice broke apart as she spoke. Matt was inherently relieved he couldn't see the hurt on her face. It was the only blessing he could hold onto with his blindness. He never wanted to hurt her, but believed this was a necessary evil. She had to move on without him. "It's been a couple weeks. You can't give up yet. Ren said it would take some time. Your body needs to heal, and only time can give that to you."

Yeah, Ren, the great Dr. Sousa, who acted as if he knew it all but wasn't any more infallible than anyone else was. His law partner, Daniella Brosen, loved the good doctor, had always loved him. They seemed to be rekindling their relationship and taking it in a different direction than the friendship they had in high school. Matt was happy for Dani, honestly, but he was irritatingly jealous of it. He'd wanted that with Claire. Now he didn't think he'd ever have it with anyone ever. He hated who he was now and knew it wasn't a good place to begin something as fragile as a relationship.

"I don't care what he had to say. What matters is what I want and know in this moment." He turned toward where he thought she was and lifted his head. "I may or may not regain my sight. That isn't the bottom line right now. You want to know what is? I'm sick of you being here in my house, invading my space, and ordering me around like I'm a child. I'm supposed to be *your* boss. So find someone to replace you. I want you gone by dinner."

It might turn out to be the worst decision he ever made, but he believed it was the only one he could make. His feelings for Claire made him second guess everything. One thing he was certain about though: she wouldn't move on with her life if she was always taking care of him. She was wonderful, and he was far from it.

"I don't know what crawled up your ass and turned you into a raging prick, but you're right. I don't have to deal with it." Her voice sounded like it had an edge of steel behind it. Good for her; it was about time she stopped being the calm and comforting caregiver. Claire leaned down, her hair whispering across his face and leaving tiny tingles of sensation. Her declaration shocked him more than anything. "If you want to battle me every step of the way, counselor, game on. I'm willing to give as much as I get, but you should know—I plan on winning the war."

Holy hell, she was sexy. He wanted to yank her into his lap and ravage her in every way possible, but that wouldn't be conducive to his plan. She couldn't see this as a challenge or she'd never back down. As much as he liked the idea of entering into a clash of wills with her, it couldn't be allowed.

"We're not at war." He waved at her dismissively. "That would imply this mattered to me. You don't, and never did."

A lie, but she couldn't know the truth.

"You can act like a repulsive jerk all you want, but I see you for who you are. Everything you are has always been visible to me. The truth has been evident since the moment we met, and nothing you do or say will make it ring false now. We all have inner demons we conceal from the world. There's no hiding when you believe there is nothing worth keeping your walls up for." She hammered her point home. "But make no mistake, I'm not your punching bag. As much as I care about you, I can't be the person you beat up on every day."

Pain shot through him at her words. He hated hurting her, even when it was necessary. In the long run, she'd thank him for it though. "I never asked you to be. Leave and you won't have to be the proverbial punching bag ever again. It would be easier for us both if you weren't here."

"I didn't say I was leaving."

She had to be smiling. Her face was a blur, and fine details were lost to him, but he could almost make out the outline of her lips. Matt started to grin back in response, but managed to hold it in. Claire was a fighter and wouldn't give up easily. It was one of the qualities he admired in her. She made a damn good legal assistant. He should have known she wouldn't go because he'd ordered her to.

"Then what was all that nonsense you were spouting?" He frowned. What new tactic was she about to unleash on him? "I thought you'd finally seen reason and was about to bow out before the real skirmish began. I wouldn't hold it against you if you did."

"So generous of you." Claire snorted. "I'll pass."

"So?"

"So what?" she asked. "Oh, you want to know what I have planned." She laughed. It was so lovely to hear that his lips twitched in amusement. "And spoil the surprise? What kind of idiot do you take me for? You're the best strategist I know. It would be moronic to give you a heads-up."

Damn, he admired her. He'd hug her if she'd not see it as encouragement. "Not very sporting of you."

The cool breeze was doing nothing for his overheated skin. He had to get his hands on her. No, he couldn't do what he wanted. Claire wasn't meant to be mauled in desperation. If he was ever lucky enough to have her, she was to be savored. She was the finest of women and should be treated accordingly.

"Well, I never said I'd be fair." Her tone was light and filled with amusement. It left him with giddiness flowing through his veins. "You know the saying."

"No, I can't say I do." He waited on bated breath. The banter was so good he couldn't get enough of her. "Why don't you enlighten me?"

She leaned in close and ran her hand across his thigh. He hardened to the brink of pain. If he reached up he could pull her into his lap and kiss her senseless. Matt wanted to, but refrained from acting on it. If she knew how much she affected him he'd never win this war they started. He'd be putty in her hands, and she'd be able to mold him as she pleased. He almost begged her to do it. One moment of insanity might be worth it for the lifetime of pleasurable memories.

"All's fair in love—and war." Her hot breath caressed his ear. "And Matt, make no mistake, this has nothing to do with merely one of those, and everything to do with both."

Without another word, she left him to think about her parting shot. What the hell had he managed to get himself into this time?

USA TODAY BESTSELLING AUTHOR

DAWN BROWER

CAN THEY ERASE THE IMPRINTS
OF BETRAYAL?

Passion
& LIES

For everyone hoping for a second chance. May the one you love be generous enough to give you one.

PROLOGUE

*V*ivian Miene had everything she could possibly want. The perfect career, the perfect man, Eric Black, and the perfect future—she'd worked hard for the first, and luck had sent her the second, the third had been assured by the prior two. She couldn't imagine anything that could possibly make her life better. Except all the secrets she kept, the ones that could destroy her perfect life.

The darkness that loomed over her happiness... Eric was a key witness in a case against the leader of a known drug cartel. He had no idea that she kept secrets from him. Her duty was to protect him and she'd been assigned to become close to him. Never had she believed she would fall in love with him. Their relationship started out for all the wrong reasons. Vivian prayed that he would forgive her for the lies she'd told. He didn't even know her real name...

"Via," Eric called out to her as he stepped through the doorway of his loft apartment. "Where are you?"

She stared out the window in Eric's bedroom over-looking Seattle. Vivian loved the view. Vivian turned toward Eric as he entered the room. He was the most gorgeous man she'd ever laid eyes on. Dark midnight locks and eyes the color of the Caribbean Sea on a body honed with hard muscle. That gorgeous physique was what had drawn her to him, but it was his heart that had made her fall deeply in love. Vivian smiled and met him in the middle of the room. He pulled her into his arms and pressed his lips to hers.

Vivian leaned into him and he deepened the kiss. He lifted his head and smiled down at her. "I've needed that all day," he told her. "I missed you."

"It hasn't been that long," she said. "A few hours nothing more."

"Any second I'm away from you is too long," he replied with a hint of delight in his tone. "I hate when I have to leave you."

Vivian leaned her head against his chest. She reveled in his warmth and strength. He made her feel safe and wanted. She closed her eyes and took a deep breath. Savored his musky scent and imagined that there was nothing that could tear them apart. She had so many secrets and feared he'd hate her when he heard them all. She had one that he might like, but she wasn't quite ready to believe it. Vivian needed more proof to believe in it herself.

"Are you sad?" he asked.

"No," she answered. "I'm happy." Vivian glanced up at him. "Tell me about your morning. Did it all go well?" This was the part she hated. She was an agent for the FBI and had been working with them since her graduation from college. Her official title was that of a profiler. She had an uncanny ability to see into the evilest of minds. They used that ability in the investigation of Miguel Santiago. Which, in turn, led them to believe Eric was the key that would lead to Miguel's arrest. Eric had intrigued Vivian before ever meeting him. She knew every little detail and volunteered to stage a meeting. She had to know if the information in his file was true. The more she knew of him the more she loved him. Reporting everything to her superiors killed a part of her.

"Better than expected," he said. "We're invited to a charity ball tonight." Eric rubbed his hands down her back. "How do you feel about dressing in a sexy dress and accompanying me?"

She nibbled on her bottom lip. "I might be interested in what you're proposing." Vivian trailed her fingers down his back. "As long as we can leave early and have a little fun at home afterward."

"I like how you think." He grinned. "I cannot make any promises. You know how those things go."

Vivian returned his smile. She wanted to stay with him in the loft forever. Forget whatever the outside world had to offer... It would be so nice. If wishing made it so... "We can try at least."

"That we can," he agreed. "Now I only came home because I forgot my laptop. I'd love to stay..."

"Go," she pushed him away. "The sooner you finish your work for the day the sooner you will be mine."

Eric kissed her quickly and then stepped away. "You make things difficult. I will return shortly before we're to leave for the benefit." With those words he spun on his heels and left snatching his laptop as he walked out. Vivian blew out a breath and prayed she was making the right decision. She loved Eric. Perhaps it was time to be honest with him.

VIVIAN WORE a dark gray tea length dress with silver sequins that outlined the deep V-neck and waist of the dress. The silky material swirled around her legs as she walked. She paired the dress with silver strapped half-inch heels. Vivian wanted to be prepared for any possibility and had no desire to run in stilettos if needed.

Eric circled her waist with his arm and pulled her close. "I must introduce you to the man in charge."

Vivian swallowed hard. This was the moment of truth. Well, not the complete truth, but the moment when she'd finally meet Miguel Santiago. All the work she'd done had been leading to this point. A part of her wanted to turn around and leave. To pretend that she wasn't lying to the man she loved and that all of this was a horrible dream. Her life was perfect—apart from the lying and secrets.

"Miguel," Eric called.

"Ah," a man said as he turned toward Eric. He had tanned skin, dark hair, and chocolate brown eyes. He was almost...pretty. "Who is this lovely woman by your side?"

"This is Vitoria Martel," Eric said.

"Please call me Via," Vivian said. She hated the false-hoods, but they were necessary.

Miguel lifted her hand and pressed his lips to the backside. "It's a pleasure to make your acquaintance."

It took everything inside of her not to yank her hand away from him. This evil man dared to press his lips to her hand. She suppressed her disgust and pasted a smile on her face. Vivian hoped it didn't look as false as it felt. "It's wonderful to finally meet the man Eric works closely with."

"I hope you've come to have fun. There is plenty of food and champagne." He gestured toward the waiters circulating the room. "Help yourself and enjoy the evening's entertainments."

With those words he nodded and left Vivian and Eric alone. "There are a lot of people here." She met Eric's gaze. "Do you know everyone here?"

"I do not," he said. "But I do see someone I need to speak with. Will you be all right on your own for a little while?"

"Of course," she said and snatched a glass of champagne from a tray as a waiter passed. She lifted it up in a salute. "I'll be fabulous, but do hurry back."

Vivian had her suspicions but kept them to herself. Instead she took a sip of her champagne and kept her attention on Eric's movements. He moved through the crowd with ease, and then disappeared through an exit. Vivian cursed and set the champagne down. She had to find him and figure out what he was up to.

She followed the same path Eric had until she reached the doorway. She slipped through the exit and darkness spilled over her. It took a moment for her eyes to adjust, then she started down the corridor. She followed the path until she reached another doorway. She opened it and it led to an outside garden. Eric was in a heated conversation with another man. Vivian couldn't make out the man's face. Was it Miguel?

She moved closer hoping to catch snippets of the conversation. Their voices were muffled. A sound boomed around them and Eric flew backward. Vivian screamed as he hit the ground. She ran toward him as pain shot through her. Vivian stumbled and then fell forward. Her body bounced against the stone path as pain became a part of her. She couldn't reconcile what had happened. Had she been shot? Was Eric all right? He hadn't seemed to be when he fell. A tear fell down her face as she gave in to the pain and lost consciousness.

CHAPTER 1

Two and a half years later...

Eric stared down at his unconscious friend, Wes Novak, and frowned. He'd been too late. Miguel had Vivian, and probably her twin Vitoria. He'd messed up. His plan had went sideways a long time ago and he should have come out of hiding. Vivian was more important than anything to him. He'd faked his death to save her. He'd thought if he were dead she'd be safe. He'd always known who she was—Vivian Miene. The love of his life. Even when she had pretended to be Via Martel he'd known. At first it had entertained him that she claimed to be someone else, and then it terrified him how much she'd come to mean to him. He should have told her the truth. Eric should have taken her with him when he disappeared. So many mistakes... He couldn't dwell on them now. He had to save her and to do that he would need Wes's help. He picked up a nearby cup, filled it with water, and dumped it over him. The water fell over Wes's face and he jolted upward sputtering. "What the hell..."

"Rise and shine, princess," Eric said in a taunting tone as he kneeled before him.

Wes wiped the water dripping from his eyes and looked over. Shock spread over his face as he stared at Eric. He rubbed his eyes attempting to clear them. "I have to be seeing things."

"Nope, I'm really here," Eric reassured him.

"I don't understand—how is this possible?"

"It's a long story, and one we don't have time for right now." Eric stood and held out his hand. "You need to get up, we have something to take care of."

Wes remained unmoving. The shock hadn't completely subsided and Eric was at a loss on how to handle the situation. He never meant for Wes to discover he was alive. It was an asshole move, but it had been for his friend's benefit. Anyone that knew he lived was in danger. Eric didn't want anyone to pay for his mistakes.

"Tori..." Wes glanced frantically around the room as he came completely to his senses. Of course his thoughts would go to the woman he loved.

He couldn't meet Wes's gaze. God he hated this. "Yeah. Miguel has both of them. We need to get them back." Damn it all. He had made too many mistakes. "Miguel thought Tori was Viv. I'm sure he was surprised to realize she had a twin." And that was when everything started a fast downward spiral he had been unable to stop.

Wes jumped up. "How are we going to get them back?"

"I have a plan, but I need you to come with me or else

it won't work." Miguel had figured out Eric was alive. He'd taken the twins to force him out of hiding. Well, the bastard got his wish. Eric was coming for him and this time he would pay for his crimes.

Eric prayed his plan worked. He didn't doubt Wes would help. He might hate the sight of Eric, but he loved Vitoria. Wes would do whatever it took to save her, the same as Eric would to save Vivian. It was a risk, but one Eric was willing to take.

Wes snorted. "Why should I trust you?" he asked.

"Because you always have—you know me. Please Wes, help me." Eric hoped that their previous friendship was enough. That Wes would be able to look past his doubts and see that for the most part he was still the same man. His lies cannot be what destroyed all of the trust between them.

"I don't know if I can."

That was fair... Eric would probably feel the same way if their roles were reversed. But he needed Wes so he had to find a way past his innate doubts. "I know you have feelings for Vitoria. Do you want to allow him a chance to hurt her?"

"Why do you care?" Wes asked.

That was simple. There was only one reason he had returned. "Vivian. I love her. I thought if I stayed away, Miguel would leave her alone, I was wrong." Eric paused, scrubbed his hands over his face. "I have to get her back." He had to find a way to make amends with her...

"Okay what do we do to get them back?" Wes's voice held resignation in it as he spoke.

Relief flooded Eric. He'd believed Wes would help, but a part of him had to consider he might say no. "Do what I say. Come on. I know where he took them. I'll explain the plan on the way."

"Why don't you tell me first? I'd like to have some idea of what I'm getting into?"

Eric groaned. He didn't want to give his friend a play by play and waste what precious time they had. Why did he have to have all the answers first? Eric wanted to shake some sense into him. "We don't really have time for this."

"Make time," Wes demanded.

"Wes, please, I'm begging you. Just come with me."

"Fine, but I don't like it. You'd better tell me everything on the way."

"I will." Eric nodded.

Wes followed him outside and got into the passenger side of a black Ford Escape. Eric put it in drive and squealed out of his parking space. They drove in silence for several minutes, but Wes didn't stay that way for long.

"Were you ever going to tell me?" Apparently Wes wasn't going to let that go until after they saved the women they both loved.

"What?" Eric asked, attempting to play innocent.

"That you were alive." Wes stated simply.

"No, I didn't plan on ever coming back. I got wind of what Miguel was up to a few days ago." He'd had someone watching Miguel. Any information about him that was considered pertinent was sent to Eric. Most of his movements were innocuous, but when he went on a date that resembled Vivian it had been considered important. Very important to Eric...

"Where have you been all this time?"

Eric sighed. "I've been working for the CIA. I haven't even been in the states. Please understand, I can't tell you more than that." He had always worked for the CIA but most of the work he'd done had been analytical, until Miguel Santiago. That needed a more hands on approach... His entire life changed because of that man. The person Wes knew became someone else. He'd had to in order to survive. Eric had a lot of regrets, but losing his best friend and the woman he loved topped that list. He wouldn't apologize for protecting them though. They deserved a good life and they were far better off not having Eric be a part of it.

"Fine, I won't ask," Wes told him. The edge in his voice suggested he didn't like it one bit though. "As long as you understand I still have questions and would like for you to one day volunteer the answers."

"If I could tell you I would..." There was so much he wished he could tell Wes. One day maybe he'd be able to, but that day was not this one.

"Don't start." Wes held up his hand stopping him from continuing. Not that Eric knew what he'd have said anyway. He was at a loss and there were no words that would make any of it right. "Explain to me how we're going to save Tori and Vivian."

"I know a guy on the inside." Hopefully he was still there... Miguel might have uncovered his mole. "I have other agents on standby, but they can't get there for an hour at least. Once we get the women out, they're going to storm in and arrest Miguel."

"Sounds too easy." Wes sounded skeptical and Eric didn't blame him.

It probably would be a shit show, but he didn't want Wes to go in any more frightened than he probably already was. "I hope it will be, but I don't think it will be as simple as it sounds."

Eric pulled down a side street and parked his vehicle. He killed all the lights and stared at a house in the distance.

"Is that where they are being held?" Wes asked.

"Yeah." He stared at the house where Vivian and Vitoria were being held.

"What are we waiting for?"

A miracle... He'd need all the help he could manage to get through this with the women, and the two of them alive. "A text signaling it's okay to go in."

As he spoke, Eric's phone began to vibrate. He nodded to Wes and opened his door. Wes followed him out joining him on the sidewalk.

"All right, this is what we're going to do. I'm going to go in and distract Miguel. You're going to go to the bedroom Vivian and Vitoria are being held in and get them out. Bring them back here and drive away as fast as possible."

Wes stopped and stared at him. "Wait. What? I'm not leaving you here."

"I'll be fine. I have backup coming in remember?" He needed Wes to follow his plan. If he went off book things might go even more sideways than it already had.

"I don't know..."

"Just do it, okay? I need you to make sure Vivian

makes it out of there. Please, I'm begging you, don't argue with me, Wes."

Wes nodded in agreement and followed Eric into the house. They entered from the back. The man Eric had in the house gestured for him to follow. Eric went in the opposite direction toward the front of the house.

Wes went up the stairs and into the room the man gestured toward and Eric went in search of Miguel. He found him in his office. Miguel sat at a desk, a gun in his hand. He directed it at Eric, and Eric kept his own gun focused on Miguel. He should have handled the situation better, but it was too late to go back. He moved closer into the room and remained silent. There had to be a way to get the upper hand. Wes and the two women entered the room with another man behind them. Eric didn't turn when they entered. He kept his own gun focused on Miguel.

"Found them trying to escape." The man behind Wes, Vitoria, and Vivian said.

When the man spoke, Eric turned his head. His displeasure was apparent on his face that they'd not escaped as he'd hoped they would. Eric hardened his features at the sight of them. Wes failed his one task. Eric had to act, do something to fix it, and ensure their survival. Eric jumped over the desk and tackled Miguel attempting to knock him out. They struggled over Miguel's gun. A gun fired, the sound of the shot echoing through the room. Eric punched Miguel and subdued him.

Screams echoed through the room. Eric turned to see what the commotion was all about. Wes grabbed a heavy statue and clocked a guy in the head. The man fell in front of him, his head bouncing off the floor with a hard thud. Wes swayed as he studied the man on the floor, then hit the floor next to the man he'd just knocked out.

"Oh God, Wes, are you okay?" Vitoria rushed to his side.

"You worried about me, sweetheart?" Wes's voice shook as he spoke.

Tears were falling down Vitoria's face. She wiped them away with her hands. "Why'd you have to go and scare me like that?"

"I'm going to be fine. It's a scratch."

Wes held his hand over his shoulder, blood dripping through his fingers. He glanced up and met Eric's gaze.

"He doesn't look good." Eric frowned. Eric retrieved his phone and dialed. He demanded an ambulance. Wes would not die.

Wes ran his fingers across Vitoria's cheek and wiped away a tear falling over it. "I love you, Tori."

"Wes?" Vitoria said his name anxiously.

Wes lost consciousness and Vitoria's sobs grew louder. Not long after that the ambulance arrived to carry Wes to the hospital.

He went over to Vitoria and said, "An ambulance pulled up. They are going to take Wes to the hospital. It looks like the bullet went through his shoulder." Eric laid his hand on Vitoria's arm. "I have Miguel and his associate in handcuffs. They're both going to go away for a very long time."

"Good. They should," Vitoria replied. She glanced at

Vivian crying on the other side of the room. "What the hell is this all about?"

Eric shook his head. "This isn't the time to talk about all of this. We need to get Wes to the hospital." He hated he made Vivian cry. Eric wanted to hold her but he didn't think she'd let him.

"Yes, we do," Vitoria agreed. "I'm not letting you off the hook though. He has a bullet in him because of your incompetence."

"Leave him alone, Tori," Vivian ordered

Vitoria met her sister's gaze. "You tried to warn me, didn't you?"

Vivian nodded. "I did."

"You didn't try hard enough." Her words filled with bitterness. "I was in danger, and all you did was leave a few messages. I always knew you didn't really care about me. It's disappointing to find out how little I do mean to you."

"It's not like that—"

"No, it's exactly like that."

Eric should say something, defend Vivian, but he didn't know how, and he didn't know Vitoria. The paramedics came into the room in a rush. They pulled a stretcher along with them. "Where's the injured individual?"

"He's over here," Vitoria replied.

They went to work on him. Once they had an idea on his condition, they hauled him onto the stretcher and wheeled him out.

"Wait, can I come in the ambulance with you?" Vitoria asked.

"Are you family?"

"No—but…"

"Sorry ma'am, you'll have to meet us at the hospital."

Tears began to spill out of her eyes. Eric took a deep breath. This was something he could fix… "I'll take you to the hospital, Vitoria." Eric grabbed her arm. "Come with me, I have a vehicle outside."

Vitoria yanked her arm out of his hands and seethed, "This is all your fault. I'm not going anywhere with you."

"Don't be stupid Tori. You want to be with Wes, and Eric's giving you a way to get there," Vivian coaxed.

Eric didn't know why Vivian was helping, but he was grateful.

"Fine," she agreed. "He can take me to the hospital."

"I'm glad you're seeing reason," Eric replied.

"Yeah, I'm still not going to forgive you anytime soon. In fact, you two can call his brother and ruin his wedding night by informing him of Wes's condition."

Eric groaned. Dallas was going to be livid… "I can do that on the way to the hospital." He turned to Vivian. "You're coming with us."

"Why the hell would I do that?"

"I want you both to get checked out," he replied.

"You can go to hell," Vivian retorted. "I don't have to do anything you tell me to."

"Viv…"

"Don't even start, Eric. I'm really pissed off at you right now." She folded her arms across her chest. "I'm not about to forgive you because you bat your pretty eyelashes at me."

"This has nothing to do with forgiving me." He hardened his expression as he stared at her. "I don't expect you too."

"Right, how stupid of me." Vivian rolled her eyes. "You didn't bother to tell me you were alive. Why would you want to seek any kind of absolution? It's clear you never loved me."

"Viv—that's not it at all." Eric reached for her.

"Come on Tori, let's go outside and wait for his royal jackass to come out to drive us to the hospital."

"I can come with you now—"

"Don't rush on our account." Vivian glared at him. "I know you have better things to do with your time."

Eric remained silent. They both had a right to their feelings regarding him. He joined them in the car and drove them to the hospital. He stayed silent the entire time. All through Vitoria's pleas to be taken to Wes, through Wes's family joining them...mostly, and even when Vivian glared at him from across the waiting room. He broke that silence when Vitoria seemed reluctant to go into to see Wes. "You should go in."

Tori glanced back at Eric. "I want to."

"What's holding you back?" he asked.

"I don't know." Her voice wobbled as she spoke

Eric nodded. "I get it. You're afraid the doctor was lying and he isn't going to make it. Don't make the same mistakes I did. Go see him."

Vitoria stared up into Eric's eyes. He'd given Vivian up to save her. Perhaps Vitoria understood. Vitoria opened up the door and walked inside to look at Wes, Eric stood directly behind her. His face was pale, yet peaceful. She raised her hand and caressed his cheek. His eyes fluttered open. "Hey, sweetheart."

"If you're trying to get my attention, this wasn't the way to go about it." Vitoria folded her arms across her chest and glared at him.

Wes laughed and then coughed. "Don't make me laugh. It hurts too much."

"I'm sorry…"

"Don't be," he squeezed her hand. "I love you."

Vitoria glared at him. "You're such an asshole."

"I tell you I love you and you insult me?" Wes shook his head.

"Yes, you don't do that."

"What? Admit how much I adore you?"

It hurt a little to witness this declaration of love between them. Eric wanted something like this for him and Vivian. He didn't think he'd find it though. He tuned them out for a little bit, but when he brought himself back to the present he smiled. He was happy for Wes.

"Glad to see you're going to be all right." Eric laughed and turned to leave.

"No Eric, wait," Wes called.

He walked over to the bed. Misery flowed through him. This was all his fault. "I'm sorry, Wes. I thought you'd be able to get Vivian and Vitoria out unnoticed. I didn't intend—"

"It's fine, Eric. You don't need to apologize to me. I think you have someone else you need talk to."

Eric stared at him. "What do you mean?"

Wes grinned. "Vivian."

"Yeah, I have a lot of explaining to do."

"No time like the present to start," Wes said.

Eric nodded and left the room. Maybe they'd be able to work things out between them. Somehow he didn't think it would be easy though... Sometimes second chances weren't given, and he didn't think Vivian would be easy to convince he deserved one.

CHAPTER 2

Three months later...

Vivian stared at her hair. It had grown out over the past few months and the red streaks had faded. The scarlet coloring not quite as bright as when she'd first had it done were a reminder of how preoccupied she'd become. Perhaps she should go to the stylist and have her hair color changed completely. The blonde was a little...blah, and she felt even more so. Perhaps it was because of Eric. He had tried, at first, to gain her forgiveness, then gave up as fast as he started.

Why did she have to love him?

She groaned and closed her eyes. She had to get Eric out of her head. He didn't love her. If he had he'd never have left her alone. Left her to have their baby without him. She could forgive the secrets and the lies. It would be hypocritical of her if she didn't. She had told her fair share of them. He had called her Vivian. Not Via. Vivi or

Vivian. He knew who she was. Had he always known? Did he know about Gabriel too? If he did, and still stayed away, that said more than anything that she, and their son, didn't matter to him.

"Momma," Gabriel said as he wobbled into her room. He was so little. Barely two years old and so precocious. He was also a tiny version of his father. It hurt to look at him sometimes. The reminder of the man she loved... Before it was because she believed Eric dead, now she ached deep inside because she wasn't as important to him as he was to her.

"Yes, baby," she said. "Did you have a bad dream?"

Gabriel had been down for his nap for the past hour. He usually slept for at least two hours. He was a good sleeper so something must have awakened him. He toddled over to her with his arms up. "Up, up," he said.

Vivian picked her son up and cradled him in her arms. He was growing so fast. Before she knew it he'd be past the days of wanting to cuddle with her or seek comfort in her arms.

"Do you want me to read you a story?" she asked.

"No," he said. "Momma?"

"Yes, baby." She rubbed her fingers through his dark curls.

"Juice," he said in his little boy voice.

Vivian smiled. Gabriel loved juice. "Sure," she said and set him on the floor. "Let's get you some juice." She left her room and headed to the kitchen with her son following close behind her. Vivian opened the refrigerator and pulled out a carton of apple juice, then carried it over to the counter. She pulled one of Gabriel's special cups out of the cupboard and filled it half way with water and the other half with juice. If she allowed him to he'd drink nothing but juice and it would run right through him. This was her compromise. "Here you go sweetie," she handed the cup to Gabriel. "Would you like a snack too?"

"Yesss," he hissed out the word. "Watch cartoons?"

"Sure," she said. "I'll put them on for you and then get you a snack." Vivian went to the living room and turned the television on. She clicked on a children's network and one of Gabe's favorite shows was already airing. It featured a happy blue dog that helped the host solve mysteries. Gabe loved that dog. Maybe she should consider getting him a puppy... She shook her head and dismissed the thought. Vivian didn't have the time for a dog. "There you go," she told him. Gabe snuggled up on the sofa with his sippy cup and stared at the television. Vivian left him alone to make him a snack.

She grabbed some grapes out of the refrigerator and peeled the skins off. She had a weird fear he'd choke on them so she peeled them and sliced them in half. She sliced a banana and some strawberries and made him a nice fruit cup. As she was leaving the kitchen her doorbell rang. Vivian frowned, set the cup on the table by Gabe, and then went to see who was visiting. Maybe it was her sister, Tori. They had been making an effort to repair their relationship. She was glad for that. Vivian had a rough couple of years and it would have been nice to have her sister around for them.

Vivian opened the door and froze. Not Tori... "What are you doing here?" Her heart beat heavily inside her chest. She didn't know how she was still standing upright.

"I thought if I gave you enough time…" Eric shoved his hands into his pockets. "Can we talk?"

She was suddenly conscious of how terrible she must look. Her hair was limp and the color fading. Her torn jeans were loose on her hips and her t-shirt had seen better days. She hadn't expected company and if it had been anyone other than Eric she'd have been all right with how she looked. He on the other had was every woman's fantasy. His dark jeans fit perfectly and his black shirt clung to his muscular chest. She wanted to run her fingers through his black hair and lose herself in those turquoise eyes. She held back. Barely. "I don't think we have anything to talk about."

"That's not true and you know it," he told her. "I made mistakes…"

She snorted. "That's an understatement. Look, you're right, we do have things to discuss." He had to know about Gabriel. "But now is not a good time.

"Please," he begged. "I…" He swallowed hard. "We had something good. If its possible I'd like to find our way back to that."

He wanted a second chance? "I don't know if I have anything left to give you. When you…died." It was her turn to swallow hard. "I had to pick up the pieces of my life. The pieces of me…" She glanced away. "I was broken but I had someone else to think about other than myself. Somehow I found a way to move on, to be strong, without you. If you want to be a part of Gabriel's life I won't stop you. But you and me" Vivian gestured between the two of them. "There's no going back to the past. All we can do is go forward."

She moved away from him and shut the door. Vivian didn't want to deal with him. She couldn't handle it. Not when she wasn't even remotely feeling her best...

*E*ric stared at the closed door uncertain what he should do next. He'd waited too long. She wouldn't be reasonable. Wait... What was she talking about? Who was Gabriel? Eric lifted his hand and pounded on the door again. She didn't open it so he repeated the action until finally she stood before him again.

"What the hell is wrong with you? I told you this wasn't a good time."

"Gabriel," he said.

"Is that what all the ruckus is about? You want to finally meet your son?"

Eric felt as if he'd been punched in the gut. He had a son. Why hadn't anyone bothered to tell him that? His informant only watched Miguel to ensure he didn't go after Vivian. No one mentioned she had been pregnant. He wouldn't have been able to stay away if they had. She was—had been vulnerable. He was such an asshole. "I didn't know..." The words came out on a harsh mumble.

Eric cursed under his breath. "Let me in." He didn't wait for her to invite him in this time. Eric pushed past her and walked into the living room. A small boy sat on the couch eating fruit and watching a cartoon. His son...

"Eric?" Vivian came to stand beside him. She placed her hand on his arm. "You really didn't know?" Her voice was hoarse. "At least I know you would have cared about him. Do care..."

"I care about you," he insisted. "I never stopped loving you. Going away—doing what I did—it was to protect you." He swallowed hard. "I didn't want to leave."

She frowned. "There had to be a better way to handle it all."

He shook his head. "There wasn't. You were in danger as long as I was alive." Eric scrubbed his hands over his face. "We need to talk about it all. Now. It's past time."

She nodded. "You're right. Follow me I'll make coffee. Gabriel will be fine watching his cartoons for a little while."

Eric did as she instructed and went to the kitchen with her. As she fussed with the coffee preparation he sat at the table. Her home was cozy, comfortable...inviting. A nice place to raise a child. "Why did you leave the FBI?"

"I didn't realize you knew about that."

"I knew everything before I left. I worked with the CIA for several years after I earned my degree...as an analyst. If not for Miguel I'd still be working behind the scenes."

"What was different about him?"

"The numbers," he said. "No one understood how he hid his money and moved it. They needed me on the inside to find the evidence. I was the only one that would be able to recognize it when I found it. I didn't get it all before it got to hot for me to be there. To make my death believable they listed me on the case files as a key witness making me expendable to Miguel and therefore making my execution more believable."

"He said he didn't order it…"

"That's because he didn't. It was made chaotic for a reason. So my handlers could retrieve my dead body and send me overseas without anyone the wiser." It had been a mess from start to finish. He hated hurting her. He should have found a reason for her to stay home that night. It would have been much safer for her. "You were never supposed to be injured. A stray bullet hit you." God. She could have lost the baby. Thank God she hadn't.

"That was what made it real for me. I wasn't seriously wounded and they confirmed what I suspected about my pregnancy. I thought it was possible but was too afraid to find out…" She blew out a breath. "I never would have kept that from you. All my lies were weighing on me. If I'd known that you…" She sighed. "It doesn't matter now. What happened is in the past. It seems I was the only one truly in the dark."

"I promise that I won't keep anything from you ever again. You're my everything. I want to be with you and I felt that way before I knew our son existed. He only makes me want it more. I'll do anything. Tell me what you need from me and I'll make it happen. Please."

Eric didn't know what else he could say or do to make her realize how much he loved her. Had always loved her. She was the only woman that would ever hold his heart. She was his everything.

"I don't know…" She walked over and set a cup of coffee in front of him. Black the way he'd always liked it. "There was a time I dreamed of this. Having you here begging me for another chance. I'm not so sure that it's as easy as the fantasies I had. This is real life and real life is never a smooth path."

"I understand," he said. "All I want is a chance. Can you give me that?"

She nibbled on her bottom lip. Vivian was still the sexiest woman he'd ever seen. He would walk over Legos or hot coals for her. Whatever torture device she set up for him he'd endure it. He would find a way to relieve her apprehension because he never intended to leave her again.

"I'm not going to make you any promises. I want to say I'll let you in again. I want to believe I can trust you." She blew out a breath. "But at the end of the day it is too complicated for that. It's going to take time. Do you think you can give that to me?"

"Baby," he began. "I can do anything. Let me prove it to you."

Her lips twitched upward. "All right then. You have your second chance. Don't waste it." She drew in a breath and released it. "I'm not making you any promises. Consider this a probational period. You have a lot to prove to me." She glanced toward the room their son was in. "You will always have a place in Gabriel's life, but I don't have to let you in mine."

Eric grinned. That was his Vivian. She never pulled a punch to save someone's feelings. He could always count on her to be as honest as she was able to be. "I don't intend to." He took a sip of his coffee. What he wanted was to pull her into his arms and kiss her senseless. That wasn't possible for a couple of reasons. One of them being their son in the other room... If Eric kissed her the way he wanted to it might lead to things a little boy shouldn't witness. Then there was the fact she might not want his kiss...yet. He could wait for her though. She was worth it. Would always be the one he loved. He would prove to her that she wasn't wasting her time with him. He would make the best of this second chance.

"Come with me," she said. "It's time for you to meet your son."

Eric stood and followed her to the living room. Gabriel glanced up at them as they entered the room. "Hey baby," she said. "There's someone I want you to meet."

"Who you?" The toddler's soft voice sounded almost accusatory. Eric didn't blame the boy. He was the interloper in his son's world.

He walked over to the boy and kneeled before him. "Who do you think I am?" That sounded stupid but he was curious what Gabriel thought of him.

The boy shrugged. "Momma's friend."

Eric hoped he'd be more than that to Vivian. One day he hoped to ask her to marry him. This was their new start though. He could be patient. The best things were worth waiting for and working to keep. "I am that." It was a beginning at least with his son. Eric wasn't certain he was ready to call him dad or even understood what that meant.

"This is Eric," Vivian said. "He's your papa."

"He is?" The boy's eyes widened. "Like I've always wanted?"

Vivian nodded. "He is."

"I thought he was gone forever," Gabriel stared at him warily.

"So did I," Vivian said softly. "But he came back to us and he wants to spend time with you. Are you all right with that?"

He nodded. "Will you watch Blue with me?"

Eric stared at the television and frowned as a blue dog hopped across the screen. He didn't know what he was about to get into, but he'd endure anything for his son and Vivian. "Absolutely," he agreed. "Tell me about this Blue character."

He joined his son on the couch and Vivian sat on the chair nearby. Eric would have preferred she sat next to him but it was enough, for now, that she stayed in the room. She might only be doing it to make sure Gabriel was all right with him; however, it didn't negate the fact she stayed at all. This was his family and he would ensure he stayed with them always.

CHAPTER 4

Five months later...

It was a warm late autumn day and Vivian thought it was perfect for an afternoon at the park. Gabriel loved playing in the park, and there were several other children there his age. He ran around with them, up through the play area, and then down a nearby slide. His laughter echoed back to her and she smiled. That was her boy. He was fearless and welcoming. He played with any child that wanted to be around him. She hoped he'd always be that inclusive.

"He looks like he's having fun," Eric said as he sat down on the park bench beside him. "Thank you for letting me know you would be here."

Vivian was trying since they had their first discussion. She wanted him to have a place in Gabriel's life. So she included him in any activities whenever possible. That was the least she could do. Plus a park was a public place and it eased some of the tension between them. He claimed he wanted to be a part of her life too. She wished she believed that as much as he proclaimed it. So far she hadn't seen any actions from him that convinced her.

"I think we should go away together," Eric said. "The three of us."

She lifted a brow. "Is that so?" What did he hope that would do? A vacation would not fix all of their problems.

"It is," he reiterated. "It would be good for us to do something as a family. Something that we have to do together without interruption."

She frowned. Vivian wasn't sure how she felt about that situation. She understood his motivation. Here, at home, she could toss him out. But if they went away together there was a good chance they'd be sharing accommodations, and certainly travel together. "I'm not certain it is a good time for me to get away. The gallery is busy this time of year, and besides Tori and Wes's wedding is real soon." That was an excuse. He probably knew it too, they could always go after the wedding. She wasn't ready for what he suggested. They weren't at that juncture, and he damn well knew that too. She had loved working with the FBI, but after she had found out she was pregnant she'd decided it was far too dangerous. Her baby had already lost a father and didn't need to lose a mother too, and God, when Miguel had kidnapped her and Tori...her son could have been an orphan. Thank God he'd been with a sitter that night and not in danger. When Eric and Wes had shown up to save them she'd never been so relieved in her life, or so mad. Eric had lied. She couldn't forget that.

When she'd opened her gallery she hadn't looked back.

She had done what she had to. How could he reconcile Eric's supposed death with reality now? She had loved him so damn much, and mourned him until she made herself sick. Vivian had pulled herself together when she wanted to crawl into a hole and die.

Now though, Eric was alive and well. Gabriel had both of them. She could make a different choice, but she wouldn't. Vivian wouldn't change the choices she'd made; however, she'd never been so uncertain what she should do with her present, or her future. Eric made her question everything.

"You don't have someone there that can handle the day to day for a weekend?" Yup, he didn't believe her. She really didn't care either. He stared at her as if he could see right through her. It could be a little unnerving when he glanced at her in that way. "And I didn't mean today. I'm in the wedding," he reminded her. "I can't leave until after it regardless."

"No," she said firmly. "I can't find anyone else.' Vivian did not care if he believed her either. This would all be on her terms, not his. "Besides I would rather Gabriel had more time to know you before we plan what constitutes a family vacation." So what if it had been months. It hadn't been enough, and damn it, she wanted him to work harder. He owed her, and he owed his son too.

The muscle in his cheeks clenched. He didn't like her proclamation, but too damn bad. He had to accept it. Some pills were hard to swallow for a reason. This was too big to be cavalier about. "All right, but I reserve the right to change your mind."

"You're welcome to try," she told him. "I am, as always, making no promises to you."

They sat in silence as Gabriel played. Their little boy wasn't paying attention to either of them. He had other things on his mind, and his parents did not play a part in them. He laughed, he ran, and he chased... In short, he was a regular little boy having a grand time at the park.

For Vivian it was an entirely different experience. It was hard to ignore Eric's presence. Even with a park full of other parents, both male and female, she couldn't shake the feeling of having him by her side. Her whole body came alive when he was near. She talked a good game, but she wasn't fooling herself. Her love for him never died. How could it have? He had been everything to her and when he was gone she nearly fell to pieces, had fallen to pieces if she were honest with herself. Gabriel forced her to pull them back together. There were still minute fractures in her soul though. A person doesn't ever fully recover from the loss of the love of their life. Even if he found a way to return.

"He's so vibrant," Eric said to her. "So full of life. He's a little miracle."

"He's been my miracle since I learned he was growing inside of me," she said softly. He was her savior too, but she'd never say that much aloud. That was too much for one small boy to handle. She lived for him. "Gabriel is my little angel." It was one of the reasons she'd named him as she had. He was her strength and reason for being.

"Would you allow me to take him for the day," he asked. "Just me and him?"

Vivian opened her mouth to object, but then closed it.

She wanted her son to know his father. They should have time together. It would be good for both of them. Besides she had no real leg to stand on. Eric wasn't a bad man. He'd been put in an untenable position. She didn't like his choices, but he would never intentionally hurt Gabriel. "When would you like to?" It hurt to share her son with him like this. It shouldn't, but it did. Gabriel had been her lifeline for so long.

"This weekend?" It came out as more of a question than a statement. Perhaps he realized how hard it would be for her to be parted from their son.

"This weekend is fine," she told him. "When you have a better idea call me and we'll settle a time and day."

Eric grinned. "Maybe afterward we can do something as a family too."

They weren't a family. Not really… That would imply Eric and Vivian were a couple, but they were far from being that any time soon. "I'll consider it." She couldn't do anything but that. She constantly thought about what it would be like for them to be a fully functional unit. She started to say something else and froze. Gabriel fell to the ground and stopped moving entirely. She bolted forward on instinct. This wasn't normal and her heart raced in her chest. Eric was beside her in an instant. Her baby…what was wrong with her baby?

ERIC STARED at the stark white hospital room. The beep beep of machine around them didn't ease the nervousness overruling his system. What was wrong with his son?

Why had he dropped suddenly and lost consciousness? He was running a fever. That much had been obvious when he'd felt his skin. There was a rash on his torso too. Had he caught a virus of some sort?

Vivian was pacing the room. He should do something to help her but he had no idea what he could do. She was even more anxious than he was. God. He had just found out he had a son. What if he lost him before he had a chance of knowing him? What would this do to Vivian? She had all but stated having Gabriel had given her a reason to go on living? Would she give up on life if she lost her son?

Eric shook those thoughts away. They were not, would not, lose their son. They had all been through too much already for him to accept that even as a possibility. "The doctors will help him."

"I know," she said. Her voice was steady but it was clear as day to him she wasn't. He stood and went to her side, then wrapped his arms around her.

"Darling," he said softly and kissed her forehead. "I'm here. Relax a little." There was not much he could do for her. He'd move heaven and earth if it was in his capabilities. He loved her and his son so damn much.

"I can't," she said. Her voice was barely above a whisper. "That's my baby there and he is sick. How could I have not known he was sick?"

He didn't say anything for several seconds. Eric just held her and rubbed her back. He was no medical professional and had no idea what ailed his son, but he could do this much for Vivian. She had to do everything on her own for too long. He was there now and he would do his part. "Sometimes illnesses seem to happen suddenly. He was playing and acting normal. How could you have known?" He rubbed her back again. "Have you developed prognostication over the years that I'm unaware of?"

She chuckled softly. "No." There was a small hint of a smile there. It wasn't much but he'd take it. They had to keep calm if they were going to be there for Gabriel.

"Then stop beating yourself up about this. The doctors will figure out what is wrong with Gabriel. All you can do is wait and let them do their job."

Eric wanted to help Gabriel as much as Vivian did. He understood that medical diagnosis wasn't in his wheel-house, but that didn't stop him from wishing he could make his son well. He needed Gabriel to be better as much as he needed his family to stay whole. He fully intended to be a part of both their lives for the unforesee-able future. They were his.

"That is easier said than done." She pulled out of his arms. He felt the loss of her immediately. Vivian was trying to put those walls back up and he couldn't let her. It was a fucked up thing, but the illness of their son was helping them bond again. He wasn't so benevolent to not use that to his advantage. Vivian was the love of his life. He would do anything to keep her by his side now that he could claim her once again.

"I realize that," he said softly. "Words are sometimes easier than actions. We still try." He had to believe that if he had any chance of winning back her love.

Her lips wobbled a little. "That's true."

"Then keep holding on to hope. He's our son isn't he?"

He lifted a brow. "He's a strong boy and he will make it through this."

She nodded. "I want to believe that."

"Then believe it," he told her. Eric refused to believe anything less and he needed her to believe it too. "Wait to hear what the doctor has to say before you start believing in worst case scenarios."

She nodded. "I'll try. It's all I can do."

"It's all any of us can do baby," he said as he reached for her again. "Let me hold you."

She seemed reluctant but then stepped into his embrace. He held on to her as if his life depended on it, and perhaps it did a little bit. His entire being was rocked by this development. Eric had believed he was making some sort of progress with her at the park. Everything had gone to hell when Gabriel had collapsed.

His son was lying in a hospital bed fighting for his life. Eric had never felt so helpless in his entire life. This wasn't supposed to happen. Not to Gabriel... That boy should be playing, laughing, and just enjoying his young life. Illnesses happened, but not like this. Whatever was attacking Gabriel's young body was no normal sickness.

The door swung open and a doctor walked in. He had sandy-brown hair and olive green eyes. Eric recognized him instantly. He had been one of the doctors on Wes Novak's case. "Hello, Dr. Ellwood." Ian Ellwood was one of the hospitals top cardiothoracic surgeons. Why was he in Gabriel's hospital room? "What's wrong?"

Dr. Ellwood frowned. He glanced from Eric to Vivian and then to Gabriel. "One of the pediatricians on your son's case called me for a consult. They think your son might have a condition that would fall under my expertise?"

"Something is wrong with his heart?" Panic filled Eric's chest. "He has a rash and a fever. How could that possibly relate to his heart?"

He wanted to pull his son into his arms and rock back and forth. What if his heart was failing. He'd been trying to stay calm for Vivian's sake, but now... He was fast losing his hold on his control. He would break if he lost Gabriel, much like Vivian said she broke when she lost him. Was this to be his punishment for not being there for his son sooner?

*V*ivian had never known fear like this. It was coursing through her veins and amping up the panic and fear exponentially. If her son was far sicker than she could ever anticipated... She swallowed hard. Eric had been calm and reassuring until Dr. Ian Ellwood walked into the room. With his entrance his fear spiked to Vivian's level. They couldn't both break down at the same time. One of them had to be strong for Gabriel.

She placed her hand on Eric's arm. "He will be all right. He has to be." Then she turned to the doctor. "Tell us what is going on with our son."

"It could be nothing or rather not what the doctors believe it might be." Dr. Ellwood sighed. "I'm only here for a consultation and we will run more tests. I don't want to worry you more than necessary. I'd rather not name their suspicions when it might be wrong."

"And I'd rather know what we might be facing then have something sprung on me at the last second," Eric told him. "I work better when I have all the facts."

"I agree with him," Vivian countered. "What does the pediatrician think might be wrong with Gabriel." She wanted to be prepared and as soon as she had the probable diagnosis she wanted to research it. She would know everything there was to know when she next discussed Gabriel's condition with the doctor.

Dr Ellwood met her gaze, then turned toward Eric. A resigned expression filled his face. "I don't like to work this way, but I understand why you would want all the information. I need a promise from you both before I go forward."

"Anything," Vivian said. She had to know what was happening with her child. "Gabriel is all that matters right now. I'll promise you whatever you need for his sake."

"Me too," Eric said. He'd been quiet for the most part. The stoic side of him had come out in full force.

"I don't want you to let fear rule you," he told them. "Even if this is what the pediatrician believes, it is not a worst case scenario. At least not in terms of the condition." He blew out a breath. "In some cases the disorder might be quite serious. I don't want you to misunderstand me. It's always serious, but some cases are more severe than others."

"All right," Vivian said. "I understand. Now explain what this disorder is."

He smiled slightly. "You are quite tenacious when you set your mind to it."

"I am," she agreed. "Now I'd like to know what is going on. Please quit stalling." Her patience, what little she'd had to begin with, was wearing thin. The good doctor had better start talking soon or she might wring his neck.

"I intend to tell you everything," Dr. Ellwood said. "But I wanted you to understand that if, and that's a big if, Gabriel has this condition it is not a severe case. If he had come in later it might have turned into one, but we will be catching it early."

"So if he has whatever you are stalling to tell us," Eric began. "He should make a full recovery."

"That's what I believe, but I also haven't examined him yet. I've only read through the notes in his chart." Dr. Ellwood shoved his hands into his pockets. "I need to check him myself and order more tests to make a complete diagnosis."

Vivian ran her finger through her hair. She'd already made her long locks into a snarled mess with her anxious habit. "Fine. Tell us what you think it might be and then examine him. I need to know."

Dr. Ellwood took a deep breath. "This might be Kawasaki disease."

Eric furrowed his brows. "What is that?"

"To put it simply it is an illness that affects children. The disease causes inflammation of blood vessels, especially the coronary arteries. Unfortunately males are 1 and a half times more likely to get it over females. That is one of the reasons we are concerned he might have it."

Vivian froze at those words. "It is affecting his heart then." That made sense considering what Ian Ellwood's specialty was. Eric had jumped to that conclusion at first too. But to hear it… That made it all the more real. "How is it treated? What happens if it gets more severe?"

Ian sighed, again. "We're not going to look to the worse case scenarios." He frowned. "If he has this condition, which we have not established yet, we'll start an I.V. treatment of immunoglobulin and aspirin. That should help immediately."

"And if it doesn't?" Eric asked.

"Then we'll move on to phase two. Possibly and addition of steroids. All of that will have to be assessed as we move forward." He met Eric's gaze. "Now I really must examine him."

Dr. Ellwood didn't wait for their permission. He moved over to the bed where Gabriel slept. He'd been tossing and turning earlier, but now he was eerily calm. Vivian's heart raced inside her chest. She prayed her little boy would be all right. This condition sounded so serious. How could he have possibly gotten it? Was it something she had done? She needed so much information but she didn't think the doctor would give her anymore. He was already frustrated by her insistent questions.

Eric stood behind her and wrapped his arms around her waist. They both watched the doctor. He looked at the rash that crawled up Gabriel's back and had spread up to his neck, then he felt around his neck. Vivian didn't know what he was looking for on her son, but she hoped whatever it was he didn't or did if it helped her son. She was so damn conflicted. After he was done he pulled out his stethoscope and placed it against Gabriel's chest. Through the whole exam Gabriel didn't wake. She couldn't help wondering if that was a good thing or a bad thing.

Dr Ellwood finished and turned to them. "I've done my part here. I'm ordering a few tests."

"And?" she asked expectantly.

"So far I agree with their assessment but I am not

prepared to make a diagnosis without the tests. They'll help me make a more accurate diagnosis." He frowned. "I know you want answers and I will get them for you. I just need you to be patient a little while longer."

With those words he excused himself and left Eric and Vivian alone with their son. As soon as he left Vivian pulled herself away from Eric and pulled out her phone. She had some research to do.

ERIC HADN'T LIKED anything that the doctor had to say. Not one word. But what could he do? The doctor was only doing his job, and what a hell of a job he had. Eric wouldn't want it. To look at people everyday and have to tell them their loved one might possibly die? That was what he was saying without actually voicing the words. Gabriel was very sick. That much had been obvious for a while now. Eric just hadn't wanted to face that fact, but now he had to. Vivian would need for him to be strong. She kept trying to push him away, but she needed him. Now more than ever…

She was sitting in one of the chairs in the small hospital room typing away on her phone. She kept stopping every now and then to read something and mumble under her breath. He expected she was researching everything she could about this disease their son might have. He didn't blame her. A part of him wanted to do the same thing, but he'd let her have the honor. It kept her mind busy for a little while and she needed that.

"Do you need me to get you anything?" he asked.

"What?" She glanced up but she wasn't really looking at him. Her focus was entirely on her phone. "No, no," she replied absentmindedly. "I'm fine."

Eric rocked back on his heels. He loved her so damn much. Had never stopped loving her. His love for her only grew in the last few months. She was so strong, brave, and amazing. What she'd gone through... His heart ached for the pain he caused her. He understood how much Gabriel meant to her. She would not survive if something tragic happened to him. Their son was her world. Eric would like to believe she felt the same way about him, but he doubted she did. She'd had to set aside her feelings and live so their son would. That had to have been difficult for her.

"I'm going to go for a walk. If you change your mind..."

"Go," she said and shooed him away. "I know how to reach you."

It hurt a little how easy it was for her to dismiss him. He shoved those feelings aside and stepped out of the room. He drew in a deep breath, then released it. He needed to talk someone that wasn't so close to this situation. Eric headed to a nearby waiting area and pulled out his phone. There was only one person he could count on. He flipped through his contacts and pressed on the name that he needed, then waited for the call to go through. It didn't take long for Wes Novak to answer.

"What's up?" Wes asked.

"I hope I'm not interrupting anything..." He swallowed a lump in his throat.

"Not at all," Wes reassured him.

"Can you bring Tori to the hospital. I think Vivian might need her right now."

Wes was quiet for several seconds and then asked, "What happened?"

Eric slumped down into one of the seats in the waiting room. He could feel tears starting to form, but somehow managed to suppress them. He'd never felt so hopeless before. This was an all new experience for him. Wes was one of his closest friends. He'd known about Gabriel before Eric, but kept his silence. He didn't blame him. Eric had lied to Wes as well as Vivian. Trust was hard to earn back. He was working on that...repairing all the relationships he'd damaged with his deception. He needed Wes, but he also knew that Vivian would need her twin. She wasn't leaning on him so she might lean on Vitoria. They'd been repairing their relationship too and Vivian now trusted her twin much more than she ever did growing up. It was amazing what could happen in a short span of time.

"It's Gabriel," his voice cracked as he spoke. "He's..." Why couldn't he get the words out. "It's bad."

"How bad?" Wes asked.

"Dire," Eric replied. "Bring Tori."

Wes blew out a breath that echoed through the phone. "Is there anything I can tell her? She'll freak without more information. She adores her nephew."

"He's very sick." Eric paused and considered what to tell him. "I don't want to get into it over the phone. Dr. Ian Ellwood is one of his doctors." Wes would understand the meaning of that. He was acquainted with the doctor and considered him a friend.

"Christ," he said. "All right. Give us a half hour and then we will be there. Vitoria will want to be there for Vivian as much as Gabriel."

"I thought she might," Eric answered.

"Try to relax," Wes said. "I realize that might be difficult, but at least try. We will be there soon."

"Okay," Eric said. "I'll be waiting." He ended the call and shoved the phone back into his pocket. It shouldn't take them long to arrive. Vivian might be angry with him for calling Wes and having him bring her sister, but she might also be relieved. He wasn't sure anymore what to expect from her. She'd done her best to remain as distant as possible from him. Even when she promised to give him a chance...she really hadn't. Now their son was fighting for his life. Eric was very afraid he might lose them both.

*V*ivian stared down at her son. His fever was lower. That had to be a good thing anyway. The medicine they were giving him was working. She prayed he didn't have this condition they feared he had. Dr. Ellwood had been right. If he did have it, then they caught it early enough. For those that they hadn't caught early it was too late...those unlucky children died. Vivian wouldn't be able to handle the death of her child. She felt so bad for those individuals that had lost their children. It had to be so unbearable. How did a parent survive such a loss? She hoped she never had to find out.

The door to the room clicked open. Vivian assumed it was Eric returning. He'd been gone for a while. She could have handled things with him better. He was only trying to help and she kept pushing him away. She understood she shouldn't, but couldn't stop herself. He hadn't been there and his connection to Gabriel wasn't nearly as strong as hers. She was being...difficult. He had made choices without considering her or the consequences. It was hard for her to let go of those feelings. She'd been trying, and failing, for days no weeks. That kind of anger and betrayal was hard to let go of. She had to work harder to set it aside though. For her son...Gabriel needed to have his father in his life. He would sense tension between them. Even if she could never forgive Eric enough to be with him, at the very least she had to find peace with him. Gabriel deserved that.

"How is he?"

Vivian jerked around and faced her twin. She was identical to her. A mirror twin really, but she didn't have the red streaks in her hair. Vitoria was far too refined for something she deemed low class. Her twin was all about image. It made sense considering the sort of business she'd started. She was a full service PR firm and worked with the rich and famous, mostly athletes. They all had an image to maintain.

"How did you know?" Vivian hadn't realized how much she needed her twin until that moment.

"Eric called Wes," she said softly, then moved to her side. "Why didn't you let me know?"

"I couldn't..." She hadn't believed her twin would care enough to come. There was so much bad blood between them. They had gone years without speaking. They had only begun to repair that relationship recently. She should have tried with Vitoria much sooner. The had lost so much time as sisters. Why did she always push people away? What purpose did that really serve her? She isolated herself when she could have a loving family.

Vitoria hugged her. "I understand. It's hard to let go of old habits." She stepped back and met Vivian's gaze. "But

I'm here now and I'm not going anywhere. You're my sister and I expect you and your son to be a part of my life."

"I appreciate that." It was hard for Vivian to admit she needed anyone. "I'm glad Eric called Wes. I should thank him."

"How are things between you and Eric?" Vitoria had no expression on her face and she tried to keep her tone light, but Vivian realized what she was doing. This was her sister trying to weasel her way in and dig for information.

"We're…" How did Vivian put it. "Not there yet."

"Do you want to be?" she asked softly. "Do you still love him?"

"That's not the question that needs to be answered." Vivian had never stopped loving Eric. He would always be the love of her life. She couldn't imaging spending her life with any other man. Trusting him was the real issue, and that wasn't even clear cut. She did trust him to a certain extent. What she couldn't be certain of is if she could trust him to stay. She realized that was a little irrational. His sole reason for leaving, faking his death, no longer existed. In theory that should mean he had no reason to ever leave her again. "I can't shake this feeling I might lose him again."

"Is that even a real possibility?" Vitoria went to glance down at Gabriel. She loved him as much as Vivian did. She had built a relationship with Gabriel and Vivian appreciated her twins efforts in that regard. "Do you think Eric would leave him?"

She shook her head. "No I don't. But a son is different.

He's part of him isn't he?" Her lips wobbled a little bit. "What if that's enough or what if..." She couldn't say the rest. Admit her fears aloud. What if it all came true because she spoke it aloud.

"Sweetie," Vitoria said. "You won't give life to your fears by saying them."

"How did you know?" Vivian asked.

"It's all over your face." She cupped her cheek. "Tell me what is going on with Gabriel. Eric didn't tell Wes much."

Vivian swallowed the lump that had formed in her throat. Her emotions were all over the place and she had no idea how long it would take her to regain her normal control. She'd worked so hard to not be the type to give into them. She'd had to be so strong for far too long. "What did he tell Wes."

"Just that Gabriel is very sick and Ian is one of his doctors."

"That's right..." She frowned. "You are sort of friends with him aren't you?"

"Wes's sister is closer to him than we are," Vitoria answered. "But we have socialized together. He's good at what he does."

She nodded absentmindedly. "I've heard that."

What should she tell Vitoria? Dr. Ellwood had said Gabriel might not have this condition. Should she wait until she knows for certain? Vivian took a deep breath and decided to tell Vitoria everything. She would need her sister, and it was better if her twin had all the information available. The time to keep secrets was long gone and had no place in their relationship any longer.

***

Eric paced the waiting room. He wanted to go check on Vivian and his son, but he also realized she needed time with Vitoria. It killed him that he wasn't what she needed. His decisions had put him where he was and while he didn't like it, he had to accept it. Vivian needed more time to realize that he wasn't going anywhere. He belonged by her side, with Gabriel. He knew it, and in time she would too. He loved her and would wait as long as it took for her to want him in her life.

"So it is clear you're super anxious," Wes drawled. "But what else is going on with you?"

He stopped, turned, then glared at Wes. "Why are you so calm?"

"Probably because it is not my son fighting for his life right now. I can relax easier and accept Ian is not going to let Gabriel die."

Eric closed his eyes and prayed for patience and a miracle if needed. Normally he wasn't a praying man. He took action and found a way to solve the problem. The fact that he had resorted to praying said a lot about his current situation. "I want to believe that."

"Then do it," Wes demanded. "Ian is a damn good doctor. If he is needed then he will do whatever is in his power to save your son. He did with Colt after his accident. He'll do it for your soon too."

"I forgot he was the doctor on Colt's case." Colt Lewis was Wes's brother-in-law. He had married Colt's sister, Emma, in a spur of the moment Vegas wedding. One they had both kept secret at first. When it had come out it had rocked Wes's family hard. They had thought Colt and Emma's relationship over for good. They had all believed he had cheated on her, but he hadn't. "How is Colt and Emma doing?"

"They're fine," he said. "Still can't believe she married him. He's been doing some physical therapy...which she is overseeing. He might not be able to make it to training camp this month. He's got a ways to go. There is always a chance he'll never play again. His injuries were quite severe." Wes sighed. "He's determined, and while Em is scared, she's supporting him. He's ready to accept the doctor's determination if need be. He doesn't have a death wish...but..."

"Football means a lot to him," Eric finished for him. "I get that."

"And so does my sister," Wes replied. "It's not an easy path for either of them."

"What about that other quarterback?"

"Paxton?" Wes asked. He shrugged. "He's gone through his PT. I think he might be starting again. Vitoria would know more than I do."

This was all small talk to avoid the real issue. His son's illness. It was good to forget for a few brief moments how fucking terrified he was. He scrubbed his hand over his face. "Dr. Ellwood thinks Gabriel has a condition that could affect his heart."

"How serious is it?"

"I don't know," he answered. "I didn't look up all the gory details, but I am certain Vivian has. She was glued to her phone when I left the room. The doctor doesn't think we need to worry too much. If it is this disease, it's the early stages and they caught it quickly."

Wes tilted his head to the side. "But you are still worried?"

"Wouldn't you be?" His tone was a little high pitched as he spoke. "It's my son."

"That he is," Wes said in an even tone. "One you didn't know you had not that long ago."

"Would it matter to you?" Eric asked. "If you found out you had a son. One that was a toddler and was sick would you not care?"

Eric was so damn lost. He didn't know if he was coming or going. He had been so focused on winning Vivian back. He had never considered that he might lose Gabriel. He was so little and full of life. It seemed like nothing could touch him and Eric had counted on that.

"No," Wes said. "I couldn't walk away. I am only trying to understand your headspace. You are usually so cool headed and it's a bit disconcerting to see you so unsteady."

Eric chuckled, but not in a humorous way. No this laugh was full of all his anxiety and fear mixed with a bit of insanity. That was what the entire situation was driving him to. "I have never had so much to lose before."

"I understand that," Wes told him. "And I am here for you. Whatever you need just tell me and I'll do my best to make it happen."

If only it was that easy. Eric didn't have any answers and hell, he didn't have much in the way of questions either. He just had a bundle of nerves and fears he couldn't shake. Wes couldn't help him with any of that. He had to find his own way to the light.

"Perhaps I should check on Vivian and Gabriel. That might go a long way to helping me right now."

"Then lets go." Wes walked over to his side. "I'm sure Vitoria has had enough alone time with her sister. They might welcome the interruption now."

Eric grinned. "Vivian barely mentioned her twin when we were together. They didn't get along."

"Sometimes they don't now," Wes replied. "But they're better than they were."

"I've noticed. It gives me hope." Eric opened the door to the waiting room and exited with Wes behind him. "She is capable of having a solid relationship with Tori now when before that was impossible. It means I have a chance of winning her again."

"You always did," Wes told him. "She loves you. That was never the problem. Just give her time and she'll let you know when she wants you to be a full part of her life again. You owe her that much."

"I know," he said quietly. "And she's worth the patience that will take."

They walked in silence toward Gabriel's hospital room. There wasn't anything else to discuss. Wes was there for him and that was all that mattered at that moment. The rest of his energy would be focused on one thing...Gabriel, and once his son was in the clear Eric would not stop until Vivian admitted they belonged together. This was his family, and nothing would stop him from reuniting them completely.

CHAPTER 7

*V*ivian was curled up in the recliner, and Eric stood near the bed by Gabriel. Tori stared out the window. Silence had become normal for them all. They had discussed everything there was to discuss, and Vivian had to admit she was exhausted.

Wes walked in with a tray of drinks. "I have coffee for everyone. I doubt its very good, but it should give us a boost ." He handed each one of them a disposable cup filled with the black nectar. How had he known how they all liked their coffee? Vivian certainly hadn't given him any instructions. She glanced at her sister and frowned. Tori must have been his source. Vivian could respect that. She took a long slow drink of her coffee. Wes had been right it was no gourmet blend but it would do.

"Is there any news?" Wes asked.

Eric shook his head. "No we are still waiting."

The door swung open and a nurse walked in. She had midnight dark hair pulled up into a high ponytail and sea-green eyes. She was beautiful and seemed like she'd fit right in as a fashion model instead of blue scrubs. "Hello," she greeted them. "I'm Gabriel's nurse."

"Lila?" Wes turned at stared at the nurse. "I thought you worked in obstetrics?"

"I do most of the time," she told Wes. "But they were short staffed in Peds and I offered to help. I love working with kids." She went over to Gabriel's bedside and took his temperature and checked the rest of his vitals. "His fever is still down so that's good. I think the tests they ran should be back soon. When they are the doctor will come in to talk to you."

"Thank you," Vivian said. "Do you have any idea how long they will take? It seems like we've been waiting forever as it is."

Lila opened her mouth to answer her, but shut it completely when the door opened and Dr. Ellwood walked in. He was reading a chart and hadn't yet looked at any of them. When he lifted his head he met Lila's gaze and frowned. "What are you doing here?" He seemed angry at the sight of the nurse. What the hell did he think Lila had done? It was such a strange reaction.

"Leaving," she replied curtly.

The room hadn't exactly been filled with warmth with all worry to go around, but the temperature dropped several degrees with their frosty greeting. "That wasn't very professional," Vivian said. "I don't know what is going on between the two of you but leave it out of my son's care."

"You're right," Dr. Ellwood said quickly. "It will not happen again. I'll speak with Lila later." He returned to looking over the charts. "So there is good news."

Vivian could use some good news. She'd been a tight ball of nerves for most of the day. Worry over her son was becoming unbearable. She took a deep breath then asked, "Does my son have the condition?"

"He doesn't," the doctor told her. "That's why I wanted to run these testes. Kawasaki is a difficult disease to diagnose. His fever is already down and staying that way. It's a good sign. The rash will go away too. He can go home today but if his fever spikes again or the rash worsens I want you to bring him right back."

"All right," Vivian agreed.

"Remember to breathe," Dr. Ellwood told her. "He's going to be fine and that's all that matters. Make a follow up appointment with his regular pediatrician."

She nodded. "I will."

"Good," the doctor told her. "Now I'll send Lila back in with some paperwork. Once Gabriel is awake he'll be discharged. Sit tight and hopefully you'll be able to go home soon."

The doctor left them alone. Eric blew out a breath and pulled her into his arms. "Thank God."

"I was so scared," Vivian told him.

"Me too," he said. "But you heard the doc. He's going to be fine."

Vivian now understood why the doctor hadn't wanted to discuss any worse case scenarios. She had worried and researched something that was not affecting her son after all. He wouldn't have to worry about any of it placing stress on his heart. He was fine. Sure he had a couple more days of healing, but all in all he was a healthy boy.

Vivian stepped out of Eric's embrace and faced her sister. "Thank you for being here."

"I'm glad my nephew is going to be all right," Vitoria said. She smiled warmly. "Do you want us to stay longer?"

"No," Vivian told her. "Go home. You have a wedding to prepare for in a few days."

Tori had been debating between having her sister or her best friend stand beside her as she said her vows. In the end Vivian had insisted Tori ask her best friend Ginnifer to do it. Vivian and Tori were still finding their way with each other. Ginnifer was the better choice.

"You're right." She nibbled on her bottom lip. "I understand if you skip the festivities. Gabriel comes first."

"We will wait and see. He's supposed to be the ring bearer. He's not going to want to give up that privilege easily."

Tori laughed. "All right. Let me know will you?"

"I will," Vivian promised.

After that Tori and Wes left them alone with Gabriel. Her and Eric did not speak. There wasn't much to say, and Vivian was exhausted. Not long after that Lila came back in with the discharge papers. Vivian signed where she needed to and stuffed the instructions into her purse. Then Eric picked Gabriel up and carried him out of the room. They would be home soon, and her son could sleep in his own bed. She knew he would be all right, but she couldn't stop the fear from filling her. It would be a long time before she would be able to shake completely free of it.

***

Three days later...

It was Tori and Wes's wedding day.

Gabriel was doing much, much better. The rash had faded a lot and he hadn't had a fever in two days, and still Vivian was keeping Eric at arm's length. He had to shake her out of the fear taking root. The thought of losing Gabriel shook her far more than he liked. He couldn't help feeling a little bit responsible for it.

He walked into the hotel where the wedding was to take place. He was Wes's best man. If Gabriel had been as sick as they feared he would have had to back out. Instead he was able to keep his promise, but part of him wanted to run. Not away from the ceremony, but toward Vivian. He needed her.

"There you are," Dallas Novak said. "Wes thought you'd bail."

He lifted his lips upward. "I made a promise. I keep my promises."

"Sure you do," Dallas said. He might be Wes's brother but that didn't mean Eric had to like him.

"Where is Wes?"

"Inside," Dallas replied as he jerked his thumb toward the event hall. "Everything is going as planned. Vivian is in there too with Gabriel."

That is what he really wanted to know but hadn't been certain how to ask without looking stupid. Perhaps Dallas wasn't as bad as Eric believed him to be. "Thanks," Eric said. "I'm going to go talk to the groom." And perhaps Vivian too if she'd let him.

Eric brushed past him and went into the event hall. Wes stood by the altar area and Vivian was indeed by his side. Gabriel looked absolutely adorable in his little black tux. He was running around the front of the room making zoom zoom noises. His son was definitely feeling much better. Those scary moments in the hospital almost seemed like a lifetime ago now.

He crossed over to Wes and Vivian with purposeful strives. She was wearing a light blue dress. Her hair was pulled up at the sides with the rest of the golden locks falling loose. The red tipped edges seemed a little brighter than they had been before. Eric stopped in front of both of them. "Who's ready for a wedding."

"I am," Wes said in a jovial tone. "I cannot wait to make Tori my wife."

Vivian chuckled. "She's more than willing to assist you in that particular endeavor."

"We should be starting soon. Guests have been arriving for a while now and the seats are filling quickly." Eric glanced back to the chairs lining up in perfect rows.

"I should probably take Gabriel back to the waiting area. He will need to be ready to walk down the aisle soon."

"Vivi wait," Eric said. "I was hoping we could talk."

She nodded. "I want to talk to. But not now, after the wedding."

"All right." He could argue but he wouldn't. He could be patient and this day was supposed to be about Tori and Wes. Vivian picked up Gabriel and carried him out of the room. Eric took his place next to Wes. "I'm sorry I was almost late."

Wes grinned. "You're right on time. That's all that matters." He slapped Eric's back lightly. "Besides Dallas was prepared to fill your place if need be. It would have been fine. I'm glad you're here though."

Not long after that the ceremony began. Gabriel walked down the aisle proudly holding a pillow with the rings on it. The flower girl had done her duty and sprinkled pedals down the aisle.

When Tori walked down the aisle, Wes held his breath. She looked beautiful, but she was almost an exact replica of Vivian. How could Eric not find her lovely. They said their vows honoring to cherish each other always. Eric was a little jealous of that. He wanted to have that kind of unrelenting love with Vivian.

They kissed each other as husband and wife, then went down the aisle in a rush of happiness. The reception would follow in a room next to this one. It should be a wonderful night. Eric didn't feel wonderful. He stood at that altar and stared as people exited the room. There was only one thing he wanted. His family.

"What are you waiting for?"

He glanced down to see Vivian and Gabriel. "You," he said simply.

"Well I'm here." She smiled. "And I have a question for you."

"Oh?" Eric hoped he had the right answer to it.

"Do you love me?"

"More than I can possibly say." He was a little choked up.

"Good," She said. "I love you too. I think it's time I stopped running from that."

Was he dreaming? This was what he wanted and it seemed too good to be true. God help him if his mind was playing tricks on him. "Are you certain?"

She nodded. "I am. I want to be happy and I can't ever truly be happy without you." Vivian stepped closer to him. "I also think we need to take that trip. It would be good to do something as a family."

"We could make it a honeymoon," he offered.

Vivian chuckled. "One thing at a time dear," she said. "Though it might be more prudent to make it a road trip. We could head to Vegas, and if you're lucky enough I might say yes by the time we get there."

Eric groaned. "Can we leave now."

"No," she told him firmly. "It's my sister's wedding. I'm not leaving until the very end." She stepped even closer so there wasn't much space between them. "But there are a couple of things you can do tonight."

He lifted a brow. "Such as?"

"You get to dance with me," she told him. Vivian nibbled on her lip. "And you can kiss me whenever you want. In fact, I insist you do so right now."

Eric knew a good thing when he saw it, or heard it, and he wasn't going to waste this opportunity. He leaned down and pressed his lips to hers, and he could swear fireworks went off. There would be no more lies between them, only passion, and love. So, so much love.

ACKNOWLEDGMENTS

This is where I thank my editor and cover artist, Victoria Miller profusely. She helps me more than I can ever say. I appreciate everything she does and that she pushes me to be better…do better. Thank you a thousand times over.

Also to Elizabeth Evans. Thank you for always being there for me and being my friend. You mean so much to me. Thanks isn't nearly enough, but it's all I have, so thank you my friend for being you.

Big thanks to Sherry for doing a wonderful proofread. I appreciate your help more than I can say. Thank You.

EXCERPT: DESIRE AND JEALOUSY

DARING LOVE BOOK TWO

USA TODAY BESTSELLING AUTHOR

Dawn Brower

PASSION AND SUSPICION ARE
A DANGEROUS COMBINATION

Desire
& JEALOUSY

PROLOGUE

A crack of thunder echoed around Allison Duvall as she parked her car outside the apartment building. It was a sleek building recently built to cater to the elite who could afford the exorbitant cost of owning one of the posh living spaces. She could never afford to live in that building, and part of her never wanted to. The people who could had always looked down their noses at her. She wouldn't even be there if she didn't have to. Unfortunately, her prime client had chosen to change his residence, and had then did his damn best to ghost her.

Paxton Kerry, the quarterback for the Seattle Starlings had become the bane of her existence. Part of her was regretting her decision to become an agent in Vitoria Miene's management firm. She wanted to move up, but she hated that her first client...her test...was proving to be far more difficult than she had anticipated. It had started well, and then took a nosedive faster than she could blink. Paxton was determined to destroy his life, and Allison's as well.

She took a deep breath and stepped out of the car. Rain descended on her in droves. She flipped open her umbrella, but it did little good. Allison was soaked through and the umbrella offered little protection. She cursed and dashed to the entrance and rushed inside. Shivers rolled over her as she shook uncontrollably. Sometimes she wondered why she'd left New York and moved across country. It rained more than she liked in Seattle, but at least most of the time, as long as she planned for it, it didn't cause any major issues. She might be currently drenched, but she could still corner Paxton.

Allison shook her umbrella and closed it. Her teeth chattered, and a lock of her copper-gold hair fell over her eyes blocking her line of sight. She brushed it to the side, then moved farther into the building, nodded at the man tending the desk, and then headed to the elevator. When Paxton had been more congenial he'd given her his codes and spare key in case of an emergency. So far he had not asked for them back, but he might after this visit. He would not appreciate her calling him on his bullshit, but someone had to do it. She stabbed her finger on the button for Paxton's floor, then leaned against the elevator wall. Allison closed her eyes and took a deep breath. It had been a long day, and it was barely morning.

The doors dinged open and she forced herself to move forward. Paxton was the only one on this floor, and the elevator opened to his apartment. Nothing but the best for his royal pain in the ass. The stench of alcohol stung her nose as she inched her way into the main area of the apartment. Empty liquor bottles covered almost every surface. Some were upright, but most were tipped over on their sides. By her estimation there had to be at least a dozen bottles, maybe more. A bowl of popcorn had been spilled over on the floor and some of it had been crushed into the carpet.

Had he had a party?

She moved farther into the room. A man laid sprawled on the hard floor near the balcony doors. One door was slid open and sheer curtains rustled in the wind as rain soaked through the opening leaving a small puddle on the floor. That same puddle was trailing toward the man, and soaked the side of his shirt. His dark hair was disheveled, and also wet. How was he still sleeping?

Allison cursed under her breath, not for the first time that morning. She rushed over to his side and knelt before him. At least she wouldn't have to worry too much about getting wet considering her run through the rain. She shook him. "Paxton," she called out to him. He didn't budge. Fuck. She placed her forefinger to the inside of his wrist and checked for a pulse, then breathed a sigh of relief when evidence of a steady heartbeat thumped evenly. Still, she had to find a way to bring him to consciousness.

She nibbled on her lips and stared down at him. He was a handsome man, even in this state she could appreciate that. His cheekbones were perfectly chiseled and his lips tempted her in ways she didn't want to admit. A part of her had always wondered how his kiss might taste. Of course that had been before he'd been injured and sidelined. He'd been happier, cockier, and a blaze of light that called to her soul.

Since his injury, and through his physical therapy, that

light had dimmed significantly. Her heart broke for him. She truly cared about him and wanted to help him move forward, whether that was as a quarterback for the Starlings, or something else. He shouldn't waste his life, and she would make sure he realized he still had a future. Allison leaned over and cupped his cheek. At that moment his eyelids fluttered open and her gaze met the evergreen depths of his eyes. He blinked a few times and then groaned.

"Good morning, sleeping beauty," she said. Allison tried to keep her tone upbeat, but had a hard time with it. Her lips wobbled a little as she spoke. "Come on, get up, we have work to do."

"Go away," he mumbled. The stench of his breath nearly bowled her over. He needed a shower and to brush his teeth. He reeked of two day old whiskey and stale pizza. "I don't want you here." His voice held the tone of a petulant child who refused to leave his warm bed and prepare for a day at school.

Allison glanced down at him, not for the first time, and frowned. "You cannot be comfortable. You are wet, and laying on marble flooring." He rolled over to face away from her. The trail of water had gone up his back like a line of sweat after a hard workout. She placed her hand on his arm and his skin felt chilled. "Paxton quit ignoring me. Get up now."

He groaned again, but slowly pushed himself into a sitting position. "What are you doing here?" His green irises were rimmed with red and looked gritty either from lack of sleep, too much partying, or perhaps both... "I didn't give you access to my apartment so you could invade my privacy."

She expected that. "This is a wellness check. You've missed three physical therapy sessions and five planning sessions with me. How long did you think you could avoid me?"

"Has Emma been tattling on me?" He scrubbed his face with the palms of his hands. He met her gaze. "I don't need either of you up in my business."

Emma Novak-Lewis had taken over Paxton's physical therapy at the Starlings. She was married to Colt Lewis, the second string quarterback that had taken over when Paxton had been injured. She hadn't married Colt until after both of those had happened. "Emma cares about you and wants to see you back playing for the team. They currently have both of their quarterbacks sidelined. At least we are currently in the off season. You know that Colt is recovering from surgery after his car accident. Do you really want to make Emma's life harder right now?"

"She can handle the strain," he replied flippantly, but his distain didn't reach his eyes. He cared about Emma too. They were friends and had grown close since she joined the medical team for the Starlings.

"You can act as if you don't care all you want, but I don't believe you." The rain had finally stopped and sunlight streamed through the balcony doors. She flung them open and let the light pour over him. He lifted his arm to block the light as he squinted furiously. "You're not that dark," she said vehemently. "Deep down in your soul you have more to offer the world than you allow yourself to give. Some people you show it to. I've been lucky enough to see it. Don't hide from the world."

"Fuck the world," he spat out, then pushed himself up on to his feet. "It hasn't exactly been kind to me of late."

"Sometimes you're such a dick." She placed her hands on her hips and glared up at him. "Get your head out of your ass and stop feeling sorry for yourself. Go shower you reek."

His nostrils flared and anger sparked out of his eyes. His lips formed a thin line as he breathed in and out several times. Paxton appeared as if he wanted to say something, but he held it in. He spun on his heels and left the room. She prayed to shower and change, but she'd give him a little space for a few moments at least. If he wasn't back in thirty minutes she'd check on him.

While he was gone she retrieved a trash bag and started cleaning up. As she was tossing the last empty liquor bottle into the bag he strolled back in. She checked the clock—twenty minutes. His hair was wet and sleeked back, and he'd changed into dark wash jeans and a green shirt the exact shade of his eyes. The result was devastating to her female libido. Damn he was gorgeous. Too much for her to handle at times.

"I have a maid service for that," he told her. "Leave it for them."

"How can you live like this," she replied with disgust. She reached for the bowl of popcorn, dumped what remained inside of it in the bag, then set it back down. "Do you have a broom?" She stared at the crushed kernels on the floor. "or a vacuum?" She had a feeling they wouldn't come up easily off the carpet and they might need to be pried loose.

Paxton crossed over to her and snatched the bag from her hand and tossed it to the side. Through gritted teeth he said, "I told you to leave it."

She glared at him and pursed her lips in displeasure. Allison hated messes and it irritated her she couldn't clean this one. "Would it really kill you to let me clean it."

"Yes," he answered.

"Why?" She lifted a brow. "Do you enjoy living in squalor?"

"I'd hardly call this apartment squalor." he replied dryly. Paxton shoved his hands into his pocket. "Now tell me why you are really here so you can leave."

"God you're an ass."

"Thanks," he deadpanned. "I do try."

"I can tell." She rolled her eyes. "I am here to check up on you. I didn't lie. Emma said to make you go to see her. You have to keep up your therapy."

"I don't want to."

The petulant child had returned in spades… "Too bad. You're going."

"What if I convince you that I don't need to go?"

That was a new one. What game was he up to? "I don't think that is possible."

"I bet I could." He removed his hands from his pockets and took a step closer. "And I don't think it would take much to convince you."

She swallowed hard. There was a wicked gleam in his eyes that turned her insides to jelly. Allison feared he might be right, but not for the reasons he stated. "You're wrong," she insisted. "Your doctors have clearly stated that injury was extensive and without therapy you're not playing again."

He shrugged. "There are other games, and some just as enjoyable as throwing a football. Maybe I've moved on."

"Have you?" She furrowed her brows. "I don't believe it. You're in denial and it is time you snapped out of it." Paxton closed the distance between them until there were barely inches separating them. She took a step back until she hit a wall. There was nowhere to go. He'd cornered her between a rock and hard place, and she wanted to lean into the hard depths of his body and stroke him everywhere. "What are you doing?"

"Proving a point," he said huskily. He leaned down and pressed his lips to hers. She'd always wondered what his kiss would be like, and now she knew. It was better than she'd imagined. It was fire, longing, and desire that set her body alight with need she'd been fighting for too long. She kissed him back because it didn't occur to her to do anything else. Why deny herself this one opportunity to have her deepest yearning.

When logic finally sprouted inside her head she realized her mistake and pushed him away. "Don't," she murmured, but wished she could have begged for more.

He leaned down so his mouth brushed her ear. His hot breath caressed her lobe and she nearly moaned. "I know you want me," he said. "Why else would you be here."

She closed her eyes and prayed for strength. Somewhere she found it and shoved him away from her. "I'm here because you're my client and I need you to go to your physical therapy. Now quit fighting the inevitable and trying to weasel your way out of it. I'll call Emma and tell her to expect you."

Allison headed to the elevator and held her breath until she reached it, then slowly exhaled. She turned to him. "Don't make me come back here."

He chuckled. "You know you want to."

She grimaced. "Please." Allison shook her head. "Don't act as if that was all for my benefit. You kissed me to entice me into doing your bidding. It won't work." It almost had... She pushed the button for the elevator. "I'll call you after physical therapy to schedule our next meeting. You're going to stop this downward spiral and improve your image. This cannot go on or you won't have a career to lose."

"All right, boss." He saluted her. "And next time we kiss...it won't stop."

She left that hanging and stepped into the elevator because she feared he was right. His kisses were addicting and now she wished she'd never had that taste. Paxton Kerry might prove to be her undoing... No, he was her undoing, and it was time she admitted that. She'd fallen in love with him.

AFTERWORD

Thank you so much for taking the time to read my book.
Your opinion matters!
Please take a moment to review this book on your
favorite review site and share your opinion with fellow
readers.

www.authordawnbrower.com

ABOUT THE AUTHOR

USA TODAY Bestselling author, DAWN BROWER writes both historical and contemporary romance. There are always stories inside her head; she just never thought she could make them come to life. That creativity has finally found an outlet.

Growing up she was the only girl out of six children. She raised two boys into productive young men. There is never a dull moment in her life. Reading books is her favorite hobby and she loves all genres.

She is active on Facebook, Twitter, and Instagram. To follow her or can find more about her check out her website for the pertinent information:

www.authordawnbrower.com

[BB] bookbub.com/authors/dawn-brower
[f] facebook.com/1DawnBrower
[twitter] twitter.com/1DawnBrower
[instagram] instagram.com/1DawnBrower
[g] goodreads.com/dawnbrower

HISTORICAL

Stand Alone

Broken Pearl

A Wallflower's Christmas Kiss

A Gypsy's Christmas Kiss

Marsden Romances

A Flawed Jewel

A Crystal Angel

A Treasured Lily

A Sanguine Gem

A Hidden Ruby

A Discarded Pearl

Marsden Descendants

Rebellious Angel

Tempting An American Princess

How to Kiss a Debutante

Loving an America Spy

Linked Across Time

Saved by My Blackguard

Searching for My Rogue

Seduction of My Rake

Surrendering to My Spy

Spellbound by My Charmer

Stolen by My Knave

Separated from My Love

Scheming with My Duke

Secluded with My Hellion

Secrets of My Beloved

Spying on My Scoundrel

Shocked by My Vixen

Smitten with My Christmas Minx

Vision of Love

Enduring Legacy

The Legacy's Origin

Charming Her Rogue

Ever Beloved

Forever My Earl

Always My Viscount

Infinitely My Marquess

Eternally My Duke

Bluestockings Defying Rogues

When An Earl Turns Wicked

A Lady Hoyden's Secret

One Wicked Kiss

Earl In Trouble

All the Ladies Love Coventry

One Less Scandalous Earl

Confessions of a Hellion

The Vixen in Red

Lady Pear's Duke

Scandal Meets Love

Love Only Me (Amanda Mariel)

Find Me Love (Dawn Brower)

If It's Love (Amanda Mariel)

Odds of Love (Dawn Brower)

Believe In Love (Amanda Mariel)

Chance of Love (Dawn Brower)

Love and Holly (Amanda Mariel)

Love and Mistletoe (Dawn Brower

The Neverhartts

Never Defy a Vixen

Never Disregard a Wallflower

Never Dare a Hellion

Never Deceive a Bluestocking

Never Disrespect a Governess

Never Desire a Duke

CONTEMPORARY

Stand alone:

Deadly Benevolence

Snowflake Kisses

Kindred Lies

Sparkle City
Diamonds Don't Cry
Hooking a Firefly

Novak Springs
Cowgirl Fever
Dirty Proof
Unbridled Pursuit
Sensual Games
Christmas Temptation

Daring Love
Passion and Lies
Desire and Jealousy
Seduction and Betrayal

Begin Again
There You'll Be
Better as a Memory
Won't Let Go

Heart's Intent
One Heart to Give
Unveiled Hearts
Heart of the Moment
Kiss My Heart Goodbye

Heart in Waiting

Heart Lessons

A Heart Redeemed

Kismet Bay

Once Upon a Christmas

New Year Revelation

All Things Valentine

Luck At First Sight

Endless Summer Days

A Witch's Charm

All Out of Gratitude

Christmas Ever After

YOUNG ADULT FANTASY

Broken Curses

The Enchanted Princess

The Bespelled Knight

The Magical Hunt

EXCERPT: NEVER DISREGARD A WALLFLOWER

NEVERHARTTS BOOK TWO

a loud noise reverberated through Lady Theodora Neverhartt's bedchamber. She inhaled a deep, sharp breath as she sat upright. A storm. Thunder and lightning always left an uneasy feeling in her stomach, and this time was no different. She hated them, and had for as long as she could recall. At five and ten that seemed like a lot of years, and in some ways, it seemed like none at all.

She slid her legs over the side of the bed and pulled on her wrapper. As long as there was a storm raging outside she would not get any further sleep that night. To help her pass the time she would retrieve a book from the library. Teddy didn't bother with a candle. She'd become accustomed to traveling the halls of her family home in darkness. Her father, the Earl of Seville, was often short of funds. That meant they didn't always have the income necessary to run a viscount's estate properly. It was best to preserve the candles for when they truly needed them.

Besides she had grown up there and knew the layout well. A candle wasn't necessary.

A roll of thunder echoed around her and she jumped again. Teddy swallowed hard. She could do this, she could...and perhaps, if she told herself that enough, she'd believe it too. Teddy took a deep breath and continued down the hall and slowly made her way down the stairs. When she reached the bottom, she let out the breath she hadn't realized she'd been holding, then turned down the hall leading to the library.

Light spilled out of her father's study. Was he awake or had he left a candle burning? Either way, it made her stomach turn. That light was not a good omen. She hoped he had not drowned his difficulties in a bottle of brandy. She hated being around her father when he was inebriated. His drunkenness was hard to bear and made her uncomfortable.

Could she slip by his study without her noticing?

Maybe. But she wasn't certain if she could. If her father noticed her she'd have to extricate herself somehow, but it would not be easy. She would have to try her best to pass by unnoticed. Teddy didn't want to return to her chambers without something to distract her from the storm. It would be a tension-filled night without the diversion. She'd like to prevent that if she could.

She started down the hall again, this time on her tiptoes. Teddy stayed close to the wall, on the opposite side of her father's study, hoping he wouldn't notice her as she scurried past it. She kept her breathing as even as possible. Her heart raced faster and faster with each careful step she took. The study was only a couple footsteps away. She held her breath and placed a tentative step, then another, until she was on the other side. She let out the breath once she reached the other side.

"Who's there?" her father called out, slurring his words as he spoke.

Drat. She hadn't gone as unnoticed as she had hoped she would. Instead of answering she kept going. The library was close and she could slip inside. When she reached the library she rushed inside and across the room. Lightning struck, illuminating the many shelves lining the back wall. She went over and plucked a book off, not looking at it. Teddy didn't care what she read, as long as it kept her mind occupied.

She turned to leave but stopped suddenly. A large man filled the doorway. It didn't look like her father, but it was dark. Perhaps she was mistaken and imagining things.

"Well, well," the man said. "What do we have here. Looks like Seville was right. One of his brats *is* wandering around the house. What did you hear?"

"Noth..ing," she stumbled over the word as she spoke. "I came for a book." Who was this man? Why was he so concerned about what she may have heard? "I promise I heard nothing."

He sighed. "What am I going to do with you." He stalked forward and grabbed her arm.

"You're hurting me."

He shook her and laughed maniacally. "I haven't begun to hurt you."

The book she'd been holding slipped to the floor. He reached over and cupped her breast. "You're a ripe young thing, aren't you? So innocent."

A tear slipped down her cheek. He squeezed her breast. Teddy tried to pull away, but he had a tight grip on her arm. "Let me go," she demanded. Why was he hurting her? She hoped and prayed he didn't force her to do something she didn't want to do. She understood that men often took what they wanted from a woman. She'd overheard a maid talking once about a man taking advantage of her. It had scared Teddy and she'd learned far more than she'd ever wanted to that day. At least until now...

"When I'm done with you. Have to make sure you keep your mouth shut tight, don't I?"

She slapped his face. "I told you I didn't hear anything."

"I don't believe you," he said as he rubbed his cheek. "You're feisty. I like it when they fight me. Thank you for making it more of a challenge, not that it'll do you any good. I *will* have you." Some light illuminated the area from a flash of lightning. It gave her a terrifying glance at the nefarious gleam in his eye. He wouldn't stop. Nothing would prevent him from hurting her.

Teddy shook uncontrollably. He was so large and strong. She had no real chance of fighting him. He would hurt her, and she feared she would never recover from it. How would she survive this?

"Let my daughter go," her father said. She turned toward the sound of his voice. She was relieved to see him even if he was a little wobbly on his feet, but his words came out clear.

Teddy wanted to burst into tears but held them in. She'd wait until she was alone. Somehow, her wastrel of a father was there to save her.

"I don't think so," the man said. "She could've heard us."

"Teddy is a good girl. She doesn't eavesdrop on conversations, and even if she had, she'd hold her tongue. Let her go."

"Fine," the man said harshly. "But if she speaks...I'll handle it, and I will not ask for your permission." He let Teddy go, and she fell to the floor. She crawled on her hands and knees and used the table to help herself to her feet.

"Go to your chambers," her father ordered. He didn't look at her as he barked the words at her. "And don't come back down."

Teddy didn't need to be told twice. She didn't look back, and she didn't stop to retrieve the book. Nothing would be able to calm her after that. Her body would be, if it wasn't already, covered in bruises come morning. When she reached her bedchamber, she clicked the lock in place, crawled into her bed, and gave into the tears burning at the back of her eyes. She sobbed the entire night, not once falling asleep.

It was a night she'd never forget even when she wanted to. It taught her men were not to be trusted. They could, and would, take advantage of her. As much as she wanted love, she would never give her heart to a man. They'd only abuse it, and Teddy would not give them the opportunity to crush her. It was far better to spend her life alone. She had her family, her sisters and brother would always be there for her, and save that, she could always depend on herself.

CHAPTER 1

Three years later…

A bead of sweat trailed down Teddy's forehead. Why was it so darn hot? She still couldn't believe she'd allowed herself to be convinced this was a good idea. Billie had married for the second time and was blissfully happy, and hoped Teddy would find that same level of bliss. Her sister hadn't stopped to consider what Teddy wanted.

She didn't want a season, or elaborate ballgown, or even suitors. Teddy had no desire to find love or give herself to any man. Being a wallflower saved her, in her mind, from a fate no woman should willingly sell herself to: marriage. It was an institution designed to subjugate women, and she refused to freely enter into the bonds of matrimony.

"Ouch," she mumbled.

"My apologies, my lady," one of the seamstresses

pinning her hem said. "It is imperative you remain still so I do not intentionally stick you with the pins."

"I'm trying." Teddy glared at her. "How much longer will this take?"

She'd been in Madame Auclair's modiste shop for a while, finishing the final fittings on her gowns.

"It won't be much longer, my lady," Madame Auclair said. "A few more pins and then we can remove this gown." Her French accent was thick as she spoke. "Please endure our ministrations a few more moments."

Teddy hated this. Hated being difficult. Hated that there was even a need for new gowns. Why couldn't she stay in the country and settle in...to her spinster life? That was what she wanted. If only her sister would actually listen to her. "I'm being as patient as I can be." She closed her eyes and counted to ten, hoping they'd be done by the time she reached the final number.

"That's not entirely true," Billie said as she strolled into the room. "You, dear sister, are capable of deep-seated patience. The issue is you don't wish to have pretty new gowns or a season at all." Billie turned to Madame Auclair and asked, "Are you truly almost finished?"

"I am," Madame Auclair confirmed. "One more pin and...there. We can remove the gown now."

Teddy breathed a sigh of relief. "Thank heavens...I feel as if I'm suffocating."

"You are not," Billie chastised. "You're not usually this dramatic. Leave the histrionics for the twins."

Chris and Carly were melodramatic on a good day. At least they were safely tucked away at finishing school, and hopefully learning much needed manners. They probably would never conform in any typical way, but they might at least learn some restraint. Carly was the worst though. She led poor Chris into more trouble than any young lady should. "Thankfully neither one will be around to watch me fall on my face. You know they would do their best to make me miserable."

"True," Billie replied, then waved her hand. "It matters not because, as you said, they're not here. But I am, and I'll be with you through everything." Madame Auclair and her assistants helped Teddy out of the dress and carefully placed it on a hook for final stitching later. "A season won't be as painful as you believe. It might even be...fun."

"Fun?" Teddy quirked a brow upward. "You and I have very different ideas of what constitutes fun. Being snubbed and enduring and empty dance card is not anything remotely entertaining. Why must I do this again?"

"Zachary thinks..."

"Your husband has no idea what it is like for a woman on the marriage mart. He would've successfully avoided matrimony altogether if he had not been confined to a country estate with you." She glanced at Billie and said wryly, "He fell in love despite his best efforts at avoiding it."

"It helps that I'm irresistible," Billie replied cheekily.

Teddy's lips twitched. "I suppose there is that."

"My lady, let me help you into your gown," Madame Auclair said. She held Teddy's blue and white muslin day dress before her. She slipped into it, and Madame Auclair started fastening her buttons. Soon she'd be able to leave this overheated dress shop. "There," she said as the last button was slipped into its corresponding hole. "You're all done."

"Wonderful," Teddy said. "Now we can go home."

"The ball gown is ready for you to take with you now," Madame Auclair told her. "The rest of the dresses will be delivered after we're finished with the last of the alterations."

"Thank you," Billie said, then turned her attention to Teddy. "See, it wasn't nearly as terrible as you thought it would be." She grinned. "Now to go home and start preparations for the ball tonight."

Teddy rolled her eyes and held her thoughts inside. Billie would only fuss even more if she explained how much, again, she hated balls, soirees, or society functions in general. "I understand why you're excited," Teddy began. "You never had a proper season. Father gambled away all of the family fortune. We had no dowries or funds to support a season. This is your launch as much as it is mine."

"In some ways, I suppose that is true," Billie conceded. "I'm an old matron now though. It won't be the same." She grew silent as they exited the modiste shop. "Zachary really does believe this will help. I do listen to you, and I understand it'll be uncomfortable. If it truly becomes unbearable, you can end your season early. All I ask is that you at least try before you give in."

Teddy frowned. Had she been that terrible? "I am acting like a brat."

"Only a little bit," Billie said. She held her hand up with her thumb and forefinger almost touching. "Zach will give you your dowry to do with as you please if you don't want to use it to find a husband. Neither one of us wants to see you unhappy. We want you to explore all your options before you settle on one path."

"All right," Teddy said reluctantly. "I'll stop complaining." She wasn't promising to try though. She had no desire to find a husband. Teddy was a wallflower, and a wallflower she'd remain.

EZRA HALSEY, Viscount Carrolton, stared at the crush of people in the ballroom. Why had he agreed to attend this ball again? Oh, right, his sister, Amelia... It was her first season, and as the head of the family, he had to attend the bloody season with her. It wouldn't look good if he didn't at least make an appearance at some of the society functions.

He needed a drink, and none of the warm punch Lady Windley found acceptable to serve her guests. No that would not quench his thirst. It would only make him want something else. He needed something stronger, that would burn as it traveled down his throat. It would help him suffer through this evening's entertainment. The mothers with marriageable daughters would expect him to dance with their insipid offspring. Perhaps he was being harsh with that description, but he couldn't find any that deserved a better depiction.

"You look as if you're itching to bolt at any moment," a man said.

Ezra turned and grinned. His friend, the Duke of Graystone, stood beside him. His reddish gold hair was brushed back, and his green eyes nearly sparkled with mischief. He was dressed in almost all black. His shirt and starched cravat were a bright white. "Why the blazes are you here?" A ball was the last place he expected the duke to be. He avoided marriage more than any of them did. "The mamas will pounce at the sight of a newly minted duke."

He grinned. "They'll be too late. As I already have a wife and cannot have more than one. It would be frowned upon."

Graystone had married. The world was really about to end. "Surely, you jest."

"Marriage is not something I would ever speak lightly about. I married a fortnight ago by special license. I am officially not in the market for a wife."

Ezra lifted a brow. "I didn't realize you were ever in the market for a wife."

Graystone chuckled. "Because I wasn't. It's amazing how love will change your perspective."

"Who did you marry?" The last Ezra was aware, Graystone had gone to his new country seat and… "Please tell me you didn't marry your uncle's widow."

"All right I won't," he grinned.

Ezra stared at him baffled. Surely… No. He had to have misunderstood somehow. Graystone had been completely against marriage. What could have changed?

"Good lord, you did. Have you lost your mind?"

"Perhaps," Graystone admitted. "But I have no regrets. Billie is the love of my life, and she is going to be the mother of my children. I'm happy. Be happy for me."

Ezra shook his head. He hoped that Graystone

wouldn't come to regret his decision. In Ezra's experience nothing good came out of marriage. Sometimes he wished his sister wasn't so set on finding a match. He'd always take care of her, so she didn't *need* a husband. "I wish you nothing but the best. What happened after I left with Sheffield? Foxworth was supposed to stay back for moral support."

"He did stay for a bit. Don't worry so much. Everything happened as it was supposed to." He tapped him lightly on the shoulder. "You should consider finding a nice lady and getting leg shackled."

"Be quiet," Ezra hissed out. "One of them might hear you."

"Whom?" He lifted a brow. "The marriage-minded mamas with daughters to spare?" Graystone chuckled. "I hate to tell you this, my friend. What I say doesn't matter. They already have their greedy eyes set on you. You're wealthy, titled, and come from what they deem a respectable family. Any one of them would gladly throw their offspring at you in the hopes you'll take a liking to them and propose on sight."

Ezra rolled his eyes. "Who are you and what did you do with my friend?"

"I'm the same person I've always been. Am I not speaking the truth?"

He hated to admit that Graystone was right. "You are," he agreed. "They'll know I'm here for Amelia, but they will still try to corner me at every turn." He hate society functions for that reasons. "I've no desire to marry and nothing is going to change that."

"Be careful," Graystone warned. "I used to spout the

same rhetoric. Marriage wasn't for me, until it was. Billie changed everything. You don't know with any certainty that your mind won't change too. The right woman, love, and the possibility of a happily ever after makes all the difference."

Ezra didn't want to argue with his friend. "Love made you want something different. It won't for me." He didn't believe in romance, and didn't want anything of that nature for himself…ever.

His parents had married for love…or so he'd been told. They had been happy for a time too. Until they weren't. He remembered them fighting. A lot. He used to cover his ears with his hands in an attempt to block it all out. Not long after that, his father had imbibed way too much brandy and went riding. He broke his neck when he fell off his horse. His mother had mourned him, but she had almost seemed relieved. As if she were finally free from her obligations to him.

"I'll let you figure it out for yourself," Graystone said. "We all have to come to our own realizations. In time, I think you will change your mind." He shook his head lightly. "I didn't want to love Billie. I fought it every step of the way. But now…she's my everything." He smiled. "I must go find my wife and her sister. Try to enjoy yourself."

With those words, the duke walked into the crowd. Ezra supposed he should quit lurking on the edge of the crush and go find his sister and mother. He wanted to do none of it. He took a deep breath and stepped forward. No time like the present to enter the lion's den. Perhaps he'd survive his first foray into society this season. Somehow, he doubted it.

Order Here:
https://www.
books2read.com/NeverDisregardaWallflower